Nine Fi...g

The Good Wolves

Tony Bowman

Cover Design

Anthony Spivey

ISBN: 9798394038617

DEDICATION

For my grandmothers, Ressie Bowman and Lillian Spivey

Table of Contents

Foreword

I've been writing almost constantly now for nine years and, sporadically, for twenty-two years before that. I'm working on my twenty-fifth (and twenty-sixth and twenty-seventh novels concurrently) across three different pseudonyms. Most days I write at least a thousand words, some days many more.

Tony Bowman is my main brand and I'm getting ready to release my eighth novel under that name in May, Nine Fingers: The Good Wolves. The Bowman books usually take a lot longer to write than the other works. They have to percolate for some reason.

I've been replaying the scenes in Good Wolves in my head for seven years now, scenes I haven't typed out till now. Until I type them, they replay in my mind, sometimes over and over again, sometimes disappearing for months before manifesting again like ghosts in mountain mist.

Once I type them, they're gone. My subconscious discards them, somehow satisfied once they have been recorded. I finish typing the scene and I no longer hear Rat cracking jokes over Valkyrie's intercom, Ward Rickman is no longer walking toward Bedford in the rain, and I can no longer see a bus load of Draugr passing me on a snowy road.

The problem is the scene never completely describes the image in my head.

I've talked about this before: representing multi-dimensional scenes in lower-dimensional media. At the very least, a book is a projection of a four-dimensional story onto a one-dimensional stream of words.

Data is lost in that projection.

I've experimented with different formats: audio books and, most recently, graphic novels. They're slower to create - my goal has always been to be a one-man band in this gig, so I've had to teach myself voice acting, audio engineering, and now digital art. I enjoy it all, though I'm not all that good at any of it.

I always return to the written word. For some reason, flawed as my words are and as low-tech as the one-dimensional stream is, novels still have the ability to show you the action, emotion, and inner turmoil better than the other mediums.

Nine Fingers: The Good Wolves has finally percolated enough and the ghosts are talking. The words are flowing again. Does that mean I can go on to Nine Fingers: Bedford Blues and finally tell the last story of my werewolves? (Well, maybe not the last… there is one more story to tell after Bedford Blues)

I'm not sure, other voices are whispering in my ear. I can hear Valkyrie's twin diesel engines, Appalachian witches cackling… it's crowded in my head and sometimes very loud.

One story at a time, that's the best I can do.

Nine Fingers was a western with werewolves, Nine Fingers: The Beast of Bray Road was a werewolf mystery. Nine Fingers: The Good Wolves is a thriller. Nine Fingers: Bedford Blues will be a coming-of-age story.

And, Nine Fingers: Apocalypse?

It will be pure chaos.

Tony Bowman
16-April-2023

Playlist

"Hey Brother," Avicii
"Let The Storm Descend Upon You," Avantasia
"City Of Heroes," Kiske Somerville
"Break In," Halestorm
"Some Kind Of Monster," Beyond the Black
"I Will Stay," We Are The Fallen
"Rise Up," Smash Into Pieces
"Don't Fear The Reaper," The Spiritual Machines
"Sleep Well, My Angel," We Are The Fallen
"Goodbye," Takida
"Daylight," Shinedown
"Vox Populi," Thirty Seconds To Mars
"Enchantress," Two Steps From Hell
"Snake Eyes," Mumford and Sons
"Darkness At The Heart Of My Love," Ghost
"House On A Hill," The Pretty Reckless

ACT I

Heroes and Villains

"It is true, we shall be monsters, cut off from all the world; but on that account we shall be more attached to one another."

— Mary Shelley, Frankenstein

Tony Bowman

Wolves

Detroit, Michigan

Why does it have to be about fire? Anna thought.

Nothing else bothered her. Not rogue werewolves, not bullets — but fire terrified her.

She knelt in the alley and sniffed the air. There was a fire nearby. She could smell the smoke, the rain aroma of the fire hoses. Red flashing lights reflected off puddles at the end of the alley from the fire engines.

Anna closed her eyes, shutting out the data she didn't need, focusing on the things she needed. The smell was there: kerosene and sweat, sulfur and deodorant.

The arsonist had passed this way, but was he leaving the fire or had he been on his way to set it?

She opened her eyes and brushed her auburn hair away from her face. Her yellow eyes widened, and she absorbed all the light the darkness contained. The sun had set hours before, but, to her heightened senses, the alley was bright as day.

There. A footprint. Men's, size eleven. It pointed toward the lights at the end of the alley.

Toward the fire.

She traced the outline of the print with her fingers. "He was here. No more than a half hour ago," she said into the microphone clipped to her blouse.

"Okay," Karen's voice said in her ear. "Go around the corner and see what the firemen are saying."

Calm. Karen was the alpha, and her voice had that effect on her. Her heart rate slowed. She felt invincible.

Saliva dripped onto her hand.

She looked up.

A werewolf was leaning over her, strands of slobber leaking from his great muzzle.

She reached up and punched his massive chest with her small fist, "Gross, Swede. Back off, will you?"

Swede growled and sat back on his haunches.

She stood up. Even crouching, Swede towered over her.

When I'm in human form, that is, Anna thought. She hated being in human form, especially when Swede wasn't. Being human made her feel small.

But, only on the outside.

Swede's tongue lolled, and Anna smiled. The black-furred werewolf was far friendlier as a wolf than as a human.

The two remaining members of the pack ran into the alley.

Layla skidded to a stop beside Swede, her claws scratching along the pavement.

Paul followed close behind, still in human form. They had been checking out an alley on the other side of the block, but they came running when they heard Anna's message.

Layla crouched by Swede and rested her shaggy head on his massive shoulder.

Anna turned and jogged to the end of the alley. She peered around the corner.

Firemen crowded the street beyond. They were battling the blaze with dozens of hoses.

The lower four floors of the apartment building were burning out of control, the work of the man she and the pack were chasing.

She turned her head slowly, listening to the conversations on the street. Apartment residents stood in a group on the other side of the police barrier. She caught pieces of their conversations, lamentations about lost pictures, lost jewelry, lost things.

Had she ever been like that? Worrying over possessions? She thought she had, but she couldn't remember it. All that mattered was the pack and her mother in Virginia.

And the arsonist. He mattered. He killed people. He had to be stopped. She was going to kill him.

She saw the fire chief. He was sixty yards away, but she focused on him, tuned out all the noise. She listened.

Anna spoke into the microphone, "He says they've lost control of the fire. The accelerants the arsonist used. They can't put them out."

"Okay," Karen said. "There's nothing we can do here. Anna, Paul, check the alleys to the south. See if you can pick up his scent."

"He's here," Anna said. "He has to be. He'd want to watch the suffering." She scanned the crowd.

They had no idea what the man looked like.

But they knew what he smelled like.

Anna stepped toward the crowd.

"Good thinking," Karen said. "Paul, work the crowd with her. Layla, Swede, stick to the shadows and check out the alleys."

A woman screamed.

Anna turned and looked back toward the fire chief.

A woman in a t-shirt and sweatpants was talking frantically.

Anna looked up at the building, "Karen, there's a little boy still in the building. He's only four." She jumped the barrier. "I'm going in."

"No! Work the crowd," Karen said. "Swede, go after the kid."

Anna listened as the frantic woman spoke to the police chief. "He's on the sixth floor, Swede. Apartment six-eighteen. His name is Aidan."

***

Swede reached the end of the alley in four strides. He stood up on his crooked legs to his full height of nine feet and looked around the corner. Flames poured from the windows on the first four floors.

This was going to hurt.

The street was crowded with firemen on each side of the building.

So much for stealth.

Swede ran into the street on all fours. All eyes were on the burning building. No one screamed as the huge werewolf ran toward the flames.

He jumped over the firemen, and they did take notice. They screamed, a few dropped their hoses.

Swede's six-inch-long claws drove into the bricks twenty feet off the ground and then he was climbing. Flames from the second floor engulfed him, and he felt his fur burn away.

The skin of his hands blistered.

He kept moving up, past the third floor.

He was on fire now; his skin was blistering. He ignored the pain.

Ten minutes in these flames and he would be reduced to ash, but he had no intention of staying.

12

He cleared the flames and felt a blast of cool water.

Swede looked down.

The firemen were directing the hoses toward him.

He wasn't sure whether they were trying to put out the flames or knock him off the building.

Either way, he had stopped burning. The pain stopped, and the werewolf virus worked its magic. The blistering faded, and his skin healed within seconds. Black fur erupted from his follicles.

By the time he reached the sixth floor, all trace of the burning was gone.

"Swede? Can you hear me?" Karen's voice asked.

The sound came from a speaker attached to the harness that crisscrossed his chest and back.

He slapped at the button in the center of his chest, signaling that he could hear her. The worst part about being in werewolf form was being unable to speak.

"Good. Well, at least we know the harness is fireproof," Karen said. "Wipe off the camera lens. I can't see."

Swede wiped off the lens on his left shoulder with the back of his paw.

"Better."

Swede kicked in a window on the sixth floor and climbed inside.

***

Anna took the right side of the street while Paul worked the left. She could see his gray hair moving through the crowd. They would work their way to the center.

And, if either of them got close enough, they would tear the arsonist's throat out – crowd be damned.

She looked over her shoulder.

Layla was watching them from the alley, ready to move if things got dicey.

Anna looked up at the building and hoped Swede was okay.

***

The flames had not reached the sixth floor, but it was filled with smoke. The fifth floor had caught fire – Swede could feel the heat rising through the hallway tile.

He stood outside six-eighteen. He slammed his palm against the door, and it fell off its hinges. It collapsed on the carpeted entryway, and Swede stepped over it.

"Aidan? Can you hear me?" Karen called through the speaker on Swede's harness.

He could be unconscious, Swede thought. The apartment was thick with smoke.

He walked into the living room. Easter toys covered the floor and tables: Easter baskets, multicolored plastic eggs, an adult sized rubber Easter bunny mask complete with long ears.

Easter Sunday was only three days away.

"Swede, he might be frightened of you," Karen said.

***

Anna was near the center of the crowd when she smelled the kerosene. He was close.

Paul nodded at her from twenty feet away. He could smell it as well.

She looked from face to face. They were all watching the flames.

Anna and Paul closed in.

***

Swede opened the bedroom door. He was reflected in a mirror on the opposite wall.

He was wearing the Easter bunny mask.

"Great, you look like a monster jack rabbit," Karen said over the speaker. "Aidan? Are you in here?"

Swede looked around. This was the master bedroom, not a child's room.

He walked back into the hall and opened the other bedroom door.

The little boy was sitting in the middle of his bed, stuffed animals piled around him. He screamed.

"Aidan. It's okay. I'm not going to hurt you," Karen said. She had lowered the pitch of her voice.

14

"Who are you?"

Swede held up a red plastic Easter egg in his clawed hand.

"I'm the Easter bunny."

***

Anna and Paul were facing each other. The smell was strong, but no one was there.

"How's this possible?" Anna asked.

"I don't know," Paul said. He shook his head and looked around. "I can smell him like he's right here."

They both looked down at the pavement at the same time. There was a red nylon backpack between them. It smelled of kerosene.

"Oh, my God," Anna said.

"What's wrong?" Karen asked over the earpiece.

"There's a bomb on the street," Paul said.

"Bomb!" Anna screamed.

People began to run in all directions, leaving Paul and Anna alone with the bag between them.

"What do we do?" Anna asked.

"We have to get it away from here. We have no way of knowing how powerful the bomb is," Paul said.

"Just back away," Karen said. "Picking it up might set it off."

Anna looked around. The crowd was still too close.

Fire terrified her.

Anna grabbed the backpack and ran toward the empty alley to the south.

"Damn it, Anna," Karen said.

"I've got a plan," Anna said as she ran past the crowd into the alley.

"Just throw it in the alley."

Anna slid to a stop in front of a green dumpster. The top was plastic, but it would have to do. She opened it and dropped the bag inside.

She slammed the lid and backed away.

Nothing. No explosion.

"Maybe it wasn't a bomb," Anna said.

She heard a cell phone ring. It was coming from the dumpster.

15

"Son of a bitch," Anna whispered.

The dumpster exploded.

***

Swede ran down the hall toward the stairwell; the little boy tucked under his arm. He put his hand on the stairwell door, and his skin sizzled.

He growled. The fire had reached the sixth floor.

There was a window at the end of the hall, and he looked down. The fire raged on the floor below. By himself, he could easily have leaped out the window and fallen the sixty feet to the ground below.

The boy would never survive the fall.

He couldn't climb down, the child would be incinerated.

Swede kicked out with his right foot and sent the window flying into the smoke-filled sky. There was a roar behind him.

The fire, hungry for oxygen erupted from the other end of the hall, a wall of fire seeking the air.

But Swede was already in motion. He climbed out the window, hooked the claws of his right hand into the window frame and swung to the side. He dug the claws of both feet into the side of the building just as the wall of flame passed him on the right, burning the hair from his right arm.

He climbed, past the seventh floor to the eighth. His feet dug into the building as he pulled himself up with his right hand. The child clung to him.

He rolled onto the roof.

***

Anna opened her eyes.

Paul was leaning over her. He was saying something, but she couldn't hear it. Her ears were still ringing.

She began to beat at her clothes with her palms, "Fire! I'm on fire!"

Paul grabbed her hands. He mouthed the word "No."

And then she could hear him.

"No, no, Anna. It's okay. The dumpster contained the blast. The flames went straight up. You're not burning."

16

"I'm not burning?" Anna whispered.

"No. It blew you out of the alley about thirty feet, but you're not burning," he looked back toward the street. "We have to get out of here."

Anna looked up. Police and EMTs were rushing toward them.

She took his hand and stood up.

The ground began to rumble.

***

Swede stood up on the roof just as the building started to lean.

Not good, Swede thought.

"Swede, the building is collapsing," Karen said over the speaker.

Tell me about it.

Swede's part of the roof was beginning to sink while the other end was starting to rise. He ran toward the rising side.

"It's sixty feet to the next roof; you can't make that."

Watch me.

The roof behind him was falling away. He ran faster.

At the edge of the roof, Swede launched himself into space.

***

On the ground, everyone stopped running toward the alley.

Anna looked up.

A dark shape hurtled through the air over the street as the building began to fall in on itself.

Swede, Anna thought.

***

Swede tumbled in mid-air, turning his back to the approaching building. His left arm held the kid tight against his chest. He was falling faster than he had hoped.

If he could break their fall with his own back, the boy might live.

His back and shoulders hit something. He felt it give and then shatter. Glass fell around him.

He had flown through a window in the building across the street, and he hit the floor. He felt his right shoulder break as he slid across the hardwood.

17

Everything was still for a moment. There was the sound of the collapsing building across the street. Swede lay there for a moment, feeling his bones knitting in his shoulder.

The little boy moved and looked up at him, "Are you okay, Easter bunny?"

Karen's voice came through the speaker, "Is the Easter bunny breathing?"

"Yeah," the little boy said.

"Then Easter bunny is just fine," Karen said.

Swede stood up.

An elderly woman sat on a flowered couch. She stared at them wide-eyed.

The camera on Swede's chest pointed toward her.

"Sorry about the window, Ma'am," Karen said.

Swede rotated his right shoulder. He felt the bones grind and pop as they slid back into place. He picked up the kid and ran through the door.

People were standing in the hallway, and they screamed as the nine-foot-tall rabbit ran past carrying the little boy.

Swede ran down the stairs to the front lobby.

***

Anna and Paul slipped away down the alley. The rescue workers were too busy with the collapsed building to worry about the burning dumpster.

***

The little boy walked out of the building and into the crowd. He tugged on his mother's pants leg.

She screamed and hugged him, "How? How did you get out?"

He turned and pointed over his shoulder at the lobby of the other building, "The Easter bunny."

A rubber rabbit mask was lying on the steps.

***

The Hunted

Karen Arthur watched the red dots moving on the screen - one dot for each member of her pack superimposed on a map of downtown Detroit. The pack headed south away from the collapsed apartment building.

She rubbed her blue eyes and leaned back in her chair. *One of the pack almost incinerated, another almost blown up - good work, Karen*, she thought.

The array of monitors around the map screen showed the view from each of their cameras. She could tell from the angle that Anna and Paul had changed into wolf form when they joined up with Layla and Swede.

"*Our natural form*," Anna would have said.

And she was right. Anna was spending more and more time as a wolf. Even though they were almost as strong in their human form, even though their senses were just as sensitive, it didn't feel right.

There was a longing to run with the pack, to be free of this human world and simply be what they were.

Karen felt it the same as the others.

But they had to live in the human world. The pack was needed.

It had been five years since Karen Arthur had chosen sides.

She had been turned and molded by a mad man, Hayden Oswald. He and his pack had done horrible things.

Karen had done horrible things herself.

But five years ago in Bedford, Virginia, Karen had sided with Ward Rickman's pack, and together they had killed Hayden Oswald and his followers.

Karen had formed her own pack, and they had spent the last three years tracking down and destroying rogues – werewolves originally part of Hayden's pack who had gone insane.

Karen rolled back along the steel floor of the panel truck and looked at the bulletin board. Rows of names, each with a red 'X' drawn over it.

All save one: Todd Stearn.

They had searched for Stearn for six months and found nothing. Either he was the stealthiest rogue in history, or he was dead.

She hoped for the latter.

She stood up and walked to the back of the panel truck. She opened the rear doors and stepped out into the cold March wind. Karen could smell the smoke from the apartment building.

Clyde Hubbard was leaning against the outside of the van. "Where are they?" he asked.

"Working their way south. They haven't caught the scent yet," she pointed to the earpiece and microphone on her right ear.

Clyde had been with her for five years. He had stood with her at Bedford and hadn't left her side since.

He was the only member of the pack who wasn't a werewolf, not that Karen hadn't offered. But truth be told, he had put down more rogues with his silver-tipped arrows than anyone else in the pack.

Smoke rose into the air above the buildings to the north.

Karen sighed.

"They'll find him," Clyde said.

"I know. That's what I'm afraid of," Karen said. She looked at the words stenciled on the van above Clyde: Detroit Express Delivery. "We're going to have to repaint the van before we leave."

"You know, you're turning into a real worrier."

She shrugged off the comment. "What the hell are we doing here, Clyde? This is an arsonist, not a rogue werewolf. We should leave this to the police."

"He's killed a dozen people. Maimed two dozen more. They've had six months to catch him, and they haven't. Our people can do better."

"It's not our fight. It's not worth losing one of our own."

Clyde laughed. "Bullshit. This is what the pack was made for – I ought to know, you're the one who told me, remember?"

She nodded, "I just want them to be safe."

"Werewolves can't be safe."

***

Running. Anna felt free, even though she had to stick to the alleys. She had caught a whiff of kerosene on the air, and she followed her nose. The alley flashed by.

She danced over a homeless person who slept against a brick wall to her right. The man didn't move in his sleep, even as four, nine-foot-tall monsters passed by.

They were the wind, and all Anna wanted to do was run and keep running. Find the Michigan woods – they had to be out there somewhere. Run into the mountains and leave civilization behind.

Kerosene. The smell brought her back, made her focus. She slid to a stop. Layla, Swede, and Paul stopped behind her.

Swede raised his head and sniffed the air, confirming what Anna already knew: the arsonist was close. Very close.

Anna lowered her head and growled.

Fifty yards ahead, a man climbed onto a motorcycle at the end of the alley.

The pack moved as one, charging down the alley. There was no mistake: the kerosene smell was strong.

The motorcycle started with a rumble, and the man pulled onto Grand River Avenue.

No! Anna thought as she reached the end of the alley. He was speeding away, almost lost in the heavy traffic.

She tapped the button on her chest, alerting Karen they had found him.

And lost him, Anna thought.

She turned and looked at the others. They were panting.

Paul had lain down in the dirty street, stretched out like a gray snowbank.

Swede looked at her, cocking his great black head sideways – the universal look of all canines who wondered what you were going to do next. He was smiling.

Anna smiled back.

To hell with playing it safe. Give the humans a show, she thought. She turned and ran out onto Grand River Avenue.

The other three followed.

***

"What in the hell are you doing?" Karen yelled into the microphone.

21

She had run back into the van when she heard the beep in her earpiece.

And now she was watching four red dots moving fast down one of the busiest streets in Detroit.

She heard the driver's door open, and Clyde jumped behind the wheel.

"What's going on?" he asked.

"Anna. She's leading them right down Grand River Avenue!"

Clyde started the van and pulled out fast. "We're moving."

"Anna, let him go and get off the street. It's not worth being discovered," Karen said.

Anna answered with two beeps. No.

"Damn it, Anna."

***

This is a lot more fun than running through the alley, Anna thought.

They ran between the cars. The street was packed from red light to red light.

Anna watched the motorcycle far ahead.

The arsonist was guiding his motorcycle between the cars as well. He was three lights ahead.

People were screaming and blowing their horns as the werewolves passed by at a gallop.

The pack reached the first red light and did not slow down. Two lanes of cars approached on the left, and Anna leaped over both lanes.

She landed on the hood of a Toyota and pushed off, leaping the next two lanes with ease.

Layla and Swede followed close behind. Layla jumped the first two lanes, but Swede fell short.

He tore through the canvas roof of a jeep.

Layla stopped in the crosswalk and looked back.

Swede was tangled, and he kicked at the tan fabric. He fell into the back seat of the jeep.

The jeep swerved but didn't slow, carrying Swede away to the west.

***

22

He's a big boy. He can take care of himself, Layla thought. She turned to follow Anna.

There was a car in front of her. The driver sat behind the wheel holding up his smartphone. He was filming her.

Layla grinned. She threw her head back and howled.

He dropped the phone as she leaped onto the hood. The front tires exploded from the impact. She bent her legs and jumped, flying over the four cars beyond.

***

Anna was one red light away when the man on the motorcycle looked behind him. She doubted he could tell what was chasing him from this distance, but he obviously thought something was.

He turned right at the red light and headed toward the river.

Anna followed him onto Randolph Street. The cylindrical towers of the GM Renaissance Center glowed to the south.

Layla was right behind her, and Swede darted out of an alley to her right, a tatter of the jeep's cloth roof still wrapped around his left foot.

She looked back over her shoulder.

Paul was a block behind, unable to match the speed of the younger wolves.

They ran between the cars. The street was filled with the sound of shrieking pedestrians and blowing horns.

The Renaissance Center loomed larger ahead.

Where is he going? Anna thought. The only things to the south were the tunnel to Canada and the Renaissance Center.

***

"Damn it," Clyde said. "Traffic's slowed to a crawl. It'll take us an hour to catch up with them."

The line of cars down Randolph Street wasn't moving at all.

"No," Karen growled. "Turn left and wait for us at the entrance to 375."

Clyde looked over his shoulder.

Karen was already naked, and the change was coursing through her body.

"Oh, great," Clyde grumbled.

Blonde fur erupted from her skin and her jaw stretched filling with long white fangs.

Clyde slapped a button on the dashboard.

The rear doors hissed open, and Karen leaped out the back.

She stood on her hind legs and stared at a woman in a Prius behind the van. The woman's eyes were wide.

Take a picture, sister, it'll last longer, Karen thought as she ran around the side of the van. She dropped to all fours and loped down Randolph Street to join the pack.

***

The man who smelled of kerosene was heading straight toward the tunnel to Windsor, Canada. A line of American flags marked the entrance to the tunnel – a concrete canyon with a four-lane road that disappeared into the gloom as it went under the Detroit River.

The road was clear beyond the red light and Anna ran faster.

At the last instant, the rider veered left. He sped down the narrow road that led by the Renaissance Center.

Mistake, Anna thought. He was headed straight to the river.

The four werewolves ran after him. The massive glass towers of the Renaissance Center rose above them.

The arsonist reached the end of the road and leaned to the left, his knee a few inches above the pavement. He disappeared around the corner.

Anna's rear claws caught in the asphalt as she did a sliding turn, tearing gouges a foot long in the road.

She could see him again.

He had jumped off the bike, and he was running through a set of glass doors into the Renaissance Center.

Smooth jazz was playing on the street outside. A band was playing under a small tent by the river. On the other side of the wide water, the lights of Windsor sparkled.

People were walking on the street by the jazz concert.

They screamed and jumped out of the way as the werewolves crashed through the tall glass windows on the ground floor of the Renaissance Center.

***

Let Them Burn

The side of the Renaissance Center facing the Detroit River is called the Wintergarden. It is a mall with a glass enclosed atrium five stories tall. The open area in the center is surrounded by palm trees to make the patrons feel warm in the frigid Detroit winter.

The arsonist stopped in the center of the atrium and stared at the four werewolves who stood in the glittering remains of the shattered windows.

He blinked. He shook his head. He had thought he was being chased by the police.

The four monsters closed on him, ignoring the broken glass under their massive paws.

Warm urine ran down his leg as his bladder let go.

He held the detonator tight in his left hand, the wire running up the arm of his motorcycle jacket to the pack on his back.

People ran in all directions, screaming.

"Stay back," he yelled. "I'll burn them. I'll burn them all."

***

Anna smiled, pulling her lips back from her fangs as she lowered her head. Drool fell on the tile beneath her chin. She loved it when they pissed themselves.

She took a step forward.

"No, wait," Clyde's voice came from the speaker on her harness. "Paul, circle left. Layla, circle right. I want a look at that bomb on his back."

***

Clyde had parked near the entrance to 375, and he sat in front of the monitors. The angles changed as Paul and Layla flanked the arsonist.

The man turned left and then right, facing the two werewolves.

"I'll do it. If I let my thumb off this button, they all die."

Clyde looked at the backpack. Aluminum pipes were sticking out at odd angles from the pack, giving the man the appearance of a porcupine. The tubes were dimpled all over with tiny holes.

"Fuel air," Clyde whispered.

Anna took a step toward the man.

"No! Anna, listen to me," Clyde said. "That bomb on his back is a fuel air bomb. It sprays out a cloud of flammable vapor, and a spark ignites it. It'll suck all the air out of the area in an instant. He'll bring the whole damned building down."

***

Anna looked around.

People were running, most running away, but some running into stores, hiding. And how many people were in the towers above? They would all burn.

This had been his plan; his endgame should the police ever corner him.

Anna took a step back.

Swede looked at her.

She didn't need to hear his voice to know his question, *What now?*

Anna began to sidestep to the left.

The others followed, and they formed a circle around the man. They moved in a clockwise orbit around him.

"Stay back!"

He was going to do it. She could see it in his eyes. This was indeed his endgame, although Anna doubted this was the way he thought it would play out.

They stopped circling him when Anna had put him between herself and the river. Swede was directly opposite.

The man turned his back on Swede and faced Anna.

Anna smiled.

Swede howled.

The man spun and Anna moved.

She was on him in an instant, her clawed right hand closing on his hand, the one holding the detonator.

26

She lifted him off the ground and ran as he screamed.

She crushed his hand, feeling the bones break as she forced her thumb over the detonator button.

She darted through the shattered windows and onto the street.

She ran past the jazz band that had stopped playing.

Anna reached the river's edge and jumped, carrying the still screaming man with her.

The surface of the river flashed past.

And, then they were in it, diving deep. He still screamed as Anna's strong legs kicked, pushing them deeper into the dark water.

Her ears popped from the pressure.

She looked into the man's eyes. His screams had stopped.

Anna pushed him away and rose.

The remains of his thumb floated away.

Pressurized kerosene rushed into the river around him.

Anna kicked and rose.

The river exploded.

***

No! Karen thought as she ran toward the river.

The road shook as a geyser of water shot thirty feet into the air.

Karen jumped off the concrete sidewalk and dove into the water.

***

Anna was asleep in the tub. She was in her mother's old house in Elkhorn, Wisconsin. She had a headache that just wouldn't stop.

Her eyes were closed, and she felt herself slip into the warm tub.

She felt herself sink lower and lower.

She felt hands on her, under her arms. Someone was pulling her up out of the deep tub. Their legs kicked behind hers, and she kicked as well, helping.

They broke the surface.

She looked back over her shoulder.

Karen's blue eyes stared back at her above the fanged muzzle.

Anna shook her head and pulled free.

Together, they swam toward the Renaissance Center.

***

Paul and Swede knelt by the river and pulled them out.

Karen fell on her back panting.

In the distance, she could hear sirens.

She got to her feet.

Anna rolled onto her feet as well.

Karen leaned forward, caught the flesh at the back of Anna's neck in her teeth and bit down hard, drawing blood.

Anna yelped and rolled away.

Karen shook herself like a dog and ran in the direction of the van.

The others followed with Anna staying at the rear.

***

The first thing you lose as a werewolf is modesty, Anna thought.

The five of them transitioned back into human form in the back of the van and pulled on their clothes as Clyde drove through the night away from Detroit.

The second thing you lose is your fashion sense.

Their clothes came from Walmart and thrift shops – because, sooner or later, they would be discarded in some back alley.

She had been partial to the blouse she had been wearing tonight. It was lying in an alley near Grand River Avenue. She hoped the next owner would value it as much as she had.

Karen was staring at the wall of the van as she dressed. She hadn't made eye contact with Anna since dragging her out of the Detroit River.

Anna knew the bite on the back of her neck was all the alpha felt she needed to say.

It wasn't fair. Yes, she had disobeyed, but they had stopped a madman. It had been worth the risk.

She almost wanted Karen to yell at her. The silent treatment was much worse.

Karen shoved past her and sat down in the passenger seat beside Clyde.

Anna looked out the window as the lines in the road flashed by. She felt a hand on her shoulder.

Paul squeezed gently and whispered, "She'll get over it."

Anna nodded and watched the road.

***

They had driven over an hour north before cutting west and doubling back to the south. Karen wanted to make sure nobody had managed to follow them. By one AM, they were at the abandoned warehouse on the outskirts of Ann Arbor where they left the motorcycles.

There was one Harley for each of them – bikes originally belonging to Hayden Oswald's gang. They would take turns driving the van, each loading their bike in the back when they took their turn.

One side of the warehouse roof was caving in, but the other side was dry and relatively clean.

They gathered outside the van as Clyde slid the big door shut behind them.

"We'll leave Michigan at first light," Karen said.

Swede ran his fingers through his long black hair, "Where we heading?"

Karen shook her head, "Just south. Kentucky maybe. Or Virginia. We need to lay low for a while."

Swede smiled and pulled Layla close, "Hear that, baby? Mountains."

She wrapped her hands around the back of his neck. "I like to play in the mountains."

"Me too," Swede said as he picked her up and threw her over his shoulder. He put her on the back of his bike and climbed on in front of her.

"Where are you two going?" Karen asked.

"Bar," Swede said as Layla wrapped her arms around his waist.

"It's one in the morning," Karen said.

"Means we got an hour, right baby?"

"You bet," Layla said.

Swede started the bike, and they headed out through the collapsed side of the building.

Anna began to walk away.

"Where are you going?" Karen asked.

Anna shrugged, "Find some place to sleep."

29

"No. You're repainting the van."

"What?"

Karen's eyes flashed, "You're repainting the damned van. That stunt you pulled put us on the Internet. We're not going to take the chance that someone got a picture of the truck. Get out the paint and the sprayer and get to work."

"That'll take hours."

"Should have thought about that before you decided to lead a wolf parade down Grand River Avenue," Karen said as she stalked away.

"I can paint it, Karen," Clyde said.

She glared at him.

"Or, not," he said. He looked at Anna, "Sorry, kid."

***

Anna carried the paint sprayer out of the van and dropped it on the concrete floor, "Paint the van? I'm a damned hero."

She looked up. Paul was leaning on the side of the van smiling at her. He held a book in his hand.

Anna stared at the concrete floor, embarrassed that she had been talking to herself. "Why does she hate me, professor?"

Paul laughed and shook his head, "She doesn't hate you, Anna."

"Everybody else can run into an inferno or jump off an eight-story building, and she's like, no problem. That's just Swede being Swede. She's harder on me than anyone else."

Paul sat down and put his back against the van. "Two reasons: one, she's harder on you because she expects more from you. Take it as a compliment."

"Why? She wants me to act like an alpha – tough shit, my eyes are yellow, not blue."

Paul shook his head, "Being the alpha only means she keeps everyone from going rogue. She holds the pack together. It doesn't mean you can't be a leader. You've seen how we work in the field – everyone follows your lead. She wants you to lead us well, Anna, that's all."

Anna thought about that for a moment, "So, I guess leading us down a crowded four-lane was a little dumb."

Paul laughed, "Oh, I don't know. Now, grabbing hold of a man with a bomb strapped to his back and jumping into the river with him – that was a little dumb."

Anna laughed. "Seemed like a good idea at the time."

"If it's any consolation, I personally think you saved everyone in that building."

Anna nodded, "Thanks, professor."

Anna reached down and opened the paint reservoir. She stopped and stood up, "You said there were two reasons."

"Yes?"

"Well, what's the second?"

"She's harder on you, my dear, because she sees a lot of herself in you. We're always harder on those who remind us of ourselves."

Anna looked down at the floor. Paul always had a way of putting things in perspective.

"Now, what say I help you paint this van," Paul said as he stood up and picked up one of the cans of paint she had retrieved from inside the truck.

He frowned at the can, "Hot Pink?"

Anna smiled, an evil twinkle in her eye, "Yeah, hot pink."

***

Karen was sitting on the curb outside the warehouse. Bats were flittering around the thick trees. Her sensitive ears could hear the sonar sounds, and they reminded her of the sound of tree frogs.

Clyde sat down beside her and handed her a cold bottle of beer.

She looked at the label, "Imported. What's the occasion, redneck?"

"I would've brought you a Pabst, but I figured you were more likely to drink the prissy, fancy crap," Clyde said as he took a drink. He was looking at his iPad.

"Let me guess, we're all over Twitter and Facebook?"

"See for yourself," Clyde said. He handed her the tablet.

There, in high definition, was Layla throwing back her head and howling. "Oh, for God's sake." She handed it back.

"Yeah, this was online for all of, oh, two minutes. And, then it disappeared."

"What? How did you do that?"

"Hey, darlin', I'm good, but I ain't that good. Somebody scrubbed the Internet clean. I managed to download this while you guys were at the Renaissance Center. Disappeared almost immediately."

"Who would do that?"

Clyde took another drink, "Somebody with a sack load of pull. If I was to put on my tin-foil hat, I'd say we're talking NSA, black helicopter, scary bastards."

Karen sighed, "As if this night couldn't get any worse."

"Which would you prefer? A billion people watching us on Facebook or some government knuckleheads who couldn't find their ass with both hands? I'd choose the bureaucrats."

"I'd prefer neither," Karen said, and she downed her beer. "What the hell is wrong with that damned kid?"

"She's nineteen, Karen. She's got at least two more years before she grows a brain. Ease off a little."

"Ease off?" Karen hissed. "She almost got them all killed. She could have brought the whole Renaissance Center down."

"That's one way of looking at it - the other way is she saved everybody in the center."

"If she hadn't chased him…"

"Yeah, I know. Maybe he would have just gone home tonight but let me share a little bit I've found out about our arsonist. The cops traced his motorcycle to one," Clyde pulled up an image on his tablet. "Albert Foxworth, age thirty-seven. Now, earlier tonight, Mr. Foxworth placed a bomb in that apartment building. He put it in the front lobby."

"I already know this…"

"I ain't finished. He then walked outside and used the intercom to call the little boy's mother – she just happened to be the only single parent in the building. He told her he had a delivery she needed to sign for. She went down to the lobby and stepped outside just as the bomb went off."

"Jesus."

"Yeah, see he wanted to make sure she couldn't get back to her four-year-old. He wanted the boy to burn. Must have staked out the building for days to find the right one to target. He might not have had red eyes and claws, but he was a monster nonetheless."

Karen nodded.

Clyde shrugged, "Maybe you're right. Maybe he wouldn't have gone to the Renaissance Center if they hadn't chased him. Then again, maybe that was where he was headed in the first place – especially considering he tried to blow up everybody on the sidewalk at the other building. I think he wanted every fireman, cop, and paramedic in Detroit tied up when he took down the Renaissance Center."

He took her hand and squeezed it, "Which makes every one of you damned certified heroes, even if Anna doesn't use her head all the time."

"Yeah, well, we need to work on that last part. She's still too reckless."

Clyde laughed, "You mean like diving into thirty feet of water when you can't swim?"

Karen grinned, "Werewolves can swim – it's instinct. At least, I hoped it would be instinct."

"Yeah, maybe so, but you and I both know Karen Arthur would drown in a kiddie pool. Now that's reckless behavior."

She took his half-finished beer out of his hand, "Point taken, Mr. Hubbard."

***

Karen woke to the sound of birds chirping. She had slept under a tree near the warehouse.

Clyde lay on the grass five feet away. He rolled onto his back and snored.

Karen smiled at his skinny frame in his thirty years out of date western shirt complete with pearl snaps instead of buttons. By his admission, Clyde was scrawny, just a little over five foot nine and weighing in at a buck thirty on a good day after a full meal.

She had asked him three times in five years to let her turn him. He had refused each time. A rogue werewolf, Clayton Ambrose, had killed both his father and brother. Their memory kept him from accepting her offer.

She picked up a pine needle and ran it over his upper lip.

He slapped at his face and snored again.

Karen bit her lower lip to keep from laughing and then stuck the pine needle up his right nostril.

Clyde began frantically slapping at his face. He began to sneeze and cough and then raised straight up, "What? What? I'm up."

He pulled the pine needle out of his nostril and frowned at Karen.

She fell onto her back and laughed.

"Ha, ha, hilarious," Clyde said as he threw the pine needle at her.

"Don't throw that thing at me, it's got snot on it," Karen said and laughed louder.

Clyde lay down beside her and started tickling her ribs, "Yeah, let's see how you like it."

Karen screamed, "Don't you dare!"

He rolled on top of her, "Yeah, you can dish it out, but you can't take it."

She smiled up at him.

He leaned in close.

She turned her head to the side, "We should get going."

Clyde sighed. "Why? What would it hurt? Just once, Karen."

She touched his lips with her index finger, "One day."

He leaned over and whispered in her ear, "Life's short, Karen. I'm patient, but I'm not that patient."

She rolled away and stood up.

"He sure did a number on you," Clyde said leaning on his elbow.

She didn't have to ask who he meant. Hayden Oswald had indeed done a number on her. "You have no idea."

***

Karen stood in the warehouse and scowled at the van.

Clyde walked up beside her and whistled. "If you were wanting inconspicuous, I think they missed the mark."

Paul and Anna were leaning against the front wheel on the passenger side, passed out on each other's shoulders.

The van was bright pink from top to bottom. The words "Kentucky Pride Ice Cream" were written in big festive letters on the windowless side of the truck.

Below the words was a giant cartoon depiction of an ice cream cone with stick figure arms and legs. They had painted a big, toothy grin below round eyes on the single scoop of ice cream that made up the character's head.

Below this, they had painted the words, "Eat Me!"

Swede walked over beside Karen and stretched, "I like it."

***

Heart of Darkness

Joseph Marlow leaned forward and tried to determine if this would be the switchback turn that sent his rental car careening down the side of Spears Mountain. He had almost chosen a compact car at Charlottesville Airport. Instead, he had taken the upgrade to a mid-size Ford. In retrospect, that had been a mistake. The car was too big for the somewhat paved goat trail he was following.

The GPS on his phone had repeatedly tried to re-route him away from this one lane road that climbed the side of the mountain in a nauseating series of almost one-hundred-eighty-degree switchbacks. Unfortunately, his destination was at the top, and there was only one road.

Mountain laurel and pine clung to the sides of the mountain. Less obstinate vegetation would have given up and left the ground bare.

He managed another switchback and saw the sign: US Government Property. No Trespassing. Use of Deadly Force Authorized.

The sign was old and weathered like the mountaintop itself.

The road widened and Joseph found himself in a parking lot, shrouded by a copse of oaks and pines. A handful of dusty cars and trucks were parked in spots that might once have been drawn out with paint. Only ghosts remained.

A small, bald man sat on the curb in front of the only visible structure: a concrete roofed Quonset Hut that extended into the mountain top.

The man was wide across his middle. His dark suit was rumpled, and his head was red from too much recent sun on nearly bare skin.

He was intent on a book in his hands, and he did not look up when Joseph pulled into a space near him.

Joseph stopped the car and got out, carrying his only two bags: a briefcase and a small gym bag.

He walked up to the man on the curb.

The man peered up at him, squinting in the bright sunlight, "Doctor Marlow, I presume?"

"Yes."

"Edward Price," the smaller man said. He stood up and waved the book at Joseph. "Heart of Darkness – do you like Conrad?"

"As I recall, I did. I haven't read it since college."

"I adore this book," Price said. "Must have read it a dozen times." He caressed the cover as if it were a lover. "Lot of time to read up here. Closest town is Buckingham, and I swear they roll up the streets when it gets dark. And the drive? Atrocious."

"Yeah, I noticed."

"But, the air," Price said, and he drew in a deep breath. "Smell those Virginia pines. God, I don't spend enough time out here. Do you like spaghetti?"

"Spaghetti?" Joseph asked. He was beginning to understand why Uncle Sam needed a psychologist out here.

"It's spaghetti night. Our chef has this wonderful recipe for his sauce, mixes in maple sugar and vodka. It's to die for."

"Mr. Price, if you don't mind, I'd like to know why I've been requested?"

Price stared up at him. "They didn't tell you?"

"No. They just put me in a Jetstream and flew me from Dulles to Charlottesville."

"We have patients for you," Price said as he led the way toward the Quonset Hut.

Joseph rushed to catch up to him, "How many people are here?"

"About two dozen caretakers and a handful of… residents," Price said as he opened a heavy iron door and ushered Joseph inside.

The room was empty except for what appeared to be an elevator door. Price pressed his thumb against a rectangular piece of glass to the right of the elevator.

The door beeped and slid open. They stepped inside the bright elevator.

"I'll get your thumbprint added to the system in a few days. Until then, one of the staff will have to accompany you to the surface."

"Surface?"

Price smiled and pressed the only button on the control panel. The doors hissed shut and the elevator began to descend.

"The mountain is basically hollow. Created quite a stir when they carved it out back in the eighties. Ronald Reagan, God bless him, he did have a flair for the dramatic."

The back of the elevator was a window and Joseph took a step back.

The inside of the mountain was indeed hollow. He was staring out at an immense cavern, with concrete terraces ringing the inside.

"Five thousand feet deep. Nuke plant in the basement – of course, we don't use it. We get our power from the grid. This was supposed to be the last stand for the good old USA should the Reds drop the bomb. You know, there's actually a runway with sliding doors at the halfway point. Used to be a half dozen Harrier Jump Jets in here. Magnificent anachronism – I keep telling them they should open it up for tourists, it'd be bigger than Kings Dominion."

"You say there are only two dozen people here?"

"Yes, it was abandoned for over two decades. We needed a secure facility, and it was available."

"What organization are you with?"

Price stared at him for a moment, "We don't have a three-letter acronym. We have ties to the CIA, NSA, NRO, DOD, but we operate under the radar."

"You mean without oversight?"

"God, I hope so. Have you ever had to answer to a congressional committee? I'd rather have my teeth pulled without Novocaine."

The elevator doors opened onto a gleaming white corridor. A bored guard in black overalls sat at a rusted metal desk.

Price nodded as they walked by.

They stepped into a huge courtyard with a glass roof. The cavern opened above them, disappearing into the darkness.

Price led him across the courtyard and into another hallway.

"We only occupy this small section," he looked at his watch. "The staff is at dinner right now. Let's meet one of your patients."

Price knocked on a door.

"Come in," a man's voice said.

The room looked like a military barracks. There was a line of empty bedframes. Only one had a mattress. The bunk had been made meticulously – you could have bounced a quarter off it.

A tall man in olive drab fatigues stood by the bunk. He snapped to attention when he saw Price.

"At ease, Gunny," Price said. "Doctor Marlow, may I present Gunnery Sergeant William Dobbs."

"Pleased to meet you," Joseph said.

"Sir," Dobbs said. His blonde hair was cut in a flat top above curiously yellow eyes.

"Gunny Dobbs will be your first patient. You're here to assess his mental faculties."

"Nothing wrong with my head, sir," Dobbs said.

"Absolutely not, Gunny. Dr. Marlow is just here to dot the I's and cross the T's, isn't that right, Doctor?"

I don't know what I'm doing here, Joseph thought.

Price squeezed Joseph's arm, "Isn't that right, Doctor?"

"Yes, that's right. Just routine, Gunny."

"Gunny, I think the good doctor would like a demonstration, if you'd be so kind."

"Sir, yes, sir!" Dobbs said. He started unbuttoning his shirt.

Price stood in front of Joseph. "Doctor, what you're about to see is going to be upsetting. I need you to stay perfectly still. You're going to want to run, but I assure you there is no danger whatsoever."

"What?"

"Unless you run. Then there is danger. Sometimes they can't help themselves when people run." He stepped aside.

Dobbs had dropped to all fours on the floor. His clothes were piled neatly on the bed beside him.

And, then he began to change. His knees bent backward with a pop that made Joseph jump.

Price grabbed Joseph's arm, "No sudden moves, Doctor."

"What the hell is going on?"

Dobbs' chest began to expand. And his jaw changed shape. It grew into a muzzle, bristling with long, white teeth.

"Dear God," Joseph whispered.

"Welcome to Project Lobo," Price said.

***

The Boy

"We're in Ohio, just a little south of Springfield," Karen said into her cell phone.

They were stocking up on supplies and gas at a Gas'N'Go convenience store.

Karen held the cell phone against her ear with her shoulder. She had her hands full of snack food and soda – a constant appetite for munchies was one of the side effects of being a werewolf.

"Did you hear about Detroit?" she asked. A moment later she said, "Yeah, that was us."

Karen leaned down and read the front page of a World News tabloid. The headline read "Werewolves Stalk Motor City." Below that was a column titled, "Hillbilly Vampires Terrorize Appalachia."

"Luckily, it looks like the tabloids are the only one's reporting on it," Karen said as she balanced a pack of powdered doughnuts on top of her cheese puffs.

Clyde walked up shaking his head, "Give me that before you drop them on the floor." He took the cheese puffs and doughnuts from her.

"Thanks," Karen said.

"Is that Ward?"

Karen nodded.

"Tell him I want a bottle of wine."

Karen rolled her eyes, "Where in the hell is he supposed to send it?"

"We can drop by the farm in a few weeks."

"You heard that, right?" Karen said into the phone. "Ward says he'll save you a bottle."

"Tell him to kiss Missy and Loretta and the baby for me," Clyde said as he laid Karen's food on the counter.

"Hey, is that Ward?" Swede called from across the store.

Karen shook her head, "Am I the only one with a cell phone? Call him yourselves for crying out loud."

"That'll be six dollars and twenty cents," the woman behind the counter told Clyde.

He dug in his pocket and handed her a ten.

"Honestly, Ward, you had the right idea. Stay put, keep the pack small. These jerks are driving me insane."

Karen laughed at something on the phone.

The front door opened and a tall teenager in a tan windbreaker walked in as Clyde was walking out.

"Hey, lady, you got any Yoo-hoo?" Swede asked.

The woman spoke with a Spanish accent, "Yes, last cooler on the left, bottom row."

"Gracias, Senora," Swede said as he walked farther back in the store.

"De nada."

The teenager walked past Karen.

She turned and stared at him as he walked up to the counter.

"What?" Karen said into the phone. "No, we're going someplace called the Breaks Interstate Park between Eastern Kentucky and Virginia. Ward, can I call you back?"

Something was wrong. The hair on the back of her neck stood up when the young man walked past. She put the cell phone in her back pocket and stood up.

The woman behind the counter smiled at the teenager.

He had short black hair, and Karen figured he was about seventeen. He had his hand in the pocket of his windbreaker.

"May I help you?" the cashier asked.

The boy's eyes flickered from side to side. He pulled a thirty-eight special pistol from his windbreaker pocket, "Give me the money in the register."

The cashier took a step back.

"Listen, I don't want to hurt anyone. I just need the money in the register, okay, lady?"

The cashier crossed herself and began to pray in Spanish.

"Please, don't point that gun at her." Karen said as she walked up beside him.

The boy stumbled backward and pointed the gun at Karen. "Stay back!"

Karen moved to stand between the boy and the cashier. "You need to be very careful with that gun. That's an old Saturday night special. It has a hair trigger."

He pointed the gun at the cashier again. "I just need money."

"I know. Look, if you're going to point that at her, at least take your finger off the trigger, okay?"

The boy's eyes were darting around like he was watching a ping pong match. He took his finger off the trigger and put it on the trigger guard.

Karen smiled, "There. That's better. You know, this is a really bad idea, right?"

The kid was breathing heavily, and Karen could hear his heart racing.

"I just need money for gas." He looked on the verge of tears.

"I'll give you gas money," Karen said.

Swede walked up to the counter and set down his bottle of Yoo-hoo. He looked at the cashier. "That's a buck fifty, right?"

The woman stared at him.

"Swede?" Karen asked.

"Yeah?"

"We're a little busy here."

Swede leaned on the counter and stared the boy up and down, "Want me to kill him?"

The kid pointed the gun at Swede.

"No," Karen said. "I'd prefer it if *nobody* died."

Swede shrugged. He put two dollar bills on the counter, "Keep the change."

He walked out the front door.

"Madre Dios," the cashier said.

Karen looked over her shoulder at the cashier and read her name tag. "Rosa, right?"

She nodded, "Si."

"You have kids?"

"Si, cuatro," Rosa said.

Karen turned back to the boy, "Hear that? She has four kids. Now, I know you don't want to shoot her."

"I just want the money."

"I already told you I will give you money."

The front door opened, and Clyde stepped inside. He held his compound bow, a silver tipped arrow aimed at the boy. "What are we doing here, Karen?"

"Take it easy, Clyde. This is almost over," Karen said.

The boy's hand was shaking.

Karen put herself between the boy and Rosa again. She held out her hand. "Give me the gun."

He pointed it between her eyes, "No way."

"Karen…" Clyde whispered.

She pointed at Clyde, "I got this."

She leaned forward and put her forehead on the barrel of the gun, "What's your name?"

"Bobby Jennings," his hand was shaking.

Karen whispered, "Bobby, you and I both know this gun isn't loaded." She reached up and took the gun out of his hand. She pushed it into the waistband of her jeans.

Bobby started to run, but Karen caught his right wrist and twisted his arm behind his back. She pushed him against the counter.

Rosa stared at them wide eyed.

"Now, you tell this lady you are very sorry for scaring her," Karen said.

"What? Ow!" Bobby said as Karen twisted his arm higher. "I'm very sorry."

"Good start," Karen said. "Rosa, is there anything this young man can do to make this right, short of going to jail?" She pointed to the gun in her waistband, "The gun wasn't loaded."

All fear was gone from her eyes. "Si, my church is two blocks down the street. I want him to go there and confess his sins."

"You want me to *what*?!" Bobby asked.

Karen lifted him off the ground by his arm, "Say, 'yes, Ma'am' and 'Thank you.'"

42

"Yes, Ma'am. Thank you," Bobby grunted.

Karen dragged him toward the door.

Clyde lowered his bow and stepped aside as Karen pushed Bobby out the door. He tipped his baseball cap to Rosa, "Buenas Noches, Senora."

"Buenas Noches."

***

Karen pushed Bobby down on the sidewalk. "Sit."

Anna walked out of the back of the van and stared at the boy sitting at Karen's feet. "Who's that?"

"Criminal," Clyde said as he walked up behind Bobby and tapped him on top of the head with an arrow.

"You said you needed gas money. For what?" Karen asked.

He pointed to an old Honda motorcycle near the street. It was red and white. The rear fender was held together with pink Bondo.

"Well, that's a piece of shit," Clyde said.

Karen handed Clyde a ten-dollar bill. "Go give Rosa this ten."

"What for?" Clyde asked.

"Ten dollars' worth on pump two. For the kid's bike."

Bobby looked up, "For real?"

"Yeah, for real," Karen said. "Hey, Swede, get rid of this." She threw the gun to Swede.

He caught it in one hand and crushed it.

"How did he do that?" Bobby asked as he watched the pieces fall on the pavement.

"Magic," Karen said.

***

They rolled down the street following the van. Bobby rode between Karen and Anna.

"You guys some kind of motorcycle gang?" Bobby yelled.

"Something like that," Karen said.

The van pulled up to the curb and the motorcycles stopped behind it.

"Why are we stopping?" Bobby asked.

43

Karen pointed to the left of the van. Saint Michael's Catholic Church was a gray stone building.

"Huh?" Bobby laughed. "You can't be serious. I ain't even Catholic."

"You made a deal," Karen said. "Go find a priest and confess."

He shook his head, "You're crazy."

"Swede, escort Bobby here into the church," Karen said as she lay down on the seat of the Harley.

"Let's go, little fellow," Swede said as he climbed off his bike.

"Okay, okay, I'm going," Bobby said as he put down his kickstand and stalked away toward the church.

Swede sat back down on his bike.

Clyde got out of the van and walked over to Bobby's bike. He broke off a piece of Bondo. "This thing is a piece of shit. You're sending him on his way after this, right?"

Karen looked up and smiled.

Clyde sighed and took off his baseball cap. "You have got to be shitting me."

"I got a feeling," Karen said.

"Yeah, I got a feeling too. Bike's a piece of shit. Kid's a piece of shit."

"No, he's not," Karen said as she closed her eyes.

"You know, he's going to need a bike – this thing won't make it twenty miles."

"I know, Clyde." She looked at the others. "Okay, listen up. I want this kid in the pack."

There was a groan from Swede.

"Knock it off. The Alpha decides," Clyde said.

Swede lay back on his bike and rolled his eyes.

Karen smirked at him. "I don't want him freaking out or worse, running off. So, nobody goes wolf in front of him."

Swede raised his hand.

Karen sighed. "You don't have to raise your hand, Swede."

"What if we're attacked?"

"Then you can go wolf."

"What if I just get bored?"

Karen gritted her teeth. "Then go wolf away from the kid. Try to remember how you felt when you first understood werewolves were real."

Swede smiled. "Baby, you remember the first time you saw me go wolf?"

Layla walked over to the motorcycle and swung one of her long legs over Swede before lying down on top of him. "Vividly."

"Great," Clyde said. "Werewolf lust in front of a Catholic Church. We're all going to hell."

Layla giggled and Swede put his hands on her hips.

"Geez, get a room, you two," Anna grumbled.

Swede smiled up at Layla. "You know what that sounds like to me, baby?"

"What?"

"Sexual frustration."

Layla laughed and bit her lower lip.

"Seriously, Anna, it's not good for you."

Anna flipped him off with both hands and walked back to the van.

***

Joseph sat in the empty cafeteria across from Price as the small man ate his spaghetti with a fervor.

Price had been right, the spaghetti was good, but Joseph had barely eaten any.

He had just seen something that shouldn't have been possible.

"Don't run," Price had said.

Not running had been almost impossible. Dobbs had transformed into a nine-foot-tall monster out of a horror movie right in front of him.

Werewolf. It was impossible – yet, he had seen it with his own eyes.

"Are you going to eat that?" Price asked as he reached for another slice of bread from the basket between them.

Joseph pushed his half-eaten plate of spaghetti toward Price.

Price dipped the bread in Joseph's plate. "That was indelicate of me earlier. Now I've spoiled your dinner. You have my apologies. We take the werewolves for granted down here. I should have eased you into all this."

"Did you say *werewolves*? You mean there are more than just Dobbs?"

Price stopped chewing and swallowed, "Oh, yes. We have three now — at one time, we had fourteen."

"What happened to the others?"

Price wiped his mouth with his napkin. It came away red with sauce, "The others are gone."

"Where?"

Price scratched his head and leaned back. "They died."

"How did they die?"

"Quietly."

Joseph looked at Price's eyes. They looked dead and cold, like a shark's eyes.

"Was Dobbs born like this?"

Price returned to eating, "No. He volunteered to be infected. They all did. They all agreed to become 'Die Gute Wolf.'"

"*Die Gute Wolf?* Is that German?"

"Yes. It means 'the good wolf' – it was a Nazi secret weapon from World War II. God only knows where they got it from. They were circling the globe looking for occult weapons in the 1930's. You know they had a secret base at the South Pole? It was a little valley heated by geothermal vents."

Joseph shook his head, "That was a hoax."

Price laughed, "Yes, and they didn't create a werewolf serum either… yet, here we are."

"Okay, you're trying to make me believe the Nazis had the ability to create werewolf super soldiers and still lost World War II?"

"Oh, they had the ability to create them. They just had the same problem we're having."

"Which is?"

"Controlling them."

Joseph leaned back, "Dobbs seems pretty obedient."

"Dobbs bleeds red, white, and blue. Following orders is ingrained in his brain," Price said. He pushed the plates away. "When someone is infected with the werewolf virus, their eyes turn one of two colors:

yellow or blue. Yellow-eyed wolves are followers like Dobbs. Good soldiers."

"And the blue-eyed wolves?"

"They're assholes."

"What?"

"Seriously. They don't follow orders. And, worse, they influence the followers. We have to separate the blue-eyed wolves from the yellow-eyed wolves. Luckily, only about one in ten develop blue eyes. We only had one."

Joseph wasn't sure he liked the word 'separate.' He doubted it was as innocent as it sounded. "So, once the blue-eyed wolf was separated from the others, what happened to the rest?"

"At first, they were fine. We used the group on a few classified missions. They can tear down brick walls, they're virtually invincible – they re-grow lost body parts. It takes silver to kill them, or beheading, or burning them to ash."

"You're serious?" Joseph asked.

"Yes. They would have revolutionized warfare. Of course, then they all went psychotic and started killing everything in sight."

"What?"

"That's the punchline to this whole damned joke. The blue-eyed wolves give off some kind of pheromones or brain waves that keep the yellow-eyed wolves from going insane. We weren't able to isolate the mechanism. The followers started to succumb within about a month, some lasted longer – Dobbs has gone almost three years. You're here to try to keep him sane."

"What about the other two?"

"One of the two already has red eyes – that's how you can tell they're gone," he pointed to his left eye. "Their eyes turn red. The other one is two maybe three weeks away from losing her mind – her eyes are turning."

"Perhaps I should work with one of them first?"

"No. Once the eyes go red, they'd as soon kill you as look at you."

"But you said the woman's eyes weren't completely there yet. Maybe I can help her?"

Price drummed his fingers on the table, "Fair enough. You can see her tomorrow morning. She'll be behind six inches of glass. Do what you can, but Dobbs is your priority, Doctor. Keep him from losing his marbles."

Price stood up, "Oh, one thing. I almost forgot." He took a nine-millimeter pistol from his jacket pocket and laid it on the table in front of Joseph.

Joseph looked at the pistol as if it might bite, "I don't like guns, Mr. Price."

"It's loaded with silver bullets. Better to have it and not need it than need it and not have it."

Joseph picked up the gun and looked at it. "I thought you said she'd be behind six inches of glass?"

"She will be. Dobbs won't."

***

Bobby Jennings walked out of the church and squinted against the setting sun. He half expected Karen Arthur's crew to have abandoned him and taken his bike.

He wasn't sure if he was glad or disappointed to find them there in the parking lot waiting for him.

The scruffy looking little guy, Clyde, met him on the sidewalk. "Roll your bike over to the van and load it in the back. You're riding with me."

"I'd rather ride my bike, if it's okay?"

"Look, kid, we've got a long way to go, and that bike of yours won't make it fifty miles. Load it in the back. I'll see if it can be salvaged when we get where we're going."

Bobby looked at the pink ice cream truck. Something didn't sit well with giving up his mobility and getting in a stranger's van.

"You guys sell ice cream?"

"No," Clyde said.

"Bobby," Karen said. "Clyde's right. Just load up in the van."

Bobby nodded. He didn't trust many people, but for some reason he trusted her.

He pushed his bike to the back of the van and opened the rear door.

Clyde's bike was locked down on the left side of the van.

Clyde walked up beside him and pressed a button under the bumper.

A steel ramp began to extend under the bumper and angled down to the pavement.

"See the wheel locks?" Clyde asked.

Bobby nodded. There were clamps attached to the floor.

"Push your bike into place and press the red button on the floor. The clamps will lock in place."

"Okay," Bobby said as he pushed the bike up the ramp. "This is a sweet setup. Where's the ice cream freezer?"

"I told you, we don't sell ice cream," Clyde said as he pressed the button under the bumper again and the ramp retracted.

Bobby lined up the bike and pressed the button in the floor. The hydraulic clamps closed on his wheels. "What are you guys into? Drugs or something?"

Clyde climbed into the back of the van and closed the rear door. "No. You some kind of junkie?"

Bobby shook his head. "No, but I got no problem with the business, if you get my meaning?"

Clyde stood toe to toe with him. "Listen up. We don't deal drugs. Got it?"

Bobby looked down at him. "Yeah, I got it. Sorry. But, I mean, what do you guys do?"

"We're hunters."

"Hunters?"

"Yeah. Big game hunters."

"You mean like tigers and shit?"

Clyde blinked. "Tigers? Where the hell would we find tigers, Bobby?"

Bobby rolled his eyes. "No, I mean *like* tigers. Mountain lions or bears, you know?"

"Yeah, we hunt stuff *like* tigers. Dangerous stuff."

Bobby nodded. "Cool."

"Don't touch anything," Clyde said as he pushed past him toward the front of the van.

Bobby looked around. Beyond the motorcycle 'garage' was an area with two chairs and a set of desks and consoles. It looked high tech with computers and monitors.

Bobby sat down in front of one of the consoles and spun around in the chair. He put his hand on a keyboard attached to the desk.

"Hey! What did I say about touching stuff?" Clyde yelled as he sat down in the driver's seat.

Bobby yanked his hands away from the keyboard. "Sorry, geez."

Clyde pointed at the passenger seat. "Up here."

Bobby moved to the passenger seat and sat down.

"Belt."

Bobby nodded and put on his seat belt.

Clyde scowled at him from the driver's seat.

This was going to be a very long drive.

***

Price led Joseph through a maze of brightly lit corridors. "Your quarters are in this wing, but I wanted to introduce you to one of your colleagues before you turned in." He knocked on a door.

"Yeah?" A woman's voice said from the other side.

"Dr. Geffman?" Price answered.

"What do you want, Price?"

"I wanted you to meet your new colleague, Dr. Marlow."

The door swung open.

A middle-aged woman with thick, round, black plastic glasses the same color as her hair stood in the doorway in a white lab coat. She smiled up at Joseph.

"Dr. Marlow, this is Dr. Angelica Geffman. It would take me five minutes to go through all her degrees and alma maters..."

"Yeah, don't do that, Price," Angelica said. She held out her hand.

Joseph took it and smiled.

"You're the head shrinker?" She asked.

Joseph laughed. "Yeah."

"I'm the mad scientist trying to figure out what makes them tick. Come on in." She pulled Joseph through the door.

Price started to follow.

She blocked the door. "Price, this is going to be a lot of boring, doctory type stuff. Don't you have a senate subcommittee to lie to or something?"

Price laughed. "Fine, Angelica. I'm putting him in Stevenson's old quarters - can you see he gets there?"

"No problem," Angelica said.

"Goodnight, doctors," Price said as he turned away and walked back down the hall.

Angelica watched him walk away before closing the door. "Weird little toad," she said under her breath.

Joseph laughed.

Angelica smiled. "You can talk about him all you want in here - I sweep it daily for bugs."

"What?"

"Bugs. Little bastard has bugs everywhere. He's paranoid. Had them all over this office and my quarters until I started tearing them out."

Joseph frowned. "Are you serious?"

"As a heart attack. He's crazy as a loon. I would have thought you picked up on that?"

Joseph looked away.

"Oh, yeah," Angelica said. "Yeah, you've got his number."

"He's like every other intel guy I ever worked with."

Angelica laughed. "No. Believe me. He is not. When the boogeyman goes to sleep at night? He looks under his bed for Edward Price. Everybody in Washington is scared shitless of him. Watch yourself."

Joseph nodded.

She grinned. "You met Gunny Dobbs?"

"Yes, I did."

"He put on the dog for you?"

Joseph chortled. "One way to put it. What can you tell me about him?"

She took his arm. "Come into my la-bor-atory," Angelica said dramatically.

The room was large and filled with equipment, some things Joseph could recognize like an electron microscope, other things were a complete mystery to him.

She led him back to a desk. Behind it was a clear, plastic bulletin board filled with pictures of soldiers. All had red X's through them with the exception of Dobbs.

To the right of the soldiers' pictures was a picture of a young woman with long brown hair in a braid. She wasn't smiling. Her eyes were yellow.

Angelica nodded toward the picture. "Paula Danvers. Lab technician. Used to be a friend of mine."

"She's the one Price told me about? He said she's kept inside a prison cell of some kind?"

Angelica shook her head. "Yeah. Six inches of glass, and steel reinforced concrete. Anything less and she could tear through it."

He stared at her.

"Oh, I'm totally serious. I've seen them knock down walls, toss cars around, jump thirty feet in the air." Angelica sighed. "Tear people apart."

"How is any of this possible?" Joseph asked.

She pointed at him. "Now, there's the million-dollar question. How indeed?"

"Do they have wolf DNA?"

"Not an ounce. If you look at their genetic structure, it's 100% human. I've tested all of their DNA, and, while they're in human form? The DNA sequence is no different than you or I. But when they become Lobos? Their genetic structure is completely different, totally alien to anything else on earth."

"You mean their DNA changes when they transition into a werewolf?"

She nodded. "Something re-writes their entire genetic structure on the fly - but there's more. Even though in human form, you can't find anything abnormal in their DNA? They have abilities beyond humans. They're super-fast, incredibly strong, better eyesight, hearing, smell - whatever this thing is? It operates beneath the DNA level, like a second genetic code." She held out her hands. "That's what I'm doing here. I'm trying to crack this second code, figure out how it works."

"Price wants invincible soldiers," Joseph said.

"Well, that's not what I want. This super-retrovirus or whatever it is? It repairs inconsistencies in the base DNA. Beyond that? It regenerates lost limbs and damaged organs. The Lobo virus? If we can take it apart and understand it? We're talking about a cure for cancer, the common cold, Alzheimer's, heart disease - a cure for everything that plagues mankind. Lose a finger and it'll grow back, damage a kidney? Your body will replace it."

"My God," Joseph whispered.

"That's why I'm still working despite my loathing of Edward Price."

Joseph looked at the soldiers with red X's over their pictures. "Did they all volunteer for this?"

"Yes. All except Paula. Dobbs scratched her - that's all it takes in Lobo form. One scratch, one bite, and the retrovirus goes to work."

"He scratched her?"

Angelica nodded. "Oh, he said it was an accident. Not that I believe him - he's as crazy as Price."

He nodded toward the board. "Price said the others died?"

Angelica looked away. "Yeah, they *died*, all right. They went insane. One right after another after Price took away the alpha. Then Price and his goons put them down."

"He murdered them?"

Angelica frowned. "Yeah, but... when they go insane? Killing them is a mercy, trust me."

"I doubt they saw it as a mercy."

"Look, Marlow, red eyed wolves will kill everything in sight. They're serial killers with superpowers. I believe in 'Do No Harm' same as you, but if you let them live? They're going to do harm."

***

What Bobby thought was going to be a long trip turned out to be a short one. He fell asleep before they left Ohio and woke up when Clyde parked the van in southwest Virginia.

"Wake up, kid. We're here," Clyde said as he slid open the driver's side door and dropped onto the smooth blacktop.

Bobby stretched and yawned before climbing out his side.

The scent of pine filled the night air. He smiled up at a canopy of stars.

It was at least fifteen degrees cooler here than it had been in Ohio.

***

Virginia

Karen Arthur walked down the path from a lodge with stone walls and roughhewn timber. She held up some keys. "I got four rooms. One for me and Clyde, Bobby? You're sharing with the professor. One for Anna." She handed out the keys as she spoke and then she turned to Swede and Layla. "For you two. Other side of the lodge."

Swede reached for the key, and she snatched it back. "Keep the noise down. Don't break anything. Do not get us thrown out. Understood?"

Swede laughed. "Never!"

Karen glared at him. "Swede, Topeka?"

"Not our fault," Layla said with a barely disguised smile.

"$5000 in damages and you two spent the night in jail. Not happening this time."

"The bed was weak," Swede grumbled.

"It ended up on the roof, then it fell five stories onto a Buick."

Swede shrugged. "An *old* Buick..."

"Old just like the people inside it, Swede," Karen said.

"Hey! They weren't injured."

She pointed at him. "I swear to God, Swede."

He abruptly hugged her, and Layla wrapped her arms around both of them.

"We'll be good, I promise," Swede laughed.

"Get.Off.Me," Karen grumbled.

Swede and Layla backed away.

Swede yawned. "Don't worry about us, we're exhausted, right, baby?"

Layla smiled up at him and pressed tight against his chest. "Oh, yeah. Straight to bed."

"Good grief," Karen hissed and turned around.

Anna was standing in front of her. She held out her key. "I don't need this. Get your money back."

"Take the room."

Anna looked behind her. "Deep woods? Just made to run through..."

"Anna, take the room."

"I need to run, Karen." Her eyes were huge and yellow in the dim light.

"Fine. Run and then get some sleep in the room."

Anna shook her head. "Whatever." She stalked away with her knapsack on her back.

***

Clyde stared at the room. It was rustic but clean. There was a problem, however. "Two beds?" Two queen size beds sat side by side in the middle of the room.

"Yes, two beds," Karen said as she dropped onto the first one and lay back, her motorcycle boots still touching the floor.

"Karen, I've been sleeping right next to you for, like, five years now."

"You still will be."

"Same bed, normally."

Karen laid her right arm over her eyes. "We're not a couple, Clyde. There was a room with two beds, and I took it for us."

Clyde tossed his knapsack by the other bed. "You're exasperating, you know that?" He walked past her toward the bathroom.

"I'm being a realist. We're not right for each other."

Clyde laughed. "Yeah, well, to paraphrase Anna, 'Whatever'." He slammed the bathroom door behind him.

***

"So, you're a teacher or something?" Bobby asked from his bed.

Paul Collins was sitting at the room's small desk. He looked up from his laptop. "I'm a college professor, or I was."

55

"Like community college?"

"No, a little college called Yale." He returned to staring at his laptop.

"Yale? That's like a university, right?"

"No, it isn't *like* a university, it *is* a university."

"What'd you teach?"

"Archaeology."

Bobby rolled onto his stomach. "Cool! You mean like Indiana Jones?"

Paul stared at him. "No. Nothing like Indiana Jones. I don't own a whip or a leather jacket. Though, I do look quite dashing in a fedora."

He turned back to his laptop.

"So, you study the Egyptians and shit?"

Paul closed his eyes. "The Greeks actually. Ancient Greece. Bronze Age and prior going back to about 7000 B.C."

Bobby stared at him.

"Really old Greek shit," Paul said and turned back to the laptop.

"Like Zeus and Apollo and all that, right?"

Paul looked up. "Yes... and earlier. You know about the Greek Pantheon?"

"Sure, I played God of War, and Clash of the Titans was way cool."

Paul gritted his teeth. "I swear to God, if this was Karen's idea of a joke..."

"Huh?" Bobby asked.

Paul laughed. "Nothing. Get some sleep, Bobby."

Bobby sighed. "I can't. Slept too long in the van. I'm going to take a look around."

Paul seemed to be mulling that over. Then he said, "Don't go far. There are some high cliffs here in the Breaks. You'll see what I mean when the sun comes up. Stay near the lodge."

***

Anna ran through the star filled night, the breeze blowing back the auburn fur of her wolf form. There were campsites nearby, but she gave them a wide berth.

As apex predators went, Anna was even more silent than most. There was an art to not breaking branches and avoiding loose rocks, and she had become an expert in the three years since Karen had turned her.

She ran down a dry creek bed and launched herself twenty feet in the air, landing nimbly on a moss-covered limestone boulder.

A startled bear rose up on its hind legs a few yards away. It didn't growl, recognizing her for the danger she was. Instead, it turned and disappeared into the underbrush.

Anna smiled, her lips pulling back from her fangs.

Then she ran off deeper into the forest.

***

Karen stood on the balcony and watched the woods. She stood with her hands on the timber railing of her third-floor balcony.

Clyde walked out of the room and stood beside her. "She out there?"

Karen nodded. "About a mile. She's running along the ridgeline."

"You want to run with her?"

Karen smiled. "Yeah." She sighed. "But she needs some time to herself."

"You're doing a good job with her, Karen."

Karen scoffed. "Raising a kid is damned frustrating. I'd rather fight a rogue."

Clyde laughed. "She's not a kid anymore. Damned near twenty. She's strong, and that's from you."

"She's reckless."

"Yeah, I know somebody else who's reckless."

"Not anymore. I'm a domesticated wolf. At least I have enough sense not to show half of Detroit that werewolves aren't just something in a Twilight movie."

Clyde shuddered. "Fluffy werewolves. Those sissies ever saw a real werewolf they'd sparkle themselves to death."

Karen laughed. "She could've died in the river, Clyde. What the hell made her do something that stupid?"

"Natural born hero. Also like somebody else I know. All of you, actually."

Laughter filled the night air.

Karen closed her eyes and shook her head.

Clyde laughed. "Swede and Layla are fooling around on their balcony, aren't they?"

Karen shook her head. "So far, they've done it everywhere but the bed. I'd really like to be able to turn off the super hearing sometimes."

"You should try it sometime," he said with a grin.

"Don't start."

***

Bobby walked down the hillside away from the lodge.

He paused when he saw her standing just beyond the trees.

Anna was naked, pulling her clothes out of her knapsack.

He just stood there and stared for a moment, her golden skin lit by the moon and stars.

Then he realized he was staring and turned away.

She walked past him in jeans and t-shirt as she pulled the pack onto her back. "Get a good look, perv?"

"I... sorry, I didn't know you were out here."

"Well, now you do," she said as she continued up the path.

***

The Lady in the Glass Cage

The next morning, Dr. Joseph Marlow stood in the courtyard and looked up through the transparent ceiling at the hollowed-out mountain above. Somehow, sunlight was shining down from on high.

"It's for our circadian rhythms," Angelica said. "Daylight bulbs. They put them a couple of decades ago because people were getting wacky down here with no sun." She pointed up. "Then they added the plants on the terraces ringing the entire cavern."

"Hanging gardens of Babylon," Joseph said as he stared at the tropical plants growing high above.

"Yep. They do a good job of cleaning the air." She walked with him down the corridor. "Look, before you go in? A couple of ground rules. Paula's easily agitated. I'll be watching, and if she shows signs of a psychotic break? I'll come over the intercom and tell you to stop. If I do that, I need you to turn around and walk out. Understood?"

"Sure."

"If she starts tearing the cell apart, we have a cocktail of nerve gas and silver iodide vapor we can release into her room..."

"Nerve gas?!"

"Relax. It'd kill us instantly, but she just takes a nap till her body flushes the silver iodide. If we have to release it the vents in the glass will close, you'll be perfectly safe on your side of the glass."

She paused outside the cell door.

He put his hand on the knob. "Aren't you coming in?"

Angelica shook her head. "I'll watch from the control room. She... doesn't like me much anymore. I mean, I'm the one who's always running tests and poking her with needles, so I get it."

Joseph nodded and stepped through the door.

The room beyond was a narrow corridor about thirty feet long and six feet wide. There was a small desk midway down with a chair facing a glass wall.

On the other side of the glass was a larger room of about thirty by twenty.

The walls were gray concrete, and the 'furniture' was also made of concrete - a bed and a long chair with green rubber pads for cushioning.

There was a bathroom stall with a white curtain where the door should be and a shower stall beside it. Water dripped from the shower nozzle.

Paula Danvers was standing on her hands in the corner, her eyes closed, brown ponytail hanging down.

"Miss Danvers?" Joseph asked.

"Shh. I'm counting." Her voice was soft and melodic and came through the small vents drilled in the glass.

"Counting?"

She had her eyes closed and she nodded. A moment later, she opened them.

Joseph swallowed.

Paula Danvers' eyes had an outer ring of yellow and an inner circle of blood red. She smiled. "I was counting your heartrate - 97 beats per minute. You're frightened." She swung her legs down gracefully and rose to her feet, the ponytail swinging as she did so.

She was dressed in a plain gray sweatsuit. "Scared of the big, bad wolf?"

Joseph smiled. "Should I be?"

"If you have half a brain. Do you have half a brain?"

He shrugged. "Two halves or so they tell me. I'm Dr. Joseph Marlow."

"Uggh," Paula said as she turned and walked back to her concrete couch. She sat on it cross-legged. "What sort of doctor are you? Endocrinologist? Proctologist? Zoologist?"

"Psychologist," Joseph said as he sat down in the desk chair.

"I was hoping for a gynecologist. At least I might get some action. Been a long time."

Joseph set a file folder on the desk in front of him and opened it. "Sorry to disappoint."

She sat up straighter. "Oh, you haven't disappointed me yet - that will come later."

"Paula Marie Danvers, 28, from Perry, Iowa."

"Deceased," Paula said.

"I'm sorry?"

"Deceased. Officially, I died crossing the street in Richmond. Or did I drown in a bathtub in Roanoke? I forget." She turned her head to the side. "What? Don't they have that in my report? How they told my parents I was dead after Dobbs gave me wolf herpes? How's Dobbs doing? Those eyes turning red yet? I hope they give us adjoining cells. Better yet, just put him in here with me and I'll kill him."

She lay down. "Or he'll kill me. Either way it'll be a relief."

"On a scale of one to ten, how angry are you?"

She rolled over and stared at him. Then she burst out laughing. "Are you fucking serious?"

He nodded. "Yeah, I am."

She leapt off the couch and slammed against the glass with a dull thud.

Joseph almost fell backward in his chair, but he managed to grab hold of the table.

She grinned triumphantly, her upper lip busted by the impact with the glass. Her blood dripped slowly down.

An instant later, the cut had healed on her lip.

"Hmm, that heart is really beating now. Makes you feel alive, doesn't it? Fear?"

"It's an eye-opener. Now, on a scale of one to ten..."

"Eleven. It's always eleven. Every second of every minute of every hour, Joseph," she said as she walked away. "You're staring at my ass, aren't you? It's okay. Men do. Some women too."

"You're very attractive."

She jumped back onto the couch and sat cross-legged again. "Can you say that? Is that allowed? Will they take away your psychology secret decoder ring for saying that?"

"Why are you angry, Paula?"

"Why am I... Have you been paying attention at all, doctor? They let Dobbs infect me, told my parents I was dead, and locked me in the deepest dungeon of Mordor. They're going to kill me once they finish sticking me with needles and letting you shrink my brain." Then she yelled, "Yes, I know you're there, Angelica. I can smell you in the control room. You smell like regret and menopause."

"You don't like Angelica?" Joseph asked.

"No. I don't. She let them do this to me. And you're helping Price, so you're on my shit list too."

"You want to hurt me?"

"Hurt you?" She frowned. "No, I want you to come into this room with me. I won't even turn wolf, doctor. I'll just tear your skin off your body one little bit at a time with my fingernails. I'll strip you down to your muscles and nerves and blood vessels, and then I'll pick away all the little connective tissue between them until you're just a screaming, disgusting thing that I've turned inside out."

***

"Still think you can help her, doctor?" Price asked as he walked down the hallway with Joseph.

"Absolutely," Joseph said.

Price took his arm. "Dr. Marlow, I'm not sure you quite understand. She just told you she wanted to filet you like a salmon.

Paula Danvers is never leaving her glass house. You are wasting your time and mine."

"Look, Price, you've got Miss Danvers in solitary confinement. She believes Dobbs purposely did this to her..."

"She's delusional..."

"Be that as it may, she believes it. She's angry, Price, and that's normal. But she's engaging with me - she wants help, despite the front she's putting up."

Price laughed. "Of course, she does! She wants you to open the cell door and let her out so she can make a xylophone out of your bones. That is after she rips everyone else here to pieces. She's a red-eyed wolf - a psychopath."

"No, she isn't. Not yet, anyway. Look at it this way: if I can reach her, if I can help her control her rage? That means we would have a therapy to get red-eyed wolves back on the team. Think about it. Your perfect soldiers would be manageable, Price."

***

Bobby wouldn't make eye contact with Anna at the breakfast table.

They had gone to a restaurant near the lodge called The Rhododendron, and Karen had paid for a country breakfast for all of them: ham, scrambled eggs, gravy and biscuits, and potatoes.

Bobby had eaten his within a minute and a half.

The others had stared at him.

"I... I haven't had real food in a while," he had stammered.

Karen just smiled and told the waitress to bring him another plate.

If Anna was angry with him for seeing her naked last night, she didn't give any indication. She was sitting by Swede and Layla, and they were laughing at each other's jokes.

He looked around the table. It was an odd mix - not that he had a lot of experience with motorcycle gangs, but none of these people fit the bill of what he thought a gang was about.

Clyde was staring at him.

Okay, maybe he fit the stereotype. He had formed an instant dislike for Bobby.

***

Karen paid cash and headed toward the front door of the restaurant. The others were already outside.

Clyde was waiting on the restaurant's porch. "We stayin' for a while?"

Karen nodded. "Yeah. Best to lay low for a few days. Besides, I don't know about you, but I'm tired."

"Let him go," Clyde said.

"What?"

"The kid. Cut him loose."

"What is your beef with this kid, Clyde?"

"I don't have one. I mean, other than the fact he's a damned thief..."

"Clyde, you saw him in there. That boy's been starving. He was desperate in Ohio."

Clyde shook his head. "You know, just because somebody could be a werewolf, it doesn't mean you have to make them one."

"He's one of us, Clyde."

"Just hear me out. That boy could have a normal life. Let's give him some money and send him on his way."

"Now I get it..."

"He's not like the others, Karen. We're not giving him anything he needs."

"Just because his body's not broken doesn't mean his spirit isn't. Remember Layla? We send him on his way? He'll be knocking over convenience stores in six months, only maybe this time the gun is loaded. He's one of us."

***

Bobby looked over his shoulder at Karen and Clyde talking on the restaurant porch.

"They're talking about you."

Bobby turned around - he had almost walked into Anna sitting on her Harley.

"You think?" He asked.

She nodded. She was wearing small black sunglasses and a white T-shirt. "Yeah."

"What are they talking about?"

She turned her head to the side. "Sending you packing. Karen wants you to stay, Clyde wants to leave you on the side of the road."

"Why does that guy hate me so much?" Bobby asked.

"Probably thinks you're a perv."

Bobby sighed. "Hey, I said I was sorry, okay? I mean, what were you doing running around in the woods naked at 3:00 in the morning?"

"Wicca. I'm a witch. I was communing with nature."

"Really?"

"No, moron. Get on."

He looked at the bike. "Where are we going?"

"Away from old people. You want to go or not?" She opened her saddlebag and handed him a helmet.

"Where's yours?"

"I don't wear one. Get on."

Bobby put on his helmet and climbed on behind her.

She pulled out and he wrapped his arms around her waist.

"Don't wait up," she yelled as they passed by Clyde and Karen.

***

Lobo-1

Joseph's quarters had an office attached to it, which Price had outfitted with two overstuffed leather chairs. The room was large compared to most of the base: a square fifteen by fifteen feet.

Joseph still felt far too close to Gunnery Sergeant William Dobbs. The man stood at attention beside his leather chair while Joseph sat in his. "Have a seat, sergeant," Joseph said.

"If it's all the same, sir, I'd prefer to stand. And, also, sir, if you don't mind? Could you please refer to me as either 'Gunnery Sergeant' or 'Gunny'?"

"All right, Gunny. I didn't mean any disrespect."

Dobbs' eyes were focused on a spot on the far wall. "I didn't take it as disrespect, sir. It's obvious you weren't in the military. I took no offense."

"You don't have to stand at attention, Gunny. This is informal."

Dobbs relaxed a fraction, but he kept his eyes on the far wall.

Joseph opened the folder on his lap. "Gunnery Sergeant William Dobbs. Born November 8th, 1985, Huntsville, Alabama..."

"Roll Tide, sir," he said and finally a slight smile broke his stoic expression.

Joseph smiled back. "Joined the Marines on your eighteenth birthday. Trained at Parris Island, marksmanship level expert, made sergeant in two years, gunnery sergeant in nine. Pretty impressive."

"Thank you, sir."

"Deployments in Iraq and Afghanistan. Distinguished yourself everywhere you went."

"Some people are cut out for war, sir."

"What happened in 2012?"

Dobbs frowned. "Sir?"

"2012 - nothing in this folder after 2012." Joseph closed it.

Dobbs nodded. "I'm afraid that's classified, sir."

"I see..."

"I'm sure Mr. Price can fill in any gaps, sir."

Joseph shook his head. "I'm sure he will if necessary. Tell me about your life outside the military."

"Outside, sir?"

"Yeah, I mean your file tells me about your military career up to 2012, but nothing other than your time in the Marines. Do you have ties with family?"

"My parents are dead, sir."

"Friends?"

"Only in the corps, sir."

Joseph nodded. "What about interests? Hobbies?"

Dobbs' eyes began to flicker back and forth. "Hunting, sir. I enjoy a good hunt. I like the outdoors."

"Don't like being cooped up in here?"

"No, sir. I'd rather be in the field."

"How often do you get to leave the base?" Joseph asked.

"At least once a week, sir. There's a lot of forest out there. Good hunting."

"When you say hunting, you mean you hunt in wolf form?"

This time Dobbs smiled wide. "No better way to hunt, Dr. Marlow."

"What do you hunt?"

"Deer, the occasional bear. Took down a coyote last time. People."

"I'm sorry?"

"People, doctor. Occasionally, I hunt people."

Joseph stared at Dobbs' smiling face. "You mean in the woods here?"

Dobbs laughed. "No, sir. I mean when they let me off the reservation to run an op. The Lobo is the ultimate anti-personnel weapon. One day we'll have a team again and we can start making a real difference."

"The team - how well did you know the team, Gunny?"

"Like brothers, sir."

"Hard to be the last man standing?" Joseph asked.

"No, sir. Losing the team was a terrible loss. We did some good work." He took a deep breath. "But they were weak."

"Weak?"

"They couldn't handle it - the power, the bloodlust. It consumed them."

Joseph nodded. "But not you?"

"No, sir. I adapted. Discipline, sir. Discipline is always the key. They lacked discipline, I have it in spades, sir."

"Well, I think that's enough for today, Gunny."

"Good day, sir." He turned away and walked toward the door.

"Oh, Gunny. One thing: what's it like?"

Dobbs stopped in mid-stride. "What's what like, sir?"

"Hunting in wolf form?"

Dobbs looked over his shoulder. "Freedom, doctor. It's freedom. Freedom from the world and all its vices. Freedom from judgement." He smiled.

And that smile chilled Joseph to the bone.

***

Bobby held on to Anna as they sped down Virginia route 460 beside Levisa Fork. The riverbed looked like it had been widened artificially as it snaked through the dark, steep mountains. The road followed the river, and the flat curves at the speed Anna was taking them were nerve wrenching.

"You wanna slow down?" Bobby yelled.

"Why?"

"You're gonna splatter your brains all over these hills."

She laughed and gunned it harder.

Bobby closed his eyes.

His hands encircled her hard muscled waist as he held on for dear life.

"Don't be afraid. If we fall? I'll catch you."

"You're a maniac!" Bobby yelled.

She slowed and Bobby opened his eyes.

A road sign announced the small town ahead as Grundy.

"You been here before?" Bobby asked.

"Passed through it on our way to Bedford a couple of times."

"What's in Bedford?"

"Friends. And my mom."

"You from there?"

"What? Bedford? No. I'm from Wisconsin."

***

"When we get to Bedford? I'm leaving her with Ward and Loretta," Karen said as she sipped her coffee on the restaurant porch.

"You can't do that, Karen. She's an adult," Clyde said.

"Yeah? Well, adult or not? She's a yellow-eye… she has to stay with a blue-eye. If she can't stay with me? She has to stay with Ward."

"You'll break her heart."

"Yeah, better a broken heart than dead. I can't do this anymore, Clyde. She's a distraction when we're trying to do our jobs."

Clyde laughed. "You know what you are?"

"No, and I'm pretty sure I don't want to know," she grumbled.

"A helicopter mom. One of those soccer moms who runs around with Bactine and Band-Aids in her purse in case her kid gets a boo-boo."

"Say that again and I will kick your skinny ass off this porch," she said as she sipped her coffee. "I am not her mom. That's my whole point. She goes to Bedford? She'll have Ward, Loretta, and her real mom. Maybe she'll grow up a little."

Clyde shook his head. "Sure, she can go try to recapture her childhood in Bedford. This kid who just chased down a serial arsonist, jumped in the river with him… and a bomb, got blown up by same… and that was just an average Thursday night. Sure… Bedford… she can pick grapes for Ward and Loretta." He walked over and put his hand on the back of her neck and massaged it. "She's grown, Karen. She's going to skin those knees… Anna can carry her own Bactine."

Karen leaned her head back. "That feels good."

"I'm good with my hands. You should take advantage."

Karen laughed. "God, hillbilly, do you ever give up?"

"Someday, I just might."

She stared out at the woods. "If she's having sex with that boy? I'll kill her."

"It'll be a double homicide," Clyde said. "Because I'd kill him too."

***

Joseph walked into Dr. Angelica Geffman's laboratory.

"How's our resident Dr. Freud, today?" Angelica asked as she deposited something in a pipette into a test tube.

"I just met with Gunny Dobbs," he said as he leaned against Angelica's lab bench.

"Piss yourself? No judgement, I've pissed myself at least three times out of fright when I've been in the same room with him. Pretty sure he enjoys the effect he has. "

"No, I managed to control my bladder… his file is whitewashed, isn't it?"

Angelica laughed and smiled behind her safety goggles. "Tom Sawyer himself couldn't have done a better job. Just an All-American… monster."

Joseph looked around the room. "You wouldn't happen to have the *real* file, would you? Or know where I can get it?"

"Why, Dr. Marlow? What do you take me for?" She nodded her head to her right. "Right top desk drawer under a box of tampons and a half-used tube of Preparation H."

Joseph stared at her.

Angelica rolled her eyes. "Doesn't do any good to lock a desk drawer in a place where the devil has all the keys. I need other ways to hide my shit... relax, I didn't use the Prep-H. The tampons though..."

Joseph laughed. He was really beginning to like Angelica Geffman.

He sat down at Angelica's desk. True to her word, the unmarked folder was under an open box of Tampax and a wrinkled tube of Preparation-H... she'd made sure to coat the outside of the tube with a layer of the ointment. "Really?"

"Hey, deterrents are ugly."

He opened the file and began reading.

Joseph stopped smiling midway down the first page.

***

The only movie theater in Grundy, Virginia was located in the community center. It had three screens - two were showing romantic comedies, one was showing a superhero flick.

Anna didn't ask what he wanted to see. She simply walked up to the ticket booth and bought two tickets for the superhero movie matinee. Then she led the way to the concession stand and bought Bobby a Coke, a popcorn, and a box of Raisinettes... again, without asking what he wanted.

She bought herself two hotdogs, a bag of Red Vines, a large Coke, and a tub of popcorn which she proceeded to drown in oil.

"I don't like Raisinettes," Bobby said.

She snatched them out of his hand and laid them on top of her barrel of popcorn.

"Are you actually going to *eat* all of that?" Bobby asked.

"I'm hungry."

"We ate like an hour ago."

"What? Now I have three moms? You don't want your popcorn? I'll eat it too," she said as she stalked away toward the theater.

"No, I want the popcorn." He looked at the movie poster outside the door. The poster was full of people wearing Spandex outfits, masks, and capes. "You really want to see this movie?"

"Oh, because I'm a girl you think I want to see one of the RomComs?"

Bobby shrugged. "I don't know... most would."

"Yeah, well, I'm not most girls. And I'm really tired of people telling me what to do, how to act, how to think!" Her yellow eyes seemed to glow in the dark.

"Hey... I'm sorry. It was really nice of you to take me to the movies and buy me all this. Thank you."

She tapped her foot and looked embarrassed. "You... can have my Red Vines if you like."

Bobby smiled. "We can share."

"Don't think this is a date or anything. You're... just the closest to my age, okay? I can't relate to the rest of them."

"No, no, I didn't think it was a date at all." Had he? He wasn't sure. If she made a point of saying it *wasn't* a date, did that mean it *was* a date?

She turned around and went into the theater. "Keep your hands to yourself in here. You touch my boobs, I'll punch you in the face."

"I... believe you. Are you always this intense?"

"Yes."

***

"He's a psychopath!" Joseph said as he leaned over Edward Price's desk.

Price smiled. "Would you mind lowering your voice a few decibels?"

"You gave me a file that had been redacted!"

"The reason I ask you to lower your voice isn't because I don't like your tone - I don't; however, that pales in comparison to the fact the Gunny Dobbs has hearing to put a bat to shame, and he really doesn't like people pointing out his mental challenges."

"*Challenges*? Challenges?! He's murdered seventeen people."

"He's a soldier..."

70

"Not the enemy! His own men. Most before he became a werewolf. He was implicated in the death of his fiancé…"

"They never took that to trial…"

"He killed a drill instructor…"

"Accidental fall…"

"He pushed the man off a seventy-foot tower!"

"Dobbs says the man stumbled."

Joseph shook his head. "Dobbs spent more time in Leavenworth than in the Marine Corps. Dishonorable discharge and life in prison. Hell, he wasn't even a Gunnery Sergeant!"

"He is now. Where did you get all this information, doctor? I doubt if Dobbs was this forthcoming."

Joseph sighed. "William Dobbs is a dangerous psychotic. He doesn't have an ounce of empathy in him, Price. What in God's name were you thinking pulling that man out of a maximum-security prison?"

"He is the only one, Dr. Marlow. Out of all the good soldiers who volunteered? West Point graduates, men with degrees in engineering, mathematics, science? Dobbs, the psychopath I pulled out of Leavenworth's mental ward, is the only one whose eyes haven't turned red. The only one who can be used as the weapon we intended. The only one who will follow orders…"

"And, what happens when he stops following orders, Price?"

"Then we will put him down, the same as we put down the others before him. So, do your best to keep the man sane…"

"*Sane*? Have you listened to a word I've said? He isn't sane, Price!"

"Manageable then. Keep him manageable."

Joseph shook his head. "He needs meds. Strong…"

"No. They won't work. Werewolf metabolism burns through the strongest anti-psychotics in minutes."

Joseph laughed. "Then I have no idea how you've kept him from slaughtering everyone in this facility."

"Simple. We let him hunt, doctor."

Joseph nodded. "Yeah, he mentioned that. He said sometimes he hunts *people*, Price."

"Bad people, Dr. Marlow. As a matter of fact, we're sending him out on a hunt tonight." He looked at his watch. "Come to my office at say, 10:45 PM. And I'll show you why we need lobos."

***

Bobby sat to Anna's left in the darkened theater. Bobby had lost track of the movie's plot - now he was only paying attention when something on the screen exploded.

The rest of the time? He was trying to stare at Anna without letting her know he was staring. Because, pretty as she was? She was downright terrifying.

"Watch the movie. Stop looking at me," she whispered as if reading his mind.

"Sorry."

She glanced at him out of the corner of her yellow eyes.

Yellow. He had never known anyone with yellow eyes before.

"Movie's boring," Anna said as she put her Coke in the armrest cupholder.

"Yeah, want to go?"

She shook her head. "Still eating popcorn."

"Okay."

"Are you a good kisser?"

"Um... huh?"

"Kisser. Are you good at kissing?"

"I don't know. I guess."

She stared at him. "You have kissed a girl, right?"

"Of course, why...?"

"Some guys are all tongue. It's like kissing a German Shepherd. I don't like it... which is ironic in an odd way."

He squinted at her.

"Never mind," she said. "Come here."

He leaned forward. Her eyes seemed to be glowing.

"Keep your tongue in your mouth," she said. She kissed him gently.

She pulled away then and left him with his eyes closed.

He opened his eyes and smiled. "I thought you said this wasn't a date."

"It isn't. The movie's bad and I'm bored."

"Oh," he said and laughed.

She moved in to kiss him again. "You're not bad. I can work with this."

"Should I keep my tongue in my mouth this time too?"

She laughed. "You just sit there. I'll handle the tongue stuff."

***

Window of the Soul

Joseph walked into the observation room beside Paula Danvers' cell.

She was sitting naked on the foam rubber mattress.

Joseph turned away quickly. "I'm sorry. I didn't know you weren't dressed. I'll come back."

"Why?"

"Because you're naked."

He heard her moving. "Two sessions in one day? To what do I owe the pleasure?"

Joseph put his hand on the concrete wall. "Are you dressed?"

"No."

"Could you please…?"

She laughed. "No."

"Look, Paula. I want to help you."

She laughed again. "How? You want to help me? Open my cell door and step back, Dr. Marlow. I promise I'll kill you last."

Joseph sighed. He turned around.

Paula Danvers was standing just behind the glass smiling at him. "We lose all our modesty when we change. Among other things."

"What else?"

"Empathy. Fear. That makes me a sociopath, right?"

Joseph sat down in the chair and rubbed his hair away from his eyes. "I honestly don't know."

Paula smiled and pointed at him. "You finally saw the real William Dobbs, didn't you? You know he's completely insane now, right?"

Joseph nodded.

"Then you know what I'm becoming," she said, and then she walked back to her bed and sat down.

He shook his head. "I only know one thing: there are only two people in this place I trust. You and Angelica."

She laughed. "You are *so* fucked. Me? You trust me?"

He shrugged. "In a way."

"I will kill you if I get out of this cell."

"Yes, and I believe you. I trust you are telling me the truth. I think there are a lot of people in this place who would kill me if they had the inclination. Dobbs and Price chief among them. They just aren't as forthcoming."

She nodded. "Price needs you to keep his dog of war on a leash. To Dobbs? You're just prey… like you are to me." She shook her head. "But you trust Angelica? That's dumb. I made that mistake. That's how I ended up in here."

"She says she had nothing to do with it."

Paula leapt off the bed and slammed her palms against the window. "She didn't do anything to stop it! She didn't do anything to get me out of this cell!" Paula began to pace.

"What was she supposed to do, Paula? Let you go? You're dangerous."

"At first, I thought she would cure me. She didn't," Paula growled. "Then I thought she would at least kill me!" Her voice became lower with each word.

She stretched her neck and it cracked. Her mouth filled with fangs. "I tried to kill myself. Want to see?"

"No," Joseph said.

She ran to the small, curtained restroom and came back with a razor. "Funny, huh? Normally they wouldn't give a prisoner a razor."

"Don't," Joseph said.

"But, for me? It doesn't matter," she said. She put the razor to her throat and drew it across.

At first there was a thin red line.

Then blood began to gush down over her chest.

Joseph jumped up and put his hands on the glass. "Put pressure on the wound! I'll get help."

Paula stared at him, her eyes like bullseyes of yellow and red. Then she laughed, a gurgling sound that came as much from her ruined throat as from her mouth.

The blood slowed, became a trickle.

Then the line on her throat grew fainter.

She threw down the razor and wiped her neck with her hand.

Other than the blood drying on her chest, no trace of the damage remained.

She spat a mouthful of blood on the floor. "I can't kill myself, and Angelica won't do it for me." She wiped her lips on the back of her hand. "The virus won't let me die. I'm 'Die Gute Wolf', practically invulnerable." She turned away and looked at the concrete wall of her cell. "I was supposed to be better. All of us? We were supposed to be better."

She walked back to the toilet and emerged with a mop and bucket. She nodded toward the huge pool of crimson on the white floor. "You think this is bad? A few weeks ago, I was throwing shit at the window. Learned really fast not to do that - Price didn't care, and… heh… one of my superpowers is my sense of smell, so… poop is not a smell I like to be locked in a confined space with, you know?"

Paula began swabbing the blood toward a drain in the floor. "Blood though? Oh, I like blood." She took a deep breath. "Blood makes me feel all tingly." She smiled at him and shrugged. "But I like to keep things neat and tidy."

Joseph finally felt his heartbeat slowing after Paula's faux suicide. "Do you trust me, Paula?"

She leaned on the mop. "Oddly? Yeah. I mean, you're a complete idiot if you think you can help me…"

He sat back down in the chair. "I do think I can help. I do not believe that you are a slave to whatever color your eyes are turning. I do not believe that a person cannot learn to overcome this bloodlust. You were a lab assistant, a scientist, reason through this, Paula."

Paula laughed. "*Reason through it*? Okay, doc. Here's my reasoning: my hormone levels are off the chart. They are clouding my judgement. I am both manic and depressive… at the same time! I want to tear everything apart - you included. I want to make the world bleed."

Joseph leaned forward. "Yeah. And you realize it. You understand *why*, Paula." He smiled. "I can't help Dobbs. Nothing will help Dobbs. He isn't horrified by what he does, because he never cared to begin with. But, you? You don't want to be what you say you're becoming. Together? I think we can make sure you don't have to be."

Paula shook her head. "You know, Price hears everything said in here, right?"

Joseph nodded. "I do. I don't care."

Paula sat down on the floor in front of the window. "You better care. If you can't help Dobbs? He'll kill you."

Joseph nodded. "So, what do you care?"

Paula shrugged. "If he lets Dobbs kill you? I won't get to do it."

"Let's start with some breathing exercises," Joseph said. Then he sighed. "Is there any way I could get you to put your clothes on?"

"Would it make you more comfortable?" Paula asked.

"Yes."

"Then, no."

***

Anna dragged Bobby into her room at the lodge and closed the door behind her.

"I thought this wasn't a date," Bobby said.

She pushed him against the wall with a thud and kissed him hard.

"Whoa! Hey," Bobby said when they come up for air. "You're… really strong."

Anna laughed. "You have no idea." She pulled his T-shirt over his head.

"Hey, can we… slow down a little?" Bobby asked.

"Are you serious? How old are you?"

"Eighteen."

She took a step back. "Wait, are you… you know?"

"What?"

"I mean, it's perfectly okay if you are…"

"Are what?"

"You know… if you don't like girls."

He laughed. "No, Anna, I like girls. I like you."

76

She smiled. "Thank goodness. I mean, it would really suck if the only guy my age in the pack wasn't into me."

"*Pack?*"

"Are you a virgin?" Anna asked.

"No, I'm not a virgin. What do you mean, *pack?*"

"You know, the gang," Anna said. She started taking off her top. "We have to be quiet, I think the professor is in his room."

Bobby burst out laughing.

She paused with her fingers on the clasp of her front closing bra. "Usually, men don't laugh when I start getting naked."

"No, no... it's just. You called him 'the professor'. Made me think of Gilligan's Island."

Then she started laughing. She shoved him on the bed and lay down on top of him. "Okay, so Paul's the professor. That would make Clyde the Skipper."

"Who's Karen?" Bobby asked.

"Hmm? Ginger?"

Bobby shook his head and ran his fingers through her hair. "No. You're Ginger."

She smiled. "Ginger man are you?"

"I wasn't before."

"Keep it casual, Gilligan."

"Gilligan?! What? I'm the idiot?"

"You're the new guy. New guy's always the idiot." She cocked an eyebrow. "Don't knock it. I had a thing for Gilligan."

"Oh, I see. So, Karen's Mary Ann?"

"Yep."

"And... Swede and Layla are... the Howell's?"

Anna pursed her lips. "Not unless Thurston and Lovey were getting it on like a couple of rabid monkeys in heat in that straw hut of theirs."

Bobby laughed. He stroked her cheek. "It's nice. What you have? A family... a pack."

"How long has it been since you had a family?"

Bobby shrugged. "I never have."

"Huh?"

"Foster home to foster home. Turned eighteen and out the door I went. Just me and my bike." He shook his head. "See how well that turned out?"

She sat up. "Well, you're one of us now."

"Yeah, hate to break it to you, Ginger. Nothing is permanent."

She shrugged. "What if it could be?"

"What do you mean?"

She stood up and took a step back from the bed. "I… want to show you something."

He sat up on his elbows. "I… actually saw it all last night. Not that I'm complaining, and I definitely want to see it again."

"You… um… didn't see *everything*." She undid her bra and let it fall to the floor. "You just have to promise not to freak out, okay?"

***

Karen sat at the small desk in her room with the iPad on her lap and swiped up. She was looking for any potential werewolf sightings. She had learned a long time ago to ignore the mainstream news - if they did report on something that matched a werewolf attack, it usually was weeks after the fact.

The best sites were on the fringe, pages like The Redbud Revue and Voices in the Darke - though it was very difficult to separate the nuts from the real sightings on these forums.

"Do Vampires Avoid Warm Climates?" was the headline on Voices in the Darke.

"No, because vampires don't exist, morons," she whispered.

"What did you say?" Clyde asked from his bed.

"Nothing. Looking for leads on Todd Stearn," Karen said.

"Oh," Clyde said. He went back to sharpening his silver arrowheads and staring at the wall toward Anna's room.

"Stop it. You're the one always telling me how she's an adult…"

"Tell me you're okay with her messin' with that little shit."

Karen had heard them return from their bike ride thirty minutes before. They had gone straight to Anna's room.

"He has a name: Bobby. And Anna's a grown woman."

"She needs a good, respectable guy. Not some failed armed robber."

Karen laughed. "That kid hadn't eaten in several days and there were no bullets in the gun."

"Scrawny and stupid."

"He's taller than you," Karen said.

"Height ain't the point!"

Karen laughed. "You'd have made a good father, Hubbard."

"Still might if you got your head on straight."

"Doesn't have to be with me, hillbilly."

"The hell it doesn't. I need a tall blonde to overcome this short gene of mine."

Karen shook her head and laughed harder.

Someone knocked on the door.

Karen stood up and opened the door.

Anna was standing outside. She bit her lip and looked at her feet. "I need help."

***

The first thing Karen noticed was the strong smell of urine in the room.

She turned and looked at Anna who walked in behind her. "You didn't!" Karen said.

She shrugged. "He… we were getting along good, and I thought it was, you know, the right time."

"What'd he do? He hurt you?" Clyde said as he walked into the room behind them with an arrow in his hand. He wrinkled his nose. "What's that smell?"

"Piss," Karen said.

"Piss… Oh, for God's sake, Anna," Clyde grumbled.

"Do I smell piss?" Paul said as he walked in the room.

Anna threw her hands up in the air. "God, I have no privacy."

"Where is he?" Karen said.

Anna nodded toward the back of the room. "Bathroom. He locked himself in after he… you know… had an accident."

"Who pissed?" Swede asked as he walked in with Layla.

"Somebody, just kill me, please?" Anna whispered.

"Bobby had an accident," Karen said.

79

Swede looked thoughtful for a second. "You showed him your wolf?!" He bellowed with laughter. "Hey, baby, for once it wasn't us who screwed up!"

Swede and Layla high-fived and fell together on Anna's bed.

Karen looked at Paul. "Can you go get some clean clothes for Bobby from the room, please?"

"Sure," Paul said and walked out.

"I'm having deja vu," Karen said as she knocked on the bathroom door. "Bobby, it's Karen. Are you okay?"

"Go away!" Bobby said.

"Come on out, kid," Swede yelled. "We promise not to eat you."

"I can't promise that," Layla said.

"Wicked, wicked woman," Swede laughed and kissed her.

Karen gritted her teeth. "Not helping." She turned toward the bed. "Shouldn't you be breaking your own bed or something?"

"Already have," Swede said. "Shitty thing couldn't handle two werewolves."

Layla smiled. "We were very acrobatic."

"Out! Both of you! Now!" Karen yelled.

"Jeez, talk about sexual frustration," Swede said.

Layla laughed as they left.

Paul passed them in the doorway with a bundle of clothes. "I think these are relatively clean in comparison to the other garments in his satchel," Paul said.

Karen took them from him. "Thanks, professor. I'll take it from here."

She looked at Clyde. "You, out."

"What did I do?"

"You have… negative energy."

He scowled. "The hell does that mean?"

She tapped her finger on the arrow in his hand. "You are literally brandishing a weapon. Go!"

He turned toward the door and shook his head. "Swede's got a point on that whole sexual frustration thing."

Anna looked miserable. "I'm so sorry. I thought…"

Karen put her hand on Anna's shoulder. "You didn't do anything wrong."

"Really?"

"It's always hard and it's always awkward. You used your best judgement. Sometimes everything just goes to…"

"Piss?"

Karen laughed. "Yeah. Sometimes it just goes to piss."

***

Karen closed the door as Anna stepped out, then she walked over and laid the clothes outside the bathroom door.

She backed up ten feet. "Bobby? It's just me. Everybody else is gone. I laid a change of clothes outside the door."

"I'm not opening this door," he said from inside.

"Listen, I'm standing way back, okay? I promise you it's safe to open the door and get your clothes."

"She's a monster. Anna, she's not human."

"I know, Bobby."

"She showed me."

"I know. Bobby, please, just get your clothes. No tricks. I promise."

"Are you a monster too?"

Karen sighed. "Yes."

"Are you going to kill me?"

"No! Absolutely not, Bobby, you are in no danger. Not from us, not ever."

The door opened and Bobby quickly grabbed the clothes. Then he slammed the door and relocked it.

"What are you people, anyway?" Bobby asked.

She could hear him changing his clothes through the door. "Werewolves."

He was quiet for a second. "I thought werewolves only came out under a full moon."

Karen laughed. "No, that's just in the movies. We can change anytime we want. We're shapeshifters."

She heard water running.

"Were you born like this?" Bobby asked.

"No. I was turned into one."

"Anna?"

"I turned her into one."

"Clyde?"

"He isn't one."

"Professor Paul?"

"I turned him."

The water stopped running. "Swede?"

"I turned him too."

"Layla?"

Karen laughed. "Swede turned her. But I approved." She sighed. "You can come out, Bobby. I promise I will not hurt you."

"How do I know?"

"Bobby, honestly? I could tear through that door like it was tissue paper. If we wanted to hurt you? You'd already be dead. Come on out."

The doorknob turned and the door opened.

Bobby charged out with the top off the toilet tank held high over his head. He swung it at Karen's head.

She caught it with her right hand, and it stopped a foot from her skull. Karen looked from the tank lid to the boy's frightened face. "You put this right back where it belongs. I already have to pay for a damned broken bed, and I am not paying for a broken toilet on top of it."

***

Karen and Bobby sat side by side on the edge of the bed. It had taken her a half hour of explanation to calm him down to this point.

"So, you don't eat people?" Bobby asked.

"No. Not recently, anyway."

He looked at her.

"It's… complicated."

"You do kill people sometimes, though, right?"

"Yes. Bad people. We hunt bad people and sometimes we kill them."

"Like who?"

Karen shrugged. "Terrorists, violent criminals - other werewolves who go insane and start killing humans."

"But you're the good guys? Right?"

82

She laughed. "Bobby, I don't know. We do what we do because it feels like the right thing to do. We save a lot more lives than we take. I don't know if that makes us good guys or not."

"Sounds like it does."

She took a deep breath. "I didn't want you to find out this way. We were going to ease you into knowing. Anna thought you were ready."

He shook his head. "Definitely not ready." He rubbed his eyes. "I can't believe I peed myself in front of the hottest girl I ever met."

Karen laughed. "Oh, she'll get over it."

"Not sure I will."

Karen patted his shoulder. "Yes, you will."

She felt him stiffen under her touch. He was still terrified.

"Why'd you take me in?" Bobby asked.

"You needed a hand."

"Yeah, but that's not all is it?"

"No. I'm the alpha." She pointed at her blue eyes. "You can tell by the eyes. Anyway, some alphas, they can tell who should be turned and who shouldn't."

"You want to make me a werewolf?"

"Yes. Listen, it's your decision. Whatever you decide? That's how it will be, okay?"

He smiled. "You won't eat me if I say no?"

Karen laughed. "I promise you, we will not eat you."

"So, all of you chose this?"

Karen nodded. "Swede, he lost both legs saving some kids on a railroad track…"

"Wait, what?"

Karen smiled. "The werewolf virus, it makes people whole again. Paul, for instance? We found him because of a talk he did online - all about werewolves and the ancient Greeks. We went to talk to him and found out he had Multiple Sclerosis…"

"Not anymore?"

"No. Not anymore."

"Layla?"

Karen laughed. "Uh, absolutely nothing wrong with her… physically. Her spirit was almost broken, though. Swede met her at a, well, a strip club in Vegas. He fell in love and asked me to see if she could be one of us."

"You just meet someone, and you know?"

Karen nodded. "It's a feeling. They feel like family."

"What if somebody gets turned who shouldn't be?"

"It doesn't work out well. They leave the pack and turn rogue… fast. Or they just kill indiscriminately without their eyes turning red."

"How long do I have to make this decision?"

She smiled. "Aww, honey, as long you need."

Karen stood up. "Just think about it."

"Karen? What about Anna?"

"What about her?"

"What's her story on being turned?"

Karen smiled. "Why don't you ask her that?"

***

The Op

Price led Joseph into a darkened conference room near Price's office.

Two large screens made up the back wall of the room.

The screen on the right was blank.

The screen on the left showed a map of the United States. A glowing yellow line stretched from Maryland to someplace in central Texas.

"That is a CIA owned C-17 that flew out of Andrews a few hours ago. It's carrying Lobo-1 at 45,000 feet," Price said.

"Lobo-1?"

"Gunny Dodd. What are his vitals, Dr. Geffman?" Price asked.

Angelica looked up from her monitor just in front of the big screens. "Heartrate is 40 beats per minute, body temperature 95 degrees Fahrenheit, respiration… hell, I can barely tell he's breathing."

Price looked at Joseph. "We like to fly him unpressurized for the last hour before a drop."

"*Unpressurized?* At 45,000 feet?! That would kill…"

84

"A man? Absolutely, but not a lobo. Gunny is just having a nice rest before his HALO drop."

"HALO?"

"Acronym stands for High Altitude Low Opening - Lobo-1 is going to jump out of the plane at 45,000 feet and then freefall to 3,000 feet before opening his chute. Most HALO drops are from 35,000 feet down to 3,500. Lobos can jump from higher altitude without oxygen and land harder without damage."

"Is this some sort of training exercise? That's Texas."

"You know your geography," Price said. "And, no, this is not a training exercise."

***

Dodd opened his eyes when the ramp opened on the C-17. He stood up and walked to the rear of the plane. He rubbed away a crust of ice in his left eyebrow. "Lobo-1, radio check?"

"Reading you five by five," the communications officer said over his headset. "Switch on headset camera."

Dodd reached up and flipped a switch on the headset. "Camera on."

"Roger that. Lobo-1 good to go. Thirty seconds to drop."

"Roger." He looked out at the night sky.

"Three… two… one…" A light by the ramp turned green.

Dodd ran off the ramp and stepped into the sky.

***

"You're running a black op on US soil," Joseph said.

"Yes, doctor, I am. Switch the map to the satellite feed," Price said.

The view changed to an overhead view of a rural landscape. The dark green and black landscape was interrupted in places by blobs of white - people, highlighted by their heat signature.

"And you're performing satellite surveillance of US territory for covert operations - also against the law," Joseph said.

"Are you going to bitch or are you going to watch?" Price said. "And we're not conducting that surveillance - that's from a British spy satellite, so, technically we're not breaking the law."

85

"I think you're violating the spirit of the law if not the letter."

Price laughed.

"These people on the ground? Who are they?"

"Terrorists, doctor."

"What kind of terrorists?"

"That information is classified."

Angelica glanced at Joseph, and that glance said, *"For the love of God, shut up before he kills you."*

***

Five miles southwest of Selma, Texas

It was Saturday night, and Saturday night meant it was Heath Yarbrough's turn to patrol the perimeter of the Jehovah's Path Conclave. His buddy, Richie Durham, was somewhere on the east side of the conclave's property on the other ATV.

They were the two youngest 'Faith Defenders' in the conclave, which meant they drew the shit duty of patrolling twenty-five square miles of scrub brush and gopher holes while everybody else was up in Selma or Bowie having fun. He turned his head and spit snuff into the wind as he drove his ATV down the dark path.

In a year of patrolling, all he and Richie had seen were armadillos, coyotes, and the occasional wild boar. A few of the guys had spotted curious ATF agents using night vision goggles.

Or so they claimed - Heath wasn't sure the ATF or even the Wise County Sheriff's Department gave a rat's ass about Jehovah's Path. The conclave was ten trailers, two barns, three ham radio antennas, and a satellite internet connection in the middle of nowhere. Thirty-five people in total with about seven hundred guns, none of them fully automatic (despite Richie and Heath's best efforts with a semi-automatic Uzi nine-millimeter that, now, thanks to their gunsmithing, was capable of firing only a single round before jamming).

"Hey, H-Bomb, you see anything?" Richie asked over Heath's headset.

"I spy with my little eye, something beginning with the letter… B."

"Um, brush?"

86

"That'd be it, over."

"Patrol one and two? You two use proper radio protocol, please?" Pappy Reynolds said over their radio.

"Roger that, Calvary Base," Heath said. "Patrol one in sector 3, nothing to report, over."

"Patrol two in sector 1, nothing to report, over," Richie added.

"Calvary Base, acknowledged."

Heath topped the next rise, and, when the ATV's headlights angled down, they illuminated a pair of yellow eyes peering out from the brush.

Heath skidded to a stop halfway down the small hill. The eyes were gone, but he had definitely seen an animal's eyes reflecting back at him from the thicket.

He drew his Marlin guide gun rifle from its holster by his right leg. He levered a .45-70 round into the chamber before turning on the small, powerful spotlight on the ATV's left fender. He aimed the powerful beam of light into the brush. He turned off the ATV's engine.

A coyote, maybe? If it were, it had to have been a big one. The eyes were too far apart. With the Marlin to his shoulder, he scanned slowly to the left.

The wind was blowing from the southwest.

Something fluttered in the breeze just beyond the light's reach.

Holding the rifle to his shoulder with his right hand, he angled the spotlight up.

A large piece of fabric was blowing in the wind.

No, not fabric. It was dark green and billowed like silk.

"What the hell?" Heath whispered.

He could see the cords attached to it.

Parachute, he thought. *It's a parachute.*

He keyed the headset microphone. "Richie? There's something out here."

"Repeat?" Richie said.

"There's something out here. There's a parachute."

Pappy Reynolds broke in. "Did you say a *parachute*, over?"

"Yeah... yeah, it's a parachute."

"You still in sector 3?" Richie asked.

"Yeah, just past the dry stream on the other side of the hill. Something isn't right."

"I'm heading your way," Richie said over the roar of his motor.

Heath moved the searchlight beam to the right.

Something crouched at the bottom of the hill.

Something with yellow fur and blazing yellow eyes.

Heath had both hands on the rifle as the shape rose.

"No… no, that ain't right," Heath whispered. "That' ain't… it ain't right."

A massive wolf stood on its hind legs staring at him, the long pink tongue lolling between its sharp fangs as the creature panted, the great chest heaving.

The monster lowered its head and growled.

Heath had stopped breathing and his heart was pounding.

Finally, he gasped and pulled the trigger.

The bullet went wide, kicking up dust behind the monster and to its left.

It didn't even flinch.

Heath levered the Marlin and fired again.

This one hit the creature left of its center of mass.

A black spray erupted from the monster's back as the bullet made a much larger exit wound than entrance.

It dropped to its knees. Then it fell onto its back staring straight up at the star filled Texas sky.

"We heard a gunshot. Was that a gunshot?" Pappy Reynolds asked over the radio.

"I shot it," Heath said as he climbed off the ATV with the rifle still trained on the collapsed creature. He levered his third round into the chamber.

"Shot *what*? What did you shoot?" Pappy asked.

"I don't know." He walked slowly toward the shape, the spotlight illuminating him from behind.

He kept the rifle pointed at the monster.

"Was it a boar?" Richie asked.

"No. No, it… I don't know. Some kind of wolf, maybe?"

"*Wolf*? There ain't no wolves here," Pappy said.

Heath stopped. He didn't want to get any closer to the monster lying on its back with its legs bent under it. It wasn't breathing, it wasn't moving, but everything in him told him not to get any closer.

"I'll be there in two minutes, Heath," Richie said.

Heath stared at the monster's head. Something was shining beside its left eye.

He took a step closer.

It was wearing an olive-green headset. There was a red blinking light beside what had to be a camera lens.

"What…?" He was standing over it, staring into the monster's lifeless yellow eyes and the shiny camera lens.

The huge right arm rocketed up, the clawed hand open.

Heath felt a moment of searing pain as the claws and then the hand itself entered his abdomen just below his navel.

The hand twisted inside him, tangling in his intestines, and then ripping down violently.

Heath watched as his insides poured onto the ground.

He dropped to his knees.

The monster sat up and looked into his eyes, the hot breath blowing back his hair.

Then the monster's face turned to the side, it's jaws locked on his throat and closed.

The world began to tumble over and over as his head came off and rolled away from his body.

***

"Oh, dear God," Angelica whispered.

"Give me a status on Lobo-1," Price said.

"What?"

"Status on Lobo-1, Dr. Geffman? If you can't do your job, I can have you relieved."

"He's… heartrate normal. Respiration… normal…" Angelica's voice was cracking.

"That was a kid, Price! That was a sixteen-year-old kid!" Joseph said.

"Enemy combatant. He shot Lobo-1 first."

"Dodd wasn't in any danger! There was no reason… Jesus, that was a child."

"You obviously know nothing about modern warfare, doctor. I've seen kids half that age strap on a suicide vest…"

"That kid was no soldier, no suicide bomber. He didn't even know what he was looking at!"

The communications officer looked up from his screen. "Lobo-1 is on the move, sir."

***

Dodd ran up the hill, the taste of the boy's blood on his lips. He could hear the second ATV approaching, and, if he timed it just right…?

The ATV came over the top of the hill and Dodd lashed out with his right paw.

The startled rider's head came off with a spray of arterial blood and flew over the man's shoulder as the ATV and the rider's body continued down the hill before it ran into the first ATV and flipped over.

Dodd didn't stop. He turned southeast and ran toward the cluster of trailers near the center of the property.

By this time, Price's techs had cut the landline and blocked the conclave's satellite internet. Two miles away, an unmarked truck was blocking their HAM radio signals as well.

Dodd pulled back his lips from his muzzle and smiled as he ran. He was blooded and free. For the next hour, he would be able to kill without interference.

Someday soon, he would finish a job like this and then he would keep running. The next time they ran an op near a major city? He would disappear into the heart of it.

Oh, and then there would be blood. So much blood.

He would pile the bodies in the street. He would make a throne out of his victims' skulls.

Price or someone like Price would kill him eventually.

But the fun he would have until then?

He loped into the cluster of trailers.

Twenty-seven heartbeats.

There were vehicles beside the trailers.

He ran by a pickup truck and slashed at the front left tire with his right paw.

The tire exploded and the front of the truck collapsed down on the dented rim.

A small car was behind it and Dodd grabbed the rear bumper and flipped it over without slowing. The windows shattered leaving diamonds of broken glass on all four sides.

Trailer doors began opening and men emerged, most carrying rifles.

Dodd ran into the gloom beyond the trailers then circled back.

He ran straight toward the side of a red and silver single wide trailer. He launched himself into the air. His feet touched the roof of the trailer and he kicked, flinging himself skyward.

Thirty feet in the air he tumbled before landing on all fours on the small trailer they were using for a radio shack. He slapped at the narrow aluminum tower with the HAM antenna beside the shack and snapped the bolts and guy wires, sending it crashing to the ground.

A nine-millimeter bullet whistled by his ear.

Dodd dropped to his knees on the trailer roof. He leaned over and saw a fat, bald middle-aged man staring up at him from the radio shack's small metal porch.

Dodd reached down and closed his hand on the sputtering man's face.

He looked into the man's eyes as the nose crushed inward, his cheekbones collapsing. Finally, the skull popped like an overripe melon and the man's body fell on the metal platform, his limbs still twitching.

Dodd raised his neck and howled, splitting the night air with the sound of a wolf amplified a hundred times.

The night came alive when the defenders, now clearly seeing what they were fighting, opened fire.

Bullets tore into Dodd's flesh, each slug burning a path through his insides. Lungs, heart, intestines were all pierced in seconds as Dodd stood up, blood spraying in clouds from the exit wounds.

Dodd fell off the roof and face down onto the bare earth beside the shack.

***

"Lobo-1 is down," the communication officer said.

The screen was black, the camera lens down in the dirt.

"Heart has stopped, respiration zero," Dr. Geffman said.

"He's dead?" Joseph asked.

Price chuckled. "Not his first time."

The camera shifted.

The image changed to the night sky - they had rolled Dodd onto his back.

Men and women with rifles stood in a circle around him.

"What the hell is that thing?" One of the women asked.

"Some kind of wolf," a man answered.

"He's wearing some kind of headset," another man said. His face filled the camera. "Son of a bitch. That's a camera. Somebody's watching this."

A woman pushed into the frame. "Hey, assholes! Your monster is dead!"

In the conference room, Dr. Geffman stared at her console. "I have a heartbeat. Slow."

"He's healing," Price said. "Imagine that. Shot at least ten times with high powered rifles and the virus is fixing him."

"Heart rate increasing… no respiration," Geffman said, then she scoffed. "Dodd is holding his breath."

The defenders arrayed around Dodd were taking turns laughing at the camera.

Suddenly, there were screams as Dodd grabbed the woman on camera by the throat and squeezed. Her neck broke in a sickening, muted snap.

***

Dodd jumped to his feet. He grabbed a hunting rifle from the nearest man, spun it around and then drove it barrel first up and into the man's abdomen, spearing him and then lifting him high into the air. He tossed man and rifle aside.

Then he spun on his right foot, his paw slashing out, and beheaded three men with his claws.

Those who remained dropped their rifles and tried to run.

Dodd ran after them.

The first man he slashed across the shoulders.

The man fell to the ground, writhing in pain.

A woman came next. Dodd loped after her on all fours. He turned his head to the side and bit into her calf.

She screamed and fell flat on her face in the dust.

The last man was almost to a trailer when Dodd caught him. He spun the man around and drove his claws into the man's guts, disemboweling him.

Dodd stepped away and let the man fall to the ground trying to hold his insides in place as he crumpled.

Dodd stepped back slowly, letting the headset camera record what was happening.

The three injured defenders were writhing and screaming as their bodies began to stretch and change.

***

"My God," Joseph said as he watched the three injured begin to transform into werewolves. "He infected them."

The woman screamed as her hips folded inward and her pelvis snapped. Her mouth was filled with sharp fangs.

"I thought you told him not to do that," Dr. Geffman whispered.

"I did," Price said. "He's… improvising again."

The disemboweled man's wounds began to close as dark brown hair covered his face and arms.

"I don't understand. Why would he…?" Joseph whispered.

"He's like a damned cat playing with his food," Angelica Geffman answered.

***

The man with the slashed shoulders was growing out of his clothes. He rolled onto all fours and stretched his back, ripping through what was left of his shirt.

Dodd pounced on him.

The man squealed in anguish as Dodd's jaws closed on the back of his neck.

He bit down.

The newly formed werewolf's head tumbled away in a fountain of blood from the ruined neck.

Dodd leaped over the woman who was struggling on her back, blonde fur covering her exposed skin as her clothes tore.

Dodd reached the man he had disemboweled just as he rose up on his hind legs.

He snarled at Dodd and slashed out with his new claws.

Dodd dodged the blow and kicked out with his right foot into the man's mid-section. The werewolf's spine snapped.

Then Dodd grabbed the werewolf's head and wrenched it from his shoulders before tossing it aside.

The female stood and shook. She stared at her clawed hands.

Dodd circled her slowly.

She lowered her head and snarled at him.

She ran toward him, and Dodd sidestepped, tripping her. She slid face first through the dirt.

He continued to circle her slowly as she got back to her feet.

She ran at him again.

This time he spun around and caught her from behind, locking her in a tight embrace.

She struggled against him, but he was much stronger.

And, better trained. He roared and locked his jaws on the side of her throat, let her feel his teeth.

Let her know the end was coming.

He bit down and jerked his jaws to the side.

The woman's head flew off and he dropped the body in the dust, savoring her taste on his lips.

***

Joseph turned away from the screens.

Price stood expressionless beside him. "Call him in. The cleanup crew can handle anyone left."

"Yes, sir," the communications officer said. "Lobo-1, exit the field. Mission accomplished."

"Oh, sweet Jesus, no," Angelica Geffman whispered.

Joseph turned around.

Dodd's camera was focused on a trailer.

Children's terrified faces looked at him through the window.

"Call him off, Price," Joseph said.

The communications officer spoke into the microphone again. "Lobo-1, you are ordered to stand down. I repeat, stand down, Lobo-1."

Dodd walked toward the trailer.

"Call off your fucking dog, Price!" Joseph yelled.

Price pushed the communications officer aside. "Gunny Dodd! Exit the field. You are not authorized…"

The camera spun around.

Dodd had taken off the headset.

His wolf face stared down at the camera, his breath fogging the lens.

Then he dropped the headset on the ground.

The camera was focused on a small rock a few inches from the lens. Nothing else was visible.

"Stop him, Price! For the love of God…" Joseph said.

"How do you propose I do that, Dr. Marlow?"

Angelica Geffman looked into Joseph's eyes as the screaming began.

***

Joseph sat on the hallway floor outside the conference room and stared at the far wall.

Dr. Angelica Geffman walked out and sank down beside him.

"Do you want to know why Dodd's eyes haven't turned red, Angelica?" Joseph asked.

"Why?"

"Because he was already insane when they turned him. A cold-blooded psychopath. And Price has given him a license to kill… no… he's given Dobbs a license to *slaughter*, Angelica."

She nodded.

"And you helped him."

She nodded again.

"Why?"

She sobbed. "Because I'm a coward. I'm terrified of him."

"One silver bullet is all it would take…"

"Not Dodd. I'm terrified of Price," Angelica said. "You have no idea what he is, Joseph."

"I'm leaving here in the morning. I'm going straight to the Washington Post with everything I have on Project Lobo."

Angelica laughed. "You try to leave and Price will have you shot before you reach the surface. If by some miracle you make it past the spec ops guys? He'll send Dodd after you. Dodd will make a pinata out of you, a literal pinata, Joseph." She took his hand. "You think I haven't tried to find a way out of this? We can't leave, Joseph. There's no escape from Project Lobo other than a body bag."

"I won't help him. I won't work with Dodd."

"Yes, you will. Because, if you don't? Paula Danvers is dead. Price finds your weakness - do you honestly believe he just let you work with her because you asked? He read you like a book. You've got a serious case of Sir Galahad syndrome. He'll use her against you."

Joseph sighed. "And your weakness is you think unraveling this werewolf virus will create wonder drugs and treatments to save lives."

"That… and cowardice. I'm very serious about that, Joseph. I place a high value on my own hide."

"Let's say we succeed in making these 'lobos' manageable? Give Price his super soldiers. Do you think there will be anything left of the world we know to save?"

"I don't know." She reached into her lab coat pocket and pulled out a USB drive. "But there's another piece of this you don't know about." She handed him the drive.

"What's this?"

"Lobos. Lobos who Price can't control."

***

Bobby stepped out of Anna's room and onto the porch.
Anna was leaning over the railing looking into the woods beyond.
"Hi," Bobby said.
"Hi."
"Listen, I'm sorry."
"No! No," Anna said. "I'm sorry. That was a horrible way to introduce you to what we are. I… I'm not good at this."

Bobby smiled. "I thought… we were going to… you know?"

She nodded. "Yeah, well, we were… we are… I mean if you still want to with me?"

He reached out and stroked her hair. "Yes, I still want to." He shook his head. "Although, I don't know why you'd want to be with me after I pissed myself."

Anna laughed. "Uh, let's see. When Karen showed Swede the wolf? He screamed, high pitched, like a little girl."

"No!"

"I swear to God. And Paul? He puked. Seriously, her arm started growing you know with the skin stretching and… Paul just lost his lunch."

Bobby laughed. "What about you?"

Anna shook her head. "I shot Karen."

"What?!"

"Yep. Silver bullet even. Clyde nearly killed me. She forgave me. Right then and there."

"She turned you?"

Anna nodded. "Later. Yeah."

"Tell me about it?"

She took his hand. "Walk with me. It's a long story."

Anna led him into the woods and told him a story about revenge and pain, fire and redemption.

A story equal parts horror and wonder.

***

Karen and Clyde watched them walk away into the night.

"Looks like you're going to grow the pack," Clyde said.

Karen smiled. "He's growing up. They both are."

"He's still a punk."

***

The Pack

"This feels weird," Anna said as she pulled her t-shirt over her head.

97

She and Bobby stood in the moonlit meadow under a canopy of stars.

"What's weird about it?" Bobby said. He was fidgeting, trying not to look at her and trying not to *look like* he was trying not to look at her. He couldn't figure out what to do with his hands. Bobby desperately wanted to look cool, but he didn't look cool, and he felt decidedly uncool.

"You're staring," Anna said as she stood in her bra and panties.

"I'm sorry. Am I not supposed to stare?"

She laughed. "No, you should watch. I mean, that's the whole point, right? To see me change?"

Going to the woods to make love had turned into going to the woods to see Anna turn.

It was just something they needed to get out of the way.

"Is it weird because you're doing this with me watching?" Bobby asked.

"I… guess."

"But you change in front of the others all the time."

"Yeah, but they're not…" She stopped and then she blushed.

"Not what?"

"Not… you."

He smiled. "You like me."

"Shut up."

"You do. You like me."

She rolled her eyes. "Duh, I came out here to have sex with you. I think the 'like you' is a given."

He started taking off his clothes.

"What are you doing?" Anna asked.

"I don't know. Maybe you'll feel more comfortable if we're both naked?" He pulled his t-shirt over his head.

"Oh… wow… okay."

"Something wrong?"

She shook her head. "No, nothing. Just… nice, you know muscles and… whatever. You're… um… not as skinny as I thought you were." She quickly unhooked her bra and let it fall to the ground.

He stared at her.

"Feel free to tell me I'm not hideous."

"Oh! No. You're beautiful. Perfect."

Her mouth dropped open. "Oh, my God. You're a virgin."

"Huh? No!"

"Don't lie to me. You have never seen real live boobs in your life!"

He sighed. "This is embarrassing."

She laughed. "Oh, no. No, it isn't embarrassing, it's sweet."

"Great, now I'm sweet."

She took his hand. "Hey. It's okay. I like being the first." She kissed him hard, pressing her body against his.

He took her in his arms and held her.

Then she took a step back. "Do not pee. Okay?"

He laughed. "I won't pee again. Promise."

She pushed down her panties and stood naked about five feet away from him. Anna rotated her neck clockwise and it popped.

"Does it hurt?"

She shrugged. "I guess. The first time is the worst. It's like your body has to learn how to become the wolf. Pelvis is the most painful - it splits. But the virus heals you so fast the pain only lasts a few seconds. Hurts like hell for those few seconds though."

She began to grow, her spine lengthening, the vertebrae separating.

Bobby squeezed his hands into fists.

She looked at him and smiled, her mouth growing wider, her teeth lengthening. "I... won't be able to talk... when I'm done," she growled.

Auburn hair began spreading quickly over her body.

Her hips folded inward as her legs became crooked.

The change rippled through her arms as muscles grew and convulsed. Long obsidian claws sprouted from her fingertips.

She stretched her jaws as her mouth became a muzzle.

And, then she was done.

The wolf towered over him.

She dropped onto all fours and panted, her breath clouding in front of her. She walked toward him slowly, head down.

He looked into her eyes - Anna's yellow eyes. Had they changed? No.

Bobby smiled. He reached out and ran his hands through the fur at her neck.

She licked his arm and rubbed her face against him.

He held her there, feeling her breath on his chest.

Bobby felt her change, the fur receding, her body becoming smaller in his arms.

A moment later she smiled up at him, human once more.

"That was…"

"Equal parts horror and wonder. That's what Karen calls it."

He nodded. "More wonder than horror."

She smiled. "Oh, I'm going to show you a lot more wonder."

He laughed and kissed her.

***

Joseph sat on the floor of his dark room with his back against his narrow bed. He turned the USB drive Angelica Geffman had given him over and over in his fingers.

What he had seen tonight would haunt him for the rest of his life.

Dodd was insane. He was a monster.

But Price? Price was worse. Dodd was a mad dog, had been one long before he had been infected with the Lobo virus.

He needed to be put down, humanely, before he killed anyone else.

Price though? Price was the monster who controlled monsters. Dodd might have been the claws, the teeth, the jaws… but Price was the brain.

Joseph had spent nearly two decades consulting for the government. He had met men like Price and Dodd before. Serial killers and sociopaths.

But, at all other times, those men had been in cages, not running covert ops with Uncle Sam's blessing and support.

And now, Joseph was trapped. He was locked in this mountain prison with the two most dangerous men he had ever known.

Angelica Geffman was not a coward. She was a survivor.

Joseph needed to find a way to survive as well.

He picked up his laptop and opened it. He turned off the Wi-Fi - would that be enough to keep Price from spying on him? Most likely not.

He pushed the USB drive into a port on the side of the laptop.

The key was filled with files. He began to open them.

File after file of newspaper reports, field reports, and video files.

SERIAL KILLER PLUNGES TO DEATH ON APPALACHIAN TRAIL.

SHERIFF'S DEPUTY AND FAMILY DEFEND WINERY AGAINST BIKER GANG.

HUSBAND AND WIFE SERIAL KILLERS DEAD IN WISCONSIN.

Every report had something in common: Lobos. Werewolves.

A grainy picture of a pretty blonde on a motorcycle, her hair flowing in the breeze. A woman with piercing blue eyes. The caption read "Karen Arthur, Alpha Lobo."

Then more stories: dead terrorists, more dead serial killers, massacred drug gangs.

More pictures of people with yellow eyes.

And then, the final file: a compilation of cell phone videos showing werewolves racing through traffic in Detroit.

Joseph pulled the USB drive out of the socket and closed the laptop.

Werewolves who weren't insane, following an alpha.

He sat in the dark. What had Paula said? *"I was supposed to be better. All of us? We were supposed to be better."* This was better. This was hope.

***

"Mr. Price? The team in Texas are asking if they should move in?" the communications officer asked as he followed Price down the hallway.

Price spoke without looking at him. "No. Tell them to wait until morning. He's overstimulated. If they go in now, he'll take them apart. Just tell them to keep the area contained. Once they've secured Lobo-1 tomorrow? Have them spray down everything in the compound with accelerant. Then call in a drone strike with Napalm. Burn it to ash, understood? No forensic evidence."

"Story for local law enforcement?"

Price stopped and pondered for a moment. "Religious zealots. They got involved in the Meth trade. We went in because the children were endangered, and the zealots blew themselves up rather than surrender - standard bullshit. Play up the religion angle. Media loves their Jim Jones Kool Aid moments. Good for ratings."

"Yes, sir," the officer said as he walked back to the conference room.

Price stood and looked down the empty hall. Tonight had been a great dry run but losing control of Lobo-1 at the end was unacceptable.

He needed the Lobos to be precision weapons, but Dodd was increasingly a nuclear option: cleanup was a nightmare, and the fallout was unacceptable.

Soon, he would need to euthanize Gunny Dodd.

It was time to revisit the question of alphas.

***

Bobby lay on his back in the warm grass. Anna lay in his arms, her head on his shoulder.

She whispered in his ear. "What did you think?"

He smiled. "Which part?"

She punched his ribs. "The sex, dummy."

He laughed. "Incredible."

She rose up, straddling him. "Right answer." She sat back and stretched. "We have to be careful."

"Because…?"

"Well, Bobby, you see, when a man and a woman really, really like each other and get super friendly and naked with each other? That's where babies come from."

He rolled his eyes. "Yeah, I know that part. You're on the pill though, right?"

She laughed. "Doesn't work for us."

"What?!" He said and started to set up.

She pushed him back down. "Human meds don't work on us. Not only that, Layla had a tubal ligation ten years before she was turned - guess what happened the first time she went wolf? Everything... down there... went back to factory default."

"Oh, my God," Bobby said.

"Yep. Lots of little werewolves running around if we aren't careful."

Bobby burst out laughing. "A litter?"

She punched his chest playfully. "Very funny. Just wanted to make a full disclosure if you decide to join the pack sometime."

He pulled her down so her face was on his chest. "So, I can decide any time, right?"

"Yes. But you can take your..."

"Now."

She sat up. "What?!"

"Now. Right now."

"Bobby, listen, we just had sex so you're not thinking clearly."

"I'm thinking clearly, Anna. All my life, I've been looking for something to belong to..."

"You don't have to be a werewolf to be part of the pack. You're in..."

He smiled. "I want to be one of you. I want to be like you."

"Um... maybe... Karen should do it. I... I've never turned anyone."

He took her hand and kissed it. "I want it to be you." He smiled. "Two firsts in one night."

She stared down at him.

"Please. It has to be you."

Anna took a deep breath. She held up her left hand.

Bobby watched as the bones in her hand began to lengthen, the skin darkening. Auburn fur covered it in seconds.

And, then the long, obsidian claws grew from her fingertips.

He reached up and put his palm against hers, interlacing their fingers.

"You're sure?"

He smiled and nodded, guiding her hand down to his chest.

"It only takes a scratch," she whispered.

"I know." He closed his eyes.

He felt the burning pain as her claw sliced into the skin of his bare chest.

He arched his back as the burning sensation spread across his body.

Her lips found his and she kissed him.

Then she whispered. "Don't fight it. It doesn't hurt as bad if you relax."

His teeth felt too big for his mouth.

She framed his face with her hands. "I'm here. It's going to be okay."

Bobby could smell everything. The grass beneath them, the dirt in which the grass grew. The smell of the pines above them. The wind through those pines, and that wind brought with it the smell of the lodge - a million smells all mixed together.

But, above all? Her.

"Bobby, look at me," she said.

Her voice was like thunder to his sensitive ears.

He stared into her eyes. The night seemed as bright as day now. Her eyes! Yes, they were yellow, but there was more. A rainbow of colors that he couldn't see before.

Weren't dogs colorblind? Hadn't he read that somewhere?

She was transforming with him, her smiling face elongating, becoming the wolf.

He screamed but it came out as a howl. Something was wrong with his hips. The bones were...

Snap! His pelvis split down the middle and folded in on itself.

He passed out, he didn't know how long.

But he awoke with her nuzzling against his face.

Bobby rolled over and onto all fours.

There was no pain now.

He felt strong. He shook all over.

Anna faced him. Was she smiling? She stood up on her hind legs.
Bobby stood up as well.

He was a head taller than her.

She held out her clawed right hand.

He placed his left palm against hers. His fur was black, the claws
longer.

Anna turned away and dashed into the woods.

Bobby paused only for a moment before following her.

***

Karen stood on the porch and smiled toward the woods.

Clyde came out and handed her a cup of coffee. "She did it?"

Karen nodded. "He's one of us now." She nodded toward the
ridgeline. "They're running. I can't explain how that feels. It's like
you're the wind." She laughed and shook her head. "No, that's not
right. You're part of everything. The wind, the ground under your
feet - you can't tell where the forest ends and you begin."

"Sounds wonderful." He smiled. "I'm going to bed. Don't wake
me when you get back."

She shook her head. "I'm not going to the woods." She reached
out and took his hand. "I'm going to bed too."

Clyde looked at her.

She shrugged. "I was thinking. Maybe we could try it your way?"

He blinked. "What are you…?"

"Don't talk, hillbilly. Just come to bed."

***

Outside Jehovah's Path Conclave Near Selma, Texas
Dawn

The Blackhawk helicopter landed on the prairie outside the
compound when they caught sight of Dodd.

The long grass waved under the prop wash as the lone figure
approached from the west.

Dodd, human again and naked, walked calmly toward the
helicopter.

He was covered from head to toe in dried blood.

105

He said nothing as he climbed into the helicopter and sat down in a seat near the back.

The gunner tried not to make eye contact as he spoke into his microphone. "Air-1 reporting. Lobo-1 is secure."

Dodd stared straight ahead, his yellow eyes unwavering.

ACT II

Changes and Responsibilities

"I was benevolent and good; misery made me a fiend. Make me happy, and I shall again be virtuous."

— *Mary Shelley, Frankenstein*

A Wolf's Work

Spears Mountain, Virginia

"Good morning," Joseph said as he walked into the observation room beside Paula's cell.

Inside her glass walled prison, she rolled over on her foam mattress and stared at him. "I really hate morning people."

"Ever do ink blots?"

"Oh, go to hell, Marlow." She rolled back over and pressed her face into the foam.

"I can only help you if you choose to help yourself."

"Ever been at the monkey house at the zoo when the monkeys start throwing shit? You're about to have that experience, smell be damned."

He moved his chair closer to the glass. "Humor me. Come on. Just try. Do this one thing for me and... I promise to let you torture me to death if you break loose. I won't even put up a fight."

She sat up and stretched. "What would be the fun in that?"

He held up a sheet of paper against the glass. "What do you see in this inkblot?"

She cocked her head sideways. "Me ripping open your chest cavity and eating your heart."

"Excellent." He held up a different sheet. "And this one?"

"An elephant with two trunks."

"Very good. This one?"

She stared at the glass.

"What do you think?"

There was no inkblot on the page. Only the words: WE'RE BEING WATCHED.

"Truth," she said. "I see truth."

"Interesting." He held up the next page.

I NEED YOU TO LOOK AT SOMETHING. COME CLOSER.

"Death wish. I see a death wish."

"Most likely."

She stood up and walked over to the glass wall. She sat down. "Too close. I can hear your heart beating."

"That must be amazing."

"You think so? I want to make it stop. Still think it's amazing?"

He smiled. "When I was a kid, I once watched a black widow spider building its web. I knew what it was, knew it was deadly. But I just couldn't take my eyes off it."

"Oh, tell me about your childhood, please," she said sarcastically.

"Ink blots first." He held up the next.

THERE ARE OTHER LOBOS.

"Um, looks like... well, I just don't care."

"I have more here on my laptop." He turned the screen toward her, hoping that his body would block the security camera's view.

Or, that Price would be so bored by inkblots that he would ignore the laptop.

Joseph began paging through the stories from the USB drive.

She watched intently, leaning forward, her forehead almost touching the glass. "I see... fairy tales."

"Fascinating. And this?"

He put up the picture of Karen Arthur.

The look on Paula's face was disbelief. "Blue... no... that can't be."

"Blue, um, does that frighten you?"

"They kill the blues. How can this be?"

He shook his head and nodded toward the security camera over his shoulder.

Paula gritted her teeth. "The... inkblot... it looks like a blue-eyed wolf. They killed the only one."

"The one here... yes." He leaned closer. "How do you feel when you think about a blue-eyed wolf, Paula?"

"I hate it. I want to kill it." Tears were welling in her eyes.

"Why?"

"I don't want help. It wouldn't work."

"What if it could, Paula? What if it could help?" He played the video of Karen Arthur's pack on the street in Detroit.

She smiled. "Running. I see wolves running." She caressed the glass.

"I don't think you hate that blue-eyed wolf, Paula."

She closed her eyes. Then she got up and turned away. "It doesn't matter, Marlow. It wouldn't work."

Joseph closed his laptop.

***

Edward Price sat in his office and stared at the security camera footage.

The inkblot ruse was clever. He would give Marlow that much.

Of course, he knew about the contents of the USB key - Angelica Geffman was a brilliant scientist, but her spy craft left much to be desired.

Right now, she, like Dr. Joseph Marlow, was useful. Therefore, they both got to live another day.

***

Clyde had awoken at first light to find himself alone in the bed.

It was her way, and he accepted it.

She needed him, loved him in her way.

But when that need was satisfied? She had to be alone.

Part of him wished he'd never laid eyes on Karen Arthur. Not a major part, just a quiet part who grumbled once in a while but kept his mouth shut most times.

A wise man once said, *"You don't choose who you love."*

Brother, ain't that the truth?

He walked into The Rhododendron restaurant and found the rest of the pack already sitting down to breakfast in the back room.

Karen stood up and smiled at him, looking like a million dollars as she walked over to him, and what idiot voice kept saying he would be better off if he'd never laid eyes on her? Whoever that guy was? He was blind.

And, then she did the unthinkable. She took his hand.

Clyde stared down at her hand in his.

She caught him staring. "What?"

"Am I dying or something?" He whispered.

The rest of the pack had seen her take his hand and went dead silent.

Swede stopped chewing with his mouth full of bacon.

"Don't make this weird," Karen whispered as she led him to the table.

"It's totally weird," Clyde whispered back.

Karen sat down and glared at the others. "We're an item. All of you knew we were an item. Stop acting shocked."

Anna began to laugh and leaned her head on Bobby's shoulder.

"I ordered you that big breakfast platter thing from yesterday," Karen said.

"Needs to keep up his strength," Swede said.

Everybody looked at Swede.

"We're not making jokes about this?" Swede asked.

Layla winked at him. "Read the room, lover."

"You know I'm terrible at that," he said and kissed her.

"Swede, it's payday," Karen said.

"You got it, boss."

"Bobby, when Swede goes to the bank this evening? You go with him."

"Uh, I can go," Anna said.

"No. Swede and Bobby can manage just fine," Karen said with a smile.

"Sure," Bobby said.

Paul was staring at his tablet. "Did you see this story out of Texas? The Jehovah's Path thing?"

"No," Clyde said as he swallowed a forkful of eggs.

"Meth lab exploded in a religious cult. Killed everyone, leveled the site."

"Interesting - religious cult that's cooking meth," Swede said.

"Yes, strange in and of itself. However, what's stranger? Local out hunting a few minutes before the explosion took this picture," Paul said as he held up his find.

A naked man covered in what appeared to be blood was walking toward a black helicopter across a field.

"Zoom in on the face, Paul," Karen said.

Paul used two fingers on the tablet to zoom in.

"Recognize him?" Clyde asked.

Karen shook her head. "No. But, the eyes…"

"Shit," Anna whispered. "I mean, it's grainy…"

Karen nodded. "They look yellow to me."

"We heading to Texas?" Swede asked.

Karen stared at the screen. Then she shook her head. "No. If he got on that helicopter, he could be anywhere by now." She looked at Paul. "Professor, find out everything you can on Jehovah's Path. Talk to the guy who took the photograph, see if he can tell us anything else."

Clyde rubbed his chin. "That helicopter is a Blackhawk. Not something you buy on the open market."

"Government," Karen said.

"Maybe the same people who erased our Detroit escapade off the internet," Clyde said.

***

"Is it a good thing or a bad thing if the government is involved?" Bobby asked as he followed Anna out of the restaurant.

"It's hard to say. You remember we told you about rogues?"

"Yeah. Werewolves who've gone bad."

Anna nodded. "A few years ago, one of those rogues was found dead out in Washington State: Emil Vincenz. There were reports of some spec ops guys being seen in the same vicinity."

"So, if the government is killing rogues? That's all good, right?"

Anna shrugged. "They aren't us, Bobby. And, now when they apparently send in a werewolf to take out a religious cult?"

"Okay, but this werewolf at the cult had yellow eyes - he wasn't a rogue."

She bit her lip. "Sometimes… the bad ones. The *really* bad ones? Their eyes don't turn red. Karen knew one like that."

***

Edward Price stepped out into the light from the access tunnel on top of Spears Mountain.

The dusty cars in the small lot had been joined by something else: a shiny black Airbus H155 executive helicopter sat off to the side.

112

Peter Hutchins was Price's polar opposite.

Tall and well-manicured in his gray silk suit, he was at least fifteen years Price's junior.

"Edward. Walk with me," Hutchins said as he turned and walked toward the open field beside the parking lot.

Price caught up and fell in step with the taller man. "Mr. Hutchins, there was really no need to fly all the way..."

"Your man was seen, Edward. There will be questions. The answers to which could prove embarrassing," Hutchins said without looking at him.

"Our people have already scrubbed the image from the internet."

"And the witness?"

"We've paid him to keep quiet."

"Kill him, Price. Quietly. Cleanly... this time." He finally looked down at Price. "The board doesn't believe you actually have control of your wolf, Edward."

"He... has become problematic."

Hutchins smiled. "Is that what you call it?" He shook his head. "Children... the optics on this could be very bad, Edward."

"We have a lid on this, sir."

Hutchins sighed. "Project Lobo has a lot of promise, Edward. But people are beginning to question if you should be the one running it?"

Price stood up straight. "Mr. Hutchins, if you want someone else..."

"No, I don't. I just want you to get things under control, Edward."

***

Gunny Dodd lay on his bunk and stared straight up at the ceiling.

He hadn't been debriefed after the mission.

They had simply driven him back from the airfield, he had gotten a shower and chow, and then he had hit the rack.

He smiled.

They were afraid of him.

Not that they hadn't been before, but now they were very afraid. He liked that.

Dodd rolled to his feet.

They were going to kill him, of course.

Last night had clinched it. As bloodthirsty as Price and his goons were? Dodd had crossed a line.

When he was young, Dodd's brother had a pet boa constrictor. They had started off feeding the snake dead mice, but as the snake grew, they switched to live prey.

His brother had no problem feeding the snake dead mice, but he could not handle seeing the snake hunt a live rat. He ended up giving the snake to one of his friends.

There was something about feeding a fellow mammal to a reptile that just felt wrong to Dodd's brother.

Now, Dodd was the snake, and Price's people were getting squeamish.

They couldn't just give Dodd to some other group. They were going to kill him… at least, they were going to try.

He would have to do something about that.

***

Karen stared at the grainy image of the naked, bloody man in Texas. She used her fingers to zoom in and out on his face.

"You think it's Stearn?" Clyde asked from his bed.

Karen stood up from the desk with the iPad in her hand. She lay down beside him on the bed.

Clyde put his arm around her and held her close as she continued to stare at the iPad.

"I don't know," she said. "Age, hair color - the fact that Stearn had a military background? It all fits," Karen whispered.

He smelled her hair. "What do you want to do?"

She smiled. "I want this to be true. I want to believe the government has found some way to control Todd Stearn and that… maybe they're using him to do the job we've been trying to do."

"You think they used him to kill Vincenz?"

She nodded. "Maybe. Clyde, if the government is using Stearn, if they've found a way to keep him from going rogue? We could… we could stop."

He smiled. "Go to Bedford, buy a house, raise a couple of kids?"

She rolled on top of him. "Maybe?"

He nodded. "I like the sound of that."

"Me too." She kissed him. "It could be over. All of this could be over."

Clyde sighed.

"What?"

He shook his head. "Darlin', I did some looking into this Jehovah's Path group. They're survivalists, not some doomsday cult. Just a bunch of people sitting on a couple tons of MRE's waiting on society to collapse. Not one mention of them being involved in the drug trade…"

"You know as well as I do that things aren't always what they seem. The news media are calling them terrorists."

He shook his head. "It don't add up. These people don't seem like terrorists. Hell, they don't even look like Branch Davidians. Our contacts at ATF didn't have them on their radar. But some other government agency decides to send in a werewolf? This smells like a massive overreaction on somebody's part… or a test run for a weapons system."

She rolled off him and sat down on the edge of the bed facing away.

"There were kids in that camp, Karen."

She sighed. "We don't know they were killed."

He rubbed her shoulders. "No, we don't."

"I'm tired, redneck."

"I know you are."

She reached up and put her hand on his. "Tell everyone to be ready. We're going to hunt this wolf. When he puts in another appearance? We ride."

***

The Beast in the Dark

Kenny Andrews didn't like the job at Spears Mountain, but it beat the shit out of dodging scorpions in the Middle East. When he finished his last tour, he had signed on with Hutchins Security at about five times his Army pay. An operator with any skill could make a lot of money in the mercenary market, and Kenny was no slouch.

He hadn't bargained on becoming a cave dweller, though.

And, working for a spooky asshole like Edward Price wasn't for the faint of heart.

Kenny had seen things, things he was paid a great deal of money not to talk about. There were the werewolves on the lower floors: the soldier, the chick in the glass cell, and the other thing they kept locked up.

There had been a lot of other things, though.

The thing that looked different every time you saw it. Once it had looked like his old girlfriend, Monica - exactly like her. Only he hadn't seen her since high school.

It looked like Monica from twenty years before. Like she hadn't aged.

The thing had smiled at him, beckoned him.

One of his buddies had grabbed his arm and pulled him back - he hadn't even been aware he had been walking toward the Monica-thing.

That thing drank blood. His buddy probably saved Kenny's life that day.

It was gone now. Dissected alive, Kenny had heard.

There had been other things over the years. Some he only heard rumors about: witches, ghosts.

One of his friends had explained that evil things draw ghosts, they travel in a monster's wake like dolphins behind a boat. Like remora on a shark.

If that was the case? Spears Mountain must be packed full of ghosts.

Kenny stretched and walked across the catwalk to look down at the levels below in the hollowed-out mountain. The plants that covered the catwalk rails were nice. The mountain was in 'night mode' now, the daylight lamps turned down to low mimicking night.

His shift was over at midnight.

Kenny had one job: guard the armory. He turned around and looked at the steel door set into the rock wall. Only three people on the base could open the armory, and he was one of them.

All the Hutchins men carried a sidearm, a few carried carbines.

The heavier weapons and extra ammunition were stored in the armory.

"Evening," a man said.

Kenny spun around to see a marine standing a few feet down the catwalk from him.

Not just any marine.

Kenny put his hand on his pistol. "Gunnery Sergeant, you aren't allowed up here."

"Just out for a walk."

Kenny took a step back. "You need to leave this level right now."

The marine smiled. His eyes seemed to glow yellow in the dark. "You going to shoot me?"

"You know I will…"

"No, I don't think so."

The marine moved fast. One second, he was ten feet away. The next he was directly in Kenny's face.

There was a sharp pain in Kenny's chest.

He looked down.

The marine's hand was wrist deep in Kenny's abdomen.

"Odd sensation feeling a man's heartbeat," the marine said. "All I have to do is squeeze and you die."

Kenny was gasping for breath. He couldn't stop looking at the point where the man's hand had disappeared into his chest cavity. He could feel the fingers around his heart.

He pushed Kenny backward. "I need you to open that door for me."

Kenny's feet weren't touching the metal catwalk floor - the monster was holding him in midair.

Kenny wanted to scream, but he couldn't get enough air into his lungs.

The monster angled him toward the keypad beside the armory door. "Punch in the code."

Kenny's hand was shaking.

He felt the fingers squeeze around his heart. "I really need you to punch in that code."

Kenny reached out and typed in the code.

The light beside the pad stayed red.

"What else does it need?"

"Eye," Kenny gasped. "Has to scan… eye." He nodded toward the glass camera lens above the keypad.

The monster grunted. He pushed Kenny's face toward the camera. The light turned green.

The monster squeezed Kenny's heart, crushing it as the door swung open. "I'll need a mop," the monster said.

They were the last words Kenny heard.

***

Edward Price stood outside the barracks set aside for Gunny Dobbs. He hesitated with his hand on the doorknob.

Fear.

Price wasn't used to fear - inspiring it, yes, but experiencing it for himself? No.

He had been in the presence of many monsters in this hollowed out mountain. Monsters he personally had been in charge of procuring, both natural and man-made.

But there was something about the lobos that made Price pause before opening the door.

Gunny Dodd had a primal nature about him.

A primal nature that had slaughtered innocent lives last night. The most innocent lives imaginable.

But was he a worse monster than Price?

That was debatable.

Price opened the door.

The barracks was empty.

Price's hand immediately went to the nine-millimeter in his jacket pocket. "Gunny Dodd?" He called out to the empty room.

The barracks was cavernous, echoing.

"Gunny…"

"Right here, Mr. Price," Dodd said as he emerged from the bathroom.

He was dripping from the shower, a towel wrapped around his midsection.

Price eased his grip on the pistol. "Didn't hear the shower."

"Something you need, Mr. Price?"

"New mission. A snatch and grab in Tennessee…"

"You nervous, Mr. Price?" Dodd asked.

Price paused. "No. As I was saying, it's a snatch and…"

"You look nervous. The way you're fingering that pistol? You look troubled."

Price frowned. Dodd looked relaxed, completely unfazed by the gun in Price's pocket.

Dodd smiled. "Look, Edward… may I call you 'Edward'?"

Price stared at the man's yellow eyes. "Yes, Gunny, you may."

"Edward, last night was a mistake. I got carried away. Truth is, there was just so much blood. I think it got to me." He sat down on his bunk. "Blood lust, I guess you'd call it." He looked at his hands. "Edward, I promise I will never do anything like that again. Ended up scaring myself."

"That's… good to hear, Gunny."

Dodd nodded toward him. "You don't need that gun with me, Edward. I'm a loyal soldier, sir. I wouldn't harm anyone you didn't sanction. Not even you. You have my word." He laughed. "Truth is? Dr. Marlow has been helping me come to terms with my condition. After last night, I clearly see I need to maintain control of myself."

Price nodded. He took his hand out of his jacket pocket.

Dodd smiled. "If we're going to do some good with Project Lobo? We need to trust one another. Well, I trust you, Edward."

Price smiled a tight-lipped smile. "I trust you as well, Gunny."

"Good. Now, tell me about this snatch and grab mission."

***

A few minutes later, Price emerged from the barracks. He walked calmly down the hall. When he was satisfied he was far enough away that Dodd couldn't overhear with his keen ears, he pulled out his radio.

"This is Price. Double the guard on Dobbs. I want to know every move he makes when he steps out of that barracks."

***

"You want to *what*?!" Angelica hissed. They were sitting in her lab.

119

Joseph looked around nervously. "You're sure this room is clean."

"Yes. Were you serious? You want to break Paula out?"

"I want to take her to this Karen Arthur."

Angelica stared at him. "You're nuts." She held out her hand and extended her index finger. "Number one? Paula will kill you - hell, she might kill all of us." She extended her middle finger. "Number two? If Paula doesn't kill you? Price will. I told you before: you're being watched, Joseph. You couldn't leave on your own, much less with Paula."

"I don't think Paula will hurt me," Joseph said.

"You don't think…" Angelica started to laugh. "Oh, my God… you're in love with her."

Joseph looked away.

"Man, oh, man," Angelica said. "Don't they take licenses away from head shrinkers who fall for their patients?"

"It's not like that."

"Really? What's it like?"

Joseph shook his head. "There's good in her. I…"

"You *feel* it? I don't really think of psychology as a science, but for the sake of argument? Put on your scientist hat and think, Joseph. Every other lobo whose eyes turned red went psycho and started killing everyone around them. I knew several of them - for the most part they were good, decent people who never hurt anyone their government didn't specify as an enemy. When those eyes started going red? They turned into serial killers."

"I don't know, maybe that's the key. They were soldiers who had killed or were at least prepared to. Paula is no killer."

"She hates us, Joseph. Dodd, Price, Me especially. Even you. Open that door and somebody is going to die - and maybe not the people you want."

Joseph hissed. "I don't want anyone to die, Angelica."

"After last night? Dodd needs to die, Price too, but I'm not willing to let Paula tear you and me apart to do it," Angelica said.

They both jumped as the door opened.

"Ahh, there you are," Price said as he entered. "No doubt plotting mayhem. Can I help?"

Angelica turned pale. "We were just discussing last night."

"Yes, tragic," Price said. "Doctor Marlow, I think it's time we explored bringing in an outside expert."

Joseph frowned. "Expert? What kind of …?"

"A blue-eyed lobo. An alpha. Now we could just have Dodd nibble on our security team until we roll a blue one, but we know of three in the wild, don't we, Angelica?"

"You're going to bring in one of the alphas?" Angelica asked.

Price nodded. "That's my plan. We have a choice between the two in Bedford or the woman traveling with the motorcycle gang."

"Ward Rickman is tied to law enforcement," Angelica said. "And Melissa Ames is a child…"

"Exactly, so I need a plan for capturing this Karen Arthur."

Angelica shook her head. "Karen Arthur has a pack, Price. There are at least four other lobos…"

"Five by recent estimates," Price said.

"You're going to capture them all?" Joseph asked.

"No, doctor. We're only going to grab Karen Arthur. I don't need more yellow-eyed wolves."

"They'll go rogue without their alpha," Angelica said.

"Not my problem. Now, you two geniuses come up with a way to capture her with minimal losses, on our side at least."

***

Payday

"You were a virgin before Anna, right?" Swede asked as they made their way through the thick woods in the dark.

"Could we not talk for a while?" Bobby asked miserably. "I thought we were looking for an ATM or something?"

They had been walking for a half hour through the forest around the periphery of Grundy, Virginia, on a moonless night.

"We are," Swede said. "So, you'd never been with a woman before?"

Bobby nearly tripped over an exposed root. "Why do you want to know, Swede?!"

Swede stopped and looked at him with a solemn expression. "She's one of my best friends. I want to make sure she's happy."

"I know what I'm doing in, you know, bed, okay?"

Swede frowned. "Naah, you don't. She probably does. You most likely messed up. This is why men are supposed to lose their virginity early on."

"She didn't complain, Swede! Okay? For the love of God, where are we going?"

"ATM. I told you. Being terrible in bed is nothing to be ashamed of. You just have to learn. I have some books on Tantric sex you can borrow when we get back. Oh, and the professor has some books on human anatomy you should look through." Swede stopped by some trees and knelt down. "Stay low."

"Huh?"

Swede grabbed his shirt sleeve and pulled him down into a crouch. "Stay... low."

Bobby peered through the brush.

There was a bank beyond the trees. It was a standard branch bank: a small brick building with three drive thru lanes and an ATM in the last lane.

They were in the woods just past the ATM lane.

"Why are we sneaking up on a bank in the middle of the night?"

"Watch and learn. Trick is to wait until the cleaning crew is gone. If they're still vacuuming the bank? You hide until they're done." Swede pointed at the bank parking lot. "No cars. No cleaning crew. That means we only have to contend with the security cameras."

"What are we doing, *exactly*, Swede?"

Swede shrugged. "Payday. Now, there's always at least one security camera inside the bank pointing out through the teller window but, we're in luck, because they drew the privacy shade when they closed and obscured the camera. Nice, huh?"

"Oh, my God, we're robbing a bank!? You people made me go to confession over trying to knock over a convenience store and you're bank robbers?"

"No, no, we're not robbing the bank. Just accessing the ATM in a special way." Swede pointed toward the drive thru lanes. "Three security cameras over the lanes but the two closest to the bank can't see the ATM lane - that means we only have the one over the ATM. And, of course, the camera inside the ATM machine itself."

"I'm not robbing a bank, Swede," Bobby said.

Swede sighed. "I hear ya, I do. Look at it this way: the government is paying us. Think of us as undocumented government employees."

"What are you talking about?"

"Our pack is performing a great service for the people of this country. We take out bloodthirsty rogue werewolves, arsonists, terrorists... you follow?"

"Yeah, I guess," Bobby said.

"Good man. Now, we deserve to be paid for our patriotism, right?"

"I... suppose."

"If we were cops, we'd be paid by the government directly. But we're monsters so we... knock over ATMs, the banks are insured by the FDIC. Bank pays us, government pays the banks. Therefore, we're undocumented government employees." Swede smiled. "Simple, right?"

Bobby stared at him in the dark. "I'm going back to the hotel." He turned to go.

Swede picked up a rock from the ground. His right arm sprouted thick hair and claws.

He flung the stone, and it whistled through the air.

The security camera over the ATM lane exploded in a shower of glass and plastic.

Bobby dropped to the ground again. "What are you doing?"

"Nice throw, huh? Now you take out the camera on the ATM." Swede handed him a stone, holding it carefully in his clawed hand.

Bobby took the stone and squinted at the ATM. The camera was a shining circle an inch across and fifty feet away. "I can't hit that."

"Better hurry," Swede said. "Andy and Barney will be here within nine minutes - probably a tad less."

"Andy and Barney?"

"Mayberry's finest? The Andy Griffith Show? No? Lack of a classical education. The cops, Bobby. They'll be here in a few minutes. Throw or we don't get paid."

Bobby sighed. He felt the change ripple through his right arm.

"Eyes too. The wolf sees better."

Bobby forced the change on his eyes.

123

The lights of the bank were now brighter. The camera appeared closer.

He felt the fangs sprouting in his mouth.

"Throw it, kid."

He threw the stone and the air whistled.

The glass eye of the camera shattered into a million pieces.

"I hit it. I can't believe..."

Swede was already sprinting across the parking lot, his arms growing, the hair sprouting.

Bobby ran to catch him.

At the ATM, Swede turned and smiled at him, his mouth full of sharp fangs. "Fun part," Swede growled.

His right paw slashed downward across the face of the ATM.

The steel and plastic shredded in a shower of sparks and a shriek of tortured metal.

Swede's dissection uncovered four metal boxes in sockets within the machine.

He pulled one out.

"How much is in it?" Bobby asked.

"Full? Two thousand twenty-dollar bills - $40,000. But it's probably," he hefted it with his paw. "I'd say half that. Probably $20,000."

Bobby reached for one of the other boxes.

Swede slapped his hand. "No. Don't get greedy. One's plenty."

"But..."

"One is plenty. We take only what we need, kid." He cocked his head to the side. "Hear that?"

Bobby turned his head.

Sirens.

"Andy and Barney are a little faster than I expected." Swede laughed. "Run!"

Swede dashed away toward the woods.

Bobby followed.

Running. Swede was wrong. Tearing apart the ATM wasn't the fun part.

Running was the fun part.

He smiled, willing his eyes to change. The forest was no longer dark, it was brightly lit. Every twig, every leaf stood out in stark contrast. The scent of the pines, the smell of rabbits and squirrels.

Four hundred yards into the woods, Swede transitioned fully, his running shoes and sweats exploding into strips as the wolf fully emerged.

Swede transferred the cash box to his mouth and switched from running to loping through the dense woods.

Bobby followed suit and freed his wolf, catching up with Swede, passing him.

Later Swede would explain that they always transitioned to wolf as they ran away. The reason: when they finally brought in the dogs to track them? Once the dogs scented the wolves, they would not follow.

Dogs were too smart to chase after werewolves.

***

"You don't approve?" Karen said as she leaned against the railing at the hotel.

Bobby threw his hands up. "You didn't approve of my robbing the convenience store and, you were right, I shouldn't have done that. But…?"

"How is this different?"

"Yeah, how is it any different?"

Karen nodded. "Okay. First of all, nobody is in any danger whatsoever."

"So, my gun wasn't loaded…"

"The lady in the convenience store could have had a heart attack. She might have had a gun and you could have been shot or an innocent bystander might have been shot." Karen shook her head. "But that isn't the point. Robbing the ATMs isn't right, Bobby. It will never be right no matter how we like to spin it."

"Then why do you do it?"

"Because we have to survive. Werewolves like our friends Ward and Loretta? They can have normal jobs. We can't. Our 'job' is to hunt down rogues and now bad people as well. We're constantly moving but we still have to survive, Bobby. We're not exactly living in luxury." Karen laughed. "We only take what we need, the bare minimum, no more."

Bobby leaned against the railing and stared out at the forest.

"Things are changing. We're running out of targets, Bobby," Karen said. "For the first time? I can see the end of… all this. When the last rogue is gone? We'll stop. We'll retire to some place out in the woods like this. Start living the American dream."

Bobby laughed. "What will we do then?"

Karen shrugged. "Anything we want. You and Anna could have a couple of kids…"

Bobby looked at her in horror. "Kids?! We're only kids ourselves."

Karen laughed. "I know. My point is: this is temporary. A means to an end. And, that end? It might be a pretty great place."

***

Layla stood naked just inside the door to the room she shared with Swede.

"Not nice to eavesdrop," Swede said from the bed.

She didn't turn around. She just raised her right hand and flipped him off.

Swede laughed, low and guttural. He was half transitioned to wolf, his eyes glowing yellow and the fangs glimmering in the light from the bedside lamp.

She turned, her own face lupine, the lips pulled back from her fangs as she smiled.

Layla leaped onto the bed from across the room, landing astride her mate. "Do you ever think about it?"

"Think about what?"

"What we'll do when we settle down," she said.

He ran his clawed fingers through her thick hair. "Anything you want."

"A farm?"

"A farm?!" He laughed. "What on earth…"

"Pigs and chickens and cows. Milk cows."

"Who are you and what have you done with my Layla?"

She laid her head on his chest. "And children," she whispered.

Swede stared at her in the dim light. "First time you ever talked about that."

She shrugged. "First time I ever thought about it."

"Is that what you want?"

She smiled at him, then hid her face in his neck.

Swede laughed.

She pressed her ear against his chest to hear it. "I love that sound."

"Children, huh? Well, birth control pills don't work on you and, I suppose the rhythm method is going to fail sooner or later..."

She laughed and sat up. "Yes?"

He looked up at her. He shrugged. "What would it hurt?"

Layla lunged down and bit his ear drawing a howl.

Then she sat up, her eyes glittering. "Now?"

"No! Now... practice," Swede growled.

Their laughter continued until break of day.

***

Preparations

"The concept is pretty simple," Angelica said. "Silver interferes with the lobos' ability to heal. By mixing a strong narcotic with silver iodide, we should be able to create a tranquilizer dart that will work... at least for a short time. It's the same method we use for the... other one."

Joseph stared at her. *The other one.* The lobo he hadn't been allowed to see.

Angelica wouldn't look at him.

Something about *the other one* obviously bothered her.

"What narcotic are you recommending?" Price asked.

Angelica turned away from her lab bench. "Fentanyl. It will take a fairly large dose."

"Jesus," Joseph said. "Wouldn't a large dose of Fentanyl kill her?"

"We'll be giving her enough to kill roughly a dozen human beings," Angelica said. "With a lobo? We might knock her out for a few hours. We'll have to filter the silver iodide from her blood afterward, though - it will cause excruciating pain once the Fentanyl wears off."

"Test it on Paula," Price said.

"Excuse me?" Joseph asked. "You want to use her as a guinea pig?"

Price chuckled. "In case you missed it, Dr. Marlow? She is a guinea pig."

Joseph looked to Angelica for support but found none. She was looking at the floor.

"Why not test it on Dodd?" Joseph asked.

Price sighed. "Excellent idea, doctor. Let's go up to the increasingly more paranoid super soldier and ask him if we can shoot him up with a mickey. I'm sure he'll be very receptive to that request."

"So, you admit you've lost control of him?" Angelica asked.

"You've obviously never testified before congress. I admit nothing. If you and Dr. Marlow want to broach the subject with Gunny Dodd, feel free. I'll send flowers." He looked from one of them to the other. "No? Then I suggest you use the guinea pig."

***

"Why even ask me?" Paula said as she paced back and forth in her cell. "I'm a prisoner. You can do whatever you want."

Marlow bit his lip. "I'm asking because it's the right thing to do. I'm asking because we need your help."

She laughed. "You're pathetic."

"I think she might be able to help you."

"You're pathetic and an idiot," Paula said.

"How do you know? How do you know I'm wrong?"

"It's too late! Why can't you get it through your thick skull?" Paula ran at the glass and pounded her fists against it. "I want to kill everyone! Every second I'm awake I want to kill everyone, Marlow. I want to feel human flesh ripping. I want to taste the blood. I can hear your heart beating through this thick glass wall and, like I said, I want to make it stop."

"Why wouldn't you? They turned you into this. Then they locked you in a cell. Why wouldn't you want to kill them? Kill us? Maybe you're the sanest one of us all."

She turned away. "Open my cell, doc. I'll kill Price first. Then Angelica. I'll try to kill Dodd, but I'll probably fail - he's stronger than me. But I'll save you till last… that way if Dodd kills me? You might make it out of this alive. What do you say?"

Joseph took a deep breath. "I have to test the sedative, Paula. Please let me test it on you."

Paula laughed. "Take your best shot."

Thwip.

Paula turned around, startled.

Joseph had aimed through one of the round vent holes in the thick glass and hit her in the left hip with the dart.

"I'm sorry."

Paula pulled the dart out of her hip through the sweatpants. "You… asshole…"

She stumbled toward him.

She rubbed her hip. "It burns."

"It's the silver iodide. We'll filter it while you're asleep."

"I take it back," Paula said as she fell to her knees in front of the glass. "I'm going to kill you first."

Smiling, Joseph knelt down and put his hand on the glass. "I know."

She leaned her face against the glass. Her speech was beginning to slur. "Could've… you know?"

"Could've what?"

She was struggling to stay awake.

"Could've fallen for you. Before. Before the wolf. I could've."

He nodded. "Me too."

She squeezed her eyes shut. When she opened them, they seemed brighter. She bared her teeth. "But now? I'm going to eat you up."

Then her eyes rolled back in her head, and she collapsed into a heap on the floor.

Joseph sat with his back to the glass and stared at the wall.

***

"She's doing well," Angelica said. "Blood pressure is 110/50, heart rate 65, O2 sats are at 100%..."

She was looking at a monitor mounted outside the cell.

Paula was lying on her bench as a small, squat robot on tank treads read her vital signs.

It was unsafe for anyone to be in the room with her.

Joseph stood with his hands on the glass.

Paula's face was contorted with pain even as she slept.

"Another twenty minutes and we'll have the last of the silver out of her system. Then her metabolism will kick in and she'll be right as rain," Angelica said.

"This is wrong," Joseph said. "It's all wrong."

"No argument from me, Joseph."

"If people knew what was going on in here," Joseph whispered.

"We'd all be dead. One word of this ever gets out? Price's masters will have us all killed. That includes Paula."

"Catch 22," Joseph said.

"Catch 22." She put her hand on his shoulder. "She's going to be okay."

"I know she's dangerous but she's suffering. More than any of them, she's suffering."

Angelica stepped away and shook her head. "No, doc, trust me. She is not suffering more than all of them."

He turned and looked at her. "The other one. The one they won't let me see?"

Paula shook her head and stared at the floor. "You don't want to know. Trust me, Joseph. You don't want to know."

Price walked into the cell block. "How's our patient, doctors?"

"She's fine. The robot is working so we should be able..."

The robot crashed into the glass wall at a height of eight feet and shattered into a thousand pieces.

Paula was in full wolf form, slamming her fists against the glass hard enough to make the room shake. She turned her lupine face toward Price and howled.

Angelica and Price took a few steps back.

But Joseph put his hands against the glass and looked up at her. "Paula, stop. Stop, you'll hurt yourself."

Price was pulling Angelica toward the steel door leading out of the cell block.

Angelica held out her hand to Joseph. "Joseph, come on! If that glass gives way…"

He shook his head. "I don't care."

Price shoved Angelica through the steel door and shut it. He spun the lock mechanism and then peered through the small window at the top.

"Paula, stop," Joseph said. His voice was calm.

He was calm.

The huge lobo looked down at him. She licked her lips.

"I know," Joseph said. "I know and I don't blame you. I don't. But I promise you I am trying to help you."

She struck the glass with her huge fist directly in front of Joseph's face.

Dr. Joseph Marlow did not flinch. He did not look away.

"I'm trying to help you," he repeated.

Paula was naked, a person again. She stared through the glass at him with her half-red eyes. "Why?"

"Because I have to."

She walked away. "You're a fool."

"I know."

She looked over her shoulder at him. "You bring that blue here? She'll kill you on principal."

Joseph exhaled. "Yeah. She can get in line."

***

"Karen Arthur and her pack have been hunting rogue werewolves," Price said in the command center. He was standing in front of a wall dominated by a huge monitor. "That's how we first found out about her. We had a pair of lobos who piqued our interest in Elkhorn, Wisconsin. They had no Alpha; however, they somehow managed to control themselves to a certain extent. That is until Karen Arthur swooped in and killed them. We've followed her ever since. Through her, we found out about the werewolves in Bedford, Virginia."

"I'm confused," Joseph said from his side of the conference table. "How did you get the first 'seed' for your lobo program if all you've done is *watch* the two packs?"

"Good question," Price said. "We started looking for the same killing patterns Karen Arthur was looking for. Only, we did so with all the resources of our dear Uncle Sam - we got to our *donor* before Arthur could get to him."

"And the rest is twisted, House of Frankenstein history," Angelica mumbled beside Joseph.

Price didn't turn around, but he pointed behind his back at Angelica. "You didn't think I heard that, but I did. One of my favorite movies." He pointed toward the monitor at surveillance photos of a group on motorcycles riding down a highway. "We've been leaving Karen Arthur and her traveling freak show alone. She's done a good job of cleaning up the rogues and she's taken out some terrorist nuisances as well. But all good things come to an end."

"What happens to her pack when we take her?" Joseph asked.

"Again, I do not care..."

Angelica spoke up. "They're only a couple of hundred miles from Bedford. They'll go to Ward Rickman. He'll keep them from going rogue."

"There," Price said. "It will all be fine. Everybody lives. Happy now, Dr. Marlow?"

"No."

"Again, I do not care," Price said. "What's your problem? You and Angelica were planning on taking Paula to Miss Arthur, I'm simply bringing Miss Arthur to Paula. Mountains and Mohammed and all that jazz."

Joseph's blood ran cold.

Price turned and smiled at Joseph and Angelica. "Yes, I knew. I know everything, doctors. That's why I'm still alive in this dangerous game and the two of you are dangerously close to the precipice."

Price turned back to the images on the wall monitor. "Where were we? Ahh, yes, Karen Arthur and her obsession with rogue lobos. We're going to divide and conquer. Two lobo attacks, one in west Tennessee, one in East Tennessee. With any luck, Karen Arthur will send half her people to each. We'll take her from whichever team she joins."

"*Lobo attacks?*" Joseph asked. "What do you mean…"

"We'll send Gunny Dodd on a mission in East Tennessee while a strike team does something 'witchy' in West Tennessee."

"You're going to kill people!?" Joseph said as he stood up from his chair.

Angelica shook her head. "You're going to send that *maniac* out again? All for a fucking *diversion*? My God, Price."

Price laughed. "My poor, deluded, doctors. This government kills hundreds sometimes thousands of people per day - every government does."

"You piece of shit," Angelica whispered.

"You want your blue-eyed wolf or not?"

***

Clingmans Dome
Great Smoky Mountains National Park
Sevier County, Tennessee

Barbara Murphy eyed the can of bear spray with distrust. "This actually works?"

Her husband, Dillon, chuckled. "Yes, Babs. It works."

She shook the can, heard the contents slosh, and then examined the red spray top.

"Honey, if you shoot yourself in the eye with that stuff? It's going to be a long hike down," Dillon warned as he hefted his pack a little higher.

They were just off the path up Clingmans Dome, the highest point in Tennessee.

Just off the path.

Everywhere they went, Dillon insisted on being 'just off the path'. He hated hiking with a crowd.

So, invariably Barbara found herself tripping over tree roots and stumbling over rocks when there was a park service maintained trail not a hundred yards away.

She was wearing snake protector gaiters - copper mesh covered boots that reached almost to her knees over her khaki pants. They were heavy, unwieldy, and a total pain; however, she didn't worry about briars slashing her legs or the occasional copperhead trying to strike.

It also helped alleviate her nightmare fear: stepping down into a rattlesnake den.

Dillon wasn't wearing armored boots, just khaki pants and thick work boots.

She looked around the pine woods at the galaxy of bugs congregating in sunbeams. The green tree blanket of the Smokys spread out before them on all sides.

Barbara had insisted on bear spray. She had put her foot down at hiking the Rockies - no way she was venturing into grizzly country.

Black bears terrified her enough.

"Fine day for a hike," a man said.

Barbara almost fell backward.

The man was crouched on a rocky ledge above them. He was wearing a muscle shirt and a pair of green military fatigues.

His hair was shaved close, and he wore mirrored sunglasses.

Dillon stepped closer to her. "Yeah. How much further to the top?"

The man turned his head and looked over his shoulder. "Oh, a thousand yards. Hard going though. Not the place for civilians."

"Civilians?" Barbara asked.

He turned toward her and smiled. "You people aren't trained for this kind of thing."

"We manage," Dillon said as he led Barbara further away from the outcropping and then around the side of it. From this side, they could no longer see the man. "You heading up or on your way down?" Dillon asked.

"Me? I've been sitting here all day waiting on some damned fool to happen by."

Dillon turned toward the outcropping and unslung his pack. He pulled the nine-millimeter out of the zipper pocket.

"What are you doing?" Barbara whispered.

"Something isn't right," Dillon whispered. He pushed her behind him. "That's an odd thing to say," Dillon said out loud as he held the pistol in both hands.

"Glock 18... nice," the man said from somewhere on the ridge line above. "Didn't have you pegged for it. Cop, aren't you?"

"Memphis Police Department. I'm going to need you to come out where I can see you... real slow." He whispered back to Barbara. "Take your cell and call 911."

She fumbled in her pack. "Aren't you overreacting?"

"No, I don't think so," Dillon said. "Mister, I said to step out where I can see you."

Laughter. "I don't think you really want me to do that."

There was no service on her cellphone. "It's... there are no bars."

"Cell signals are being blocked. Little drone flying overhead. Your tax dollars at work," the man said from somewhere.

To Barbara, the voice sounded like it was coming from all directions.

"Last chance," Dillon said. "Step out where I can see you."

She put her hand on Dillon's back. "Let's go. We can just run down to the trail."

"No, actually, you can't," the man said.

He sounded closer.

"I said step..."

"I'm right here."

Barbara looked up at the ridge line.

The man was naked and smiling down at them.

"He's high or something," Dillon said as he aimed the gun. "On the ground! Now!"

"You wouldn't happen to have silver bullets in that gun, would you?"

"What?" Dillon asked.

"I thought not," the man said.

He grew. The man grew.

Seven feet, eight feet.

His arms and legs were lengthening, muscles growing. Hair sprouted everywhere as his fingernails became gleaming black claws.

Barbara screamed as Dillon fired his gun.

She saw the bullets hit.

The creature didn't flinch as the dense fur covered his body.

The face was the worst part. The jaw and nose lengthened, became a muzzle filled with long sharp teeth.

The sunglasses fell off revealing glowing yellow eyes.

The monster threw itself into the air and came down on Dillon's shoulders.

Barbara was thrown back into the bushes as her husband shattered.

His bones broke as the creature's weight drove him into the ground.

The monster crouched over him and swung its clawed, right hand.

Dillon's head separated from his body and tumbled into the bushes as blood sprayed from his ruined neck.

Barbara screamed.

The monster sat up and turned its head sideways, like some dog in a video. It seemed to be smiling at her, tongue lolling.

Then the creature reached down with both hands, drove its long claws into Dillon's rib cage and separated the two halves.

It reached in and tore out Dillon's heart.

Then it took a bite.

The monster walked on all fours over to her. Then it held the heart out to her.

The creature's face changed, becoming almost human. "Eat."

Barbara screamed again.

Then she pointed the bear spray at the monster's face and pulled the trigger.

The creature screamed in agony and rolled away, pressing its face into the mossy ground and rubbing furiously.

Barbara got up and ran down the mountainside, the bear spray can still in her hand.

She could see the trail below.

Barbara fell on her butt and slid down through the rich black dirt.

Then the monster was on her.

He landed in front of her, the great arm rocketing out. It gripped her throat and raised her into the air.

She struggled to point the bear spray toward the monster's face.

It took the can from her grasp.

She was blacking out, gasping for air as the monster's grip on her throat tightened.

The monster forced the can of bear spray into her mouth.

She felt the muscles in her jaw give way.

The monster leaned in close and began squeezing the base of the bear spray bottle.

The can exploded in her mouth.

**

Breaks Interstate Park

"Two at once," Clyde said as he looked at the iPad. "Karen, it's a trap."

"Maybe. Maybe not," Karen said.

Two hours earlier, the news had been alive with two stories about bear attacks in Tennessee: one in the Smoky Mountains, one west of Nashville.

Clyde shook his head. "Which one are we going to check out?"

"Both."

"Aww, Karen, for God's sake…"

"Clyde, we have to look into both. Once we determine which one is most likely a werewolf, we'll combine forces."

"Splitting up is a bad idea! You know this. We don't split up."

"Clyde…"

"It's a trap, Karen."

"I know! I know that."

"Then why… oh, wait a minute…"

Karen turned away. "If this is a trap, and it very likely is?" She sighed. "They're going to keep trying it until we take the bait."

"We're not responsible for that."

"Oh, baby, yes. Yes, we are," Karen said. "They killed kids, Clyde. These people? They're capable of anything. They'll kill and they'll keep killing to get what they want. We have to stop them."

Clyde threw the iPad on the bed. "Why us?! Why does it have to be us?"

"If not us? Whom?"

***

The pack gathered outside the restaurant.

"What do you think, Karen?" Paul asked.

"You know my opinion," Karen said. "We can't just ignore this. But this is the first time we've knowingly walked into a trap. I may be the alpha, but… everyone here needs to know what we're walking into."

"They killed kids," Layla said. "That last time? They killed kids. We have to stop them."

"Yeah," Swede said. "But I mean is this the way to do that?"

Anna nodded. "I'm with Layla. We have to go."

"Bobby?" Karen asked.

Bobby was looking at Anna. "Huh?"

"What's your vote?"

"I get a vote?"

Clyde laughed. "Yeah, you get a vote."

"I… we should stop them."

"Swede?" Karen asked.

The big man took a deep breath. "Maybe we shouldn't all go."

Layla laughed. "Can it. I'm going with you. And I know you're going."

"Yeah, well, maybe you don't know me that well…"

Layla shook her head. "Lover, you jumped between buildings with a toddler in your arms. You've got hero tattooed on your ass."

He grinned. "You know damned well what I have tattooed on my ass. It isn't 'hero'."

She wrapped her arms around his neck and kissed him.

"Swede?" Karen asked again.

He kissed Layla's face. "We go."

"Paul?"

"Well, I don't have 'hero' tattooed on my ass; however, I too believe these people must be stopped. I thank you, Karen, for giving us the illusion of free choice in all this."

"Huh?"

Clyde laughed. "Whither thou goest, babe. Whither thou goest."

They all laughed.

"Okay, okay," Karen said. "Clyde, you take the professor and Bobby to Nashville. I'll take Swede, Layla, and Anna with me to the Smokys."

"Wait a minute," Clyde said. "I go with you."

"No arguments," Karen said. "You're the best hunter. Bobby is too green for wilderness searching…"

"Hey!" Bobby said.

Anna poked him in the ribs. "Shut up. She's right."

Karen looked at the professor. "And Paul…"

Paul nodded. "I'm too slow. I understand and I agree with your assessment, though my ego is bruised."

"You'll get over it," Karen said. She turned back to Clyde. "I need you to lead the Nashville team."

"Karen…"

She touched his cheek. "I'll be fine. I'm a big werewolf and I can take care of myself."

"Yeah? Who's going to take care of me?"

"Bobby," Karen said.

"I'm a dead man," Clyde said.

Bobby hissed. "Hey! Come on. I'm standing right here, guys."

Karen smiled "We keep in touch via cell at all times. As soon as we eliminate one of the leads? We join back up. Understood?"

They nodded in agreement.

"We leaving now?" Swede asked.

"No," Karen said. "Both crime scenes will be crawling with cops today. We'll leave in the morning. Get some sleep."

Swede smiled at Layla.

"She said *sleep*," Layla whispered.

"I fully intend to sleep at some point," Swede whispered back.

***

"You're really good at that, Mr. Hubbard," Karen said as she snuggled against his bare chest in the bed.

"Should've seen me in my youth," Clyde said.

Karen laughed and played with his chest hair. "Popular with the ladies, were you?"

139

"Oh, darlin', there were times I had to chase them out of the trailer with a fire extinguisher."

Karen laughed harder. "You are so full of shit, hillbilly."

"Yes, I am." He kissed her head. "Actually, I was a wallflower."

"You? Never."

"True. Chaste and pure just like you."

"Oh, hillbilly, I've been a lot of things but 'chaste and pure'? No."

"You're scared aren't you," Clyde whispered.

She sighed. "You know me too well."

"No, never well enough. I don't think I could in a thousand years."

She smiled. "When it was you and I alone, at the beginning? I wasn't afraid of anything. Then… when I fell in love with you?"

"Five minutes after you met me, go on."

She poked him in the ribs. "It was a little longer than that. Anyway, after I fell in love with you? I stopped being as fearless. And now…?"

He nodded. "You're responsible for all of them."

"Anna and Bobby are so young, Clyde."

"She's tough and that boy might be green, but I think he's lived through a lot," Clyde said.

"And Swede is the toughest creature I've ever seen but… he's vulnerable, soft hearted. And Layla? Oh, Layla doesn't belong in any of this."

"They take care of themselves."

"And Paul? He's too damned old for this shit, Clyde. Half the time he can't keep up…"

"And, before you came along? He could barely walk. You think he would like to go back to his crutches? You think Swede would like to go back to being a double amputee? You think Layla wants to go back to being a stripper? And Anna… Jesus, Karen. You gave her a life."

She nodded. "I know all of that, I just… I'm afraid for them."

"That's the bad thing about being in charge. Lot of weight on your shoulders. But we have a job to do."

She rose up and smiled at him. Then she started to cry. "I'm sorry I pushed you away for so long. I can't imagine being without you. And… yeah, I was in love with you five minutes after…"

He pulled her close and kissed her.

***

Paul Collins rubbed his eyes and laid the iPad beside him on the bed. He had been reading research on Atlantis, as he usually did.

This latest text was well researched and had all the merits of a scholarly work.

It was also completely false.

He was becoming increasingly convinced the most accurate description of the fate of Atlantis was from an obscure poem from the 1960s written by an equally obscure poet: Merlin Taliesin.

A man who refused to talk to him no matter how nicely he asked. In a few years, Merlin Taliesin would be dead and the mystery of his work, Only Gods May Stay, would be lost.

Die Gute Wolf originated in the lost kingdom of Atlantis, a weapons system created in a final, desperate attempt to stop something… monstrous.

He closed his eyes. "*The demons. Not dead, but hiding, Mighty Atlantis they did slay. Foolish Atlantis I say, Not even gods may stay…*"

Paul fell asleep, the final words of the poem on his lips.

***

Bobby sat naked on the bed sheets as Anna grumbled in the bathroom. "I'm sorry," he said.

"Stop saying that."

"Yeah, but I *am* sorry."

Anna came out of the bathroom naked. "I said: Stop saying that."

"I just… I get excited."

She smiled and lay down beside him on the bed. "It's okay. But… you know birth control doesn't work and condoms…"

"Break."

"Always," Anna said. "Get the wolf in you excited and…"

"I get it. They don't make them for werewolves."

"So, you have to… not be… there… when you."

"I know, I'm so sorry," he said as he stroked her hip.

She smiled. "Stop it. I won't be… incredibly upset if that, you know, happens. I mean, I want to have kids."

"Really?" He asked.

"That doesn't mean you don't try to get out in time! Don't misread what I said! I'm not ready to be a mom and you sure as hell aren't ready to be a dad."

"I get it. I'm trying, I promise." He smiled.

"Try harder."

He nodded. "Absolutely."

"Stop smiling."

"Whatever you want." He kissed her forehead. "Want to go again?"

"We're supposed to be sleeping," Anna said.

"Yeah, well, Swede and Layla aren't sleeping. I mean… they've both screamed in their room at least five times."

"Six."

"Only three times for us."

Anna laughed. "It's not a competition."

He shrugged. "It… could be a competition."

She laughed and rolled over on top of him. "Control this time."

"Control, got it." He put his hands around her waist.

"Ow! Claws."

"Sorry."

She bit her lip and then bared her fangs. "On second thought? Keep the claws."

He smiled up at her as his jaw began to stretch.

***

Layla paused above Swede as low howls came from the direction of Anna and Bobby's room. She laughed. "Animals. They should be ashamed." Then she jerked her head to the right, changing into her wolf in seconds.

Swede licked her face and growled.

***

Ghosts

Ghosts are real.

That thought came to Karen as she slept in Clyde's arms.

They were not alone in her dream.

She could smell *him*.

The ghost that haunted her.

She thought he had given up being her own personal poltergeist, that maybe he had stepped into the light and somehow escaped the limbo he claimed to be trapped within.

She sat up in bed, unsure if she was asleep or awake.

Hayden Oswald, the psychotic werewolf who had made her all those years ago, sat in the room's cushioned chair, his face hidden in the dark.

"Robin Hood is a little short for you, isn't he?" Hayden said in the darkness.

Karen shivered and put her arm over Clyde.

"Relax. Ghosts can't kill the living. Trust me, if we could? I'd have killed that hayseed a long time ago," Hayden chuckled.

"What do you want?"

"You. A second chance. To breathe air again. Feel wind on my face. A nice, rare ribeye with a baked potato would be nice. Not much chance of any of that. Do you imagine it's me when he's inside you?"

"You weren't that memorable."

"Liar. You loved me."

"What the hell do you want, Hayden? Keep your jokes to yourself this time."

He leaned forward. "We're all here. Limbo. All of us."

"Who's *we*?"

"My crew. The ones you killed, the ones Ward killed. All of us, stuck in this limbo. Dogs may go to heaven, sunshine, but werewolves don't go anywhere. Heaven won't let us in and the Devil doesn't want us. Purgatory, like I told you before."

"I'm so sad for you," Karen whispered and then smiled.

"There she is. That's the cruel bitch who slaughtered her ex and his old lady. Good times."

"Screw you, Hayden. Now, if you can't do anything but disturb my sleep? Piss off." She started to lay back.

"I made you kill them."

She sat up. "What?"

"I made you kill them. You were drunk on me, on what I made you. You weren't responsible."

She chuckled. "Absolution from the damned? Go to hell, Hayden."

"Already been over that, sugar. Ain't no hell for the likes of us." He sighed. "I wanted to tell you that you're not responsible for the bad shit you did. I am. Don't go to Gatlinburg."

She stared at him. Why would he be telling her this? "What's going to happen?"

"I don't know. But it isn't good. It's like… It's like when you're riding your motorcycle out west and you feel that gust of wind out of nowhere that just doesn't *feel* right. Bad stuff's coming. You don't have to be part of it. You can take William Tell there and go raise hicks in Bugtussle."

"That's it? That's all you got? A ghost has a *feeling*?"

He leaned back in the chair and smiled. "What can I say? Sometimes we can see what's around the bend. Sometimes we can't… but you can be dead nuts certain if I say it's bad? It's bad."

"If we don't go, innocent people are going to die."

He hissed. "What do you care? People die every day. And what makes you think innocent people aren't going to die if you go? It's just… you won't."

"Don't you want me to die? Then I could join you in this limbo of yours. Just… Romeo and Juliet in a living hell. I'd think you'd get wood thinking of that. After all, I did kill you."

"You helped. But, in case you missed it? When 'Dumplin' had you on the ropes in Wisconsin? I'm the one who got you up off your cute ass and back in the fight."

Would Phoebe Walker have killed her that night in Elk Horn if she hadn't dreamed about Hayden?

"It wasn't a dream, baby. It was real," Hayden said. "Walk away from this vigilante shit and you'll live a long life. Otherwise?"

"Not happening, Hayden."

He chuckled. "Well, I tried. Nobody else believed you would listen either. I don't know if we can protect you."

"I don't need your protection."

He leaned forward and she could see the ruin of his decaying face. Karen shrank back.

"Yeah, longer you're here? Less of you there is. Bitch, ain't it?"

"I'm… sorry, Hayden. Not even you deserve… this."

He shrugged. "Yeah, I do. But it's nice of you to say otherwise. Good luck, blondie."

Hayden Oswald began to fade away.

"Hayden, wait…"

And then it wasn't Hayden.

A gray skinned creature stared at her from the darkness. It was gaunt and emaciated. The face had been human once.

It was dripping with silver jewelry, silver chains around its neck. The spindly fingers with their long talons each ended in sharp silver claws.

It spoke in a rasping voice. "We are coming. You and your kind will feel the cold soon. Despair."

More creatures filled the room, and she felt their silver claws tearing at her flesh.

She screamed.

The lights came on and Clyde had his hands on her shoulders. "Karen?! Karen, honey? Wake up, darlin'."

They were the only ones in the room.

She had shifted half into wolf form and her claws were inches from Clyde's ribs.

"Karen. Wake up. It's okay," Clyde said.

She transitioned back into human form. "Oh, God! Did I scratch you?"

"No, no. You didn't - it's okay."

Someone pounded on the door.

"You two okay in there?" Swede asked from outside.

"It… was just a nightmare," Karen said. "We're fine."

"Man, everybody's going at it like monkeys tonight," Swede grumbled. "Can't get any sleep."

Layla laughed somewhere near him.

Clyde brushed her hair out of Karen's face. "Are you okay?"

"Hold me," she whispered. "Just hold me."

***

The Next Afternoon
Spears Mountain, Virginia

Joseph Marlow read through the reports on the murders in Tennessee. The Nashville victim was a homeless man killed by a black ops team. They had left the dismembered body on the banks of the Cumberland River near the airport.

Actually, they had left two-thirds of the body there and brought the rest back - in order to create the illusion that some parts had been consumed.

The Smoky Mountains killing had been a couple.

Dodd had done that one himself.

Marlow wanted to vomit.

Marlow was an unwilling participant in all this; however, he was still a participant.

The Hippocratic Oath hadn't been a requirement when he graduated. He had taken it anyway along with a number of others who believed in its tenets.

Now, he had broken it.

Worse, he wanted to break it again. Gunnery Sergeant Dodd needed to die. He needed to die as soon as humanly possible.

And Edward Price needed to die as well.

Angelica sat beside him in the control center, and he could feel her trembling. She was reading her copy of the report as well.

He put his hand on hers beneath the table and she held on tight.

There were a lot of monsters inside Spears Mountain. He was beginning to believe he and Angelica were the only actual humans left inside.

They were all damned.

"The lobos are approaching the junction," one of the technicians said.

Marlow looked up at the big monitor.

It displayed a satellite view of Interstate 40 near Sevierville, Tennessee. This was the gateway to the Smoky Mountains, the intersection with state route 66.

The camera was focused on five motorcycles and a neon pink van going west on I40.

Price stepped closer to the screen. "The one with long blonde hair?" He tapped the screen. "That's Karen Arthur. I love the resolution on this British spy satellite. Make a note to send the head of MI6 a nice bottle of champagne."

"Yes, sir," the technician said.

Price looked at Marlow. "Fingers crossed they split up here." He turned back to the screen. "Otherwise, this gets complicated."

Marlow found himself praying they didn't split up.

"Four motorcycles taking the exit," the technician announced.

"Yes!" Price laughed. "One of them is Arthur." He traced his finger beside her image. "Who are the others?"

"The big one, the stripper, and the girl from Elkhorn."

Price nodded. "That means the hillbilly, the college professor, and the kid are on their way to Nashville. Radio Dodd's helicopter and tell him to standby at Clingmans Dome."

"Dodd!?" Angelica said. "I thought he was back here?"

"No. I need him onsite when we take Karen Arthur."

"Damn it, Price! He'll kill her!" Marlow cried.

"Take it down a notch, Dr. Marlow, or I'll have you restrained," Price said without looking away from the screen. "Dodd is under strict orders not to harm Miss Arthur. He's just there to eliminate any other opposition."

"You want to see if he can take out the other werewolves," Angelica said.

"Don't be silly. We've already determined he can do that. He killed the other rogues, remember?"

"Yes, but these aren't rogues! You're still running a fucking test!" Marlow said.

Price spun around. "What if I am? Project Lobo is the single most promising military project since the Manhattan Project. Pollard's research into creating sociopaths, MKUltra, Project Draugr… none of them have come close to this potential." He leaned on the conference room table. "Look at this as a means to an end, Dr. Marlow. You want Karen Arthur here to see if your pet werewolf can be cured? This is the cost."

***

Gatlinburg, Tennessee

The gateway to the Smoky Mountains, Gatlinburg, was a small mountain village deep in the lush countryside. It had been built around a ski resort but had grown into a small tourist area complete with an aquarium and its own miniature version of a Space Needle.

"I want to see the wax museum on our way back," Layla said over the radio as they rode through traffic toward the park entrance.

"Did you smell that fudge shop?" Anna said. "I'm drooling."

Karen looked around. "I want us to go silent, okay?"

"Why?" Anna asked.

"I don't know. I… I feel like maybe someone might be listening to our radios."

"Boss lady, you're sounding a little paranoid," Swede said.

"Just switch them off," Karen said. She pulled over to the sidewalk and put down the kickstand.

The others pulled in behind her.

"What's up?" Anna said as she climbed off her bike.

They gathered around Karen.

"Let's say this is a trap," Karen whispered. "And let's say they're watching us. Do we really want to ride out to Clingmans Dome in broad daylight?"

Swede nodded. "Probably not."

"What's your play?" Layla asked.

"We've got a nice, crowded town here. Let's go be tourists. And sometime this evening we'll slip off into the park. It's a twenty-mile run to Clingmans Dome."

"Less than an hour for us," Anna said.

"Unlike the humans, we don't need light to investigate the area," Swede said.

Karen smiled and nodded. "Plus, it will give Clyde and the boys enough time to get to Nashville. It will be crowded where they're

148

going. Less likely to be ambushed. Maybe they can investigate and get back to us."

"And then we can all go to the mountain," Anna said.

"Exactly."

"Yeah, well, what if Nashville is a trap as well?" Layla asked.

Swede laughed. "Eh, we've got Robin Hood and Einstein on that team... plus that dude from Twilight... not the vampire, the other one."

Anna poked him in the chest. "My boyfriend is not fluffy. Don't ever call him that again."

"Must be true love, Layla. She's defending him," Swede said. Then he grabbed Anna in a bear hug. "She grew up so fast," he sobbed.

"Let me go, you gorilla," Anna laughed.

He set her down. "Okay, onward to fudge and wax museums. God, I hope there's beer."

Karen watched them walk away, Swede in the middle with his huge arms around both their shoulders.

Something's wrong, she thought. They were in danger. It wasn't just the vision or dream or whatever it had been last night.

She *knew* it, knew it the way she knew that each member of her pack could be safely made into werewolves when she first met them as humans.

She stared up into the blue Tennessee sky.

Something was wrong.

She wanted them to get back on the motorcycles and just ride away. Head west, catch up with Clyde and just not look back.

Hayden Oswald's ghost was right: something bad was on its way.

"You comin', Boss Lady?" Swede called.

"Yeah. I'm coming."

***

Edward Price stared at the closeup image of Karen Arthur's piercing blue eyes looking directly into the satellite's camera lens. "She couldn't... I mean, she couldn't possibly see the satellite... could she?"

"The British bird is 750 miles up, sir," the technician said. "It would be impossible even for one of *them*."

149

"It's like she's staring right into your soul," Price whispered.

"You better hope not," Angelica said. "You better hope like hell she isn't."

***

The Blackhawk circled the summit of Clingmans Dome. "Spears Mountain says the targets have stopped in Gatlinburg, Gunnery Sergeant," the pilot said over the headset.

Dodd was sitting in the back with his eyes closed. "Drop me off near the summit."

"You sure? They're running out of daylight. Maybe they're waiting till morning."

"We don't need daylight," Dodd said. "I like it better in the woods, anyway. Everything stinks in this helicopter. Aviation fuel, oil, metal… you two. Everything stinks."

The pilot looked at the copilot.

The man shrugged.

"Okay, Gunnery Sergeant, you're the boss."

They set the chopper down in a clearing.

Both pilots were glad to see Dodd disappear into the trees.

***

Interstate 40
West of Gordonsville, Tennessee

Clyde drove the van with Bobby. Paul rode ahead on his Harley.

Bobby sat in the passenger seat and looked over his shoulder at his motorcycle locked in its cradle beside Clyde's. "When do I get a new bike?"

"As soon as we get back to Bedford. Ward and Loretta have several in their barn."

"How'd they get so many Harleys?"

Clyde laughed. "Liberated from some fellas who didn't need them anymore."

"Oh. You mean Hayden Oswald's gang?"

"Yeah."

150

"What was that like? I can't imagine fighting just one werewolf, much less an entire gang."

"It was… frightening. It was them against me, Karen, Ward, Loretta… oh, and their dog."

"And Melissa?"

"No," Clyde said. "She was just a kid. Still is. She hadn't turned yet. Paul says the werewolf virus doesn't manifest until puberty."

"Oh… so, if Anna and I… you know… would the baby be a werewolf?"

"Most likely. It's genetics. Now if one parent is a werewolf and the other is human, it's not 100% certain but still very likely."

"So, with you and Karen, maybe your kids won't be werewolves but, with me and Anna, almost definitely?"

"Jesus, kid, what're you worried about? Cross that bridge when you get to it."

"It's just… Karen looks at us and she just knows if we can be werewolves or not. She knows whether we'll be good or bad. How does that work when we have kids?"

"Paul says it's in the genes. If Karen says the parents will be good wolves? Their children will be too. It's some sort of ancient bloodline."

Bobby smiled. "So, our kids would be okay?"

"Good grief, you realize you two have only known each other a few days, right?"

Bobby laughed. "I can't explain it. I just saw her and… I fell in love. I think she did too. You ever heard of such a thing?"

He smiled. Then he shook his head. "Naah, that's crazy. Nobody falls in love the first minute like that. Nobody sane anyway."

***

Spears Mountain

"Chef made steak," Marlow said as he walked into the cell block.

"Hope it's human," Paula said as she got off her foam mattress and walked to the glass.

"No such luck." Marlow shivered. There had been some of the Nashville murder victim left over - it was in the freezer.

They were probably saving it for Dodd.

"No, this is good old beef."

"Like you'd serve me people," Paula said with a smile.

"No, I wouldn't. I don't think you'd eat it if it were."

"Don't be so sure."

He put the tray in the sliding mechanism used to pass food into her cell.

The tray slid inside, and she took it out.

"Mmm, smells yummy," she laughed. Then she lifted the cover over the paper plate. "Aww, they cooked it."

"Rare. I requested it especially," Marlow said as he sat down at the table across from the cell.

"Did you cut this for me? You could have just given me silverware…"

"And have you fling a fork through one of these vent holes and stab me in the eye? I'm still shocked they gave you a razor. Tsk, tsk… I'm not stupid."

"Jugular. I'd aim for your jugular. I'd hit it too."

"I'll bet."

"Your gallows humor is getting better, doctor. I'll give you that." She picked up a piece of steak with her fingers and popped it into her mouth. "They're going after the alpha? This Karen Arthur woman?"

Marlow nodded.

"And I'll bet they sent Dodd along to help, didn't they?"

"Yes."

"Good."

He shook his head. "How so?"

"She might kill him."

Marlow smiled. "There's a thought."

Her eyes widened. "What? A bloodthirsty response from Dr. Joseph Marlow? You actually wish ill on one of your patients?" She shook her head. "Maybe I'm not the only one who belongs in a cell."

"He killed children, Paula."

She paused with the steak a few inches from her mouth.

"I see that disturbs you."

"Keep telling yourself that. I'll do worse when I get out of here." She took the morsel and chewed her steak slowly.

"You know, I'm good at my job, Paula. I can read people. Even when they aren't quite people."

"Oh, here we go…"

"You haven't hurt anyone - not that you wouldn't. Oh, you're dangerous and very capable of killing. Lots of good people are capable of killing. There's nothing wrong with that. That's a survival mechanism."

"Go on. I love to hear your bullshit."

"Okay. Here's what I know about you: you'd kill Dodd. He's a mad dog. Mother Theresa would pull the trigger on Dodd. I know I would," Marlow said. "And Price?" He looked up at the security camera. "That vermin needs to die. Him and everyone like him."

"Don't do that," Paula whispered.

Marlow looked at her and smiled. "Why not?"

"Don't tempt the devil," she whispered.

"What do you care?"

"I… I don't…"

He nodded. "Please, go on. I love to hear your bullshit."

She grinned at him. "Touché."

"Now, where was I? Oh, yeah, Dodd you'd kill. Price too. Not Angelica."

She laughed. "Oh, that's where you're wrong."

"No, I'm not. You hate the people who did this to you. You hate the people who keep you in that glass box. You know as well as I do Angelica isn't responsible for any of this."

"She could've…"

"What? Could've *what*? Let you loose so you could kill people or be killed yourself? Find a cure? Don't you think she would do that if she could?"

Paula laughed. "What? You two a couple now?"

"No. A little late for that."

Paula looked away. "Wow. Your timing sucks, Marlow."

"No shit."

They both began to laugh.

She set down her tray and put her hand on the glass. "Don't ever open that door, Marlow. I'm lucid right now. I'm thinking clearly. But I can hear your heart beating and I can smell you and…"

He put his hand against the glass beside hers. "I can't imagine how bad it is for you. I can't. Just, please? Give it a chance. Once the alpha is here? She'll be in a cell just on the other side of the wall. Angelica says the two of you will be able to talk over the intercom."

"It won't help, Marlow."

"Give it a chance. Maybe just being in proximity will help. Maybe it's her voice. Maybe it's her scent…"

Paula laughed. "What are you going to do? Hook our air vents together?"

"If I have to."

She took a deep breath and shook her head. "Don't open that door, Marlow. Not ever."

***

Andrew B. Gibson Bridge
Nashville, Tennessee

Paul guided his motorcycle off the Briley Parkway on the northeast end of the Andrew B. Gibson Bridge and onto the sandy shoulder.

Clyde and Bobby followed in the van as Paul rolled down the dirt path and stopped under the bridge.

The Cumberland River flowed past, and they could hear the buzz of insects drowned out by cars passing overhead.

The brush was thick on both sides of the bridge, but Clyde could see glimpses of blue tarps, old tires, and scrap wood: the telltale signs of a homeless encampment.

He and Bobby got out of the van as Paul climbed stiffly off his bike.

"This it?" Clyde asked.

Paul nodded. "According to the police reports, the body was found fifty yards northwest."

"It was a homeless dude?" Bobby asked.

"Yeah," Clyde said.

Bobby nodded. "I slept in a few places like this." He nodded toward the encampment. "Not fun."

"What do you smell?" Paul asked.

"Huh?" Bobby said.

"Your olfactory center is as important as your vision now that you're a werewolf," Paul said. "What do you smell?"

"Dead fish. Mud. Water." He wrinkled his nose. "B.O., like... wow."

"Unwashed humans," Paul said and nodded. "Nauseating. While we have the wolves' heightened senses, we do not share that canine appreciation for stench. What else do you smell?"

"I... it's weird. It's like... perspiration but... chemical like."

"Fear, Bobby. You smell fear," Paul said. "Clyde, there are at least a dozen people in the bushes watching us. They're terrified."

"How do you know there are that many?" Bobby asked.

Paul pointed to his ear. "Heartbeats. Eventually, you'll be able to detect them, separate them, count them. It just takes practice."

"Not to interrupt his Jedi training, professor, but we're burning daylight," Clyde said. He opened the back of the van and pulled out his compound bow and arrows. Then he closed the door and locked it.

"There's no danger here, Clyde," Paul said. "I can smell the blood from the murder scene but whatever killed the man is long gone."

"Noted, professor. Shall we?" Clyde said as he walked toward the camp with the bow in his hand and the quiver of arrows slung over his shoulder.

They walked under the bridge. The camp was visible now through the thick laurel bushes - whoever lived here had beaten a hasty retreat when they saw the trio walking their way.

Small shelters and lean-tos had been constructed of whatever the denizens could find: scrap and rotted plywood, crumpled tarps, and splinter laden pallets. Old, bug-infested mattresses littered the ground.

"Hard to believe people live like this in the twenty-first century," Paul said.

Bobby shook his head. "When you have nothing else? Any port in a storm, professor."

Paul looked at him. "Indeed."

Bobby paused. "You hear that?" He whispered.

"Clyde," Paul said. "Twenty yards to your two o'clock. One of the homeless has overcome his fear."

"Gun?"

Paul sniffed the air. "Metal... not a gun. Not silver. A knife, perhaps."

Clyde reached for an arrow.

"Best not to spook the natives further," Paul said. "Bobby, take a position on Clyde's 10 o'clock. I'll go to the 2 o'clock position."

"Huh?" Bobby said.

Paul laughed. "Stand in front of Clyde to his left. I'll stand to his right. That puts us between our target and Clyde."

"I can take care of myself, professor," Clyde said.

"Yes, well, I would get a stern talking to by Karen should I allow her paramour to be killed by a knife-wielding assassin," Paul said as he took his position in front of Clyde.

"Para-*what?*" Bobby asked as he stepped to Clyde's other side.

"Paramour... lover," Paul said. "Oh, that settles it. When we get out of this, you're getting an education. I may be rusty at teaching, but it'll be better than nothing."

"Dude's moving," Bobby said.

A man wearing dirty military fatigues stepped into view through the bushes. "You CIA?"

Paul raised an eyebrow. "No. Are you expecting the CIA?"

The man's gaze darted between each of them. He had a graying, grizzled beard and there was a hunting knife in his left hand. He held it overhand with the blade edge toward them. "They sent the black helicopters in. I figured the CIA would be next. You're not cops and you're not military."

"We're not the CIA," Clyde said. The way the man held the knife showed he knew how to use it. "You Army?"

"Was. Not now. Why'd you guys kill Smiley?"

"Smiley was the man who died up there?" Paul asked.

"Yeah, you should know."

"We didn't kill Smiley," Bobby said. "We came here to find out who killed him."

"Smiley was a friend of yours?" Paul asked.

"No. Couldn't stand him," the man said. "Always had a scowl on his face."

Bobby stared at him. "Then why'd you call him 'Smiley'?"

"It's called irony," the man said.

Paul looked at Bobby and smiled. "There, see? World is full of teaching moments. Absorb them."

"Look, we're not here to hurt you or anybody else," Clyde said. "Tell us about the helicopter you saw?"

"Didn't see it. Heard it. Spec Ops job designed to come in quiet. No running lights either. But I encountered them before when I was in the suck."

"The *suck*?" Bobby asked.

"The shit, kid," the man said. "Afghanistan. Spec Ops guys use them to drop in unannounced. For some reason, they dropped in on us and killed Smiley. He was an asshole, but nobody deserves what they did to him. They carved him up like a Thanksgiving turkey, him screaming the whole time. Took trophies too: an arm, foot, his dick."

"Will you show us where they killed him?" Paul asked.

***

When a man gets torn apart on a riverbank, there should be more to mark the spot, Bobby thought.

The spot was a circle about four yards wide, stained red with blood in the lush undergrowth and ringed by yellow police tape.

Paul knelt just inside the perimeter.

The homeless man stood a few yards back, the hunting knife now in a sheath on his belt.

"What do you think?" Clyde asked as he crouched outside the police tape.

"Difficult to say," Paul said. "Could have been claws. Could have been knives."

"You some kind of tracker?" The homeless man asked.

"Something like that," Paul said.

Bobby moved along the perimeter of the tape. The ground was soft and...

He paused and stared.

There was something under a laurel branch.

He lifted it gently. "Hey, Paul?"

"Yes?"

"You need to look at this," Bobby said.

Paul ducked under the police tape and stopped beside Bobby.

There, under the laurel, was a large footprint - a footprint with long claw marks gouged into the black earth beyond the toe prints.

Clyde walked up behind them. "Is that what I think it is?" he whispered.

"A werewolf print, yes," Paul said.

"So, the werewolf was here?" Bobby whispered.

Paul stood up. "Not necessarily." He turned to Clyde. "I need to see the body."

Bobby looked at them. "We can do that?"

Paul and Clyde nodded. "We have friends," they said.

***

"We have friends who can get us into the morgue to look at a body?" Bobby asked from the passenger seat as they drove back across the bridge toward Nashville.

"Yes," Clyde said.

"Who?"

"Above your pay grade."

"You guys are always holding stuff back from me. Is it Ward Rickman? Can he get us into the Nashville morgue?"

"Probably."

"So, you're going to ask Ward?"

"No."

"Then how…?"

"We have friends. Some of those friends can get us into places we need to go."

Paul turned right onto an exit ramp.

Clyde continued straight.

Bobby looked back at the exit. "Where's Paul going?"

"Find Wi-Fi somewhere. He has to make a call."

"To get us into the Nashville morgue?"

"Yep."

***

Karen sat on a bench in a shopping area made to look like a storybook German village. This high up in the mountains, the air was cool and carried with it the smell of new pines and other, older hardwoods.

Mixed with the scent of kettle corn and buttery fudge, of course.

Anna sat down beside her and held out a caramel apple on a stick.

"Thanks," Karen said and took it.

Anna had an identical confection in her other hand. "You know the best thing about being a werewolf?"

"No, what?"

"You can eat anything you want and not gain a pound."

Karen laughed. "There is that." She looked around. "Where are Swede and Layla?"

"Scoping out make-out spots. So far, they've gotten NC-17 rated in the wax museum, the aquarium, the haunted house… I couldn't take it anymore, so I left them to their own devices."

"Well, at least they're consistent. I should have sent Layla to Nashville, but I was afraid Swede would have spent his time humping legs."

Anna laughed out loud and almost spit out a piece of her apple. When she recovered, Anna took a deep breath. "I like this place. Maybe we should settle nearby when this is all over?"

Karen nodded. "Farm right off the national park."

"Yes. All those acres upon acres of forest to run through."

"It'd be wonderful," Karen agreed.

"Yeah." Anna nodded. "Why'd you do it?"

"Hmm? Do what?"

"Split us up. We could have easily investigated both areas together. Why send the others to Nashville and the four of us here? And I know the only reason you're waiting before we go into the woods is you want to go in after dark."

Karen sighed. "You're a smart kid."

"I should be. You've been training me to lead. So, tell me the plan."

Karen nodded. "It would be almost impossible to ambush us in Nashville."

159

Anna thought for a moment. Then she smiled and nodded. "Bobby's too green. Paul's too slow. But Clyde? He has more kills than all of us."

"Clyde can protect Paul and Bobby. And you're right, he has more kills than all of us... werewolf kills."

Anna nodded. "Of course. But we won't just be facing werewolves. We may also be facing soldiers..."

"And he'd be bringing a bow and arrow to a gunfight."

"Wow. You've got this leader thing down, Karen."

Karen scoffed. "Oh, yeah, I'm doing great. Split our team, leading us blind into the woods. I'm a regular General Patton."

"If it's any consolation? I think it's a good plan."

"Thanks. I actually appreciate that. Look, I know I'm hard on you..."

"No, you're not. I've been a brat."

"Let me finish. That thing you did in Detroit? It was reckless and... over the top."

"I know. I'm sorry..."

"But it worked. You saved all those people, Anna. You. That's why you're on this team. I need you watching my back."

Swede and Layla walked into the shopping area.

Swede was wearing a Cat in the Hat top hat and Layla was wearing a bright orange pair of gigantic sunglasses.

Karen laughed.

"And those two?" Anna asked.

"I needed Swede here because... he's Swede. Throw him at a wall? That wall is coming down. And Layla? The two of them are joined. They fight as a unit. I couldn't separate them."

***

Clyde and Bobby parked on the street outside the Nashville morgue and, ten minutes later, Paul rode up and parked behind them.

He had changed into khakis and a white shirt.

Clyde and Bobby got out of the van and met him on the sidewalk.

"We'll have about an hour," Paul said as he put on a striped tie. "The coroner has been called to an accident east of here. It will take him at least a half hour to get to the location, another few minutes to

160

realize he's been duped, and another half hour to drive back in a huff."

"Is that enough time?" Clyde asked.

"I think so, yes, but we shouldn't dawdle. Now, Clyde, you're a detective from Knoxville. If anyone asks, you left your ID in the car. Bobby? You're my student assistant. Try to look smart."

"You know, you guys are really insulting," Bobby said as they crossed the street.

"There is no sin in being ignorant," Paul said. "Only in remaining so."

"Oh, that makes it so much better," Bobby said as they entered the building.

***

"This is highly irregular," the morgue attendant said as he led them toward the cold room.

"Yes," Paul said. "I'm very sorry but when the governor says jump? We jump."

The attendant stared at Clyde who was still dressed in jeans and a denim motorcycle vest. "You sure you're a detective?"

"I'm undercover," Clyde said.

They walked into the morgue and the automatic lights came on, illuminating a room filled with stainless steel tables. Bodies draped in sheets occupied some of the tables.

The back wall had three rows of refrigerated cadaver drawers.

"Which one is the victim?" Paul asked.

"Right over here," the attendant said. He led the way to the third table. "John Doe."

"Smiley," Bobby said.

"Huh?" The attendant asked.

"His name was Smiley," Bobby answered. "We found out this afternoon."

Paul looked at Bobby and nodded.

The attendant began writing on the toe tag. "Smiley. With an 'e', right?"

"Yes," Paul said as he pulled on a pair of blue latex gloves from a container mounted on the wall.

161

"Was that a first name or last?"

Paul and Bobby looked at each other.

"Unknown," Clyde said. "Just Smiley."

"Well, better than John Doe, I suppose," the attendant said. "'Course, he ain't smilin' now." He pulled back the sheet.

Most of Smiley's face was gone, the skull cracked open. His forehead, eyes, and sinus cavity had been ripped off, revealing his brain beneath.

"Jesus," Bobby whispered.

Paul walked over to the body, pulled out his cellphone, opened his voice recorder app, and pressed record. "Victim is a white male of indeterminate age. Massive trauma to the face. Frontal lobe excised." He leaned over the body. "Left arm wrenched from socket and removed... some lacerations on the scapula from a sharp implement."

"A knife?" Clyde asked.

Paul sighed. "Indeterminate." He moved down the body. "Puncture wound in left chest." He opened the wound and peered inside. "Appears to have severed the aorta. This wound came prior to the removal of the arm and the trauma to the face."

Paul looked up to see Bobby staring intently at the body.

"Are you okay, Bobby?" Paul asked.

Bobby nodded. "Never seen a... dead body before."

"Don't puke in here," the attendant said. "Bathroom's in the hall."

"I think it best you step outside," Paul said.

"I'm not going to be sick," Bobby said. He swallowed.

"Yes, I can see that," Paul said. He could see Bobby was salivating.

"Hall, kid. Now," Clyde said.

Bobby nodded and walked away.

Paul turned back to the body. "Abdomen has been torn open. Some amount of small intestines have been removed." He reached inside the body and spread the intestines apart. "Hmm... curious."

"What is it?" Clyde asked.

Paul looked up. "Liver is intact."

Clyde nodded.

Paul stripped off the gloves. "Well, that's all I needed to see. The governor's office thanks you for your cooperation, Mister…?"

"Oh, Baker. Nathaniel Baker, doctor."

Paul dropped the bloodied gloves into the biohazard disposal. "Thank you, Mr. Baker. Good day."

Paul and Clyde walked into the hallway.

Bobby was pacing outside. "I'm sorry. I thought I was going to be sick but then…"

Paul put his hand on Bobby's shoulder and led him down the hall. "It's normal. The wolf sees meat and it wants to eat."

"Even a guy *that* dead?" Bobby whispered.

"Meat's meat, kid," Clyde said.

"If you hadn't been there?" Bobby said. "I mean… would I have… you know? Eaten?"

"We can't help what we are, Bobby," Paul said. "We can only control what we do. We only eat our enemies."

"What's the verdict, professor?" Clyde asked.

"Not a werewolf attack," Paul said.

"How do you know?" Bobby asked.

"Hunger. If a werewolf had done this? It wouldn't have left the liver intact. There wasn't a mark on Smiley's. A group of men did this with knives. They went out of their way to make it look like a werewolf attack, but they didn't think about the wolf's hunger. I first suspected it wasn't a werewolf when I saw the chest puncture. That was the killing strike - delivered first, to the assailant's credit. He killed the man quickly rather than letting him suffer."

"Again, not something a werewolf would normally do," Clyde said.

They walked out of the building.

"This means the Nashville attack was a decoy," Clyde said as they reached the vehicles. "If there's a wolf involved at all? He's in the Smokys."

***

"How was Nashville?" Karen asked. She had the cellphone to her ear.

"Uneventful. Thinking about going to see the Grand Ole Opry tonight," Clyde said on the other end.

"You should."

"How's the park?" Clyde asked.

"Looks nice… from here. We're in Gatlinburg," Karen said.

"You should backtrack to Pigeon Forge. Dollywood's a lot of fun," Clyde said, referencing Dolly Parton's amusement park sixteen miles north and away from the national park.

"Maybe," Karen said.

"Lots of tourist traps around Gatlinburg. Be careful."

Karen smiled. "We will."

Clyde paused. Then he said, "I love you, Karen."

"I love you too, hillbilly," Karen said and hung up. She looked at the sun sitting low on the horizon.

It would be dark soon.

***

"Damn it," Clyde said. "Played. She played me."

"What's wrong?" Bobby asked.

"Karen. They're going in without us." He put his foot to the floor, eased into the left lane on the interstate and drew up even with Paul's Harley. "Roll down your window, Bobby."

Bobby cranked down the passenger window.

Paul looked over at the van.

"She's going in without us," Clyde yelled.

Paul nodded, then throttled up.

Clyde pulled behind him and they broke the speed limit heading east.

***

Running

Karen led Anna, Swede, and Layla to the park entrance as the sun dipped below the mountains.

"The attack in Nashville wasn't a werewolf," Karen said as they moved deeper into the woods and away from the trail.

"Clyde's on his way, right?" Layla asked.

"Yeah."

Swede smiled. "But we're not waiting for them, right?"

Karen sighed. "No. Listen, there's a high likelihood this is a trap."

"But we have to go in," Anna said. "We've been over this."

"It's the right call," Layla said. "No offense to Bobby? But if he goes with us, Anna will have to watch after him."

"She's right," Anna said. "I can't be dangerous with Bobby coming along."

Swede nodded. "And I love the professor but he's not up to this."

"Agreed," Karen said. "So... Layla? Fall back to town and wait in a crowded location for Clyde."

"What?! No way!" Layla said.

"Listen, lover," Swede said. "The alpha has a point."

"Swede, you are not leaving me behind! If this is a trap? We're going into it together."

"Baby, come on," Swede said.

She poked him in the chest. "You send me back and I'll just follow you. I will not be left behind!"

Swede looked at Karen and shrugged. "You got an idea here? Because I'm fresh out, boss lady."

"I'm just as dangerous as any of you," Layla said. "And you damned well know it."

Karen looked up at the sky. The first stars were coming out. *Could their satellites see in the dark?* Paul would know.

Too bad she hadn't asked before they left Virginia.

"Here's how it's going to play out and I don't want any arguments," Karen said. "If I say turn and run? We turn and run. Anybody goes down? We pick them up and run away. If we get separated? We meet back in Gatlinburg, wait for Clyde, and regroup."

They all nodded.

"We're going to be facing people. Maybe a single werewolf as well."

Layla shook her head. "How do we know there's only one werewolf?"

"Clyde said Nashville was 'uneventful'... no werewolf. That means they only had one to carry out the simultaneous attacks."

Anna nodded. "It tracks."

"So, as I was saying," Karen said. "One werewolf, multiple human soldiers, mercenaries, whatever they are. We've always held back with humans. Not this time. They've killed kids. They've killed innocent people just to draw us out. They wanted to be on our radar? Well, they're on it. No quarter, no mercy. Agreed?"

"No argument from me," Swede said.

Layla nodded.

"No quarter," Anna said.

"Best case scenario? We find the crime scene, maybe discover some clues as to who's behind all this? And then we go check out this Dollywood Clyde keeps talking about," Karen said.

Anna laughed.

***

Spears Mountain

"My God, watch them run," Price said as he watched the white shapes on the monitor running through the thick forest.

The British spy satellite was out of range, so a drone dispatched from Arnold Air Force Base was circling the Clingmans Dome area.

The drone's sensitive infrared camera was focused on Karen Arthur and the three members of her pack who accompanied her into the forest.

Dr. Geffman and Dr. Marlow stood behind Price and watched the wall monitor.

Price pointed at the lead white shape on the monitor. "That's Karen Arthur. See what she's doing? She's leading them due south rather than southeast toward the target area. They're going to approach the peak from either the west or the south - my money's on south."

He smiled. "Watch the other three. Constantly rotating between left flank, rear, right flank. Completely at random but maximizing their ability to detect dangers." He looked at one of the technicians. "How fast are they running?"

"Umm, I'd estimate thirty-five miles per hour," the technician said.

Price laughed and clapped. "Thirty-five miles an hour through thick forest, almost total darkness, and Arthur is navigating like she has a GPS in her head. Oh, doctors… if we had an army of soldiers like these? We'd be unstoppable. That's why this is all so important."

"Then maybe you should have worked with the blues, Price," Marlow said. "Instead of killing them and throwing in with a psychotic."

"We were at cross-purposes," Price said. "As I said, the blue-eyed wolves wouldn't follow orders."

"Goes along with having a conscience, Price," Angelica said. "You wouldn't understand."

Price laughed. "I do so enjoy our little chats. However, if you continue to poke the bear? The bear will have you both taken to a CIA black site with no name staffed by people who make me look like a saint."

Price turned to the technician. "Radio the team. Have Dodd take up position on the mountain. Everyone else is to remain airborne at a safe distance to the northeast until Dodd engages - if Karen Arthur's pack detects our Spec Ops team, she might withdraw."

"If Dodd kills Karen Arthur, all of this was for nothing," Dr. Marlow said.

"Not so," Price answered. "There are two more blues in Bedford, Virginia."

***

Two miles west of Clingmans Dome
Just across the North Carolina border

The night was so peaceful, the run so invigorating, Karen could almost have forgotten the danger.

Behind her to her left, Swede knifed between laurel bushes, leaped onto a ridge and disappeared into the darkness.

The long claws on her hands dug into the black earth and she skidded to a stop.

Immediately, her heart rate began to slow.

She panted, the long wolf tongue lolling.

Layla and Anna scrambled to her side.

Karen looked toward the ridge and growled.

Layla leaped onto the ridge and ran in the direction Swede ran.

Karen transitioned to human, and Anna followed suit.

"Think he sensed something?" Anna asked.

Karen shrugged. "Maybe. Count of five we follow. Five, four..."

Swede and Layla leaped off the ridge and landed beside them. They both transitioned to human.

"Thought I heard something," Swede said. "Could have been a bear."

"I spotted three on the way down," Anna said.

"Sorry, I guess I'm jumpy," Swede said.

Layla put her arm around his shoulders.

Karen smiled. "Jumpy is good. We all need to be jumpy." She turned and looked up the slope toward the top of Clingmans Dome. There was a concrete observation tower at the summit, but it was empty at this time of night.

She scented the air.

Blood. Human blood. Not fresh.

"Near the top but on the other side," Karen said. "That's where he killed them." She looked up into the night sky.

"Something wrong, boss lady?" Swede asked.

Karen sighed. "When they designed us? Whoever designed us? They didn't factor in airborne threats. I keep hearing plane engines... helicopters maybe. But I can't tell what's military and what isn't. Could be sightseers over our heads or..."

"Bad guys," Anna said.

Karen nodded.

Swede looked up. Then he extended both arms and flipped off the night sky. "If they're watchin'? No need to be shy."

Karen laughed. "Swede, Layla, flank left up to the summit. Anna and I'll will flank right. Meet at the top."

"We're not going to the crime scene?" Anna asked.

"Not yet. That's what they're expecting. Let's check out the high ground. Maybe take a look around from that observation tower."

Swede nodded as he began to transition. "Yeah, and look for those black helicopters."

***

Nine Fingers: The Good Wolves

Spears Mountain

"Now that's curious," Price whispered. "They're ignoring the blood and heading straight for the summit."

The white dots were making a pincer move up two sides of the mountain.

"Tell Dodd they're taking the high ground behind him."
***

Clingmans Dome

The fifth werewolf on Clingmans Dome was crouching motionless on the ledge near the location where he had killed the hikers. Dodd was controlling his breathing, feeling the breeze from the southwest in his fur… a breeze that carried his scent away from Karen Arthur and her pack.

The woman was good.

But not that good.

She should have approached from the northeast.

If she had, she would have caught Dodd's scent a mile down slope.

It would have been as simple as paying attention to the prevailing wind.

Stupid mistake.

He had picked up their scent as they passed by to the west.

Now they were somewhere behind him.

If they approached from the southwest? He'd be on them before they knew what hit them.

The radio crackled in his ear, and he almost ripped it off. He hated it. Hated all this human garbage, technological and biological.

"They're at your six, flanking left and right. They're heading up the mountain to the summit. They'll be behind you and up slope."

Dodd pulled his lips back, exposing his fangs as saliva began to drip.

He fought the urge to growl.

Then he stood and turned, bounding up the slope toward the summit.

***

The observation tower was a mid-century modern concrete structure of arching ramps leading to a central tower.

It was a remnant of a science fiction future that never happened.

Karen and Anna met Swede and Layla at the entrance to the curving ramp.

They transitioned back to human form together and stood naked on the concrete, their clothes in gym bags strapped across their backs.

There was nothing here but the wind at their backs.

Here at the summit, the Smoky Mountains were living up to their name.

A thick fog had formed obscuring the upper part of the ramp and the tower.

"Wind's behind us," Swede whispered. He sniffed. "Nothing back there."

"I don't *hear* anything either," Anna whispered. "You?"

Karen shook her head. She stared straight into the fog clinging to the ramp. "Spread out. We're going up the ramp. Slow."

"Watch out for tripwires and shit," Swede said.

"*Tripwires?*" Layla hissed.

"You know. Bomb tripwires. Like in the movies."

"Thanks for that thought, Swede," Anna whispered.

They spread out across the ramp and started walking up.

Wind at our backs, can't see more than twenty feet… way to go, alpha, Karen thought.

She stopped dead.

A massive shape was crouched on the concrete ahead.

Karen didn't have to tell the others to transition.

They transitioned at once and dropped to all fours.

The male werewolf stood up on two legs and stared at them.

Swede took a step forward.

Karen turned her head toward him and growled.

He stepped back, head lowered, saliva dripping from his bared teeth.

The enemy stared at Karen and cocked his head to the right.

Four against one, Karen thought. But he looks calm. He's not frightened. He's barely even excited.

She heard the whistle of the dart as it struck her in the neck.

Karen swatted at it as liquid fire filled her neck.

Silver iodide! Mixed with something else. The dart fell off when she slapped it, but the liquid payload had been delivered.

The ramp began to wobble and swim in her vision.

Karen staggered.

Anna and Layla ran to put themselves in front of her, shielding her from the enemy werewolf.

Swede was bounding up the ramp, roaring like a lion.

Finally, the enemy reacted.

He ran straight for Swede, and they collided, grappling like wrestlers on the ramp.

Karen shook her head, trying to clear her vision.

A narcotic. Something strong.

She growled as the spinning stopped.

She ran forward, flanked by Layla and Anna.

***

Spears Mountain

"What? How is she still standing?" Price said as he stared at the monitor. He turned toward Angelica. "You did this! Did you load a weaker dose of Fentanyl in the dart?"

"I used the same amount we used on Paula," Angelica replied.

"But…" He turned back to the screen.

The male werewolf was landing body blow after body blow on Dodd and the three women were almost on him as well.

Then Price smiled. "That bitch. Doctors, your pet werewolf was playing opossum… the dart didn't actually work."

Marlow laughed.

"Yes, very funny," Price said. "Luckily, I brought spares. Tell the Spec Ops team to fire more darts!"

171

***

Clingmans Dome

The air was alive with what sounded like angry bees.

A second dart hit Karen in the right shoulder and then a third in her right hip.

The dizziness returned and, this time, it did not stop.

She struggled to stay on her feet.

Anna collapsed beside her, darts in her right arm. She transitioned back to human form, all except for her right arm which was filled with silver iodide. "Karen? What do we... do?"

Karen couldn't transition, the dart to her neck was blocking her completely.

Layla went down screaming. The darts hit her in the small of the back and she couldn't move from the waist down while she transitioned back to human form from the waist up.

Karen held herself up with her right arm.

Swede was still fighting with the blond furred werewolf.

She saw Swede pull his arm back and drive his claws deep into the werewolf's abdomen.

"The heart! Tear it out, Swede!" She screamed. It only came out as a howl.

The blond furred werewolf howled in pain as Swede drove his claws up.

Then darts were slamming into Swede's spine.

He fell back, his claws pulling free of the werewolf's guts.

"No!" The blond werewolf screamed as he transitioned into a tall blond man with a crew cut, the stomach wound already closing.

It was the man from the Texas picture.

"No! You had no right to stop him! That was our fight! Who fired those darts?"

Karen was falling onto the concrete, fighting to maintain consciousness.

"Who fired those fucking darts?"

There were people around her. Men in boots.

172

Anna looked at her from the concrete. Her eyes kept rolling back in her head.

Layla was pulling herself across the concrete toward Swede who was struggling to get back to his feet.

"You weren't winning! I was winning!" The blond man screamed at Swede, his yellow eyes glowing.

Psychotic. He's psychotic, Karen thought.

"Gunnery Sergeant Dodd, Mr. Price says to stand down," a soldier said somewhere behind Karen.

Dodd. His name is Dodd, Karen thought. Not Stern. Not one of Hayden's crew.

Dodd took a step toward the soldier who had spoken.

The other soldiers aimed at Dodd.

He laughed. "Yeah, okay. No need for a tranq. I'm good."

He knelt over Swede. "Good fight, big guy. But I had you. You know I had you."

Swede transitioned back to human above the shoulders. "I had... your heart... in my hand... asshole."

"Swede, stop," Layla said.

Dodd turned and looked down at her as she crawled closer. "Will you look at that? Must be true love. This bitch yours, Ole? Ole Olufsen, but your friends call you Swede. Yeah, know your enemy. Art of War." He moved to crouch beside Layla. "She is yours, right? Layla Kowalski. Stripper... though I heard you used to do a lot more than strip, huh?"

"Get away... from her," Swede growled as he began pulling himself across the concrete.

"We know everything about all of you. You actually thought you could fight the government? Tsk, tsk. You're pathetic. Walked right into a trap."

Swede was dragging himself closer.

Dodd wrapped his hand around Layla's throat. "She is hot though. I mean I can't blame you for wanting this whore."

"Don't... touch her!"

Karen tried to roll toward them.

A soldier put his boot on the small of her back. "Get the medic in here. We need an IV in place. Exfil in five. Gunnery Sergeant? We need to wrap this up."

"Aww, and it was just getting interesting," Dodd said. He squeezed Layla's throat and stroked her hair with his other hand. "I'd take you home, but I don't think they'd let me keep you."

"Swede," Layla whispered. "I love you."

"Let her go," Swede screamed. "Just let her go!"

Dodd's arm transitioned and he sank his claws into Layla's face and through her sinus cavity.

He smiled as he ripped off the top half of her head.

***

Anna screamed along with Swede.

Her entire right side was paralyzed so she tried to push forward with her left leg.

Swede transitioned back to wolf, but he could barely move. He roared at Dodd and snapped his jaws, but Dodd was already walking away from Layla's body.

Werewolves were practically indestructible.

Silver, of course, could kill them if it was delivered to the right location.

A werewolf could burn to death.

Remove the heart and they would die before it could regenerate. Or remove the head.

"I don't care what he did! Get the IV in that blue!" A soldier said. "Gunnery Sergeant Dodd, stand down now! You are to go back to the chopper and prepare for exfil! That is an order from Mr. Price himself."

Dodd laughed. "Oh! My master's voice. Sir, yes, sir!" He continued laughing as he made his way down the ramp.

Anna was midway between Swede and Karen.

The soldiers were rolling Karen over and putting a needle in her arm.

Anna stared into Karen's blue eyes.

Karen nodded toward Swede.

Anna pulled herself to Swede as he reached Layla's body.

He picked up the severed half of Layla's skull and pressed it against the other half.

Anna grabbed his arm and pulled herself up beside him. "It won't work. Swede? You know it won't work."

Swede raised his head and howled.

The soldiers were trying to lift Karen on a stretcher, and they almost dropped her when they heard him.

Anna rolled onto her side.

She raised herself up on her left arm. "We're coming for you!" She screamed. "You tell your boss, this Price? You tell him we're coming. And we're going to kill you all. Every last one of you! You tell him!"

One of the soldiers looked at his watch. "In four minutes? You'll be dead anyway. Move out."

They walked away, carrying Karen on the stretcher.

**

Spears Mountain

The officer leading the Spec Ops team at Clingmans Dome had been broadcasting everything from his body camera.

Dr. Marlow and Dr. Geffman stared in silence at the screen.

"God, Price. He has to die. Kill him now while you still can," Joseph Marlow said.

"I'll take that under advisement... I truly will," Price whispered.

"What did he mean when he told the two survivors they would be dead in four minutes?" Angelica asked.

"No loose ends, doctors. No loose ends."

**

Clingmans Dome

Anna was trying to balance on her left foot. "Swede, we have to go."

He was holding onto Layla's body and howling.

"Swede, they're going to kill us. You have to let her go."

He howled and took a swipe at Anna with his claws.

A helicopter rose over the trees to the north.

175

"Swede! They took Karen. Do you see? They took her and now they're going to kill us. I need you to move, now!" She held out her left hand.

He stared at her hand and growled.

"Fine. Stay here and die. Stay here and die while the asshole that killed Layla flies off to kill someone else. He laughed, Swede. He laughed when he killed her. The Swede Olufsen I know? He's not going to lie down and die. You can die after we kill that son of a bitch." She held out her hand again.

He stared up at her with his yellow eyes.

Then he grabbed her hand.

She leaned back and pulled, sliding him down the ramp a foot at a time.

***

Spears Mountain

"Chopper inbound with Karen Arthur, sir," the technician said.

"Good job," Price said. "What's Dodd's condition?"

"Major Simmons says he went practically catatonic when they got him into the chopper."

"Are they carrying silver bullets onboard the chopper?" Dr. Marlow asked.

Price rolled his eyes. "Yes. What are you proposing?"

"Kill him, Price. For the love of God, how many more people does he have to kill before you put him down?"

"Dr. Geffman can study the blue. Maybe we can find a way to control him," Price said.

Angelica Geffman laughed. "Give it up, Price. That guy's a train wreck. He'll kill all of us sooner or later."

"Mr. Price, CIA wants to know if you still want them to fire on the mountain top?" The technician asked.

"Yes. Hit the observation tower with a Hellfire. Incinerate the whole area."

"Yes, sir."

"Two more deaths on your scorecard, Price," Angelica hissed.

***

Nine Fingers: The Good Wolves

10,000 Feet Above Clingmans Dome

The Predator drone made slow circles around the mountain, the camera in the nose swiveling to maintain view of the observation tower below.

The drone was launched from Arnold AFB, but it wasn't being controlled from there.

The pilot sat in a basement of the CIA building in Langley, Virginia.

"Can you see them?" A voice asked over the pilot's headset.

"Roger that. Two heat signatures. Looks like the smaller one is dragging the larger one away from the ramp, over."

"Make sure they're taken out in the blast. They are the target."

"Roger that."

Someone opened the door and the darkened room brightened. "I'll take it from here."

The pilot squinted. "Excuse me? I'm in the middle of an op..."

"I know," the man said. "This is no longer a company operation." He held out his ID.

"Uh... look... I'm going to have to ask someone about this..."

"No. You don't. You see this ID and you know what it means. Go get some coffee and forget about it. Forget *all* about it. Understood?"

The pilot nodded. "Yes, sir."

The pilot got up and the man took his place.

"They want to make sure the two survivors are taken out," the pilot said.

"I know. Leave," the man said.

The pilot walked out of the room and didn't look back.

***

Anna pulled Swede. He was beginning to move his legs a little. The narcotic was wearing off.

Anna looked nervously up at the sky as she pulled him a few feet further away from the observation tower.

Then the world exploded.

***

The Helicopter

"That was a big boom," Dodd said. He was leaning back against the rear bulkhead of the chopper. He hadn't spoken since they had loaded Karen onboard.

He smiled down at her.

Karen tried to turn her head toward the open door of the helicopter, but she only managed to move her eyes.

She was paralyzed, the narcotic coursing through her system aided by the silver iodide.

At some point, she had transitioned to human. She didn't think that was possible but, somehow, her wolf had receded.

She concentrated and finally succeeded in turning her head to look out the door.

There was an orange ball of fire rising above the green forest a few miles away.

Karen began to cry.

There was no way Anna and Swede could have made it.

The entire mountain top was on fire.

She turned her head back to Dodd. "I'm… going to kill you," she whispered.

The sound in the chopper was deafening.

"Sorry. Not even I could hear that." Dodd said. "Too loud. I'll bet you can hear me, though, can't you." He nodded toward the soldiers sitting around him. "They can't… the humans. They need our wolf ears. Means we can have a nice conversation, private, just the two of us."

Karen was strapped to the stretcher, an IV pumping poison into her veins. It was hard to stay awake.

"I'm going to kill you," Dodd said. "In a few minutes? I'm going to reach over and tear your heart out of your chest. So, I want you to stay awake. I don't want you to sleep through it."

She stared at him, trying to will her arms and legs to move.

They wouldn't.

"Baby, why don't you ever listen to me?" Hayden Oswald said.

She turned her eyes to the left.

He was sitting in the seat beside Dodd - though she could have sworn a soldier had been sitting there before. She was hallucinating.

"I'm a lot of things, baby, but I'm no hallucination," Hayden said. "Only you can see me, though."

"Dreaming," Karen mumbled.

"No. Not this time," Hayden said. "Turns out you blues have one foot in the waking world, one foot in the spirit world. That's why you can tell if someone is supposed to be a wolf: you can see their soul."

Hayden nodded toward Dodd. "Take a look at this one's soul... I mean, I can't see it... I can see he's got a brain full of spiders, but I can't see his soul. You can."

She looked at Dodd. "There's nothing there but a void."

"What did you say?" Dodd asked.

"She's high as a kite, Gunnery Sergeant," the medic said. "There's enough Fentanyl in her to kill everyone in Boston and half of Rhode Island. She might be reciting Shakespeare for all I know."

Hayden was staring at Dodd. "He's going to kill you."

"Let him," Karen whispered.

Dodd was staring at her lips as they moved.

"I led them into an ambush, and I knew..."

"Stop," Hayden said. "You're not a damned soldier. You're not a damned general. You did the best you could. You want to be perfect but you're not. You can't be. Karen Arthur is a good person and through all this crazy shit she still wants to see the good in others." Hayden looked at Dodd. "Even when they are psychotic freaks. I ought to know. I was your first."

Dodd lunged forward, transitioning only his right arm to werewolf form.

His claws touched her abdomen.

"Stand down!" The medic screamed.

The soldiers were raising their weapons, training them on Dodd.

"No more room for alphas. Only me," Dodd said with a smile.

Karen couldn't feel anything as his claws dug into her flesh.

And then Hayden's hand closed on Dodd's arm.

Dodd looked shocked. He looked toward the spot on his arm.

He can't see Hayden's hand, Karen thought. *But he feels it.*

"I can't… hold him," Hayden said. His brow was wrinkled in concentration. "I can't stop him."

Another hand. Bigger. Grasping Dodd's wrist.

Karen looked up into the round face of a bald man, his face red with effort.

"Here's a new sensation," the bald man said in a sing-song southern accent. "Never thought I would touch human flesh again."

Clayton Truman Ambrose. She recognized him from the news - the serial killing werewolf Ward killed in Bedford.

"Why?" Karen whispered.

Clayton Ambrose smiled. "So much to atone for. I fear my penance may never be done. I have to say it is nice to be on the side of the angels for once."

The helicopter was full of the dead, unseen by all but Karen, but whose power was definitely being felt by Gunnery Sergeant Dodd.

He strained against dozens of invisible hands gripping his arm, staying his claws. "How are you doing this?!" He screamed in Karen's face.

Many of the ghostly faces she recognized: members of Hayden Oswald's gang, rogues she had put down.

All fighting to save her from Dodd.

A woman whispered in her ear. "Evil creatures, every life they take? Those victims have a choice: to go on to whatever comes next or to haunt their murderer. The more the murderer kills, the more they are surrounded by their sins."

Karen looked toward the source of the voice and wasn't surprised to see Phoebe "Dumplin'" Walker's face looking exactly as she did on the day she almost killed Karen in Elkhorn, Wisconsin.

Phoebe nodded. "But there's a corollary to that spiritual truth. For those of us who became monsters, every werewolf who started out as a good person but went rogue? We linger here in limbo, terrified and disgusted by what we did. And we exist to atone."

Phoebe stood up and leaned close to Dodd's ear. "You're not one of us. You were a mad dog long before you became a werewolf. Someone should have put you down a long time ago. You don't have much time left. I think even you can sense that. You'll be with us soon. And the things we can do to a soul? Oh, you will beg for hell, William Dodd. You will beg for it."

Dodd jerked his arm away and shrank back into his chair.

He stared at Karen in horror.

Hayden leaned over her. "Goodbye, baby. See you around."

And, somewhere high above rural Virginia, Karen Arthur passed out.

***

ACT III

Ronin

"Heavy misfortunes have befallen us, but let us only cling closer to what remains, and transfer our love for those whom we have lost to those who yet live."

— Mary Shelley, Frankenstein

What Remains

Clingmans Dome

The forestry service firefighters arrived at the mountain top thirty minutes after the blast. The firemen spread out, making a perimeter around the inferno.

They were lucky: the ground was wet, the forest beyond green. Fresh rain was forecasted to arrive at any moment.

Still, they began building backfires to make sure they contained the blaze.

The man at the northern most end of the perimeter was dragging brush forward toward the blaze.

He had seen wildlife exiting a forest fire before. He had seen raccoons, bears, deer running from fires in the past.

Once, in Arizona, he had seen a full-grown mountain lion and her cubs dashing to safety less than five yards from where he had been standing.

But he had never seen anything like what emerged from the flaming hell of Clingmans Dome.

And he would never relate what he saw that night on Clingmans Dome to anyone.

The shape walked out of the flames on two legs. At first, he thought it was a bear, but he knew that no bear in the Smoky Mountains stood nine feet tall.

The face looked like that of a wolf, a wolf with thick black fur and yellow eyes.

That alone was the stuff of nightmares.

What was even curiouser was that the monster wolf was carrying a naked woman with long auburn hair in its arms.

The fireman stood stock still, terrified that the slightest sound might draw the creature's attention.

It stalked past carrying its burden.

When it was directly across from the firemen, the beast turned its great, shaggy head and looked into the man's eyes.

There was no menace in the look.

It regarded him for a moment and then continued walking into the deep woods.

***

"Fire!" Anna screamed in her sleep. "I'm burning!" She began to sob.

Swede licked her face, put his wolf nose against the side of her neck and snorted.

She opened her eyes.

They were in the deep woods. She was naked in Swede's wolf arms.

"Swede?"

He stopped walking and put his forehead against hers.

"Oh, Swede, I'm so sorry. I'm sorry I was cruel to you." She looked around. "How did we survive? We should have burned."

She felt him transitioning.

He laid her on the wet grass as he changed back into human form.

Swede sat down on a fallen log and laid what looked like Anna's bag on the ground in front of him. He put his face in his hands. "We did burn. That's what saved us."

"What? How?"

"My back burned. Down to my spine," Swede said. "Burned away the silver iodide and I started to heal. You were knocked out. I picked you up and carried you away from the fire."

"God..." She felt her right arm and hip.

The darts were gone.

"I... tore up your arm and hip. Drained the silver out. You changed back in your sleep. Sorry if I hurt you."

"You saved me," Anna said. She stood up and looked at him.

"Couldn't save her."

Anna burst into tears. She sat beside him on the log. "We couldn't save either of them."

Swede just looked at the ground in front of him. "I saved your clothes. Bag melted a little."

Anna reached down and tried to unzip the bag. The zipper was melted closed.

She yanked it and the bag ripped open. Anna picked through her clothes and began putting them on.

"You believe in ghosts, Anna?"

She looked at him as she pulled up her jeans and buttoned them. "Ghosts?"

He nodded. "I saw her. When I was unconscious? I saw Layla." Anna sobbed.

"I'm so sorry, Swede," she whispered.

"She was whispering in my ear. She said, '*Next life, lover.*'" He shook his head. "Why would I dream that, Anna?"

"I don't know, Swede."

"I should've made her stay in Gatlinburg, Anna."

Anna pulled on her T-shirt and sat down beside him. She put her arm around him. "She wouldn't have stayed behind."

He nodded. "We have to find Karen."

"We will."

"And we have to kill them, Anna. We have to kill all of them. Especially *him*."

"We will," she whispered.

***

Gatlinburg, Tennessee

The entrance to the national park was closed.

Clyde parked the van and got out. He walked past the line of cars queued up to turn back.

A group of hikers was standing outside the park service office.

"Any idea why the entrance is closed?" He asked a blond boy wearing a backpack.

"Ranger says there was some kind of explosion up at Clingmans Dome. Bomb or something." He pointed into the forest. "It's on fire. They won't let anybody into the park."

Clyde felt his heart stop.

There was an orange glow in the distance.

He turned and ran back to the van.

Paul met him. "What's going on?"

185

"Something happened on the mountain. It's on fire." He looked at the van. It would take five minutes to unload his bike.

Paul's bike was parked on the curb.

"Paul, I need your bike," Clyde said. He opened the back of the van and reached for his bow case.

"What's going on?" Bobby asked as he got out of the van.

"Trouble," Clyde said.

"Clyde?" Paul said.

"What?"

Paul pointed toward the park.

Anna and Swede were walking toward them.

Swede was wearing an old pair of worker's coveralls.

"Thank God," Clyde said as he put the bow back in the van.

He turned back around.

That's when he saw Anna's face.

"No… please, God, no."

***

Anna clung to Bobby as they stood on the curb.

Swede sat on the loading deck of the van, Paul crouched behind him.

Swede looked like he was in shock.

Paul looked over Swede's shoulder at Clyde. The question on his face didn't need to be voiced: 'What now?'

Clyde swallowed hard. "Swede? Can you ride?"

Swede nodded.

"How about you, Anna?"

"Yes."

Clyde nodded. "Okay. Bobby, you ride Karen's bike."

Bobby nodded. He looked at Swede. "What about… Layla's?"

Swede seemed to shrink at the sound of her name. He put his face in his hands.

"We'll put her bike in the back of the van. We won't leave it," Clyde said.

Swede looked up and nodded. "Thank you," he whispered.

"We need to get out of here," Clyde said.

"We're going to find Karen, right?" Bobby asked.

186

"Yeah, kid," Clyde said. "We're going to find her."

Bobby held Anna tight.

Anna separated from him and held out her hand to Swede. "Come on. Let's go get the bikes."

Bobby walked with Swede and Anna toward the center of Gatlinburg.

Paul climbed down from the back of the van.

"What do you need?" Clyde asked.

"Internet access. Not something public. We need to break in somewhere - I believe they'll be monitoring any local Wi-Fi and cellular access."

"I'll find you something."

Paul nodded.

They watched Bobby, Anna, and Swede walking.

"I'll stay close to Swede," Paul said.

Clyde nodded. "Yeah. Watch after him, professor. We're going to need him. We're going to need both of them."

***

Boyds Creek Elementary School
Boyds Creek, Tennessee

"Will it work?" Clyde asked.

They had pulled the van around behind a small elementary school northwest of Sevierville and hidden the bikes in the bushes nearby.

Paul looked at the wiring going into the back of the school.

He climbed up the bricks, driving his werewolf claws into the wall.

Sixteen feet up, he used his right hand and slapped a metal utility box opened.

He smiled down. "The modem and router are inside the box. Toss me the network cable."

Bobby pulled a long network cable out through the back door of the van and climbed up beside Paul.

Paul plugged the cable into the router and a yellow light came on. It started to blink. "Perfect."

They both jumped down, leaving the network cable connected.

Paul stepped into the back of the van and brought up the computer console. "We have a connection."

"Bobby," Clyde said. "Go keep watch in case the cops show up."

"What do I do if I see them?"

"Just yell. Don't hurt anybody," Clyde said.

Swede and Anna were sitting on the asphalt outside the rear of the van.

Paul knelt in front of them. "I know this is difficult, but I need you to think back to the ambush. Did anyone say anything? Did you hear names?"

Anna nodded. "Yeah, they didn't seem to care if we heard. I guess they thought we'd be dead soon and it wouldn't matter. They kept mentioning their boss. Somebody named 'Price'."

"The werewolf's name was Dodd," Swede spat. "Gunnery Sergeant Dodd."

Anna nodded. "Yeah. Definitely."

"How were the soldiers dressed? Any insignias? Names?"

Anna shook her head. "They wore black tactical gear. No insignias."

"No," Swede said. "No insignias."

"How about the helicopter?" Clyde asked.

"It was dark," Anna said. "Maybe a couple hundred yards away."

"It was black," Swede said.

Anna nodded. "Big. No lights."

"That enough information?" Clyde asked.

"Let's hope," Paul said.

"Why'd they miss?" Anna asked. She looked up into the van at Paul.

Paul stared at her. "What do you mean '*miss*'?"

"The rocket... bomb... whatever it was? If they were trying to kill us, why did they hit *behind* us?"

Swede looked up and nodded. "Yeah. Yeah, Anna's right. They hit on the other side of the observation thing from us."

"Shouldn't they have been shooting directly at *us*?" Anna asked.

Paul rubbed his chin. "Yes. I should think so." He sat down at the computer console and began typing.

***

188

Waffle House
Outskirts of Kingsport, Tennessee

Clyde stared at his food. He couldn't eat - not while she was out there somewhere.

Anna pushed his plate closer to him. "Eat. You have to eat, Clyde."

She turned to her right side and looked at Swede. "You too." She kissed his cheek.

Clyde saw Swede tear up and he looked away.

Paul walked in from the van and sat down. "Our friends answered."

Bobby looked out the window at the van. "Was it okay to use the internet in the van? I thought you were afraid…"

"Outgoing, Bobby. Listening for a response from our friends is passive."

"Packet radio," Clyde said. "Our friends answered us with an encrypted radio stream."

"I don't know what any of that…"

Anna took Bobby's hand. "You don't have to. Just know they couldn't track us. What did they say, Paul?"

"Gunnery Sergeant *William* Dodd. Dishonorable discharge from the Marines. A convicted murderer and, apparently, a man who's been dead for half a decade," Paul said.

"I can assure you he's alive, professor," Swede said.

Paul nodded. "Evidently they are using him to test our… condition… as a possible weapon."

Anna scoffed. "What kind of monsters take a psychopath and turn him into a werewolf?"

Paul shook his head. "Unfortunately, our friends don't know. If this is indeed a government project? It's off the books. No one has ever heard of it. No one in our circle, that is."

"What about this 'Price'?" Clyde asked.

"There was an *Edward* Price high up in military intelligence but his whereabouts are unknown. What our friends do know about him is that he's been involved in questionable operations for the last thirty years. Scientific and medical research that is never going to win anyone a Nobel Peace Prize."

"But no one knows where he is now?" Clyde asked.

Paul shook his head. "My impression from our *friends*? He's feared in Washington. Greatly feared."

"Anything about the soldiers?" Anna asked.

Paul shrugged. "There are dozens of military contracting companies out there. Vincell, G4Q, Hutchins... the list goes on and on. They could have been from any of them or from an unknown organization."

"In other words, we have nothing," Clyde said as he stared at his eggs.

"They're still working," Paul said. "This is everyone's top priority, Clyde."

Clyde nodded. "I know. I know. It's just..."

"Not used to feeling helpless," Anna said.

Paul cleared his throat. "As for why the predator drone missed..."

"Drone?" Anna said. "It was a drone?"

Paul nodded. "From the local Air Force base; however, it was being controlled from CIA headquarters."

"So, it's the CIA?" Swede asked.

"No. The orders were faked. The original pilot of the drone thought he was acting under CIA orders. Apparently, those orders were coming from some other group."

"Whoever this Edward Price works for," Clyde said.

Paul nodded. "I believe so, yes."

Anna looked at Paul. "You said 'original pilot'?"

Paul gave her a weak smile. "When I contacted our friends yesterday to gain access to the Nashville morgue? I... told them to keep an eye out for any operation involving the Smoky Mountains or Nashville. One of our... friends... found out about the drone dispatched to Clingmans Dome. He... took control of the aircraft and, well, he made sure the Hellfire missile missed you."

Anna smiled. "You saved us."

Paul rubbed his eyes and looked away. "I... I only wish..."

She reached across the table and took his hand. "Paul? You saved us."

He looked at her and wiped his eyes. Then he nodded.

Anna looked around the table. "No blame. Not at this table. The men responsible for this? Price, Dodd… they're the ones to blame. Not us. Not our friends. Now our job is to get Karen back. Agreed?"

Everyone nodded.

Clyde looked down at his food.

He pushed it away.

***

They walked out of the Waffle House and into the first light of dawn.

"Where do we go now?" Bobby asked.

"Helicopter was headed northeast, right?" Clyde asked.

Swede looked away toward the dawn.

Anna nodded. "I'm… pretty sure, yeah. Everything was happening at once."

Clyde nodded. "Then we go northeast. Central Virginia."

"Bedford?" Anna asked.

"No. We can't involve Ward. Not yet," Clyde said. "We'll head for Lynchburg, maybe Charlottesville."

"That may be a mistake," Paul said.

Clyde looked at him. "How so?"

"We're being watched. We suspected it from the beginning and now we know it. I have little doubt the helicopter's base is somewhere to the northeast, but if we head in that direction…?"

"They'll know we know," Anna said.

"Precisely."

"North then. Into Kentucky," Clyde said. "Lexington. Someplace urban - can't shoot rockets at us in the middle of a city. They'll have to send in troops. That will be messy for them."

Anna nodded.

Bobby headed toward the bikes and Swede followed along after him, head down.

Paul and Anna started to follow them.

"Hang back a minute," Clyde said.

191

After Bobby and Swede reached the bikes, Clyde turned and walked further away. "Follow me."

They followed him to the far end of the lot.

"Think they can hear us?" Clyde asked.

Anna looked over her shoulder.

Bobby was sitting on Karen's bike.

Swede was... just staring into space.

Anna shook her head. "No. Not if we talk low."

"Time to address the elephant in the... parking lot," Clyde said.

Paul nodded.

"What?" Anna asked.

"How long do we have until you four start to turn rogue?" Clyde asked.

Anna paled.

Paul looked toward the other two at the bikes. "There's no set pattern or schedule. But... from what I've seen? It'll start in about three weeks."

Clyde sighed. "How will it play out?"

Paul shrugged. "It depends on several factors. The length of time one has been exposed to an alpha is a major influence, temperament and mental state are also key."

"Give me your best guess, professor," Clyde said.

Paul took a deep breath. "Swede will go first."

"God," Anna whispered.

"He's devastated. He's in shock now," Paul said. "But soon he'll fall into a rage. He'll begin lashing out. And, then? He'll begin seeing us as the enemy. At that point, Swede will either leave or..."

"Try to kill us," Clyde said.

"He wouldn't," Anna said. "Not Swede."

"Anna," Clyde whispered.

"Bobby will turn next. He hasn't been around Karen long enough and he's still coming to terms with the wolf," Paul said. He turned to Anna. "I'm sorry, Anna. I don't mean to be cruel."

"You're not. You're right, I know."

Paul nodded. "Then either you or I will turn. My... philosophical nature and your will power will keep us sane for at least a month and a half. Maybe a little longer."

He turned to Clyde. "When I turn? When I even begin to turn? Clyde, you must kill me."

Clyde held up his hands. "Hang on, it's not going to come to that."

"It could. I realize that all of you, Karen included, think I'm the least dangerous of the pack because of my age. However, I'm smarter than all of you. That sounds conceited but we have no time for modesty. If I turn, I will be unbelievably dangerous. I will see all of you as problems to be solved... I'm extremely good at solving problems."

Clyde nodded. "I know. It's not going to come to that. We have a contingency plan. Karen and I talked about it a long time ago and I filed it away. We're going to look for her for two weeks. After that? We go to Bedford and join up with Ward. Nobody in this pack is going rogue. That's what she wanted and that's what we're going to do."

Anna nodded. "She really talked to you about that?"

"The five..." Clyde winced. "The four of you mean everything in the world to her. If we can't get her back? You go to Bedford, and you live."

Anna sobbed and Clyde held her.

He turned to Paul. "Give us a minute, will you?"

Paul nodded and walked toward the bikes.

"Cry it out. It's okay," Clyde said. "I want to do the same thing."

"What if we don't get her back, Clyde?" Anna sobbed.

"We're going to get her back. I just needed you to know her plan in case this happened. That's all. Now, I need you to stop crying and listen."

She sniffled. "I'm sorry."

"Don't be. You're in charge."

Anna blinked. "What?"

"You're in charge of the pack. I'm not."

"Are you nuts?!"

"Anna, doesn't mean I'm going to let you tell me what to do. You are in charge of the peanut gallery, though."

"I can't... I'm not Karen! I'm not you."

"Hey, I didn't say I wouldn't help but… sweetheart, you are the closest thing to an alpha werewolf they have now. And we might find ourselves at cross-purposes."

Anna frowned. "What does that mean?"

Clyde looked toward the van and the others gathered around the bikes. "If it comes down to saving Karen or saving the four of you? I'll choose her."

"It would never come down to that."

"I sure hope not but, if it does? You need to look out for the pack. She trained you for that. My focus will always be her."

"Us too. We love her too."

Clyde smiled. "I need you to take care of them. I can't and I won't. I either get Karen back or I die trying. You can't do that. You're responsible for the others now. It's as simple as that."

"We're going to find her, Clyde."

He nodded. "Until then? You're the alpha."

She sighed. "I can't even keep them from going rogue."

Clyde laughed. "Hayden Oswald kept an entire motorcycle gang from going rogue for years just through the force of his will. And if that son of a bitch can do it? I know you can."

"They were all insane by the end, Clyde."

"Hayden was insane. You're not. Hell, I don't know, maybe he caused all of them to go crazy. Either way, you only need to hold them together for two weeks. Then you take them to Bedford. But they'll be your pack even if it's Ward keeping them sane."

"You talk like you wouldn't go with us," Anna hissed.

He smiled. "If I can't get Karen back? God forbid if she's dead?" He shook his head. "Whole lot of people are going to die. That blood will be on my hands. Not yours." He nodded toward the others. "Not theirs."

"Well, I'll be the one who decides whether we get blood on our hands, won't I?"

Clyde smiled. "Yep. Your pack. Your rules. Now, and this is hard and it's mean, but every time you feel like you want to cry and you don't know what to do? You think about Karen and how she'd handle it."

"No more crying. Got it," Anna said, and she wiped her tears away.

"No, darlin'. Just know when it's time to cry and when it's time not to."

They walked across the lot and joined the pack.

***

Spears Mountain

Karen opened her eyes.

The room was white.

She was lying on her back on a foam mattress. She had a thin white sheet draped over her otherwise naked body.

She could hear some sort of machine whirring nearby.

Karen turned her head to the left and winced.

There was something stuck in her neck.

She gingerly touched the spot with her finger.

There was an IV in her neck, another in her left arm.

Blood flowed steadily down both clear rubber tubes and into a small robot beside her makeshift bed.

She grabbed the tube in her neck and started to pull it out.

"I wouldn't do that," someone said.

The white room had a wall of thick glass to her left.

A tall man wearing jeans and a white shirt stood on the other side of the glass. "It's filtering the silver out of your blood. You should let it finish."

"Who are you?" Karen asked.

"My name is Dr. Joseph Marlow. I'm a psychologist."

Karen looked around the room.

There was a small bathroom area and not much else.

A cell. She was in a cell.

"Where am I?"

"Spears Mountain, Virginia. It's a military installation… well, it was."

Karen leaped off the bed, carrying the robot into the air with her.

The tubes pulled out of her neck and the robot shattered against the far wall.

195

She landed in full wolf form in front of the glass wall.

She drove her fists against the wall in front of Dr. Marlow's face.

Marlow fell backward on the floor.

Karen hit the glass as hard as she could but only managed to make noise.

Marlow stared up at her. "You'd think I'd be used to that by now."

She bared her teeth and growled at him.

He looked to her side. "Going to need another robot." He stood up. "I'm sorry. It wasn't my idea to bring you here."

Karen transitioned back to human. "You killed my pack! I'm going to kill you!"

"I'm sorry about Layla Kowalski. Nobody was supposed to be hurt."

"Anna Sanders, Swede Olufsen..."

"Still alive."

Karen took a step back. "What?"

Marlow looked over his shoulder.

She followed his gaze.

There was a camera on the wall pointed toward them.

"Edward Price has been screaming bloody murder all morning. Anna Sanders and Swede Olufsen are still alive. Price's cleanup crew missed."

Karen smiled and sobbed. "You still killed Layla. You'll all die for that."

"That was Dodd. He's..."

"A psychopath. You made him. You're just as guilty..."

"I know. I cannot tell you how sorry Dr. Geffman and I are about that." Marlow put his hand on the glass.

Written on his palm were the words: WE'RE PRISONERS TOO. ON YOUR SIDE.

Karen stared at his palm. "Not sure I believe you."

"Again, I don't blame you. We tried to make Price keep Dodd away but..."

"Price is the man in charge?"

"Here, yes, I suppose." Marlow nodded toward the cell. "We have clothing for you by the toilet facilities."

She turned and walked toward the small bathroom area.

There were two plastic bags containing a t-shirt and a pair of sweatpants.

"Why am I here, Dr. Marlow?" She pulled on the pants and reached for the T-shirt.

"We're hoping to discover how you are able to keep the lobos from turning rogue."

Karen laughed and shook her head as she pulled the T-shirt down. "Well, to start off? You can't just infect a psychopath with Die Gute Wolf and expect a good result."

"Not my choice."

"Although, you can send Dodd in here and I'll see what I can do. No darts this time."

Marlow smiled and nodded. "I'll suggest that one. Doubt if they'll take us up on it."

"You might as well go ahead and kill me, doctor. Nothing is going to fix Dodd."

"There are others."

Karen stared at him. "What others?"

"Two... I think. I've only met one. She's my patient. Also a prisoner."

Karen frowned. "Crazy as Dodd?"

"No. No, not at all. She's... well, she's unbalanced but... No, she isn't crazy. She's upset."

Karen looked around. "You can't keep us in boxes. We're wolves, Dr. Marlow. We don't like confined spaces. How long has she been in a cell?"

"Nearly a year."

"Red eyes?"

Marlow looked away. "Not... completely. No. A little more red in the yellow every day."

Karen frowned. "That long?"

"That's good, isn't it?" Marlow asked.

Marlow was in love with this woman. She could smell it through the vent holes in the thick glass wall.

"It's interesting. She's a rogue or nearly one. Put her down, doctor. There's no coming back from it once it starts. You'll be doing her a favor. Has she killed?"

Marlow rubbed his eyes. "No. No, she hasn't hurt anyone."

"Then maybe she won't end up in limbo."

Marlow stared at her. "I'm sorry? Limbo?"

Karen laughed. "Oh, Horatio, there is more in heaven and earth… trust me."

"Limbo isn't scientific."

Karen lay down on the bed and closed her eyes. "You're talking to a woman who turns into a werewolf. I think you left 'science' behind when you walked into this nut house."

Marlow laughed softly. "Miss Arthur, there's an intercom on the wall behind you. If you press the button? You'll be connected to her cell. She's right on the other side of the back wall. Could you just talk to her? Please?"

"I don't owe you shit, doctor."

"No. No, you don't. She's in pain. And I don't think you're the kind of person who wouldn't at least try…"

"I told you. You want to end her suffering? Put her down before she kills, doctor."

Dr. Marlow turned and walked out through the metal cell block door.

***

Marlow stood outside the door and rubbed his eyes.

Angelica stepped out of the control room. "You tried. You did good."

He shook his head. "The vent. It's open between their cells?"

Angelica sighed. "Come on, Marlow. You heard what she said. Being able to smell each other won't cure Paula."

"Damn it! Is it open or not?"

"Yes, Joseph. It's open. They're breathing the same air. There's a foot of reinforced concrete between them."

"Well, we sure as hell can't put them in the same cell," Marlow said.

***

"I thought you and I were on the same team, Gunnery Sergeant?" Price asked.

"We are," Dodd said as he sat on his cot.

Edward Price was standing flanked by two Spec Ops operatives holding automatic weapons.

"Tell me what happened with Layla Kowalski?" Price asked.

"Enemy combatant."

"She was paralyzed from the waist down. Swede Olufsen had been similarly neutralized. Anna Sanders was down. Karen Arthur was down. Simple snatch and grab. That was the mission, Gunny."

Dodd laughed.

"Something amusing?" Price asked.

"They stopped me from killing the big one."

Price stared at him. "Camera footage told a different story."

Dodd grinned. The smile was too wide, too big. More like a caricature of a human smile.

Price swallowed.

Dodd turned his gaze toward Price, the hideous smile fixed in place. "I had him. Another few seconds and I would have taken his head. They started shooting tranq darts and spoiled that."

"So, you threw a tantrum and took Layla Kowalski's head instead?"

"He needed to feel loss."

Price shook his head.

Dodd licked his lips. "He needed to know I took everything away from him. He needed to know that. Now he'll become…" Dodd looked away.

"*Become* what?" Price asked.

Dodd turned his head toward Price. His facial features had stretched, the wolf manifesting half-way. His voice came out guttural, like a growl, "Become a man worth killing."

The men to Price's left and right took a step back and leveled their rifles.

Price took a step back as well. "Stand down, Gunnery Sergeant."

Dodd's face returned to some facsimile of normal. The mouth was still too large and wide, the teeth too jagged. "I'm not the one that let Olufsen and Sanders get away. None of this is my fault."

"Gunnery Sergeant Dodd, you are restricted to quarters until further notice."

Dodd leapt to his feet and came to attention. He saluted. "Sir! Yes, sir! I am in need of some sleep, thank you, sir!"

He continued to smile at attention as Price backed out of the barracks along with his guards.

One of the guards closed the door.

Price stared at the barracks for a few moments, half expecting Dodd to come crashing through in wolf form to kill them all.

When that didn't happen, Price looked at one of the guards. "I want two guards on the barracks at all times. One at each end of this hallway. Have them rotate every half hour. Understood?"

"Yes, sir."

"He doesn't leave. Not for any reason. No one else in or out."

The operative looked at the door. "What about his food, sir?"

"There are rations in there. Let him eat crackers and spam." Price said as his cellphone rang.

He pulled it out of his jacket pocket and walked down the hall. "Price."

"I need to speak to you, sir," the security chief said on the other end.

"Meet me in my office."

***

"How long has this man been missing?" Price asked. He could feel the walls closing in around him.

Kennith Andrews was one of the Hutchins mercenaries and he was now missing.

The chief shook his head. "At least a couple of days, Mr. Price. His buddies covered for him. They didn't want to see him get in trouble."

"He have a history of this?"

"No, sir. Kenny Anderson is first-rate. That's why he was on Armory Detail."

"Have you inspected the armory?"

"We looked sir. Nothing seems to be missing. I've changed the access code and removed Anderson's biometrics from the system."

Price nodded. "He have a woman in town? Or in one of the trailer parks?"

"No, sir. Our men know the locals are off-limits."

Price snorted. "Please. They're soldiers. As soon as they go out on leave, they're hitting anything in a tube top. Send out a team to scout around. Check the bars - in civilian clothes, please. Don't draw attention. Also, turn this facility upside down - if he's a corpse? I want him found. Bring in dogs if you must."

"Understood, sir." He turned to leave.

"Oh, and the next time anything strange happens? Unexplained disappearances or the like? Come to me immediately or I'll make you disappear."

"Yes, sir."

***

Karen paced the cell, looking for any apparent gap or other means of escape. The concrete walls were steel reinforced and not just with rebar - there were thick steel plates as well.

Steel plates with an outer coating of silver.

She found the plates by digging through the concrete with her claws.

The glass wall was too thick even for a werewolf to shatter.

There was an air vent in the wall above the toilet, but it was too small for anyone to squeeze through.

A steel hatch was set in one wall, but it was far too thick to tear through.

The sliding mechanism in the glass wall was likewise too small for her to squeeze through.

She sat down on the foam bed.

At least Swede and Anna were alive, if Marlow was telling the truth.

She was fairly certain the doctor had been sincere.

Was Hayden right? Could she see souls?

She wasn't sure.

What seemed perfectly plausible when she was delirious on the helicopter now felt less certain.

Had she actually been saved from Dodd by an army of dead werewolves? It was a comforting thought.

The notion the dead rogues were trying to atone for the horrors they committed, even if they seemed to be trapped in a hellish limbo? That meant something.

It meant by putting them down? Karen and her pack were, in a way, saving them.

She desperately wanted to talk to Ward Rickman about this. He had killed rogues who were once his friends, and she knew that weighed heavily on him.

If he knew Clayton Truman Ambrose was at peace even in his limbo prison, perhaps that would make Ward feel better about killing him that night on the Blue Ridge Parkway.

Karen rolled onto her side on the mattress.

And then there was Hayden.

Some part of her mourned for that monster.

Some part of her still loved him despite all of it.

Not the way she loved Clyde. Clyde was forever. She had always known that no matter how hard she had fought to deny it.

But there had been a spark of good somewhere inside Hayden, hidden deep. Maybe before he had been turned, that spark could have been made into something *worth* loving.

The Hayden in limbo might have recovered that spark, and, for that? She was glad.

She rolled onto her back and looked at the intercom on the back wall.

Karen blew out her breath and then drew a deep one. She rolled off the bed and walked over to the intercom.

It was a small speaker inset in the wall with a single red button below it labeled 'TALK'.

What the hell? She thought. It wasn't as if she had anything else to do.

She pressed the button. "Hello?"

She took her finger off the button.

Silence.

She started to press it again, but the speaker came alive with a hiss.

"Hi, roomie! How do you like the digs?" A woman said. "Comfy, huh? Listen, just an FYI: you have to keep it clean yourself. They just won't send in a maid. I've asked for a nice fat one and they decline."

Batshit insane, Karen thought. She pressed the button. "My name is Karen. And, you are?"

"Paula Danvers, Sagittarius, I love long walks in the woods and puppies with soulful eyes."

Karen rolled her eyes. "If I'm boring you, I'll go back to staring at the walls."

"No, no. Don't be silly. Hey, what kind of werewolf are you?"

"Huh?"

"I wanted to be one of those fluffy, snuggly kind from the Twilight movies but instead I'm sort of a combination of the ones from Dog Soldiers and David Naughton in American Werewolf in London."

Karen laughed in spite of herself. "Same kind as you. Don't know Dog Soldiers, though."

"My ex made me watch it. Should've paid more attention since I got recruited to be one, huh?"

"I'm an alpha," Karen said.

"Ol' blue eyes, huh? Prettier than mine I bet."

"How far gone are you, Paula?"

Silence.

"You can shove the bravado," Karen said. "You're scared."

"You think so? When I tear your head off, we'll find out how…"

"I said drop the bullshit. Or you can sit over there and sulk."

Silence again.

"Fine. Nice talking with you," Karen said. She walked back toward the bed.

"Yes, okay?! Yes… I'm scared."

"See? That wasn't hard."

Paula laughed. "Tough werewolf love, is that it?"

Karen shook her head. "I'm not tough. And just so you know? I'm scared too. Not about losing my mind. I'm afraid for my pack."

"They're still alive?"

"Maybe. Your boyfriend seems to think so."

"Boyfriend? Marlow? Yeah, he's smitten. Gives me those big puppy dog eyes. He'd make a nice pet. Or I could just hang his head on a wall."

Karen laughed. "That's the thing I hate the most about rogues: all of you have the same dark humor. It's monotonous."

"He thinks you can help me?" Paula said softly. "Can you?"

"You want me to lie and make you feel better?"

Paula laughed again. "No. Give it to me straight."

"I have to put you down. I'm sorry."

Paula was quiet for a moment. "Well, thanks for telling me straight. I won't go without a fight."

"Your kind never does. It won't matter. I've been doing this a long time," Karen said. "But, and you have my word on this, you won't suffer. You've suffered enough."

"Gee, thanks," Paula said. "Don't let me hurt him, please? Don't let me hurt Joseph." Her voice cracked. "Or Angelica Geffman… I don't want to hurt either of them but… I will if someone doesn't stop me. Please promise me you'll protect them."

"I lost a pack member…"

"They aren't responsible. Price is holding them prisoner same as us. Joseph wanted to take *me* to *you*. Price is the one who reversed that."

Karen frowned. She put her hand against the wall. She closed her eyes.

She felt stupid doing that. What was she some kind of sideshow psychic trying to tap into…?

Karen gasped and opened her eyes. She put her hand over her mouth to stifle a sob.

Through a foot of concrete, rebar, and silver, Karen had 'seen' Paula Danvers.

Paula Danvers should have been part of Karen's pack. She came from the bloodline.

Instead of becoming what she had been destined for, Paula had been locked away in a cage to slowly become a monster.

One more victim of Edward Price and whoever pulled his strings.

"Karen? Are you still there?" Paula asked.

Karen took a deep breath. "I'm still here. Don't worry. I won't let you hurt them."

"Thank you. Listen… when you come for me? I'll try not to fight but… I can't promise…"

God, stop talking, Karen wanted to scream. It would be cruel to tell Paula she could have been better. She could have been one of the pack.

"I'll take care of it, Paula. Trust me."

"I do. I don't know why…"

Karen smiled. "You do what you have to do when the time comes. So will I." She paused for a moment and then added, "It isn't the end, you know?"

Paula laughed. "Pretty sure it is. I'm not complaining. I welcome it."

Then Karen told her a story so insane only a werewolf would believe it.

***

Edward Price sat in his office and listened to the intercom conversation. He listened to stories of limbo and ghosts.

Ghosts.

That last part made him shiver.

The concept of everyone you killed following you, playing in your wake like some sort of demonic dolphins, clinging to you like leeches? That terrified him.

He opened his file drawer. He thumbed through it and found a folder marked "Swords Creek, Virginia."

He flipped it open and thumbed through reports from a company called Somacorp and their facility inside the Swords Creek coal mine.

The research they had done there, disastrous as it had been? That research put ghosts on Edward Price's list of possible military technologies.

It had come to nothing.

Ghosts couldn't harm the living.

Those they could harm were of no concern to Price's benefactors.

Still, the concept of your victims' ghosts crowding around you, smothering you, trying to suffocate you…

He closed the folder and dropped it back into the filing cabinet.

It was time to meet his blue-eyed wolf, superstitious nut that she now appeared to be.

***

"You're shorter than I pictured," Karen Arthur said as she looked at Price through the glass wall.

Price laughed. "I get that a lot. Personally, I've always felt my stature made me try harder to succeed."

"Like Napoleon and Adolf Hitler," Karen said with a smile.

"Dr. Marlow said you had quite the whit. Miss Arthur, your country needs you."

"Then my country should have asked nicely. My country shouldn't have killed Layla Kowalski. My country shouldn't have fired a missile at two members of my pack." Her arms transitioned and she slammed her clawed hands against the glass. "And my country sure as hell shouldn't have killed those kids in Texas." She cocked her head to the side. "But I don't think *my* country did that at all. Tell me, Mr. Price, who do you work for?"

Price nodded and smiled. "The group I work for is bigger than any single nation, Miss Arthur. However, I promise you we are working toward peace and prosperity."

Karen shook her head. "The prosperity of totalitarianism and the peace of a prison." She looked around. "I'm a wolf, Mr. Price. We like our freedom. I don't think our world views are going to mesh."

"You've done an admirable job of eliminating Hayden Oswald's rogues. Not to mention the serial murderers and terrorists you've eliminated. All things my benefactors applaud. We're trying to do the same thing with Project Lobo but on a much larger scale."

"Save your sales pitch for the politicians, Price," Karen said. "One of mine is dead. You and your pet wolf are going to die for that. If you had a brain in that undersized skull of yours? You'd kill me right now."

"I'm sorry to hear that, Miss Arthur. Truly, I am; however, you are going to cooperate with us. We're going to try to discover how you blues tick in order to recover the sizable investment we've made in Gunnery Sergeant Dodd."

Karen smiled. "By all means, send people in here to run all the tests you want…"

"No, we'll send in our little robots to do that."

Karen pointed at the shattered plastic and circuit boards on the floor. "You mean like that one."

"Yes," Price said.

"What makes you think I'm going to cooperate with you?"

Price stepped toward the glass. "Because your pack? They're hiding in Lexington, Kentucky. No one can truly hide from us, Miss Arthur. If you force my hand? The first thing I will do is place a sniper across the street from their hiding place and have them blow off Clyde Hubbard's head as soon as he pokes it out."

Karen went pale.

"Thought that would get your attention. After that? I'll have a bunker buster bomb dropped from a drone onto the warehouse they're squatting in and add a Napalm chaser - not even your people can regenerate from that combo. The press will report it as a gas main explosion. We'll probably take out a few dozen other people in collateral damage but, well, you have to break eggs to make an omelet."

"You son of a bitch!"

"My family lineage aside? If you still won't cooperate? There's always Bedford. Ward and Loretta Rickman along with their children Melissa and baby Nathaniel. I employ specialists who delight in murdering families, even werewolf families."

"You are a dead man, Price. We'll come for you. You just signed your death warrant…"

"Really? Who's going to kill me, Miss Arthur? They'll be dead and you'll be living in this fishbowl. You're holding a very bad poker hand, Miss Arthur, and I have all the aces."

Karen stared at him for a moment. Then she turned and walked back to her mattress.

"Something I said?" Price asked.

She frowned. "You win, Price. Run your tests. But I can tell you before you start? Dodd can't be saved. He can't be controlled. He was never supposed to be one of us. Nothing from me would have helped him, not even on day one."

"I'll let Dr. Geffman be the judge of that. She's an annoying bitch but she's good at what she does."

Karen said nothing. She simply stared at the wall.

She heard the cell door open and close as Price left.

Karen paid no attention. Her gaze was focused on the two visitors in her cell.

Hayden Oswald was smiling and nodding, leaning his back against the far wall. "See that look on her face? I love that look. Told you she'd figure it out fast and that's the look she gets when she figures shit out."

Clayton Ambrose smiled, standing beside him in those ridiculous khaki shorts and matching safari guide shirt. "Yes, I can almost see her allure. You chose well."

"Got to admit: at the time I was just horny. But, yeah, I chose well."

"Still an asshole, Hayden," Karen whispered.

He laughed. "And limbo hasn't changed me a bit. You take care of yourself, blondie. See you on the other side… or sooner. Guess that all depends on you."

And they were gone. Two psychopaths looking for salvation or just running a long con - she wasn't sure which. Either way, did it really matter?

Sincere or not, the two ghosts were right about one thing: Karen had indeed figured something out. The question was, could she turn that into a plan to save herself and the pack?

***

Lexington, Kentucky

The old, abandoned warehouse on Smith Street was in sad shape. The flat roof leaked like a sieve when it rained and there were rats. So, the owner hadn't looked a gift horse in the mouth when Clyde handed him $20,000 in cash for a security deposit and another $20,000 in cash for the first month's rent.

Coincidentally, a bank ATM in Nicholasville had been robbed a few nights before and the thieves had taken a little over $40,000 from the mangled machine.

If the owner had put two and two together? He hadn't said a word. He'd simply pocketed the money and enjoyed his good fortune.

Clyde had wanted someplace populated enough to make a military assault by the men in the black helicopters difficult if not impossible to achieve without witnesses.

The warehouse fit the bill situated as it was in the midst of multi-story office buildings.

Anna and Bobby rode up to the warehouse on their bikes. They circled around to the loading dock and rode directly up the ramp and into the first floor of the warehouse.

Clyde closed the double doors behind them.

All the bikes and the van were here, enclosed and out of sight.

"Any trouble?" Clyde asked as they got off their bikes.

"No trouble," Anna said. "Thai." She held up two white paper bags.

Bobby held up two more.

Anna carried her bags to the folding card table behind the van and set them down. "We've got eyes on us in the office building across the street."

Clyde nodded and stretched with his hands on his lower back. "I know. Dressed like plumbers. They've got a sniper nest on the top floor above that insurance company."

"Probably listening to every word we say," Bobby said.

"Most likely," Clyde said. He held up a piece of paper: PAUL SAYS TO ONLY TALK IN THE BASEMENT. He showed it to them and then stuffed it into his jacket pocket.

Anna and Bobby nodded.

Anna looked around. "Where's Swede?"

Clyde frowned. He pointed up. "Roof."

"Shit," Anna whispered. "I'll go get him."

"Want me to get the professor?" Bobby asked.

"No," Anna said. "Take the food downstairs. We'll eat with him."

***

Anna opened the door at the top of the stairs and stepped out onto the rotting roof.

209

Swede was standing near the edge staring across the street at the building where the 'plumbers' were.

"Been staring at them long?" Anna asked.

"Two, three hours. I lost track of time."

Anna walked up to him. She sat down on the short, raised wall at the edge of the roof. "Come eat. There's Thai."

"Not hungry."

"Is that your plan? Hunger strike and stare the bad guys to death?"

He gritted his teeth. "I was thinking maybe I'd go over there and get a little payback."

Anna nodded. "Might work. They're packing silver bullets. You know that, right? They're locked onto both of us right now with sniper rifles."

"I know."

"Also listening to every word we say so you've pretty much lost the element of surprise."

"Won't help them."

She smiled. "What? You're bullet proof now? Silver proof?" She stood up and walked to him. She looked up at him.

Then she reached up and put her hands on his face. "I loved her too. Not like you loved her, but she was my friend."

He pulled away. "They have to pay," he growled.

"They will," Anna said. "You need to grieve."

"I haven't got time to grieve."

"Right now? You've got nothing but time."

He pointed across the street. "They know where Karen is!" He hissed through gritted teeth.

Anna shook her head. "Maybe some of those guys across the street know, it's possible. But think, Swede: would you send anyone who knew where Karen was to stake us out? Knowing we might... I don't know... peel them like apples with our claws until they spilled the beans?" She smiled. "Do you smell urine? I think one of them peed." She tapped her finger on his chest. "Hey. What you're looking for? You're not going to find it up here, big guy."

He swallowed and nodded. "I know."

"Come on. Come eat. We'll kill these jerks later."

***

210

Clyde and Bobby walked down the creaking stairs into the musty basement. The room was huge. It ran the length of the warehouse. The only light was from a single work light Paul brought down from the van when they arrived, and it made a circle a few feet away from the stairs.

Concrete columns supporting the floor above stood sentinel and disappeared into the blackness of the rest of the basement.

Things moved and scurried in the darkness.

Clyde found it unnerving but no one in the pack seemed to notice.

That revulsion for things that hid and scurried innate to most people seemed to have been lost amongst those infected with the werewolf virus.

"Geez, what's he been doing down here?" Bobby whispered.

Clyde looked down.

There was a ragged three-foot wide hole in the basement floor.

"Paul?" Clyde asked.

The professor poked his head up through the hole and smiled. "Ahh, dinner?"

"What are you doing down there?" Bobby asked.

Paul vertical leaped out of the hole and landed on the edge of the broken concrete. "I'm afraid we won't be getting that security deposit back," Paul said with a smile. He was holding a network cable in his hand.

Clyde shrugged. "Never have before. Why should we start now?"

"I thought there might be underground utilities running through here," Paul said. He pointed into the hole. "I tapped around the floor down here until I found something hollow. Turns out they're using an old storm drain under the street to route electric, gas, telephone, and, most recently? Optical fiber."

"Internet?" Bobby asked.

Paul nodded. "Gigabit running right under our feet."

"You patched in?" Clyde asked.

"Just now," Paul said as he pulled the network cable over to a laptop he had sitting open on the third stair step up. He plugged it in. "We won't have Wi-Fi - anything radiating might be intercepted by

211

our friendly plumbers across the street. So, we'll be limited to this laptop."

"This might get us somewhere," Clyde said.

"It will at least let us utilize our encrypted communications."

"What's going on," Anna asked as she and Swede appeared at the top of the stairs.

"Paul got us internet," Bobby called out.

Paul turned and put a finger to Bobby's lips. "Shh! No yelling about internet. Speak quietly even down here."

"They can hear us down here?"

"If you yell, yes," Clyde said.

Paul nodded. "All they have to do is bounce a laser off the windows on this warehouse and capture the reflection. The sound of our voices will cause the windows to vibrate. The laser light will be effected by that vibration, and they can turn those tiny changes into sound. They can bug us without ever setting foot in the building."

"Shit," Bobby whispered.

Paul winked. "However, I doubt very seriously if they a) realize there is a fiber optic cable under the building, and b) believe we can exploit it in any event."

"Who do we call first?" Bobby asked.

"Food first," Clyde said. "Then we start making calls."

***

"You should have called me immediately," Ward Rickman said.

Clyde was sitting on the wooden step beside the laptop with his headset plugged in to the side. "Well, as you can imagine, we've been a little busy."

"Where are you? I'll leave right now."

"Thanks, old buddy, but… not this time."

"Are you nuts? Clyde, you guys need help…"

"I'll level with you, Ward. The only reason I called was to warn you. We're being watched and you're probably being watched as well."

"We can handle that, Clyde. But… am I on speaker?"

"No."

"Clyde… they'll turn."

Clyde rubbed his eyes. "I know." He turned and looked up the stairs. The door at the top was closed and he was alone in the basement. "Swede's irritable. He's getting a little squirrely. Anna is keeping him level so far."

"When his eyes start to turn? It'll be too late, Clyde."

"We're not there yet. I'll send him to you before that happens."

"At least tell me where you are. I can call in local law enforcement and get these 'plumbers' off your back."

Clyde laughed. "You're a good friend, Ward. But you are a terrible liar. If I tell you where we are you'll drive straight out here. You've got a wife and two kids to think about. Karen would skin me alive if I put any of you in danger."

"Okay, okay, we'll do this your way," Ward said. "I'll check around and see if I can find out any more about this Edward Price character."

"Appreciated," Clyde said. "Just make sure you encrypt everything - these people are connected as hell."

"We're going to find her, Clyde."

"I know."

***

Spears Mountain

"I'm Dr. Angelica Geffman," the short woman in glasses said as she stepped up to the glass wall of Karen's cell.

"Pleasure," Karen said without getting up from her bed.

"Would it be okay if I took some blood samples?"

"Didn't you get enough out of me while I was unconscious?"

"I've… used it all."

"Learn anything?"

Dr. Geffman laughed. "Only that I don't know Jack."

Karen sat up and stretched. "Other than attempting to save Price's pet werewolf, what are you hoping to accomplish with all this, doctor?"

"I want to understand how you work. How your body can transform itself completely in seconds - the amount of energy used to shape shift is incredible."

213

"Yeah, we're always hungry after… you could learn all of that from Paula and Dodd."

"Yes, but… if I understood the whole system? Blue-eyed alphas, yellow-eyed pack werewolves, yellow-eyed psychotics like Dodd, and red-eyed rogues? I might be able to isolate the wonderful parts of the Die Gute Wolf virus. Limb regeneration, spinal injury repair… what you are could be the miracle cure of all time."

Karen shook her head. "Not everyone is supposed to be one of us, doctor."

"I know… I mean, even that? How does that work? How do you know…?"

"Magic."

Angelica stared at her. "Excuse me?"

"Magic, doctor." Karen walked to the glass and smiled down at her. "I can see ghosts, Angelica. Talk to them sometimes. A few days ago, I wasn't sure I believed in the concept of a soul… now, as it turns out? I've been seeing souls the whole time. I can look at someone and I just know whether they belong with my pack. I looked into Edward Price's soul, and I saw nothing but darkness. I looked into Dr. Marlow's soul, and I saw light… yours too. That's why I'm talking to you, Angelica. That's why I'm going to give you my blood. I trust you to do the right thing with the knowledge you gain."

Angelica swallowed hard. Then she shook her head. "I'm not brave. I'm afraid. I can't promise you I won't help Price."

Karen nodded. "I understand that. I'm not asking you to die, Angelica. I'm not asking you to open my cell door either. But if you do? I'll do everything I can to get you and Dr. Marlow to safety before I kill everyone in this mountain."

Angelica glanced at the security camera.

"Oh, I know. He sees and hears everything. It doesn't matter. He either kills me right here, soon? Or I'll kill him. Mr. Price's weakness is he believes he's invincible. No one is." Karen sat down on the floor. "Now, send in your robot to take my blood. I won't even break it this time."

"Thank you," Angelica said. "I'll send it through. By the way? What you do? It's not magic. It's science. We just don't understand it yet."

Karen laughed. "Have it your way, doctor. Oh, I don't know if you've thought about it yet, but you will. Sooner or later, you're going to get the idea to inject yourself with my blood. You'll think by becoming a werewolf you can save us all. Don't do that, Angelica. You're a good person but you're not one of us."

***

Angelica emerged from the cell block a few minutes later with a biohazard bag filled with blood samples.

Marlow met her in the hallway. "What did you think?"

"You're right. She's amazing." She shook her head. "Do you think it's possible? Magic?"

Marlow shook his head. "No, it's science. It has to be."

"I guess," Angelica said. She wasn't convinced.

***

"You know, all I ever wanted to be was a soldier," Dodd said. "Other kids I grew up with they wanted to be policemen, firemen... and they'd change what they wanted to be from one day to the next, you know? Not me, though. I only ever wanted to be a soldier. Strong. A soldier is strong. Nothing more important than being strong. So, I enlisted as soon as I turned eighteen... the very day. And do you know what I found in boot camp? Weakness. I found weakness. There was nobody like me. The other recruits, the sergeants... all weak." He shook his head. "That's when it all went wrong. They needed to be culled... I like that word. Culled. The weak have to be eliminated. They locked me in a cell for just trying to fix what was wrong with the corps, Kenny."

Dodd was sitting alone in the dark.

He was holding Kenny Anderson's severed head in his right hand. The lifeless eyes had gone milky white, and the sallow skin of the face was beginning to sag from decay.

"You understand why I killed you, don't you, Kenny? Mercy. I'm strong and I showed mercy. You needed to be culled. Those people

215

at that cult in Texas? They needed to be culled. Weakness has to be culled. It has to be removed like… like cancerous tissue. That stripper on the mountaintop. Weak. Her mate needs to die as well… all of them… that whole pack. They need to be culled. I have to be the only one. Because I'm strong."

Dodd sniffed the air. "Damn, Kenny, you're getting ripe, son." Dodd laughed. Then he leaned his head forward and bit into Kenny's cheek, tearing off a large piece of meat.

Dodd chewed and swallowed. "Meat's still good though."

He tossed the head onto what was left of the body.

Then he stood up and stretched.

He had hidden Kenny Anderson in the space between the barracks and the mountain wall. Lucky for him, the security team didn't know about the access panel in the latrine that led to this area. All the living space in the mountain was made up of prefab metal boxes - there was dead space all around. Caverns rarely had right angles and these dead spaces allowed Dodd to go anywhere he wanted without ever appearing to have left the barracks.

It was how he had surprised Kenny outside the armory.

And now it was Kenny's tomb.

He turned Kenny's body over on the stone floor and the head rolled away into the darkness. He checked Kenny's pockets till he found what he was looking for.

Dodd smiled.

***

Revelations

"Want to see something weird?" Angelica said as she stared at her computer screen.

"Honestly? I've seen enough weird to do me a lifetime since I came here," Joseph said as he walked over to her desk.

They were in Angelica's lab waiting on the expensive machinery on the back wall to finish analyzing Karen Arthur's blood samples.

"I hear you. We are in the heart of weird. I know this is hard for a shrink but put on your scientist hat for a minute," Angelica said with a wink.

"You're a very rude doctor," Joseph grumbled.

"Since our robot nurses haven't been set up to measure brainwaves, I had Price buy me an experimental unit. It doesn't need electrodes which Paula would never tolerate. Very sensitive antenna inserted in one of the vent holes in the glass cell wall. Once it's calibrated, it can lock onto a patient's brainwaves from across the room. I moved it to Karen's cell as soon as they brought her in."

"Okay… what did you record?"

"See for yourself. When she was unconscious? Normal brainwaves. Conscious? Again, normal brain waves."

"Nothing weird there," Joseph said.

"Just wait. Now, this point?" She moved her computer mouse and a different waveform appeared. "This is when she transitioned into wolf form. Heavy activity, as expected and then her brainwaves settle into a very *not* human normal pattern."

"That's the same as Dodd, Paula… normal for a lobo," Joseph said. "Which makes sense because they're processing information from their senses differently."

"Exactly. This is how the wolf thinks." Angelica smiled. "Now, hold onto your ass, Marlow." She clicked the mouse.

"Whoa."

The screen showed brainwaves off the scale.

"What the hell is *that*?" Joseph whispered.

"That, doctor, is when you walked into the cell block. She saw you and her brain went into overdrive. I swear, there was so much energy coming out of her body the lights should have flickered."

"Why?"

"Why indeed… now, remember I told you the device had to be calibrated to the patient? Well, the data processing part of the machine is the part that has to be calibrated… the data itself? The machine stores everything. So, while it was analyzing her brainwaves? It stored yours. Here's what your brain was doing while Karen Arthur's brain was 'broadcasting.'"

She clicked the mouse.

The screen changed to show Karen's brainwaves on the top, Joseph's on the bottom.

Each spike in Karen's brainwaves resulted in a subtle spike in Joseph's.

"What... what is that?"

"Magic," Angelica said. "Her words. Not mine."

Joseph laughed. "What? Now you believe in magic?"

Angelica shook her head. "Telepathy. Marlow, the entire time you were in that room? Karen Arthur's brain was carrying on a conversation with your brain. What else do you call it? Stimulus from her side, response from yours."

"You're saying she read my mind? Come on, Angelica."

"No, what did she say? She said she can see *souls*, Marlow. This is how she sees them. Karen Arthur's subconscious was testing you, learning about you." She moved the mouse and clicked. "And, kiddo, you ain't seen nothing yet."

Karen Arthur's brain waves again, firing non-stop, waves upon waves.

"When was this?" Joseph asked.

"Now... well a few minutes ago. After she spoke to you? She called Paula on the intercom. The brainwave tsunami started then, and it hasn't let up. It's so continuous I wasn't able to see a difference when Price went in or when I went in; although, I did see our brains responding to hers... it's just that her brainwaves were moving so fast and with so much energy they just look like static now."

She smiled and clicked the mouse. "And this? This is Paula's brain, talking back to hers."

Constant activity.

"This has been going on for hours, Marlow."

He stared at the screen. "What... what does it mean?"

She put her hand on his. "Joseph, I think that Karen Arthur's brainwaves are punching a hole through reinforced concrete, a layer of steel sheathed in silver, and I think her alpha brain is trying to fix Paula."

Joseph sat down in a desk chair. "Karen said she can't be cured. No rogue has ever been cured."

"Yes, but what if Paula has the genetics to be one of them? Maybe none of the rogues had her genetic makeup?"

Joseph nodded. "And that makes a difference. That's why Paula has held on to her sanity this long!"

"Maybe."

He stood up. "I have to talk to Karen Arthur."

"Its 2:00 AM, Marlow."

He was already headed for the door. "I have to know."

She watched him go.

"Young love," a voice said behind Angelica.

She spun around.

Dodd was standing in the shadows at the back of the lab.

Angelica backed toward the door, her hand in the pocket of her lab coat. "Dodd! How the hell did you get in here?"

He stepped out of the shadows. "I disconnected Price's camera in here. This time of night it'll take a while for anyone to notice."

His mouth was dripping with blood and his fatigues were equally stained. "All that true? She can *fix* us?" He wasn't looking at Angelica. He was looking at the floor.

"I don't know." She had her hand on the pistol Price had issued to her when she first came to Spears Mountain.

Dodd rubbed his face, smearing the blood. He bent his neck to the side and the bones cracked. "I don't want to be fixed."

"Dodd? You need to leave. I won't… I won't say anything to Price. But you need to leave."

He looked around. "I'm tired of this place. Not supposed to be underground. I'm supposed to run." He smiled. "Feel the wind on my face. Tired of playing the pet. Good boy. Fetch. Play dead." He stared into her eyes. "You think you can pull the trigger?"

"I will if I have to. Silver bullets…"

"I know." He started walking toward her.

"Please, Dodd. I don't want to shoot you."

"I know."

She pulled the pistol out of her lab coat and pointed it at Dodd's chest. "Please stop. Please don't make me."

"*Please stop. Please don't make me,*" Dodd said in a mock falsetto. "Weak. Not as weak as some. But… still weak."

She pulled the trigger.

Nothing happened.

219

She tried to pull it again. "Safety. It must be the safety." She fumbled with the gun. *Where's the damned safety!*

"It's a Glock. There is no manual safety. Did you honestly believe Price would hand you a working gun?" Dodd said.

Angelica began to sob. "Please, Dodd, no."

He took the gun out of her hand and laid it on the lab bench.

Then he sniffed her.

"You haven't pissed yourself. The woman I killed in the Smokys - the first one? The one with the bear spray? She lost control of both. Disgusting. Weak."

"Please, Dodd. I don't want to die."

Dodd's jaws elongated. His fangs grew in.

He opened his mouth and growled an inch from Angelica's face.

She gritted her teeth. "Go on then, you son of a bitch! I hope you choke."

His jaws receded but the fangs stayed. He smiled.

Then he took her hand and forced it open.

He dropped a cellphone covered in blood into her hand.

He turned and walked toward the back of the room. "You don't have a way to communicate outside the mountain. The Hutchins security guys do. That's one of their cell phones. It uses a VPN and is whitelisted to pass through the facility's firewall - just the grunts' way of sticking up their middle finger to Price."

Angelica stared at the phone. "Why... why give me this?"

"Send her pack a message. Tell them where their alpha is."

"Her *pack*? You want me to tell her pack where she is?"

He paused and looked over his shoulder at her. "Yeah. Yeah, tell them. I want them to come here. I need them all to come here."

"Why, Dodd? Why would you...?"

He turned around and stared at her with a shocked expression. "Don't you understand? I have to be the *only* one. They all have to die. The other three in Virginia as well. You bring them here so I can kill them. World is only big enough for one lobo." He reached into his pocket and pulled something out. "Almost forgot. You'll need this to open his phone."

He threw something at Angelica.

It rolled on the floor in front of her: a discolored, severed thumb.

Angelica shrank back.

"You should probably put that on ice." Dodd walked into the dark at the back of the room and disappeared.

***

Karen opened her eyes from a sound sleep when she heard a voice. She jumped out of the bed and slammed against the glass wall in wolf form.

Dr. Marlow was staring up at her from the other side of the glass. "Sorry. What is Paula?"

She punched the glass.

Marlow ignored her. "I said I was sorry. What is Paula?"

She transitioned back to human form. Looking behind her, she saw that her sweatpants and T-shirt were laying in shreds on the floor. "There had better be more clothes in here somewhere."

"There are. Please, what is Paula?"

Karen blinked and shook her head. "A werewolf. Almost a rogue."

"What else?"

"Are you high or something? What are you asking me?"

"Let me ask a different way: if Paula wasn't a lobo and you met her on the street? What would you do?"

"Stop calling us lobos… sounds like we play baseball for an Arizona minor league team."

"Miss Arthur, please. What would you do?"

She turned away. "Go to bed, Dr. Marlow."

"She's supposed to be a lobo… werewolf, sorry. Isn't she?"

"It doesn't matter." Karen lay down on the bed and pulled the sheet over herself.

"I think it does. Please tell me."

Karen sighed. "Yes. Yes, she is. Or… she should've been. That's what makes it even more depressing."

"It's working."

She rolled over. "What's working?"

"Your magic. It's working. Your brain is trying to fix hers."

"My brain… whatever…" Karen shook her head. "It doesn't work. We… tried, doctor. Before. With other rogues. They don't get better."

"Were any of them supposed to be werewolves in the first place?"

"I… don't know. None of the ones I tried to cure were. And, Ward, he doesn't really have the same, I don't know, *powers* I do. It was blind luck Loretta was from the bloodline when he accidentally turned her."

"I don't believe in luck," Marlow said. "His subconscious most likely directed his actions. But that's not the important part. Your brain is broadcasting to Paula's and Paula's is answering. This is going to work."

Love is blind, Karen thought. "I hope you're right, doctor."

***

Joseph walked back into Angelica's lab. "She didn't realize any of it. Still doesn't believe it will work but, Angelica, I think…"

Angelica was sitting at her lab bench. There was an open bottle of Tequila in front of her and a water glass. She poured a half inch of Tequila with a shaking hand, set the bottle down, and downed the liquor in a single swallow.

"Angelica. Are you okay?"

Her hand was shaking as she set the glass down on the lab bench. "Dodd was here."

"What?!"

She nodded. "Came in from the back of the room. Little access hatch back there. Never noticed it before. I pushed a cabinet in front of it." She started giggling. "Like that would stop him." She pushed the Tequila bottle toward him. "Pour it for me?"

"I think you've had enough."

"Nope. Still conscious. Need to be asleep and numb."

"Did he hurt you?" Joseph asked.

She shook her head. "No. He brought gifts." She pointed to the lab bench to the side of hers.

There was a red stained cell phone laying on the white bench.

Along with a severed thumb.

Joseph nodded. "We need to tell Price."

She shook her head. "Can't. He says that phone has access to the outside. He wants us to tell Karen Arthur's pack where we are."

"He *what?*"

***

Bedford, Virginia

Deputy Agnes Gooch was going through the morning emails when her phone rang. "Bedford Sheriff's Department, Deputy Agnes Gooch speaking. Oh, hi, Beulah. No, he's very busy this morning. Can I help you?"

Agnes squinted at the screen. HOT SENIORS WANT TO DATE YOU. She thought about it for a second and forwarded it to her personal email.

"Cat? Beulah, I've told you before we don't get cats out of trees, you want the fire department. Neither Ward nor Loretta even like cats and… the feeling is mutual."

One of the emails caught her eye:

From KAnderson365@HutchinsSec.com

Subject Regarding K A

"The department doesn't own a ladder, Beulah. If you just leave Mr. Peaches alone, he'll climb down on his own."

She opened the email and stared at the screen.

"Beulah, I have to call you back. You should call the fire department." She hung up. "Ward!"

***

Lexington, Kentucky

They all gathered around the laptop screen.

"*HutchinsSec*," Paul said. "That's Hutchins Security - that answers the question of where our Spec Ops friends are coming from."

Clyde nodded. "Going to need everything we can get on Hutchins."

Paul nodded.

"*Regarding K A*," Bobby said. "Karen Arthur."

"Yes," Clyde said.

223

Paul was staring at the image on the screen. "Certainly to the point."

The email contained no text, simply a JPEG image.

A photograph of a wolf's face.

Someone had Photoshopped blue eyes on the wolf.

"But it doesn't tell us anything," Anna said. "Except that Hutchins Security is involved in this."

"Where is Hutchins corporate headquarters?" Clyde asked.

"Washington, D.C., according to their website," Paul said. "However, they have offices all over the world. It's a multi-billion-dollar company."

"So," Swede said. "We find the CEO and squeeze him till he pops. He'll tell us where Karen is."

Anna looked at Clyde.

Clyde shrugged. "He's not wrong."

"Steganography," Paul said and snapped his fingers.

Bobby stared at him. "Dinosaurs? What does that have to do with anything?"

Paul looked confused. Then he looked annoyed. "No, not *Stegosaurus*… Steganography, it's the practice of hiding data within a visual image."

"You mean there's a message written on the image somewhere?" Anna asked.

"No," Paul said. "Not drawn on the image itself. Encoded in the data for the image." He started typing. "If I open this image with an editor that lets me look at the bytes themselves."

"Yeah," Clyde said. "It might be just tacked onto the image data somewhere."

"Well, I mean I doubt if it will just be in there in plain text. Whoever sent this probably encrypted…" Paul went silent. "Hmm…. Son of a bitch… It's right here."

Clyde smiled. "Plain text. They just wrote it backward to fool any algorithms looking for keywords."

"What does it say?" Anna said as she leaned forward.

"*KA inside Spears Mountain in Virginia. She is alive. Send help. Careful, werewolf is waiting for you. Signed Dr. Angelica Geffman and Dr. Joseph Marlow,*" Clyde said.

"Where's Spears Mountain?" Anna asked.

***

A half hour later, they gathered around the laptop again.

"Spears Mountain is northeast of Lynchburg, elevation a little over two thousand feet," Paul said. "It was part of a farm owned by the Spears family who still own the land bordering the mountain on the east slope. In the early 1980s, it was purchased by the United States government."

Clyde spoke. "Our friends tell us the Reagan administration brought in heavy equipment and removed the top of the mountain, then dug down into the mountain, creating a fortified bunker."

"It was the height of the Cold War," Paul said. "There were numerous locations like this setup throughout the country - in case hostilities broke out, the President, government officials, and military leaders could go to the nearest location like Spears Mountain and have command and control for a counterattack."

"Supposedly, the place even has underground aircraft hangars," Clyde said.

"So, it is the US Government?" Anna asked. "The government took Karen."

"It's not that simple," Paul said.

"Spears Mountain has been abandoned for over twenty years," Clyde said. "But our friends have been able to track shipments of supplies and personnel through shell corporations owned by Hutchins Security to Spears Mountain. They believe Edward Price is working with or for this guy, Peter Hutchins."

Paul brought up Hutchins' picture.

"Nice suit," Swede said. "Be a shame when I get it all bloody."

Clyde nodded. "Hutchins is a real one percenter. Our friends believe he's part of a group with their hands in a lot of shady dealings. Foreign coups, gun running, drug trafficking, organized crime…"

"Real charmer," Anna said.

"Group like that would have a lot of their own *friends* in the government," Bobby said.

"At the very highest levels," Paul said.

"You're saying we picked a fight with Godzilla," Anna said.

"In all fairness," Clyde said. "They started it."

"These are people who can borrow CIA assets, spy satellites," Paul said. "They can use government agencies against us, NSA, FBI."

"And our friends can only help us so much without blowing their own covers," Clyde said.

"We're on our own," Anna said.

"Very much so," Paul said.

"What about the doctors, Geffman and Marlow?" Anna asked.

Paul turned the laptop toward her. "Dr. Joseph Marlow, Psychologist. Long time military contractor. They send him in to evaluate military personnel who have been through traumatic experiences, prisoners of war, soldiers who crack under pressure, that sort of thing."

Anna nodded. "This Dodd, he's certifiable. Do you think they brought in Marlow to be his shrink?"

"Makes sense," Paul said.

"What about the other one?" Clyde asked.

"Dr. Angelica Geffman," Paul said. He changed the image to a smallish woman with thick plastic glasses. "Brilliant geneticist, Harvard Medical School, MIT... obviously she was brought in to research Die Gute Wolf."

"And to weaponize it," Clyde said.

"Without a doubt," Paul said.

"We're wasting time," Swede said. "We know where Karen is, we know where Dodd is, let's get on the bikes."

Paul looked at Anna.

"We can't just go straight in, Swede," Anna said.

He gritted his teeth. "You said we would move as soon as we knew where to go. We know. Why in the hell are we waiting?"

"Because we can't make a move without them knowing," Anna said. "The plumbers across the street, drones, satellites. It's a miracle we even got hold of this information."

Clyde nodded. "We start rolling toward Spears Mountain? We won't even make it halfway before they take us out."

Swede punched one of the concrete columns. "What?! We're just going to sit here and do nothing? They have Karen, they killed…" His voice trailed off.

"I didn't say that," Anna said. "We're going to do something, but we have to plan this out. We can't do Karen any good if we're dead."

"What if we snuck out through the tunnel down here?" Bobby asked.

Paul nodded. "That's a good idea; however, with the technology arrayed against us? I believe it would only buy us a few hours before they knew what we were up to."

Clyde rubbed his chin. "What if we didn't go?"

"Huh?" Anna asked.

Clyde leaned against a column. "What if the pack broke up? Went our separate ways - any direction except toward Spears Mountain."

"How is that going to help?" Swede asked.

"No, wait, I think I know where he's going with this," Anna said. "Bobby and I head north, toward Wisconsin - they may think I'm heading home."

Paul nodded. "I have relatives in Alabama. If Swede and I went that direction…?"

Clyde smiled. "We look like we've given up. I'll slink back to southwest Virginia."

"Wait," Anna said. "That's *toward* Spears Mountain."

Clyde shook his head. "They're not afraid of me. I'm not a werewolf. I'm just a redneck with a bow and arrow."

"They don't see you as a threat," Bobby said.

"No, they don't," Clyde said.

"Last thing they would expect would be for us to split up," Anna said. "They'll think we gave up. Even if they figure out we were tipped off about Spears Mountain? They'll think we looked at what we were up against and quit."

Swede shook his head. "I still don't see how this helps us. We still have to get to Spears Mountain."

Anna laughed. "We'll need help."

"Shell game," Clyde said.

Bobby looked from Anna to Clyde and back. "Are you guys talking in code?"

227

And then Swede started to smile.

***

"It's a good plan," Anna said.

"Almost perfect," Clyde said.

They were alone in the basement.

"Almost?" Anna asked.

"Paul has to keep Swede from cracking. The shell game has to work out perfectly. Lots of moving parts."

Anna nodded. "It's all we've got."

"Maybe not all." He took a deep breath. "I've got an idea. I'll need your help."

"Okay, what do you need?"

"First, tell Bobby I'm taking his bike."

"That piece of crap? Why?"

"I'm going to need it. Besides, I've been working on it. And, second…"

She didn't like the second part.

***

The Bait

Blue Grass Insurance Building
Next door to the warehouse
4:00 AM

"This is overwatch. I have the girl and the kid leaving on their bikes, over," the sniper said into his headset.

"This is southside. Olufsen and Professor Collins also leaving from the opposite side," the southside sentry said over the radio.

"Advise central four of the five are on the move," the team leader said. "Stay sharp, Hubbard will probably leave in the van next."

The sniper scanned slowly left and right across the ground floor exits. "No movement."

"Drone is tracking the girl and the boy. They're making for the I-75 entrance northbound," the team leader said. "We're bringing in a second drone for the other two... satellite has them entering I-75 southbound. Overwatch, do you have eyes on Hubbard?"

"Negative. He's not moving. I do not have eyes on." He trained his scoped weapon on the roof of the warehouse. "Wait..."

Clyde Hubbard was standing on the roof with an arrow drawn. He let it fly.

It smashed through the sniper's scope, entered the man's eye, and exited through the back of his skull.

"Overwatch is down! Overwatch is down," voices called on the radio.

Clyde went back downstairs.

***

The ground floor windows shattered as flashbang grenades came through and skittered across the floor before exploding in a flash of blinding light and deafening sound.

The Hutchins mercenaries came through each entrance, a dozen men in three groups. They moved across the warehouse floor quickly, checking the corners and illuminating each dark space with their gun mounted flashlights.

"Clear," each group called out.

One group headed up the stairs. A minute later they called out clear from the upper level.

The old pink van sat in the middle of the warehouse floor. The team leader looked up at the painted cartoon ice cream cone decorated with the words "EAT ME". "Watch the van," he said. "I need a team to take the basement."

"Baker Team, on me," the squad leader said as four men headed for the stairs.

Then the van exploded.

The team leader was thrown backward twenty feet by the blast.

He slid on his back on the smooth concrete.

He lay on his back trying to process what had happened. He brought a bloodied hand up to touch the headset.

"Explosion," he said. "Explosion in the warehouse. Need evac. Help." He could taste blood in his mouth. He could hear screams all around him.

Screams that started out sharp and then went silent.
A shape moved on his periphery.
Clyde Hubbard stood over him. "That Price you're talking to?"
The team leader tried to raise his sidearm.
Clyde stepped on his hand.
His bones broke and he screamed.
It came out as a gurgle.
Clyde knelt beside him. "Body camera, huh?" He pulled it off the man's bulletproof vest and looked into the lens. "Hello, Mr. Price. You killed one of us and took another, so now I've killed, oh, eleven of yours. Twelve if you don't send an ambulance for your man here at my feet. Way I see it? We're even. The pack's broken and we're out of time without an alpha. Stop following us and we'll leave you alone. Send more troops and we'll kill them. Piss us off enough? We'll find you. Tell Karen I love her."

He tossed the body cam aside and headed for the basement.

***

Spears Mountain

"The team leader didn't make it," the security chief said in Price's office.

"Where's Clyde Hubbard now?" Price asked.

"Heading east on Interstate 64 toward Virginia."

Price laughed quietly. "We were worried about the lobos and lost our team to the guy with the bow and arrow. Ridiculous. What was the explosive used?"

"C-4, high grade and a lot of it."

"How did he survive the explosion?"

"They had excavated a hole into a storm sewer under the warehouse. He hid down there and detonated it remotely. Came up and finished off the team. Then he took his motorcycle out through the sewer. Exited in east Lexington."

Price leaned back in his chair. "Why kill them? Why take the risk? Why not just leave?"

The security chief shrugged. "Payback?"

Price looked away. "Status of the others?"

"Anna Sanders and Bobby Jennings are in a motel outside Indianapolis. Professor Collins and Olufsen are holed up in a barn near Sparta, Tennessee."

Price stared at the wall. "I want security topside doubled. Nobody goes on leave."

"Sir, the pack members are hundreds of miles away…"

"Something feels off."

***

Dodd lay on his bunk and stared up at the ceiling. Soon the lights in the mountain would come up, artificial dawn in this suffocating tomb.

He smiled.

Earlier, Dodd heard his guards muttering outside: Karen Arthur's pack was on the move.

They were coming to him.

***

Angelica tapped on the glass wall of Karen Arthur's cell.

Karen rolled over on the bed. "Let me guess? More blood?"

"Yes, please," Angelica said. She put her palm against the glass. "How did you sleep?"

Karen stared at Angelica's hand pressed to the glass wall. Written in magic marker on her palm were the words: PACK KNOWS WHERE YOU ARE. CLYDE SAYS HE LOVES YOU.

Karen fought back her smile. "It was actually a wonderful night."

Angelica smiled back.

***

The Shell Game

Shelbyville, Indiana

The Shelbyville Motel was a one level, seven room remnant of the 1950s on a frontage road southeast of Indianapolis. Anna stood to the side of the drawn curtains and peeked out.

231

The men in the SUV that had been parked all night on the other side of the frontage road left an hour before, but Anna wasn't taking any chances.

Bobby stretched under the sheet on the single queen-sized bed. "I slept. I can't believe I slept. What time is it?"

"5 AM," Anna said.

He rubbed his eyes and looked at her. "What... the hell?"

She fluffed her hair. "Like it?"

Her long auburn hair was gone.

She now had short, jet-black hair. "Punk, huh? Cut it myself."

He just stared at her with his mouth open.

"Say something," she laughed.

"I hate it. Don't ever do that again."

"Are you kidding me?"

"No. No, you are a redhead and that... no. Just no."

She climbed onto the bed and pushed him down. "You're a jackass."

He touched her hair. "How long will this take to grow out?"

"Uhh... as long as it takes me to transition to wolf and back, dummy."

He nodded. "Oh, yeah, duh. Thank goodness."

She sat up and pointed at the bathroom. "Go shave your head."

"Huh? Why?"

"Disguises. Go on. I left you a track suit and sneakers to wear."

Bobby got off the bed and walked toward the bathroom. "You want me to shave my head and wear a tracksuit? What's my disguise? Russian gangster?"

"Whatever works," she said. "Scoot, we need to get moving."

***

Bobby stepped out of the bathroom twenty minutes later with his head shaved and wearing a red tracksuit with white stripes. "This is going to ruin my image."

The room was empty.

"You don't have an image," Anna said from a distance.

"Where...?"

"Adjoining room. Come on over."

The door to the room next door was ajar.

Bobby stepped inside.

Anna laughed. "Oh, God, you do look sleazy."

She was standing in a red and purple sundress between two battered suitcases. "I packed our stuff. Ready?"

"Where did those cases come from? We can't carry those on the bikes."

"I'll explain in a minute. Right now, we need to get out of here. Close the adjoining room door."

He turned and closed both doors.

"When we get outside? Keep your face down. Don't look up. Paul says he isn't sure how good the satellites are, but he thinks the drones can count the zits on your face."

"Anna, what difference does all this make? Those guys parked across the street aren't going to be fooled by these disguises," Bobby said.

"Those guys are gone. Get the bags, follow me, and remember to keep your head down."

She opened the door and stepped into the parking lot.

Bobby stopped.

The bikes were gone.

"Where…?"

"Shh," Anna hissed. She took a set of keys out of her jeans pocket and pressed a button.

A blue Chevy pickup with dark tinted windows was parked in front of the room. Its doors unlocked.

"What? Where did this come from?"

"Bags in the crew cab. Bobby? Move."

He opened the back passenger door and stuffed the bags inside.

Anna climbed up into the driver's seat.

Bobby got in the passenger's side and closed his door.

"Windows are dark enough they can't see our faces. Relax," Anna said.

"Where are the bikes?!"

"Two people disguised as us took them while you were asleep. They were staying in the adjoining room. This is their truck. They're going to ride our bikes all the way to Wisconsin."

"More *friends*? How the hell many *friends* do we have?"

"More than a few," she said as she started the truck. "But not enough."

She backed out of the parking spot and pulled onto the frontage road. Then she took the Interstate 74 exit heading southeast.

"I want to know how we have these friends," Bobby said. "Who are they? And don't give me that bullshit about it being 'above my paygrade' that Clyde handed me."

Anna laughed. "Okay. I'll tell you everything. You deserve to know the truth."

***

Sparta, Tennessee

Swede stared through the gap in the barn door boards at the White County Sheriff's Department cruiser idling on the side of the road. "They're not cops. I know it. They're with Hutchins Security."

"Perhaps, there's nothing we can do about that now," Paul said. He was sitting on a hay bale. He looked at his watch.

5:45 AM.

If they were to stay on schedule, they had to leave this barn and leave it soon.

An hour earlier, Paul and Swede's doppelgangers had snuck into the barn and then taken their motorcycles out through the front while Paul and Swede hid behind the hay bales.

The SUV idling down the road had immediately followed the bikes with the disguised riders.

Paul and Swede were going to wait a half hour before sneaking out of the barn and heading into the woods. From there, they would transition to wolves and head north.

There was a Jeep Wrangler waiting for them in a Kroger parking lot with a full tank of gas.

Twenty-five minutes into their wait, the sheriff's department vehicle had pulled up in front of the barn.

Two deputies sat inside the cruiser drinking coffee.

"We should kill them and take the cruiser," Swede whispered.

"They may be innocent bystanders."

234

"Who just happened to pick this barn to sit out in front of while they drink coffee and eat doughnuts?" Swede's lips pulled back from his teeth.

"We'll give them a few more minutes. They'll move on," Paul said.

The deputies were too close to the barn to risk sneaking out.

"It'll be light in a few minutes," Swede said. "We'll lose the element of surprise."

"Just be patient. A few minutes longer," Paul said without looking up.

"Damn you!" Swede hissed. "I've been nothing but patient while you and Anna and Clyde have held back!"

"Keep your voice down, please?"

Swede started to transform. "Enough waiting!"

Paul was on him in a second, spinning him around and shoving him down onto the dirt floor. "Human form. Now."

"You've lost your mind, old man." Swede stood up and drew back his clawed fist.

Paul stared into his eyes. "You feel that? The anger? Maybe it's just a stage of your grief. Or maybe you're taking the first steps toward going rogue. I can't be sure which."

Swede's drawn fist began to tremble. Saliva started pouring out of his half-transformed muzzle.

"She was one of the kindest people I've ever known," Paul said. "How she could have come from where she did, seen the things she'd seen, and still be... innocent?" He shook his head. "And she loved you. I was jealous of you. God, how I envied you. I looked at you and I thought, 'That Swede, he's the luckiest man on earth.'"

"Stop," Swede groaned. "Just stop."

"What would she say to you, right now? What would Layla say if she saw you ready to strike out at me? Your best friend?"

Swede let his fist drop. "I... I'm sorry, Paul."

"No, Swede, you hold onto your anger. We're going to need it because they have Karen, and we have to get her back. To do that, we need you to be just as dangerous as you can possibly be. After that? After that you'll be able to let the anger go."

Swede nodded.

Outside, the police cruiser hit its lights and pulled back onto the road. The sound of the engine disappeared in the distance.

Paul smiled. "See. Just a couple of deputies enjoying their morning coffee. Let's get moving."

***

Spears Mountain

"For some reason, in the middle of the night, Karen Arthur's pack split up," Price said as he pointed to the big monitor in the control center. "Sanders and Jennings have just crossed into Illinois, Olufsen and Collins are in central Alabama." He shook his head. "Why would they do that? Why would they purposely be heading away from the alphas in Bedford, Virginia?"

"Maybe they don't want to draw attention to Ward Rickman's pack," Joseph said.

"Yes, but… they'll go rogue without an alpha," Price said.

"Where's Clyde Hubbard?" Angelica asked.

"Interstate 81 in Virginia heading east. Small town called Abingdon. This after he killed twelve of our men with an ice cream van loaded with C-4."

Angelica and Joseph looked at each other.

"Yes," Price said. "I think Mr. Hubbard has declared war on us. I'd have law enforcement take him out; however, I'd have to admit to a clandestine operation in Lexington. Also, he's uncomfortably close to Bedford and Ward Rickman."

"He could be headed here," the security chief said.

"How would he know about the mountain?" Price asked. "And, even if he does? Let him come. He's alone and he's only a man. If he crosses our security perimeter, we can kill him legally and nobody will bat an eye." Price tapped the screen. "No… the lobos are the threat. I just can't for the life of me figure out what they're doing. Make sure we have that British satellite at our disposal as well as drones."

"Yes, sir," the security chief said.

"Now, about Dodd," Price said. "Dr. Geffman, where are you with understanding how our blue-eyed blonde enchantress works?"

Angelica shrugged. "I've had two days, Price."

236

"Yes, and you and Dr. Marlow were burning the midnight oil last night. Oh, by the way, we repaired the camera you sabotaged in your lab. Childish. What have you learned?"

Angelica sighed. "It's not pheromones. It's brain waves. Karen Arthur's brain is broadcasting a calming signal to other lobos near her."

"But it doesn't work on Dodd?" Price asked.

"She claims it won't. We'll have to get Dodd in proximity to her to find out for sure," Angelica said.

"But not so close that Dodd can kill her," Joseph added.

"Point taken," Price said. "Do you think these 'control waves' could be duplicated artificially?"

"Sure," Angelica laughed. "All I need is a building full of MIT grads to isolate and decode the signals and a few billion dollars in funding to create the generator and we'll be all set."

"I realize you're being flippant, but I'll see what I can do," Price said. "What do you think, Dr. Marlow? How is Dodd's mental state?"

"Judging from the Smoky Mountains mission? He's paranoid, depressed, delusional, and sadistic. He's losing touch with what little humanity he possessed to begin with. I told you before: he's a ticking time bomb, Price."

"Agreed," Price said. "Chief, if we need to take Dodd down, is your team prepared?"

The man scratched his head. "I have sixteen men, all veterans, most Spec Ops. Each man is carrying ten silver bullets for their rifles, another ten for their sidearms, in addition to standard rounds."

"How many silver rounds in the armory?"

"1000 5.56 millimeter and 1000 nine-millimeter for the sidearms."

"Distribute them. If Dodd leaves the barracks? Tell them to shoot him on sight."

Angelica looked away.

"Something wrong, doctor?"

She shook her head. "Nothing. Just wondering why you're waiting?"

"He's a valuable military asset, doctor. I'm not going to flush that much money down the drain. I'm still hoping you and Dr. Marlow can find a way to get him back in line. I just want a contingency plan."

"Fair enough." She took the pistol out of her lab coat and set it on the conference table. She shoved it toward Price. "As a contingency, how about you give Joseph and I new guns… ones that work this time."

Price looked down at the pistol and smiled. "Didn't know you had firearms knowledge, doctor."

"We're scientists, Price," Angelica said. "You didn't think we'd check to see if the damned guns worked?"

***

After the meeting, Angelica and Joseph walked down the hall toward the lab.

"Nice speech," Joseph said. "Of course, we *didn't* actually check to see if the guns worked."

"I don't know shit about guns," Angelica said. "You don't strike me as being Wild Bill Hickock either."

"No, I put the gun he gave me in the closet in my quarters the first night. Haven't touched it since."

Angelica shook her head. "What the hell are Karen Arthur's lobos doing?" She whispered.

"I don't know," Joseph said. "There's no way they've abandoned her. We need to be ready."

"How do you prepare for an invasion of werewolves?"

He smiled at her and winked. "By being smart enough to tell them who the good guys are in this mountain in the message you sent. Which you were."

"Oh, sure, they're going to walk up to us, change back into people, and say, 'Dr. Geffman, I presume?'" She laughed. "They'll rip us to shreds and ask questions later, Marlow. If we make it out of this? It'll be a miracle."

***

Edward Price stood in the armory and stared at the orderly rows of rifles, pistols, and the stacked boxes of ammunition.

The Security Chief stood behind him. "When we checked the room after Kennith Anderson's disappearance? We only checked that everything was in place. Total number of firearms, total boxes of ammunition. We didn't actually open the boxes."

Price shook his head. "Every silver bullet is gone?"

"Yes, sir, both calibers. He put regular ammunition in the boxes to make them feel heavy enough. But truth be told, sir? None of my men even picked the boxes up."

"So, we have a little over 160 rounds of rifle ammunition and 160 rounds of pistol ammunition?"

"Yes, sir. Still more than enough to handle Dodd."

Price laughed. "Assuming Dodd stands still long enough for you to shoot him. Assuming your men can shoot straight. Assuming they manage to hit him in a vital organ."

"Yes, sir."

"How long to get more silver ammunition?"

"At least a week, sir."

"I'll have to hand it to Dodd. He thought this through."

The Security Chief looked at him. "You think this was Dodd?"

"Well, either that or Anderson pawned the silver bullets when he went AWOL. What's your guess?" Price shook his head. "Dodd leveled the playing field. If we try to kill him? We'll do so with limited ammunition. No, we can now assume he killed Anderson and somehow disposed of the body… he probably ate it. Here's a question for you: how did Dodd get up to this level and kill Kennith Anderson without being caught on a single security camera?"

"I'm not sure, sir," the chief said.

"Find out. Losing that ammunition not only puts us at a disadvantage for Dodd. It also puts us at a disadvantage against Karen Arthur's pack. Make sure the surveillance teams stay on them." He turned to leave. "Oh, one more thing: the team following Clyde Hubbard? I've changed my mind. Take him down. Too many moving pieces on this board. It's time to start whittling them down."

***

Clyde's Run

Tony Bowman

Interstate 81 near Buchanan, Virginia

The black SUV stayed as far behind Clyde Hubbard as it dared. The small, beat-up motorcycle was deceptively fast and maneuverable as Hubbard weaved it in and out of the traffic ahead.

Price had told the team in the SUV to expect Hubbard to turn toward Bedford County, but he had passed each turn off I81 without slowing.

"Yes, sir, we're on it," the team leader said into his headset. "Price wants him dead."

"Finally," the driver said.

"Alright," the leader said. "He's got to be close to empty. When he stops for gas, we take…"

Ahead of them, Clyde Hubbard swung his bike onto the shoulder, up an embankment, and jumped a small chain link fence at the top.

"Jesus! Follow him!" The team leader yelled.

"But the fence!"

"Go!"

***

Clyde landed the bike on the surface street on the other side of the fence.

He looked over his shoulder and smiled as the big SUV crashed through the chain link fence in a cloud of dust and bits of metal.

Let's see if you boys can drive, Clyde thought as he gunned the throttle and fishtailed. He pulled onto Parkway Drive going southeast.

***

"Where does this road go?" The team leader asked as the driver did his best to stay on the tail of the old motorcycle.

One of the men in the back was looking at his phone. "It links up with the Blue Ridge Parkway."

"He's going to try to lose us offroad," the driver said.

"Stay on him."

One of the men in the back spoke. "I've lost the drone feed."

"What?!"

***

240

Spears Mountain

"What happened to my damned drones?" Price asked as he watched the blank monitor screen in the control room.

The technician looked up from his console. "They've been recalled, sir."

"Recalled by whom?!"

"CIA Director Hansen, sir. He was just pulled into a meeting at the Capitol Building. Congress wants to know why he's operating drones over American soil?"

"How did they...?"

"The New York Post, sir," the technician said and pointed at the screen.

The monitor changed to show the New York Post website and the headline: 'CIA FLYING DRONES OVER HEARTLAND, WHY?'

"The story went live a half hour ago. Congress called an emergency session of the Intelligence Committee and the director just pulled our drones."

Price began to laugh. "They've blinded us. Stay in communication with the ground teams. When will the British satellite be in position."

"Twelve minutes, sir."

***

Bearwallow Gap
Entrance to the Blue Ridge Parkway

Clyde roared through the stop sign at Bearwallow Gap and turned east onto the parkway.

A few seconds later, the SUV skidded sideways past the stop sign and kicked up gravel on the opposite shoulder as they gave chase.

In spite of it all, Clyde Hubbard was having fun. He leaned forward on the bike as he rocketed along the two-lane road bordered by thick green foliage and trees.

He leaned to the side and passed a pickup, never letting off the throttle.

He looked in the rearview just long enough to see the pickup pull onto the shoulder to let the SUV pass.

Clyde straightened the next three curves.

He had spent two days working on Bobby's bike, modifying the engine, the suspension. He had increased the horsepower but at a cost: fuel consumption.

He was running on fumes.

In a few minutes, he would have to stand and fight.

He said a prayer the gas would stretch just a little farther.

***

The team leader shook his head. "He should have gone off road? What is he doing?" If Hubbard turned off onto one of the trails, there would be no way they could follow. He had to know that.

"Major intersection coming up in a mile," one of the men in the back said. "Peaks of Otter. "

"How many ways to go at the intersection?"

"Umm, he can continue on the parkway or turn right onto Peaks Road."

The team leader turned his head. "Where does Peaks Road go?"

The man looked at his phone. Then he looked up. "Bedford, Virginia."

"No… no, no, no," the team leader said and punched the dash. "Catch him. Run him off the road."

The driver looked at him. "Are you nuts? I can barely keep up with that bike."

***

Clyde topped a rise and saw the Peaks of Otter Visitor Center. He smiled. What he was waiting for was just on the other side of the park entrance.

***

Three police cruisers marked Bedford County Sheriff's Department were blocking the road to Bedford.

The team leader watched as Clyde Hubbard slipped between two of the cruisers and slid to a stop on the road.

Behind the sheriff's department cars was a line of Virginia State Police cruisers.

"Stop. Stop!" The team leader yelled. "Turn around and get us out of here."

The SUV slid to a stop.

Clyde Hubbard notched an arrow and drew his compound bow.

The arrow passed between the Bedford cruisers and struck the front of the SUV.

The radiator exploded in a cloud of steam.

Green trucks roared up behind the SUV marked PARK POLICE.

A tall man in a tan uniform approached the SUV, his hand on the grip of his holstered pistol.

Two women wearing matching uniforms, one young, the other older followed him carrying shotguns.

The man was wearing mirrored sunglasses. He turned his head to the side and looked at the SUVs tires. He motioned for the driver to lower his window.

The motor whined as the glass slid down.

"Just over the county line," the man said. "Welcome to Bedford County. I'm Sheriff Ward Rickman. Those are my deputies, Rickman and Gooch behind me. You're under arrest."

"On what charge?" The team leader asked.

"Reckless driving, speeding… I'll make a list."

"You're interfering with a government operation…"

"Yeah, that's what the other five fellows said when I arrested them in town this morning. I expect they're friends of yours. Thing is? Nobody in the government knows anything about this 'operation'. Out of the car, slow."

The men in the back of the SUV looked at the team leader.

Ward Rickman smiled. "Oh, please, try something." He took off his glasses, revealing his blue eyes. His mouth filled with fangs. "It'll be a short fight."

The men started getting out of the SUV.

They left their weapons on the seats.

Ward turned around.

Clyde Hubbard was already gone.

***

Spears Mountain

Dr. Joseph Marlow walked into Paula's cell block. "Hi."
She was sitting on her bed. "You're late."
He smiled. "Oh, did you miss me?"
She laughed and shook her head. "The only bright spot of my day is routine. You break the routine and what do I have? Chaos, Marlow."
"I'm sorry, there was a lot going on this morning. Let's get started. On a scale of one to ten? How badly do you want to kill me?"
Paula laughed out loud. "Today? Umm, a four. No, five."
"Hmm, marked improvement." He sat down on a folding chair near the glass. "In all seriousness, how do you feel?"
She shrugged. "Fine. Calm. I feel calm."
"Why do you think that is?"
"Oh, it's all you, doc. You're a miracle worker," she laughed.
"Really? Because I think it's Karen Arthur that's made a difference," Joseph said.
She nodded. "She says she's going to kill me." Paula chuckled. "Hard to believe that could make me feel peaceful but... here we are."
"I think there's more to it than that. Her being here is fixing you."
Paula shook her head. "Come on, Marlow."
"I've seen the brain scans. You're getting better, Paula."
She smiled at him. "I haven't thanked you. I should have, Joseph. You've been kind to me. I'm at peace with what is coming."
"I'm not," Joseph said. "You're getting better. It's not wishful thinking on my part. Can't you feel it?"
"I'm just happy it's almost over."
Joseph put his palm on the glass.
Words were written on his hand in magic marker 'KAREN'S PACK COMING. BE READY.'
Paula nodded. "Don't open the door, Joseph. Let Karen do it. I don't want you to get hurt."

***

Nine Fingers: The Good Wolves

Stantonbury, England

Rajesh Kavendi popped a biscuit into his mouth and chewed. Then he poured the tea into his paper cup and carried it carefully through the sterile hallway to room 65 West of Hempstead House.

Officially, Hempstead House was a records storage facility for MI-5.

Unofficially, Hempstead House was a satellite surveillance control facility belonging to MI-6.

Rajesh pushed open the door to room 65 West.

The room was dark with two control consoles and a massive display on the far wall.

It showed a satellite view of the eastern half of the United States.

"Hello, Mary," Rajesh said as he sat down at the console.

"Evening, Raj," Mary said.

"How's our girl this evening?"

"She's just coming up on station. Washington is following a terrorist suspect in central Virginia. Locking onto him now."

"Sounds like fun." He put on his headset.

"Switching control to your console… now," Mary said.

"I have Cassandra," Rajesh said.

Cassandra was a two billion Pound Sterling, state of the art surveillance satellite and Rajesh was one of her 'handlers'.

Cassandra's camera was focused on a man riding a motorcycle along a four-lane highway.

Rajesh moved a joystick on his console and centered the man on the motorcycle on screen. "Subject heading east on route 460 approaching Lynchburg Virginia Regional Airport."

He re-adjusted the image using the joystick. It was sliding off the screen. "Cassandra's a bit dodgy today."

"Is she?" Mary asked.

"Camera keeps moving off center."

She sat back down at her console. "No, it isn't. Camera is tracking… wait, the camera can't keep up. Satellite attitude is changing."

Rajesh brought up another screen. "Bloody… attitude correction jets are firing! Who's doing that?"

245

Seven-hundred-fifty miles above Virginia, jets of compressed gas were firing, rolling the satellite over.

"I can't stop the roll!" Mary said.

The motorcycle rider's image slid off the top of the screen. A few seconds later, Cassandra's camera was pointed into space.

"Wait, wait," Rajesh said. "Roll has stopped."

Cassandra was inverted relative to the ground.

"Okay," Mary said. "Let's see if we can re-orient… Oh, God… The mains just came online!"

"Shut them down!" Rajesh said.

"I… I can't…"

Cassandra's main engine, used only to correct her orbit, suddenly cut on.

The big satellite de-orbited, driven by its engine lower and lower until, hitting the atmosphere, it began to burn.

***

Spears Mountain

"We've been sabotaged," Edward Price said into his cellphone. He had taken the elevator to the top of the mountain and walked across the parking lot.

"They're a little more capable than you thought," Peter Hutchins said. "The New York Post was a nice move. We'll quieten that. We always do."

"I'm not concerned about the Post," Price said. "I'm concerned about them having the ability to take down a satellite. Someone's helping them and I don't mean that hick Sheriff. Someone connected is watching over them."

"We have enemies in the US Government. We always have. I'll dig around."

"I want evac. Me along with Dr. Geffman and Karen Arthur. I'll also need all Geffman's research material secured."

Hutchins laughed. "Calm down, Edward. You're overreacting. From all appearances, you have a single man on a motorcycle carrying a bow and arrow heading your way. Not an army."

"Peter, I'm blind. I'm hunkering in a bunker, and I have zero idea of what may or may not be coming for me. Dodd has completely lost his mind and is apparently eating my staff. I need to evac and salvage as much of this as possible…"

"Your teams are still following the other lobos, correct?"

"Yes."

"And they're moving away from your location?"

"Yes, but…"

"Then let my mercs do their job, Edward. You have your saferoom if things go wrong. Have the mercenaries kill Dodd and then kill Hubbard when he gets there. I'll try to find out who Hubbard's benefactor is, and we'll handle them as well," Hutchins said. "Now, for God's sake, Edward, stop panicking."

Hutchins hung up.

Price stared at the phone. "Prick," he said. "I'm going to die in a damned hole in the ground."

***

Lion's Den

Fifteen minutes later, the Security Chief stood with eight of his men outside the hallway to the barracks.

"Dead silent from this point on," the chief said. "Safeties off. Keep your fingers on your triggers. Dodd is fast. You hesitate? You're dead. Aim for center mass but the only way the silver bullets will kill him fast is the heart or the brain. When you have a shot? You take it. Understood?"

"Yes, sir," they replied.

"Move out," the chief said.

They opened the hallway door.

The guard on that end of the hallway joined them.

When they reached the barracks door, the chief raised his fist and held it vertical, signaling them to stop.

He pointed to the man behind him and pointed to the door.

The man nodded and stood beside the doorknob.

The chief held up three fingers.

He lowered one finger.

Then another.

Then the last.

The man by the door opened it and shoved it inward.

The men poured into the room guns aimed forward.

The chief looked inside.

Dodd was in his bunk, a sheet pulled around him.

The men opened fire.

Dodd's body danced under the sheet as bullets punched into him.

Blood sprayed against the far wall.

"Cease fire!" The chief yelled.

He stepped into the room. "Stay sharp," he said.

He walked over to the bed.

"Christ, what's that smell?" One of the men said.

The chief knew what the smell was. He ripped back the sheet.

Kenny Anderson's head was lying on Dodd's pillow.

The rest of him, what little was left, was wrapped in the sheet.

The chief took a step back. "Latrine. He has to be in the latrine."

The door to the washroom was partly open at the back of the room.

"We're going to open that door," the chief said. "I want two men high, two low. Then we go in one at a time. Spread out when you're through the door. Go."

This time they opened the door slowly. Two men knelt to either side pointing their weapons at the room beyond while two men stood above them and aimed high.

The other men entered the room slowly.

It was empty.

"Clear," one of the men inside said.

"Dear God," the chief whispered.

There was a small steel door at the far end of the latrine standing half open. It had been painted the same color as the wall.

Above the door, written in blood, were the words: ABANDON ALL HOPE, YE WHO ENTER HERE.

***

"There are, uh, these dead spaces between the metal walls of the living spaces and the excavated rock of the mountain itself," the

Security Chief said. "He's evidently been using these to move about unseen. It's how he ambushed Kenny Anderson."

Price stood in the latrine and looked at the words above the access door. "You know the words?"

"Dante, sir, the Divine Comedy. The inscription above the gates to hell."

"Excellent. Good to find a mercenary with a classical education. Ironic given your stupidity."

"You're right, sir. We missed it. I take full responsibility."

Price ignored the comment. "How far do these passages lead?"

"Throughout the entire base, sir."

"How many access doors like this one?"

"Forty-three, sir."

Price nodded. "Too many to cover with the men you have. How much silver ammunition did you waste on Anderson's corpse?"

"Seventy-two rounds of 5.56… none of the nine-millimeter."

"Almost half the rifle rounds gone," Price said.

"Sir, I can take men into the passages and try to corner him."

Price laughed. "As much as I would enjoy seeing you dead at this point? I need you to keep me alive, Chief. No, he wants us to follow him in. He'll rip your men to shreds."

"In that case, sir? We should evacuate. Get you and the science team out of the mountain and to a safe location."

"Oh, there's a thought. Wish I had come up with that one," Price chuckled. "Unfortunately, I've more or less been told to go down with the ship. And, if I'm going down? So are you."

"Then what are your orders, sir?"

"Tell your men topside to watch their backs as well as their fronts. Anybody takes that elevator up without my authorization? Tell them to shoot to kill. Oddly enough, given the layout, the cell blocks, my quarters, and the control room are the most secure areas - the cell blocks have reinforced walls and the other areas don't border these dead zones. Have your men form a perimeter around that. And, for pity's sake, don't waste any more of our ammunition."

***

Karen paced back and forth in her cell.

Not knowing what was going on was driving her insane.

Other than the occasional clandestine updates from Angelica or Joseph, she was left to only imagine what was happening outside her cell.

And her imagination was not comforting.

The pack was coming.

She knew Clyde would not involve Ward if he could possibly avoid it.

Most likely, the only ones coming would be the pack themselves. Price's people were watching them, would kill them if possible.

"Oh, Clyde, I'm not worth this," she whispered.

If even one of them died? She would never forgive herself.

"I don't feel it," a voice said.

Karen turned to her left, the direction of the voice.

"Who's there?"

"You know who I am." It was a man's voice.

Dodd's voice.

"Where are you?"

"In the walls. Like a rat. Scratch, scratch, scurry."

She walked to the left wall of the cell.

"I'd come in there and eat you up," Dodd said. "But they put silver in the wall. It burns."

"I know. I tested it as well," Karen said.

"Are you the type that snivels and whines when they die? The stripper, she kind of whimpered at the end. Women are weak. Useful for breeding but, beyond that? Too weak. You disgust me."

"Weak, huh? You try cramps just once in your life, asshole."

"No, not physical... a weakness of will. Of drive. Determination."

Karen rolled her eyes. "Not only a psychotic asshole, also a chauvinistic psychotic asshole."

He laughed. "Your pack are *ronin* now."

"What?"

"Ronin... it's a Japanese word. It means samurai without a master. Price thinks that will make them less dangerous. It actually makes them more formidable, though. You and I both know that, don't we?"

"Do you have a point, Dodd? Or are you just lonely and want another wolf to talk to?"

"Your pack is coming. I gave Geffman the means to contact them."

Karen frowned. "Why would you do that, Dodd?"

"I want them here. I'm going to hunt them down one at a time and cull them. None of you are strong enough to be like me."

Karen laughed. "You think you're strong? You're not strong, Dodd. You're a coward. You kill the defenseless. Swede almost killed you in Tennessee, and, oh, Mr. Dodd, he didn't know you then. He does now. There won't be anything left of you but a greasy spot when he's through."

"If he does? If he can?" Dodd whispered. "Then I deserve it. It would mean I'm too weak."

"You don't have an ounce of remorse for what you've done, do you? All the pain and suffering you've caused?"

"Should I?"

Karen smiled and ran her claw down the wall, cutting a groove. "What was it Phoebe Walker whispered to you, Dodd? In the helicopter? Could you hear it when she said, '*Oh, you will beg for hell, William Dodd. You will beg for it.*'?"

Karen heard Dodd shuffle backward behind the wall. She laughed. "Oh, yes, you heard her. You heard poor, insane Phoebe Walker whispering sweet nothings, didn't you? Maybe you thought it was your imagination? It wasn't, Dodd. It was real. It's all real and it's coming for you."

"Shut up," Dodd whispered.

"They're all there in the dark with you right now, Dodd. All the people you killed and all the werewolves who are trying to atone. I think they get hungry and I think they're going to eat your soul when you die. You tell me my pack is coming? If they are, Dodd? You're going to die soon. And then you'll belong to the ghosts." Karen laughed. "I almost pity you, Dodd. *Almost.*"

She could hear him breathing but he said nothing.

"What's wrong, Dodd? Nothing to say?"

She heard footsteps as he walked away.

Then Karen slid down to sit with her back to the wall.

She prayed everything she had just told Dodd was true.

And she prayed her pack would survive.

***

The Battle of Spears Mountain

Summit of Pruetts Mountain
Less than one mile west of Spears Mountain

Anna and Bobby stood in the trees on top of the small mountain and looked toward Spears Mountain in the east.

There was a structure on the summit of Spears. It looked like a Quonset hut leading into the mountain peak.

"It looks small," Bobby said.

"Maybe. Or, maybe the mountain's hollow and that's just the entrance."

Bobby looked at his watch. "3:30… they're late."

"They'll be here," Anna said.

They had left the pickup on the side of the road a mile away.

Anna left the keys hidden beneath her seat.

Bobby asked her why and she told him, '*If we die? Our friends will want their truck back.*'

Paul and Swede stepped out of the trees behind Bobby and Anna.

"Thank God," Anna said. She ran to Paul and hugged him. "You're late."

"Well, traffic, you know?"

She went to Swede and hugged him. "Are you okay?"

"I'm okay," he whispered. "I'm sorry I've been hard to live with."

"You? Please," Anna said and kissed his cheek.

"3:45," Bobby said.

"Did you two see Clyde?" Anna asked.

"No, did you?" Paul asked.

She shook her head and turned toward Spears Mountain. "Didn't expect we would."

Bobby looked at his feet. "Shouldn't have destroyed our phones. We could've at least called him. Coordinated."

"No, too risky," Paul said. "All we can do now is follow the plan."

252

"Exactly. We move on the mountain at 4:15," Anna said.

"What if Clyde didn't make it?" Bobby asked.

"He made it. We have to believe that and keep on believing it," Anna said.

***

East Side of Spears Mountain

The Spears family sold their mountain to the government in the 1980s, but their cattle farm still stood on the east side.

A narrow dirt path between the farm and mountain led to the main road. The path was bordered on the right by a tall fence marked with 'High Voltage' and 'U.S. Government Property' and on the left by a barbed wire livestock fence.

Beyond the barbed wire, black cattle grazed in the tall grass. They looked up at the small motorcycle with only passing interest as they gnawed grass and flicked away flies with their tails.

Clyde took off his helmet and flung it to his left as he rode up the dirt track.

He kept his eyes on the electrified fence, looking for a gap that he might use.

Beyond the fence, narrow switchback paths ran up this, the steeper side, of Spears Mountain.

The paths were overgrown in places looking like they hadn't been traversed in decades.

He almost missed seeing the old man in overalls standing in the cattle pasture.

The man had a crowbar in his hands, pulling the barbed wire tight and then bracing the bar with his hip as he tacked it in place with his hammer.

Clyde stopped the bike and dropped the kickstand. "Howdy."

"Howdy," the old man said. He pulled a blue bandanna out of his overalls pocket and mopped the sweat off his brow.

"Those cattle look fat and slick," Clyde said.

The old man laughed. "You know your cattle?"

"There was a time," Clyde said. "Black Angus, aren't they?"

253

"They are." The old man pulled another strand of barbed wire tight with the crowbar.

"Can I give you a hand?"

"I'd be obliged."

Clyde walked over and took hold of the crowbar. He held the wire in place as the old man hammered the staple into the locust post.

"You Mr. Spears?"

"Donald Spears. And you are?"

"Clyde Hubbard, sir." Clyde hooked the next strand of barbed wire down with the crowbar and pulled it tight.

"What brings you out here, Mr. Hubbard?"

"Well, sir, that mountain is where I'm headed."

Mr. Spears nodded. "You government?" He hammered in the staple and then began unrolling the spool of barbed wire toward the next post.

"No, sir, I'm not with the government."

Spears nodded. "Terrorist? Communist?"

Clyde laughed. "No, sir, not hardly."

Spears scratched at the day's growth of beard stubble on his chin. "Main entrance is about a mile around to the other side."

"Rather not go in that way."

"I gathered," Spears said.

"Do those switchbacks go all the way to the top?"

"They did," Spears said. "Cattle paths made over about a hundred years before I sold the mountain to the Army. They cut the top clean off the mountain and then built it back up. So, those switchbacks probably go almost all the way to the top."

Clyde nodded. "That fence says it's electric."

"Back when Ronald Reagan was in charge, it was. Now, though?" The old man shook his head. "That bunch up there now, they don't maintain anything. 'Course a fellow might want to test it before he takes a hold of it."

Clyde smiled. "Sounds prudent."

"Those people up there now? They aren't Army. I was Army and they are definitely not. They're sloppy. People in town say they're beat dog mean, too."

"Say they're sloppy?"

Spears nodded. "Yep. For instance, about a hundred yards down the path here? There's a gap in the fence. Had a calf get out and go right onto their property. I had to go halfway up the mountain to bring it down." Spears laughed. "You know, it was broad daylight, and they didn't even know I was there. And, when I told one of 'em when I saw them in town about the gap? They didn't do a damned thing about it."

Clyde looked at the old man and smiled. "Thank you, Mr. Spears."

"Thank you for helping with the crowbar. You be careful on that motorcycle now."

***

One hundred yards up the path, one section of the government fence was leaning forward at almost a forty-five-degree angle.

Clyde checked his watch: 4:00 PM. He opened the throttle and rode the bike through the gap in the fence. The first switchback, a flat diagonal scar of red clay in the green mountainside, began five feet up the slope and took him fifty feet up the side of the mountain.

***

Last Night

"Wait near Spears Mountain until 4:15 tomorrow afternoon," Clyde said. "Join up with Swede and Paul. At 4:15, you come up that mountain and you kill everything you meet."

Anna nodded. "We will. Where will you be?"

"Tomorrow morning, after you leave the warehouse? I'm going to get their attention. And I'm going to keep their attention all day. I'm going to keep them off you."

"It's too dangerous," Anna said. "Let me do it..."

"No. It has to be me. I need you leading that assault up the west side. At 4:00? I'm going up the east side. God willing? By the time you reach the top? I'll already be there..."

***

Clyde
4:03 PM

255

The new shocks he put on the old bike were working. He turned it into a trail bike and it was eating up the mountainside.

The cattle paths were overgrown and treacherous, but he steered around the exposed tree roots and dodged rocks as he climbed the mountain.

***

Last Night

"What if something goes wrong? What if you don't make it?" Anna asked.

Clyde shook his head. "Then you do it without me."

Anna looked away. "We try not to kill humans."

"I know but, Anna? They brought this war to us. Now it's up to us to finish it. I believe in this idea that Karen has created, all of you? I believe it's important. I believe the world needs Die Gute Wolf. I think it's something worth fighting for. Worth dying for…"

***

Clyde
4:08 PM

The switchbacks ended abruptly fifty feet from the top. Where before there had been narrow switchbacks, now there was only steep, grass covered slope.

***

Two-armed Hutchins Security men stood guard in the parking lot outside the Quonset Hut that led into the mountain.

They stepped out when they heard the sound of a motorcycle somewhere in the distance.

One of the guards inspected his rifle.

He had two magazines, both with thirty rounds. The one already loaded into the M-4 rifle was standard 5.56 Millimeter ammunition.

The magazine in his tactical vest had the same capacity, but the first ten rounds were silver.

The chief had been clear: if the elevator started up from below without him calling on the radio? They were to switch magazines and shoot whoever (or whatever) got off the elevator with silver rounds.

"They say Dodd is sneaking around down there," the other guard said as he walked up.

"Yeah, I've never been so glad to be on topside sentry duty."

"Tell me about it."

Someone whistled.

The guards spun around.

"Up here," a man's voice said.

They looked up.

A man wearing a motorcycle vest was standing on top of the Quonset Hut.

He threw an old motorcycle at them.

It was 4:15 PM.

***

"Let's go!" Anna yelled.

Anna, Bobby, Swede, and Paul ran down the slope of Pruetts Mountain.

They shifted as they ran, releasing their wolves, their clothes falling away in shreds.

They reached the empty road that wound between the two mountains and jumped over both lanes.

There was a gate ahead. It was unmanned.

On both sides of the gate, a high fence ran far away into the brush. A sign said 'U.S. Government Property. No Trespassing. Use of Deadly Force Authorized.'.

Another sign said 'High Voltage'.

They leaped over the fence, clearing it by fifteen feet.

They landed on the other side, still running as they headed up the slope at nearly thirty-five miles per hour.

Anna howled when she heard gunfire coming from the mountaintop.

***

257

One of the guards in the parking lot was a bloody pulp beneath the ruined motorcycle.

The other raised his M-4 and fired.

On full auto, the gun fired a steady stream of bullets at Clyde Hubbard.

He felt the first impact that went deep into his right lung.

A second shattered the left side of his jaw and tore out his inner ear.

The third went into his abdomen and severed his spine.

Clyde fell back.

***

Last Night

"They'll be armed, Clyde. You can't go in first," Anna said in the warehouse basement.

"I've got an idea of how to get the drop on them. I've been looking at the map. I can go up the east side of the mountain."

"They'll still have guns, Clyde!" Anna hissed.

"Yeah, that's the beauty of it, honey. They'll be armed." He held out his arm. "And, they'll be expecting a man."

Anna looked at his arm. "Oh, Clyde. I don't know…"

"I do."

***

Clyde
4:17 PM

The first time had hurt, lying there on the warehouse floor with the Die Gute Wolf virus coursing through his body. The bullets had been a love tap in comparison.

But, after the first time your hips break and fold in on themselves? It's a piece of cake.

Clyde Hubbard stood up in werewolf form and growled at the frightened man below.

He saw the look of fear in the man's eye, the scent of urine leaking down the man's thigh.

That sudden look of recognition when the man realized: he had brought lead bullets to a werewolf fight.

The guard started fumbling in his vest pocket.

Clyde jumped off the Quonset Hut and landed in front of him.

He grabbed the man by the throat and lifted him into the air.

Then he ripped the gun out of the guard's hand and caved his skull in with it.

***

Clyde smiled, his lips pulling back from his fangs as Anna and the others arrived.

He tried to transition just his head back to human form, instead he transformed fully.

He covered his groin with his hands. "I can't get the hang of this."

Anna transitioned from the waist up and laughed. "You'll get it. It just takes time."

"My eyes are up here," Clyde said.

"Quite a mess you made," Paul said as he transitioned halfway as well.

"Well, first werewolf kill," Clyde said.

"I'm impressed," Swede said. "Not by your equipment but by the motorcycle kill. Never killed anybody with a bike before."

Clyde laughed.

"My poor bike," Bobby said.

"Sorry," Clyde said.

Bobby shrugged. "Naah, it was a piece of shit."

Clyde turned toward the Quonset Hut. "Only camera is pointed down at an angle. I don't think they saw me kill the guards."

"It won't take them long to figure out something's wrong," Anna said. "Paul, that hut doesn't look big enough to house werewolves and personnel."

"No. I imagine the base is beneath us."

"Agreed," Clyde said. "A local told me they definitely excavated the top of the mountain… you don't need to do that to build a Quonset Hut."

Anna picked up the guard with the caved in skull. "Black hair?"

"Yeah," Clyde said. "Kind of black and red now."

"Swede, put on the dead guy's uniform," Anna said. "We need a look inside the Quonset Hut. Hopefully the camera isn't good enough to see the brain matter." She tossed the body to Swede.

Swede caught it and the head fell off. "Yuck, why do I always get the nasty jobs?"

***

Inside Spears Mountain

The Security Chief looked at the camera feed from the surface. "What's Mitchell doing?"

One of the guards entered the Quonset Hut and disappeared from view.

"Probably hitting the latrine," the technician said.

"There's nobody else topside, why doesn't he just piss in the bushes?"

"Maybe he's dropping a deuce?"

***

There was an elevator door at the back of the Quonset Hut and nothing else other than a second security camera.

Swede knelt off to the side and looked at the door.

Then he stood up and, keeping his head down, walked back out into the daylight.

He stepped away from the door camera.

"There's an elevator with some kind of fingerprint scanner on it," Swede said.

"Damn," Clyde said.

Bobby looked at the naked guard's corpse. "Take his thumb?"

Anna shook her head. "Doesn't matter. They'll see us all getting on the elevator."

"They most likely have a way of stopping the elevator from their side," Paul said. "We might be able to get one of us, namely Swede, onto it."

Clyde shook his head. "I'm betting they're on lockdown. They probably won't even let the guard in."

"Then what the hell do we do?" Swede asked.

260

Anna smiled. "Let's start the party."

Swede nodded. "Now you're talking."

***

"Any word on getting our drones back?" The Security Chief asked.

The technician shook his head. "Langley says no dice."

The chief looked up at the security monitor.

A werewolf with red fur was staring into the camera inside the Quonset Hut. The creature raised its right hand and extended its middle claw.

"Oh, my God," the chief said.

Anna Sanders was flipping them off.

Then the camera went black.

***

As the pieces of the camera fell on the hut floor, Anna looked at Swede and growled. She motioned toward the elevator doors.

Swede raised his arms and turned toward the elevator.

He brought down his claws and sliced through the doors.

Sparks cascaded down and metal fell away in ribbons.

The concrete elevator shaft was exposed.

Anna leaned over the edge and peered down.

She wasn't expecting what she saw.

The elevator shaft was a concrete channel thousands of feet long, open on the back.

The view through the back of the tower was of a vast cavern, brightly lit with layer upon layer of concrete terraces projecting out from the stone walls. Plants grew in massive hanging gardens on the edge of each terrace.

The terraces grew larger and larger the deeper you looked.

At the very bottom was a glass enclosed courtyard. She could see security guards running there.

The elevator was at the bottom of the shaft and two large counterweights hung on either side of the shaft near the top.

Clyde and Swede ran past her and jumped into the shaft, Clyde clinging to the left wall and Swede clinging to the right, their claws digging into the concrete as they descended.

"*So much for making a plan,*" Anna thought.

Bobby looked at her and cocked his wolf's head to the side.

Anna snarled and leaped into the shaft above Swede.

Bobby followed.

She looked up to see Paul peering over the edge.

"*Come on, Professor,*" Anna thought. "*Everybody else is making bad decisions.*"

Paul gingerly climbed out and began descending along the back wall of the elevator.

***

Price peered up through the glass of the central courtyard. He could see a pinpoint of light at the top where they had ripped open the elevator doors. "They're coming down the elevator shaft," Price said. "Tell your best shots to take up positions where they have line of sight on the shaft. Try to pick them off when they get in range."

"Yes, sir," the Security Chief said. He was staring up at the terraces. "Mr. Price? Seven levels up on the far wall." He pointed over Price's head.

Dodd was there, standing naked on one of the hanging gardens, looking toward the elevator shaft.

"Wonderful," Price said. "You ever watch a Godzilla movie, Chief?"

"Sir?"

"Not the original. One of the corny ones from back in the seventies. The ones where Godzilla is fighting a gang of other monsters? That's what this is like. Fun movies but the people on the ground end up getting crushed. We're on the ground, Chief."

"Yes, sir."

***

Angelica knocked on Joseph Marlow's door. "They're in the complex!"

Joseph opened his door. "The pack is here?"

262

"Yes, all hell's broken loose. I've closed down my lab."

"What do you mean?" Joseph asked.

Angelica just laughed. She dug in her lab coat pocket and pulled out a USB drive. "It's all on here. We need to get Karen Arthur."

"Right, let's go let them out," Joseph said.

"*Them?* What do you mean *them?*" Angelica whispered.

"You get Karen Arthur and I'll get... Paula."

"No!" She shoved him back into his room. Then she followed him in and closed his door behind her. "Joseph, no!"

"We're wasting time, Angelica."

"Are you suicidal?"

"No, I'm not. Paula is calm and rational..."

"She's playing you! Are you really that dense?"

Joseph shook his head. "She isn't playing me. I know she isn't."

"Think with the head that has a brain, Marlow!"

"What's the combination to open her door?" Joseph asked.

"I won't tell you."

"She won't hurt me, Angelica."

"We'll go get Karen Arthur and let her decide."

Joseph sighed. "Okay, fine. You go get Karen and I'll wait for you in Paula's cell block."

"Why? Why are you going there?"

"To prepare her. To let her know you're bringing Karen to her. What's the problem? I don't know the code to open the door."

"Fine. Just please? Don't do anything stupid."

***

The pack was three quarters of the way down the shaft when everything went sideways.

Below Anna, Swede howled.

Then he climbed sideways toward the open side of the shaft, his claws driving into the concrete as he crossed.

Looking out, she saw why.

Dodd was standing on a terrace below their level on the opposite side of the cavern.

He was smiling.

Swede reached the edge of the shaft and then crawled to the outside before dropping onto the terrace below.

The terrace made an arc around the inside of the cavern wall and Swede ran full speed along it toward Dodd.

Bobby was already moving to follow Swede, climbing along the inside of the shaft.

Anna followed suit, heading for the opening.

A bullet knocked a chunk of concrete free an inch from her muzzle.

The round buried a half-inch into the wall.

She could smell it: silver.

Bobby was still heading for the outside.

She reached up, grabbed his calf and yanked him back.

A two-foot section of concrete came free when she pulled him - his claws were lodged firmly in the material.

It fell from his grasp and bounced off Anna's shoulder before careening down the shaft.

The concrete chunk exploded on top of the elevator car far below.

More bullets were flying, ricocheting off the inside of the shaft.

She could tell from the smell that some were silver, but others weren't. They were mixing the rounds.

Paul howled above her.

He had shoved a set of elevator doors open and was crawling through onto a terrace.

She nodded and shoved Bobby up toward the opening.

Looking down, she could see Clyde far below continuing to descend. The shooters either couldn't see him or he was out of range.

More bullets ricocheted near her arm, and she climbed up to join Bobby and Paul.

***

"I hear gunshots," Karen said as Angelica entered her cell block.

"Your pack is here. They're somewhere above trying to make their way down. Price's men don't have a lot of silver ammunition - Dodd took it and hid it somewhere."

"Let me out," Karen said.

"Way ahead of you," Angelica said as she walked over to the heavy steel door and started pressing buttons.

***

"The pack is here," Joseph said as he entered Paula's cell block.

She sat up on her bed. "Leave. As fast as you can."

"We are. All of us. You included," Joseph said as he stood in front of the steel door.

"What are you doing?! Stop!"

"You know, one of my jobs as a government psychologist was to assist intelligence agencies in figuring out enemy's passwords and safeguarding our own passwords and codes. There's a science to it. Most people follow set patterns. Now, these door locks? They use a four-digit code."

"Marlow! Don't open the door," Paula said.

"First thing? You look at the keypad. The buttons used most often will either be worn or dirty. I had this one guy, NSA, constantly eating Cheetos. Damned cheese dust got embedded in his office file cabinet digital lock. Sixteen possible combinations once you saw the cheesy buttons."

"Marlow, please… don't…"

"Yep, four worn buttons '1257'…" He laughed. "Angelica's birth month and year? 1275… Angelica, if I were evaluating her? I'd write her up." He hesitated before pressing the buttons. "However, when she sent the message encoded in the image? She reversed the letters. You see? People follow patterns. Not '1275' but… '5721'."

He pressed the buttons.

The door beeped and the lock clicked open.

Paula rushed the door and the force shoved Marlow back against the wall.

She emerged from the cell in full wolf form.

Marlow didn't move, he just stared up into her eyes. "Listen to me, Paula."

She growled at him, lowering her head. She walked toward him.

"You're terrified of your wolf. You don't want to hurt anyone, but you convinced yourself you will."

She put her paws against his shoulders and pressed him into the wall, her jaws an inch from his face.

"It becomes a self-fulfilling prophecy, do you see? You've convinced yourself you will kill me, so your mind is playing it out."

She snarled.

"You're in love with me. Same as I am with you. I feel it. I see it. So do you. Do you smell fear on me, Paula? No, you don't. Because I'm not afraid of you."

She transitioned back to human in seconds. "You're an idiot. A complete…"

He kissed her, pulling her against him.

"I could've…" She whispered.

"But you didn't."

"She will," Karen Arthur said as she stepped into the cell block followed by Angelica.

"No, she won't," Joseph said. "You're wrong. Not about the other rogues but you're wrong about her. Werewolves with the bloodline can hold off going rogue for a long time and they can be cured as long as it hasn't gone too far."

"Respectfully, doctor? You're not an expert," Karen said. "I am. You need to step aside." She stretched her neck, and her fangs began growing in. Karen flexed her fingers and claws sprouted. "Now, step aside. I promised Paula mercy."

Joseph stepped in front of Paula. "You'll have to go through me to kill her."

"Joseph?" Paula whispered. "It's okay. I'm ready for this to be over."

"You don't know what you're saying," Joseph said. "We can beat this. I know we can. Trust me."

Karen shook her head. "In Elkhorn, Wisconsin? A woman thought she could cure a rogue, Dr. Marlow. By the end, they were both serial killing werewolves. They're in purgatory right now."

"And I'll bet neither of them were of the bloodline, were they?"

More gunfire sounded outside.

Marlow shook his head. "We're wasting time. Those men are shooting at your pack, Karen."

"Doctor, move out of the way or I'll knock you on your ass."

"Don't you touch him!" Paula roared as she transitioned.

Marlow pressed back against her. "You'll have to kill both of us, Karen."

"All three," Angelica sobbed as she ran past Karen and stood beside Marlow. "Paula, please don't kill me," she whispered.

Karen glared at them. Her claws retracted and her face returned to human. "Okay, nobody's killing anybody." She pointed at Paula. "You. Human. Now!"

Paula slid back into her human shape.

More gunfire sounded outside.

Karen looked up. "I don't have time for this. Paula, can you get these two out of here?"

"Yes."

"Fine. I'll kill you later. Get out of here," Karen said.

"Thank you, Karen," Marlow said.

"Don't thank me," she said and then she looked at Paula. "This is a temporary reprieve, Paula. I promised you a quick death. That's still on the table. But I'm telling you now: if you harm one innocent person? Just one… I'll kill you so slow you might die of old age first. Understand?"

"Yes," Paula said.

"This other werewolf Price has down here?" Karen asked.

Angelica went pale. "God, no. Just leave it to die."

"I can't trust it will," Karen said. "Where is it?"

***

Swede ran around the curved terrace, past dozens of office and lab doors.

The snipers below stopped firing at him after the first few shots - he was at the wrong angle and too far away for them to hit. They were concentrating their fire on Anna, Bobby, and Paul.

He glanced toward his three friends, saw they were crouched behind the terrace wall.

They were safe for now.

Dodd stepped off the planter and onto the terrace. He stood with his head down, in human form, arms straight down to his side.

Swede was ten feet away when Dodd transformed, flowing effortlessly into the blond wolf.

Swede leaped, stretching out his clawed hands. He crashed into Dodd and they both went rolling across the terrace.

Dodd shoved him away and stood.

Swede struck out with his left and Dodd blocked the blow.

Then Swede threw an uppercut that caught Dodd in the solar plexus, sending the blond wolf airborne.

Dodd landed on his feet four yards back, the claws in his feet digging into the concrete terrace.

Then Dodd ran straight for Swede.

***

"We have to get to Swede," Anna yelled. She had transitioned back to human.

She peered over the terrace wall in time to see Swede careen off one of the concrete walls on the other side of the cavern.

An instant later, a bullet kicked up concrete dust from the wall a few inches from her face.

She dove down as the silver bullet ricocheted off and landed on the floor beside Paul.

He leaned over and tapped it with his claw. Then he transitioned his upper body. "Ahh, so that's how they solved the tumbling issue with the silver bullets. It's a jacketing over a heavier core. Most likely depleted Uranium. That would give it almost the same ballistics as a comparably sized lead bullet."

"Seriously!?" Anna yelled over the sound of the gunfire. "Everything's going crazy and you're geeking out over the bullets?"

Paul smiled. "Haven't you noticed? They're mixing the rounds... they're running low on silver bullets."

"That's good, right?" Bobby asked.

Anna smiled and nodded.

***

Clyde crouched on top of the elevator. Somehow, the snipers had missed seeing him during the descent. They were shooting up, over his head.

Shooting toward Anna and the others.

Here at the bottom of the cavern, there was a glass enclosed courtyard. He was level with the thin glass roof.

There was no way it would hold his weight. He would either have to go through the roof of the elevator and then through its doors, or directly through the glass courtyard roof, or somehow climb around the outside of the concrete elevator shaft without the snipers seeing him and opening fire.

If he went into the elevator, he had no way of knowing if there would be a hallway full of riflemen waiting for him on the other side.

***

Karen opened the door leading from the cell block area a crack and peered into the hallway beyond.

It was empty.

She could hear gunshots in the distance.

She looked back over her shoulder. At the far end of the cell block corridor stood a door.

That door led to a sub-basement. According to Angelica, that basement held the other werewolf.

She had to take care of that one.

More gunshots.

But first? Her pack was in trouble.

***

Edward Price was a survivor. He had always been the last man standing in a countless number of SNAFUs. He had been in the crosshairs of insurgent armies, nearly blown up in failed coups, narrowly escaped being blasted into oblivion by a muttered spell from an angry witch.

He had even managed to crawl to safety when everyone working for him had succumbed to shape-shifting vampires.

But this? This was like being surrounded by superhero zealots.

In short, he was terrified.

He walked at the center of four guards including the Security Chief himself.

Their goal lay ahead: Angelica Geffman's lab.

269

"I want her subdued, not harmed. Dr. Geffman is government property," Price said.

The Security Chief opened the laboratory door.

"Angelica? Time to go," Price said.

He stared at the room.

Angelica's equipment had been destroyed. A red fire ax lay discarded on the floor.

Blood samples that had been carefully stored in refrigerators were spilled on the floor, the refrigerators themselves smashed beyond repair.

Angelica's computers were also smashed. The hard drives had been removed and an axe had been taken to each one.

Her handwritten notebooks were burned to ash in a smoldering wastebasket.

There was a single sheet of paper on Angelica's lab bench.

DIE GUTE WOLF IS NOT FOR YOU, PRICE. IT NEVER WAS. GO TO HELL.

SINCERELY,

DR. ANGELICA GEFFMAN

Price clenched his fists. "Find her. Alive! I want her alive!"

***

"Are there stairs?" Joseph asked as he and Angelica hid behind Paula.

She was leaning around the corner and looking at the next hall. "Yes," she whispered. "There are stairs. But they probably blocked them and, in any event? I am not carrying the two of you up almost a mile of stairs."

Joseph laughed.

She turned and looked at him.

"Wait, you're serious? You could carry us up?"

"Yes, but it would really suck. Especially when there's a perfectly good elevator."

"Elevator? Are you nuts?" Angelica hissed.

"I don't know, ask him," Paula whispered. "The elevator is right around the corner, but I can hear three maybe four of Price's mercenaries watching it. Stay behind me." She started around the corner.

"Wait a second!" Joseph whispered. "You can't kill them."

"Oh, trust me, I can," Paula said as she returned to her hiding spot.

"Karen said not to kill anybody," Joseph whispered.

"Karen said not to kill *innocents*. Those guys are the enemy."

Joseph took her hand. "And what if you can't stop?"

She smiled. "Then you better talk fast, Dr. Marlow. Put on your Bob Newhart act and talk fast."

***

Two hallways away, Karen leaned out from an alcove and looked up at the terrace above.

Three snipers were there aiming at the opposite terrace a few levels up.

On the far side of that terrace, Karen could see Swede grappling with Dodd.

Anna stuck her head up and one of the snipers opened fire.

Pinned down, Karen thought. She had to help them get to Swede.

She transitioned to werewolf and stepped out of the alcove. She crouched down and then vertical leaped, landing on the terrace above.

She crouched on the concrete floor.

The snipers were focused on Anna.

Karen ran straight for the snipers.

***

Swede threw his weight against Dodd and managed to spin him around. He almost succeeded in getting Dodd in a full Nelson.

Then Dodd curled his body forward, tossing Swede over his shoulder.

Swede lost his grip and slid across the concrete.

He jumped to his feet and faced Dodd.

271

Dodd's face became human once again. He began circling. "You're definitely the strongest of them. But you're untrained, undisciplined. You're like a bull in a China shop."

"*You know what, asshole? You talk too much,*" Swede thought.

Dodd had his back to the hanging garden.

Swede roared and rammed into him as hard as he could.

***

The men guarding the elevator turned away from it as Paula turned the corner behind them.

She ran at them in full wolf form.

She slapped with her left clawed hand at the first mercenary and his head separated from his shoulders.

The next man was turning his rifle toward her as she brought her right hand up, driving the black claws up through the bottom of his jaw, into his mouth, and on into his brain.

She flung him aside.

The third man fired directly at her midsection.

The bullet punched through her stomach.

Paula felt like she was on fire.

The silver bullet passed through and blew a hole the size of a tennis ball out of her back.

She staggered back and so did the mercenary.

Then she felt the wound closing.

She growled and drove her right hand forward.

Paula's hand disappeared wrist deep in the man's rib cage. She yanked her hand back and tossed his heart aside.

She was enraged as the man fell.

Paula knelt down and tore open the man's abdomen. She shoved her muzzle into the wound and began eating the liver.

"Paula?" A voice said.

She dug deeper, letting the flesh slide down her throat.

"Paula?"

She turned toward the annoying sound.

Joseph Marlow was standing behind her. Angelica hung back a little further.

She looked terrified.

272

"Paula, we have to go," Joseph said. He held out his hand.

She transitioned back to human. She swallowed a mouthful of the merc's liver. "Hungry. I was… hungry."

Joseph knelt in front of her as Angelica pushed the elevator button.

"I know and that's okay. He was a bad person. You saved us. Now it's time to go, okay?"

Paula stood up and wiped the blood from her face.

The elevator door opened.

Angelica stepped inside and pressed a button. "Come on!"

Paula let Marlow pull her toward the elevator.

She stepped inside.

The elevator's back wall was glass.

She saw a miraculous sight through it: two werewolves, one blond, one with black hair grappling as they fell from one of the upper terraces.

Dodd, she thought. And one of Karen's pack.

She smiled at Marlow and shoved him backward.

She backed out of the elevator as the doors began to close.

"Take care of each other," Paula said. "I love you, Joseph."

The doors closed.

"No!" Joseph Marlow screamed as he tried to get to his feet.

***

Clyde heard the commotion from below as he crouched on top of the elevator.

The elevator started to rise, and he reached down to tear open the roof.

That's when he saw two things at the same time: Swede and Dodd falling toward the courtyard and Karen going after the snipers.

He leapt off the elevator.

***

There were mercenaries in the courtyard. They scattered when the two falling werewolves hit the glass and shattered the roof.

The werewolves hit the tile floor in an avalanche of glass.

***

273

The snipers above were standing up now, aiming for Swede and Dodd.

They never saw Karen as she slammed into them, sending one man flying directly into a concrete piling. He exploded like an overripe grape.

The other two recovered and turned toward Karen.

She grabbed the closest man's rifle and shoved it forward against him. Then she lifted him with it and tossed rifle and man alike over the terrace edge.

The third sniper fired a shot, but it went wild ricocheting off the wall.

Karen ripped the rifle from his hands and clubbed him with the stock.

He went down in a heap.

A door opened behind her.

A bullet grazed her as she turned.

Two more men with rifles were running toward her, firing off shots as they ran.

She crouched ready to leap.

That's when she saw the werewolf with light brown fur pull himself up over the edge. He closed the distance between himself and the two mercenaries.

Then he reached out with both hands and cracked their skulls together.

They went down.

She turned her head to the side. The werewolf stared at her with bright yellow eyes.

She transitioned to human form and ran toward him.

He caught her in his arms and pulled her close, nuzzling her face with his muzzle.

"Oh, hillbilly, what have you done?" Karen sobbed as she clung to Clyde and wept.

***

Swede felt his broken hip and leg bones knitting together. He rolled onto his side.

274

Dodd was a few yards away, his arms and legs bent at an odd angle.

But not as odd as the right angle he now had in his neck.

"*Please be dead. Please be dead,*" Swede thought.

But even as he thought this, he could see Dodd's head rolling. He could hear the vertebrae snapping back into place.

Swede tried to move.

The survivor of this would be the one who could recover first.

***

Joseph was pounding his finger against the button for the lower level.

The elevator rose quickly.

He turned and looked down through the back glass. They were too high, too high to see what was going on below.

The elevator rose to ground level and the inner doors opened, revealing the destroyed outer doors.

Angelica stepped through avoiding the jagged, destroyed metal.

Joseph looked at her.

"There's nothing you can do, Joseph! You don't even have a gun!" Angelica yelled.

"I won't leave her, Angelica." He smiled at her as the doors began to close.

"I'll wait here for you as long as I can," Angelica said as the elevator began to descend once more into Spears Mountain.

***

Karen looked up to see Anna, Bobby, and Paul climbing down the inside of the elevator shaft.

High above, the elevator car was descending.

Below, the mercenaries were closing in on Dodd and Swede.

***

Swede got to his feet first. "*You lose, asshole,*" Swede thought. He stumbled toward Dodd.

A bullet struck Swede in the shoulder. The wound closed instantly.

275

Dodd howled in anger as he rose to his knees. He picked up a three-foot-long shard of glass from the remains of the roof and flung it toward the mercenary who fired the shot.

It hit him in the midsection and cut him in half in a spray of crimson.

The other mercs began firing.

Swede put Dodd in a choke hold.

He felt a blowtorch burning in his left hip.

A silver bullet had hit him there and it drove deep.

Swede fell to his left knee and lost his grip on Dodd.

Through the pain induced haze, he saw Karen and Clyde flinging mercenaries like rag dolls around the courtyard.

He tried to stand but it was no use with the silver bullet in him.

"Aiggh! Not again!" Dodd screamed. He was human once again walking through the broken glass without seeming to notice. "You're down again?! Enough then. Time for you to die."

He grabbed Swede's head in his hands and began to squeeze.

Strong claws on hands covered in gray fur dug into Dodd's shoulders and wrenched him backward, throwing him. He slid through the shattered glass.

He stood up as the gray-haired werewolf growled at him.

Dodd laughed. "Professor Collins? I didn't know you had it in you."

Paul ignored him and knelt by Swede. He drove his claws into the hip wound and Swede shrieked.

Bobby and Anna stood between Paul and Dodd, growling on all fours.

Then Paul pulled his hand free and tossed the silver bullet onto the tile.

Swede's wound began to close.

"Good! Good. I'll kill all of you!" Dodd screamed as he stood up, the numerous cuts on his body from the broken glass closing.

Swede got to his feet and howled.

"You don't get it, Dodd," Karen said.

"His kind never does," Clyde said as he shivered and returned to human form.

Paul, human again stepped to the side. "What was it he called us? *Pathetic?*"

Bobby stood up, his face becoming human. "Weak."

Anna nodded. "Time for a lesson."

Dodd turned his head, looking at each of them in turn. "Come on! Enough talk! I'll kill all of you."

Karen turned and smiled as Paula Danvers stepped into the courtyard.

Paula smiled back. "I'm not even one of them? And even I understand it."

They began to circle Dodd.

"Come at me!" Dodd screamed. "What are you waiting for, weaklings? I'll kill each…"

Karen shook her head. "No, Dodd. We're strong. Because we're together. The strength of the wolf lies in the pack."

Dodd screamed and shifted to wolf form as the pack, snarling, leapt upon him.

***

As the elevator neared the courtyard, Dr. Joseph Marlow watched the werewolves tear into Gunnery Sergeant William Dodd. He saw how their claws ripped away Dodd's skin.

He saw Swede Olufsen get behind a screaming, torn and bloody Dodd.

Swede put his massive right hand on Dodd's head and curled his claws down, driving them into Dodd's sinus cavity.

He heard Dodd's final scream as they ripped the top of his head off.

***

The pack stepped back from Dodd's corpse, changing back into humans as they did.

Swede looked at the ruined skull in his hand and tossed it away.

Then he fell to his knees and began to sob. His shoulders heaved and he wept.

Anna burst into tears and put her arms around him.

One by one, they knelt beside him.

277

Karen rubbed his black hair and raised his face up.

"It doesn't help," Swede sobbed. "I thought… but it doesn't. She's still gone."

She kissed his head. "I know."

Joseph Marlow walked into the courtyard.

Paula ran to him. "Are you insane? You could've been killed." She kissed him. "Why didn't you go with Angelica?"

"She's waiting topside," Joseph said.

"We can't leave yet," Karen said. "Two things left to do."

***

The Security Chief stood with his men outside Price's office. "Sir, we really need to get moving. We'll have to take the stairs."

"I'm aware," Price said. "I have to salvage what I can. Hold the hallway." Price went inside and closed the door behind him.

He walked to the back wall and pressed an inset button.

The section of wall slid to the side.

"Last resort," Price whispered. He started gathering his files.

***

Angelica Geffman walked out of the Quonset Hut. The western sky looked beautiful with only a few hours left till sundown.

Birds called from the pines.

It would have been idyllic if not for the crushed body parts of the two guards scattered near the entrance.

"Don't look," Angelica whispered as she kept her eyes straight ahead.

She stepped in something that squelched under her shoe.

Angelica winced.

She felt her lunch coming up.

She hurried past, not looking down.

Her yellow, convertible VW Beetle was still sitting where she parked it two months ago.

It was covered in dust and pollen.

She dug in her purse and pulled out her keys.

The lights flashed and the car unlocked.

278

She got in and sat down. Her finger hesitated over the start button.

What if it didn't start?

Price hadn't let her out of the mountain in two months.

What would she do if it didn't start?

"Come on, you German piece of shit," she whispered.

She pressed the button and the bug roared to life.

Angelica laughed. She kissed the steering wheel. "I'm so sorry I doubted you, you beautiful monument to German engineering."

Now all she had to do was wait.

***

"We've got no quarrel with you," a woman's voice called from down the hall.

The Security Chief raised his pistol and aimed toward the sound. "Is that you, Miss Arthur?"

"It is," Karen said from somewhere around the corner. "You and your men are free to go. The elevator is operational. Use it and get out."

"As soon as Mr. Price is done, we will."

"No," Karen called. "Just the four of you."

"We have silver bullets, Miss Arthur. We will kill you."

"You won't get all of us. And, if just one of us makes it? You're all dead."

The other mercenaries looked at each other.

"Don't even think about it," the Chief muttered.

"This deal isn't going to be on the table for long," Karen said. "As a matter of fact? You have ten seconds. Nine. Eight..."

The three mercenaries broke and ran down the hall away from the sound of Karen Arthur's voice.

The Security Chief turned and aimed his pistol at them. "Get your asses back here!"

They didn't slow down.

He almost fired. "Son of a bitch," the Chief muttered. He turned back toward Karen's voice.

They were standing in the hallway a few feet from him: six werewolves, Dr. Marlow, and Karen Arthur in human form.

279

He had the pistol pointed toward her, but his hand was shaking.

She didn't blink. "When they ask you if you would ever willingly face us again? You tell them the truth. You tell them you've looked death in the face and you never, ever want to see that again."

The werewolves growled, their lips pulling back from their fangs.

Karen Arthur smiled, her jaws lengthening, teeth sprouting.

"Boo," she growled.

He dropped his gun and ran.

***

The Turtle

Swede kicked Price's office door in and then quickly stepped aside.

They'd been expecting a hail of bullets from Price.

When nothing happened, Karen peeked around the door jamb.

She transitioned back to human form. "You've got to be kidding."

The others followed Karen into the office.

The back wall had slid to the side revealing a steel cylinder seven-feet-tall and five-feet in diameter.

There was a heavy glass window in the steel.

Edward Price was sitting in a padded chair inside the column. There was a speaker below the window. "My safe room. All the comforts of home."

Karen ran a claw down the glass.

It was unmarked.

"Same glass as the walls of your former cell," Price said. He pulled a bottle of red wine out of a box by his chair.

Swede slammed his fist into the steel outer wall. "Can't even dent it."

Price shook his head as he poured the red wine in a glass. "Damned well better not dent. Paid a small fortune to some eggheads at NASA for the material." He moved the wine glass in a circle, letting the wine breathe.

"Paul?" Karen asked and nodded toward the cylinder.

He examined the cylinder. "Seam there... most likely the door." He transitioned his hand and tapped the seam with his claw. "Too tight. Won't be able to pry it." He looked in at Price. "I assume it only opens from the inside once closed?"

"You assume correctly," Price said with a smile. He took a sip of wine. "I'd share my wine with all of you but then I'd have to open the door."

"He has to open it sometime," Bobby said.

"Oh, and I will. Just not now," Price said.

Paul craned his neck and peered into the window. "Air supply is self-contained, and I see CO2 scrubbers…"

"As I said, NASA eggheads." Price smiled. "I've read your work, Professor Collins. All that stuff about Atlantis? Ridiculous tripe."

"Yes, well, you're a Neanderthal," Paul said.

"What do you think, Paul?" Karen asked.

"If we had an industrial laser? Maybe. Barring that? We won't be able to extricate him."

"So, he just gets away?" Swede asked. He slammed his fist against the cylinder.

"You know? I can't even hear that in here. This thing was worth every penny," Price said as he took another sip of wine. "I'm as snug as a turtle in his shell."

Clyde nodded. "Let's just set the whole damned place on fire."

"Cook the bastard," Swede said and nodded.

"Ah, would that you could," Price said. "Back in the day when they stored jet fuel in the mountain? You might have been able to do it. All gone now. Jets are still up there in the hangar but… no fuel."

"So?" Bobby asked. "Let's just pile up chairs and shit and light it on fire."

Paul shook his head. "It wouldn't burn hot enough or long enough. I doubt if it would raise the internal temperature of the cylinder a degree."

"Very good, Professor," Price said. "There's also a fire suppression system." He smiled. "And you're quickly running out of time."

"What's that mean?" Paula Danvers asked.

"When I entered my safe room? I pressed the little red button behind my chair. The cavalry is coming."

Karen smiled and shook her head. "More mercenaries? We'll just kill them, Price." She looked at Paul. "How long can he stay in there?"

"Twelve hours give or take. Depending on how shallow he breathes."

"Cavalry will be here in…" Price looked at his watch. "Hmm, thirty-five minutes."

"We already told you we aren't afraid of your Hutchins mercenaries," Karen said.

"They're not from Hutchins," Price said. "Elements of the 82nd Airborne on their way from North Carolina. They were wheels up ten minutes ago."

Karen frowned.

"That's right, Miss Arthur. A plane load of America's finest young men. They're going to parachute onto the mountaintop. Of course, they have no idea that werewolves are real, and they won't have a single silver bullet on them. But they are tenacious." He leaned forward and smiled. "So, you'll either have to surrender or kill them. Their blood will be on your hands."

"You son of a bitch," Karen said.

"Again, with my lineage. You're positively obsessed," Price chuckled.

"Let's go," Karen said through gritted teeth.

"No!" Swede said. "He has to pay. He has to pay for all of this! Layla…"

"*Really*? How much is a stripper worth?" Price laughed.

Swede transitioned and pounded his fists against the cylinder.

Price kept smiling.

Karen put her hand on Swede's arm. "Swede. Let's go. We'll meet Mr. Price again." She glared at Price. "When he can't hide under a rock."

They turned to leave.

"It doesn't have to be like this, Miss Arthur," Price said. "We could work together. I still believe in Project Lobo."

"Hard pass," Karen said.

She looked down at Price's desk.

There was a small stack of manilla folders.

Karen picked them up. "You were in a hurry to get into your shell, huh, turtle? Project Lobo, Project Draugr... Swords Creek, Virginia?" She opened the Swords Creek folder and read.

She turned to Price. "Ghosts." She smiled. "You know, don't you?"

"Ghost stories? Stick around and I'll tell you a few. Twenty-five minutes, Miss Arthur."

She walked to the cylinder. "Let me tell you what I know, Price. Every person you've murdered? If they don't go on to what comes next? They follow you, Price. A man like you? You've killed a lot of people. Can you feel them? In your shell with you, do you feel their fingers on you?"

Price swallowed the last of his wine. "I'm perfectly fine with my ghosts, Miss Arthur. They can't hurt the living."

"Yes, Price, but you won't live forever. I know what's coming for you, Price. After we get through with you? It'll be *their* turn. I pity you." She walked toward the door.

"We'll hunt you, Miss Arthur. You won't have a minute's peace for the rest of your life. And, as for Project Lobo? I'll just start over."

Karen smiled over her shoulder. "No, I don't think you will."

She couldn't see Price's hand shaking as she walked away, but she knew it was.

***

Karen stepped into the hall and closed the door behind her. She started down the hall back toward the cell blocks.

"We need to go, now," Clyde said. "We can't kill soldiers, Karen. Those kids don't have a clue what they're walking into."

"We're not going to hurt them. But Project Lobo has to end, here, today."

"The other lobo," Dr. Marlow said.

Karen nodded.

"What other lobo?" Clyde asked.

***

When Angelica saw movement in the Quonset Hut, she almost cheered.

283

Then when she saw the three mercs run out of the darkness like they were running from the devil himself, she turned off the VW and dove down in the seat.

They ran past without even glancing toward her.

Then they piled into an SUV and kicked up dust and gravel heading down the mountain.

A few minutes later, the Security Chief followed. He was moving slower.

She glanced over the dash to find him looking at her.

The Chief had a huge wet stain in the front of his khakis.

He nodded at Angelica, climbed in one of the other SUVs and drove away.

***

The Man in the Basement

The stairs to the sub-basement were narrow.

There was a smell here: mold and damp.

And blood.

The door at the bottom of the stairs wasn't locked.

Karen pushed it open.

There was no cell here.

It was just a small room with a single light over a hospital bed.

"Oh, God," Anna whispered.

Bobby hugged her.

Paula looked away.

There was a werewolf on the bed. Hundreds of tubes and wires connected him to equipment and IV stands.

His arms and legs were amputated, the stumps encased in silver to keep him from regenerating.

His head was a ruin, misshapen, frozen in mid-transition. Mostly human on the left, mostly wolf on the right.

His blonde hair hung in wisps from his mottled scalp.

The werewolf's red eyes swiveled as he looked toward them.

He locked his gaze on Karen.

Tears began to flow from the human eye.

Karen walked to him.

"Karen? Don't," Clyde whispered.

"It's okay," Karen said. "He can't hurt anyone."

"*Follow the blue-eyed wolf or burn in hell*," the werewolf slurred. "That's what Petrov said when he made us. That damned ship and that damned dying Russian." His wolf tongue was too long for the human side of his face.

"Todd Stearn?" Karen asked.

He nodded and tried to smile. "Never thought… I'd meet another alpha."

Clyde shook his head. "The last rogue." He turned to Bobby. "The last of Hayden Oswald's gang."

Karen could see the liquid being pumped through some of the IVs - silver iodide. She reached to pull out the tubes.

"No," Stearn rasped. "Leave it. Still… dangerous. Deserve this for what I've done."

Karen shook her head. "No. No, you didn't. It wasn't your fault."

"Doesn't matter now. Please, kill me? I don't want to hurt anyone else."

Paula Danvers began to tremble. "Just like me. That's what I'll become," she whispered.

"No, you won't," Joseph said.

Stearn turned his head and looked toward the pack. He smiled. "That… that's what we were supposed to be. We could've been better. We were supposed to be better. And now? You are."

Karen sobbed and turned away.

Clyde smiled at her weakly.

When she turned back, Hayden Oswald and Clayton Ambrose were standing behind him.

"Please," Stearn whispered.

"Send him home, blondie," Hayden said. "He'll be among friends even if he doesn't have any place else to go."

She glanced behind her. The rest of the pack was looking at Stearn - they couldn't see the apparitions.

Karen moved behind Stearn. She touched his hair. Then she raised her hands above her head and transitioned to werewolf.

She brought her hands down swiftly.

Todd Stearn's head fell onto the floor.

She reached down and picked it up, laying it gently on his chest.

Karen walked toward her pack, sliding back into human form. "Open the oxygen valves in here. Make it burn. We can't kill Price, but I don't want a single blood cell left for Price to experiment on."

***

Daylight

The pack walked down the hall. Behind them, flames blew open the stairwell door.

"Fifteen minutes," Marlow said as they reached the elevator.

Clyde pressed the button and the elevator doors opened.

They stepped inside and pressed the button for the top floor.

Music began playing as they ascended.

Anna frowned. "What is that?"

Marlow looked up at the speaker in the ceiling. "I don't know. I don't remember music playing last time I rode this thing."

Swede began to hum along with the instrumental piece. "That's Rush."

"Nonsense," Paul said. "Blue Oyster Cult."

"Don't Fear the Reaper," Karen said.

Anna snapped her fingers and started singing the words. She stopped. "Come on. Don't make me sing alone."

They all started singing.

Karen smiled and Clyde held her tight.

A few seconds later, the elevator shuddered to a stop less than halfway up.

"Not that easy," Price's voice said over the speaker. "You have five minutes. It'll take longer than that to climb to the top."

"Bastard's got control of the elevator," Clyde said.

"Man, I hate that prick," Swede said. He reached over and tore the elevator doors open.

They were midway between floors.

Swede tore through the outer doors above, and they crawled out of the elevator.

Karen leaned over the terrace wall and looked up.

It was a long way to the top.

"Hmm," Paul said. He was looking at double doors set into the rock wall. He pointed above them.

A faded tin sign read: HANGAR.

They opened the doors and went inside.

Three jets sat on the floor of the massive hangar. The landing gear had long since decayed and the planes sagged on their supports.

"Those are old Harrier jump jets." Clyde pointed to the far wall. "That has to open so they could take off and land." He ran to the wall. "There must be controls here somewhere."

"Here!" Paul called out. He was standing by a control console near the terrace entrance. He pressed some buttons. "No power."

Clyde shook his head. He was standing near the center of the back wall. "Wouldn't matter. Mechanism is rusted. Water got in."

"If it's a door?" Swede said. "We can open it."

He transitioned to werewolf and threw his shoulder against the left side of the wall. Somewhere, gears began to grind.

Clyde did the same on the right side.

Paul, Anna, and Bobby ran to help.

Paula joined them.

Karen could hear metal grinding.

And then the hangar was flooded with sunlight as the hangar doors began to slide open. Outside, she could see plant and tree roots tearing away and decades' worth of dirt and rocks sliding down.

Karen smiled.

"Never been so glad to see daylight in my life," Dr. Marlow said.

"Me too," Karen said.

Paula walked back to them. She looked at Karen and nodded.

"Swede?" Karen said. "Hold the doctor."

Marlow struggled as Swede grabbed his arms from behind.

"Relax, doc," Swede said as he transitioned back to human.

"What are you doing?!" Marlow yelled.

"What has to be done," Paula said as she knelt down. She looked up at Karen. "Thank you. I was part of a pack even if it was only for a few minutes."

Karen nodded.

"No!" Marlow yelled and struggled against Swede's grip.

"Don't look," Paula said. "You'll be okay." She smiled. "I don't want to end up like Stearn. I don't want to hurt people."

"You won't!" Marlow yelled. "Karen, you're wrong about her. She's getting better."

"I'm sorry, doctor," Karen said as she drew back her right arm. It became a werewolf's limb. She stretched her claws.

"I looked at her and I knew!" Marlow screamed. "I knew. She's supposed to be one of you. I knew it. This is wrong! It's all wrong."

Karen hesitated. She looked at him.

"I know it," Marlow sobbed. "I can see it."

Karen smiled. "Maybe there's another way."

***

The setting sun painted the sky orange and purple as they ran out through the ancient hangar doors. They could hear the sound of a plane overhead.

The blue sky filled with billowing parachutes and the pack ran down the green mountainside.

Seven werewolves and a man doing his best to keep up as he laughed.

Joseph Marlow ran out of the heart of darkness. One of the wolves stopped, ran back to him, took his hand and ran with him.

The pack ran around to the east side of Spears Mountain, finding the ancient cattle trails and running along them.

On the mountain top, Angelica Geffman looked up as the men descended in their parachutes. "Good luck, Marlow," she said. She put the Beetle in drive and headed down the mountain.

Paul Collins stopped running and turned around looking at the mountaintop and the paratroopers. He became a human once more. "I'll catch up." He ran toward the west side of the mountain.

"Paul?" Karen yelled as she transitioned.

"Trust me. I'll be fine," he said as he became a wolf once again and ran off on all fours.

***

288

Angelica stopped the VW on the steep road as the two soldiers with rifles walked toward her car. She had seen their parachutes descending in front of her from two hundred yards back.

Behind the paratroopers, she could see the gate to the main road. It may as well have been a hundred miles away.

One of the paratroopers stood in front of her car.

The other walked up to the driver's side and tapped on the window.

She rolled down the window and tried to smile. "Hi. I... took a wrong turn... I was just going back to the main road."

"Dr. Geffman? We were told to detain you."

"I don't know a Dr..."

The soldier was gone.

One second, he was standing there and the next he was simply gone.

The other soldier was turning left and right in front of the car. "Frank! Frank! Where are you?"

He looked at Angelica with wild eyes.

And then he fell, dragged beneath the Volkswagen. His fingertips left scratches on the hood as he was pulled down.

Angelica rolled up her window then held onto the steering wheel white knuckled.

Something huge and gray stood by the passenger door.

Tap, tap, tap... the shape tapped on the glass.

She reached out with a trembling hand and pressed the door unlock.

The door opened.

"Dr. Geffman, I presume?"

Her eyes widened.

She turned slowly.

An older man stood smiling at her through the open door.

She nodded. "Uh huh," she stammered.

He sat down in the passenger seat and closed his door. "I'm Professor Paul Collins. I've been reading your papers on gene manipulation, and I must say they are intriguing."

Angelica was still nodding. She swallowed. "You're naked."

Paul looked down. "Ah, yes, sorry. I barely notice any more."

Angelica was still nodding. She took off her lab coat and handed it to him. "For your... lap."

"How kind. Thank you." He draped it over his lap. "We should... go. There will be more soldiers along any minute now."

She put the car in gear and headed for the gate. "Did you kill them? The paratroopers."

"Oh, no! No, no, they'll be fine. Little headache when they wake up. I try not to kill anyone I don't have to."

"That's considerate."

They reached the open gate.

Paul sighed. "I love riding in cars."

Angelica began giggling. "Feel free to... stick your head out the window if you like."

Paul stared at her and then he laughed. "Oh! Oh, that's funny. Because... werewolf... yes, very funny." He pointed at the road. "You should drive. Fast."

Angelica pulled onto the road, and they sped off.

***

Mr. Spears was loading his remaining spools of barbed wire into the bed of his truck when he saw them running down the dirt path - huge wolves running on their hind legs.

One was carrying a full-grown man in its arms, but the man didn't seem to mind.

The cattle spooked and ran for the barn.

There was no time for the old man to be scared.

He just watched the wolves run and mopped the sweat from his brow.

One of the creatures slowed and looked at him. It nodded its head and ran on to join the others.

"I'll be damned," the old man said as the wolves disappeared in the distance.

***

Two Weeks Later
Rental Cabins Outside Gatlinburg, Tennessee

"Just so you understand, my eyes may not have turned blue, but that doesn't make you the boss of me," Clyde Hubbard said as he sat in the rocking chair on the cabin's front porch.

Karen smiled as she rocked in her own chair. "Yes, dear." She was reading through the folders she had taken from Price's desk.

"I mean it. I'm still my own man."

"Of course, dear."

"That sounds very condescending. It's a very condescending tone, Karen."

"Whatever you say, dear."

He smiled and chuckled.

Anna and Bobby came out of the cabin and headed for their motorcycles. Bobby now had a Harley fresh from the Ames Winery barn.

"Who wants fudge?" Anna asked as she got on her bike.

"Ooo, me," Karen said. "Peanut butter."

"Clyde?"

"I want a caramel apple."

Bobby smiled. "It's nice hiding out in the Smokys."

"I hardly call this 'hiding out'," Paul said as he walked out of the cabin and onto the porch.

"Chocolate and marshmallow, right?" Anna asked.

Paul smiled. "Yes, please."

"Back in a minute," Anna said.

Karen smiled. "Take your time."

Anna and Bobby rode off.

"Find anything new in those files?" Paul asked.

Karen shook her head. "Ghosts, witches, demons… and these… vampire things."

"I think it's all bullshit," Clyde said. "He left that out for you to find. Just trying to spook us."

"Maybe. I hope so," Karen whispered. She looked at the drawings in the Project Draugr file and shivered. Several months before, Ward Rickman called her with a story about monsters they had encountered.

These drawings resembled what Ward and Loretta described.

Swede came out of the cabin and walked to his bike. He knelt beside it and started looking at the brakes.

"Problem?" Karen asked.

"Naah. Just feels a little loose."

She nodded. He still wasn't himself. It was going to take time.

Paul walked off the porch. "Swede, I've been meaning to talk to you."

"Fire away, Professor," Swede said as he leaned closer to the motorcycle's back wheel.

"Well, as you know I've been corresponding with Dr. Angelica Geffman…"

Swede smiled. "'*Corresponding*'… is that what you kids call it nowadays?"

"I felt very awkward when I first met her. Tongue tied, actually. And it occurred to me I probably need to brush up on my skills with the fairer sex."

"You *had* skills?"

Paul shrugged. "No, actually, I never did."

Swede chuckled and shook his head as he continued working on the bike.

"So, I think I'm in need of a… what do you call it? A flight man? A wing leader?"

Swede squinted up at him. "A wingman?"

"Exactly! Yes, a wingman. I was thinking if you would accompany me to the local drinking establishment you might give me some pointers?"

Swede sighed. "Another day, maybe, Professor." He turned back to the bike.

Karen caught Paul's eye.

Paul's slight smile said it all: 'I tried'.

Karen nodded.

"Well, whenever you would like, then," Paul said as he turned away.

Karen had learned the best way to look at a ghost was out of the corner of your eye. It was out of the corner of her eye she saw Layla Kowalski kneel by Swede and put her lips by his ear.

Swede looked up, hearing something only he could hear. He shivered.

Karen choked back a sob.

Then Layla stood up. She looked at Karen and smiled.

She walked away, disappearing in the Smoky Mountain sunshine.

"You know what, Professor?" Swede said as he stood up and stretched. "A beer sounds pretty good right now. I saw a honky tonk about a mile down the road toward Sevierville." He climbed onto his bike.

Paul smiled at Karen. "I greatly appreciate this, Swede."

"No problem, Professor," Swede said. "Class is in session and the classroom awaits."

Paul laughed and got on his bike.

The engines rumbled and they rolled away down the road.

"Thank you, Layla," Karen whispered.

"What'd you say, darlin'?" Clyde asked.

"Nothing." She got out of her rocker and sat down on his lap.

"Oh, hi there," Clyde said as he kissed her.

"Alone at last," Karen said.

Her cellphone rang in her jeans pocket.

She pulled it out and looked at it.

"Considering you just bought that burner phone yesterday?" Clyde asked. "Who could be calling you?"

"I bought it with a credit card in my name," Karen said.

It continued to ring.

"You *what?*" Clyde asked.

She pressed the speakerphone button. "Hello, Mr. Price."

"Miss Arthur, I wanted to catch the two of you before things became awkward. I hate to call people in the middle of sex," Edward Price said.

Karen looked up toward the sky. "Brits bought a new satellite?"

"We gifted it to them. Least we could do."

"I see you got my message?"

Price laughed. "Bold of you to buy a cellphone and use a credit card. I imagine you are ready to talk to me?"

"You imagine correctly," Karen said. "I think it's time we had that little talk you've wanted."

"Tired of running?"

Karen smiled. "We were never running, Price. My pack needed rest. We're rested."

"I can come to you," Price said.

"No. Washington, D.C. Tomorrow night, 8:00 PM. There's a bar called Zephyr, are you familiar with it?" Karen asked.

"On K Street? Very familiar. Nice and crowded, good choice."

"We'll see you there," Karen said.

"No, no, not *we*. You get to pick one venue, I get to pick the other. You come alone to Zephyr. Your pack can dine at Epling's on K - a nice rooftop restaurant a block from the bar. Excellent steaks, they can order them raw. I'll treat."

Karen laughed. "Rooftop, huh? So, my pack will have snipers on all sides?"

"I'm not a moron, Miss Arthur. If you want to talk to me? I want your people under surveillance. Oh, and the Rickman's won't be joining us, will they?"

"No, no, just us, Price."

"Good... oh, feel free to bring Dr. Geffman and Dr. Marlow... to Epling's of course. I want you all to myself at Zephyr."

Karen shook her head. "Don't know where Geffman is, Price. Haven't seen Marlow since the mountain."

"How about Paula Danvers?"

Karen frowned. "We kill rogues, Mr. Price. It's what we do."

Price laughed. "I'll bet that was fun. Very well, Miss Arthur. It's a date: you and I at Zephyr, 8:00."

"Yeah, just a tete a tete... werewolf to turtle."

"I look forward to it." He hung up.

Karen crushed the phone in her hands and let the pulverized remains fall on the plank porch.

Clyde shook his head. "I don't like us splitting up again."

She leaned down and kissed him. "I figured this would be how it would play out. And, after this? No more splitting up the pack. I promise."

***

The Good Wolves

Zephyr Bar
K Street, Washington D.C.

Karen Arthur parked her Harley on the street in front of the Zephyr Bar. A rain earlier in the day had wet the street so that it reflected the lights of the city.

She walked into Zephyr wearing her jeans and a white T-shirt.

Edward Price was sitting in a booth halfway back. He stood up, a smile on his cherubic face. "Miss Arthur, somehow you manage to make Walmart clothing look glamorous."

She smiled and sat down opposite him. "How was your ordeal in the safe room, Mr. Price?"

He sat down. "I only made it through one and a half bottles of Merlot before the paratroopers came to my rescue. That was devious killing Stearn like that. You took away my source of the lobo virus knowing I would have to turn to you and your pack to continue the program."

Karen nodded. "What you did to him was monstrous."

"Agreed. I'm almost ashamed of myself."

"You don't have the slightest concept of right and wrong, do you?" Karen asked. "I can't fathom you, Price."

"Quite the contrary, *right* is whatever makes money for and bestows power upon my employers. *Wrong* is whatever takes money and power away. I'm well compensated for my flexible moral views."

Karen shook her head. "And that doesn't bother you?"

Price shrugged. "Oh, in the end, I think this will all be for the best. I think the world will benefit… eventually."

***

Epling's on K
Washington, D.C.

Clyde sat with the pack around a table on the rooftop of Epling's on K. He looked over the edge of the roof. He could see the Zephyr Bar at ground level in the distance.

295

"Compliments of Mr. Price," a waitress said as she set a bottle of Merlot on the table.

Paul picked up the bottle. "Mmm, Masseto Toscana. Very expensive."

"Mr. Price said to bring as many bottles as you wanted," the waitress said.

"Oh, in that case?" Swede took the bottle and held it over a potted palm beside him. He turned it upside down and the Merlot poured into the pot. "Keep them coming."

Paul sighed. "Oh… not even a sip?"

"*Ah, cruel fate, how swiftly joy and sorrow alternate,*" Bobby said with a smile.

Paul laughed. "There. See, Robert? Education is not being lost on you."

"Talk like that will never get you laid," Swede said.

"He does get laid," Anna said, and she put her arm around Bobby.

"I was talkin' to the professor," Swede said.

"I am also getting laid, thank you very much," Paul said.

They all looked at him.

"What? She admires my intellect and I hers," Paul said.

"That and she likes the super strength, speed, stamina…" Swede said.

"Well," Paul said with a shrug. "That doesn't hurt."

They all laughed.

Clyde looked at the waitress. "You got Pabst?"

She frowned. "Is that a beer?"

Clyde closed his eyes. "Just bring me whatever is on tap."

"Should we drink or eat anything?" Anna whispered.

Clyde shrugged. "Snipers on the rooftops all around us so… why bother to poison us?"

***

Aman Hotel
5th Avenue, New York, NY

"He's with her now?" Peter Hutchins asked as he sipped his martini in the hotel room.

Hutchins smiled at the answer. "Let me know when they take out the other lobos." Hutchins nodded. "Yes, I know he wants to take them all alive but that's never going to happen. We'll be lucky to get Arthur sedated and airlifted to Area 51 North. The odds of her agreeing to join us voluntarily are negligible."

There was a knock on the door.

"My appointment is here." He listened to the phone as he crossed to the door. "If this fails? The fault falls on Price. I personally would welcome being rid of the little toad."

He hung up the phone and opened the door.

A strawberry blonde with green eyes was standing in the hallway in a short, Italian leather dress.

She smiled.

Hutchins stared at her in confusion.

The bodyguards on either side of the door were staring at her as well.

"You're not my normal Tuesday night," Hutchins said.

She laughed softly. "I'm nobody's normal Tuesday night. Cindy has the flu... trust me, she's disgusting. I'm Tamara."

"I don't like change," Hutchins said.

She shrugged. "Change is good for you but, if you want? I can leave." She turned and walked away.

Hutchins smiled. "No, don't be silly. I'm Peter."

She turned around and smiled.

He stepped aside and let her come in.

***

Price sipped his wine. "You haven't touched your meal."

"Not hungry, thanks," Karen said.

"Afraid I'll poison you?"

"No. Not that you wouldn't. You've poisoned people before. It's your preferred means of execution, isn't it? Poisoning. It's cowardly."

Price stared at her. How did she know he usually poisoned those he killed? How could she know that?

The earbud whispered in his ear. "*Alpha and Bravo teams in position. We have a solution on all targets at Epling's. Standing by.*"

"*Charlie team standing by in the alley ready to take the Alpha Lobo.*"

Price smiled. The trap was ready to spring. "So, what do you think about my proposal?"

Karen leaned back and smiled. "Very tempting. We wouldn't have to hide anymore."

"No more knocking over ATMs for a paycheck," Price added.

"Pension?"

"At the end of the day? Why not?"

Karen nodded. "We'd be like a Seal team. You'd just send us anywhere the bad guys needed to be dealt with?"

"Precisely."

"Only, sometimes, those bad guys might not be the *real* bad guys, would they?"

Price shrugged. "In my business, we deal with shades of gray."

"At best, we're special forces. At worst, assassins?"

"I suppose."

Karen sighed. "What an end for the last remnants of Atlantis."

Price laughed. "Oh, come now. You aren't buying into Paul Collins' crackpot theories, are you?"

Karen shrugged. "It has a romantic charm. An ancient civilization, dying, decaying, realizing too late that in their quest for power? They had lost their souls. So, they create us, the good wolves, one last desperate attempt to be better, to do better."

"If Atlantis ever existed, it's long gone."

"And, yet, we remain…"

***

The wait staff laid the platters of steak in front of the pack. "Five steaks," the waitress said as she tried to smile. "Very, very rare."

They stared at the bloody steaks.

"They look delicious," Paul said.

Clyde was looking down at the Zephyr Bar.

***

Peter Hutchins pressed the woman against the wallpaper. He touched her strawberry blonde hair and leaned in to kiss her.

She turned her face away.

"It's alright. You're not the first... escort... I've known who didn't like to kiss." He ran his hand up her inner thigh. "So long as you enjoy everything else." He nuzzled her neck. "I can go all night."

Tamara turned toward him and smiled. "I like that. I like a man who can last all night." She pushed him toward the bed.

***

Price looked at his watch. "As fascinating as this conversation has been, Miss Arthur? I'm afraid I'm going to need an answer. Will you accept our offer?"

Karen smiled. "One last question, Price."

"As long as it is the last, please?"

"How long have you been watching us?"

"What do you mean?" Price asked.

"When exactly did you start watching my pack?"

Price laughed. "We started watching you before you turned Anna Sanders."

"Elkhorn. You started watching us..."

"After you killed the Walkers. We had discovered them prior and were getting ready to bring them into Project Lobo when you killed them."

Karen smiled and nodded. "Phoebe would have loved that."

"Undoubtedly. And, after we started watching you, we found out about Ward Rickman's pack, Hayden Oswald, the rogues..."

"But you didn't start following me until Elkhorn," Karen said. "That explains a lot."

He frowned. "I don't follow."

"No, I know you don't." She leaned forward. "When you first talked to me... well, threatened me... at Spears Mountain? You weren't afraid."

"I still don't..."

"Because you didn't know." She pointed at him. "That's how I knew we would win, Price. Because you didn't know."

"Know what?"

"What I was doing between the time I met Ward Rickman in Bedford and killing the Walkers in Elkhorn. The first thing I did when Clyde and I hit the road after Bedford? I tracked down a man I had met along the way to Bedford. I met him in a gas station. He was a veteran and I had this... urge... this overwhelming need to infect him with Die Gute Wolf. I thought I was insane."

She laughed. "I wasn't insane." She shook her head. "When my eyes turned blue? Suddenly, I could look at someone and I just knew if they were supposed to be one of us. That man was the first member of my pack. But there were so many others, Price."

Price leaned back and stared at her.

"I see those wheels turning now," Karen laughed. "We stopped at VA hospitals, places where heroes could be found, anyplace we heard about someone doing something selfless - because, nine times out of ten, those are the people who are supposed to be Die Gute Wolf." Karen shook her head. "You thought you found my *first* pack, Price? You found me and my *last* pack."

Price stared at her wide-eyed.

"The yellow-eyed wolves would stay with me, and then? Sooner or later, we'd get a blue. And that blue would take the yellow-eyed wolves with them. Then the process would start again. Think about it, Price. Paul says our growth is exponential. It has been exponential. For years, Price. Die Gute Wolf is everywhere."

"No," Price said. "That's impossible. We would have noticed. There would be killings..."

"No, Price. My pack? The pack that stays with me? We're the only ones who hunt rogues. The only ones who kill at all. All the other packs? They just live their lives."

A waitress walked up to the table and set down another glass of wine for Price. "We serve you in restaurants," the waitress said.

He looked up in shock to see her yellow eyes.

"We tend bar," the bartender called from behind the bar showing his fangs.

A man turned on his barstool. "We do your taxes." He lowered his glasses to show his piercing blue eyes.

A cop walked by and tipped his hat to Karen. "Just a cop walking his beat." His fingers were tipped with claws.

A woman at the next table looked at him and winked a blue eye. "School teacher."

The waitress reached into Price's coat and withdrew his pistol. "Silver bullets, Karen." She crushed the gun in one hand and set it on the table in front of Price.

"Thank you, Pam," Karen said.

One by one, everyone in the bar stood up, looked at Price and left after flashing a yellow or blue eye, a fang, a claw.

A few seconds later, only Karen and Price remained in the bar.

"Government as well," Karen said. "That's how we took control of your drone at the last minute at Clingmans Dome. How we had your drones recalled and blinded you when Clyde made his run to Spears Mountain."

"The British satellite?" Price whispered.

"Kids. College students," Karen laughed. "Paul wasn't sure they could actually pull it off, but they did. They have a lot of street cred now."

"Well, I must say, Miss Arthur. You caught me with my pants down." Price smiled. "Alpha, Baker, Charlie, execute!"

The earbud was silent.

Karen shook her head. "No, Price. No more Alpha, Baker, or Charlie. Just the dead."

The door to the bar opened and Clyde walked in with the rest of the pack.

Paul Collins held a bottle of Masseto Toscano Merlot in his hand.

"Any trouble?" Karen asked without turning around.

"Naah, the other packs took care of everything. Gonna be a hell of a mess to clean up," Clyde said.

"Oh, Mr. Price has the resources, don't you, Mr. Price?" Karen asked.

Price nodded. "Check and mate, Miss Arthur. I yield. Terms?"

"I was getting to that…"

***

Tamara climbed onto the bed with Peter Hutchins. She straddled him. "You can really last all night?"

He smiled. "With you? Absolutely."

"I… really doubt that." She leaned back and rubbed her eyes.

She dropped her contact lenses onto his bare chest.

He looked down at the green lenses.

She smiled down at him with glowing yellow eyes.

Hutchins almost got out a scream before she slapped a clawed hand over his mouth.

Tamara leaned down over him and smiled with a mouthful of wolf fangs. "I normally like screamers, but I don't want any interruptions."

She squeezed her thighs together and Peter Hutchins' hips were pulverized.

He screamed into her palm.

"No. No, I don't think this will last all night," Tamara whispered.

Hutchins squirmed and whined beneath her.

"Your monster killed our friend. Your monster killed innocent children." Tamara growled. "I wish this could last all night, I really do? But I'm too pissed off. And?" She licked his face. "I'm… starving."

She closed her jaws on his forehead and crushed it.

***

Karen smiled. "Our job was to destroy the rogues, then it was to stop human killers. You and your masters, Price? You weren't even on our radar." She leaned back. "Well, you are on it now, Price."

"You're going to kill me?" Price asked.

"Eventually, yes. I want that in the back of your mind, Price. I want you to stew on that. One day, one of us will come for you but, until then? You take this message back to your masters. We're the Good Wolves. Run your companies, sell your weapons, control your shadow governments to your hearts' content. But if we find you hurting innocents to make that happen anywhere in the world? We'll come for you and your masters, and you will beg for death. Hell will be a relief."

"You have no idea who you're dealing with," Price said. "My *masters*? They control everything on earth, Miss Arthur. Do you think killing me, killing my strike teams… do you think any of that matters to the people in charge?"

Karen nodded. "A dying, decaying civilization that's lost its soul, Mr. Price? We're familiar." She stood up. "Tell your masters to mind their manners. Touch even one of my people. Harm just one of Die Gute Wolf? We'll pull down this whole house of cards."

Karen walked back to stand with Clyde. "But, if they really need a demonstration of what we can do? Ask Peter Hutchins. Or what's left of him."

They turned and left then, walking out into the night.

***

Tamara fixed her hair in the mirror. She adjusted her dress. There was a bit of intestine on her left shoulder, and she brushed it off.

She searched in her bag. "Lipstick... lipstick... damn it." She shrugged.

Tamara walked back to the bed and the pile of skin and bone that had once been Peter Hutchins. She dipped her index finger in the blood and then applied it gently to her lips.

She turned and looked in the mirror. "Perfect."

She pulled out a pair of sunglasses and put them on, then she walked to the door and stepped out into the hall, closing it behind her.

One of the bodyguards leered at her.

She smiled and licked her lips. "He said it was to die for."

Then she walked away toward the elevator.

"Lucky bastard," the bodyguard said.

***

The pack climbed on their bikes.

"What now?" Clyde asked.

"Now? We live," Karen said. "We just... live."

They rode down K Street and left the city behind.

The End

Denouement

Lake Como, Italy
One Week Later

The board sat around the oval conference table and looked at the projected computer screen on the far wall.

The screen showed a collage of pictures: Karen Arthur and her pack.

"Where are they now?" A woman asked.

Price pointed at the screen and the image showed a satellite view of a forest. "They returned to Gatlinburg, Tennessee. Miss Arthur purchased a sizable tract of land bordering the national park. They're building a large house there. Apparently, now that we are aware of the Good Wolves, they are no longer shy about being discovered. Her personal bank accounts have swollen into millions of dollars. We tried to track the sources of the funds, but we ran into a quagmire of shell companies."

"You underestimated them, Edward," a man said.

"We all underestimated them," Price said.

"And Peter Hutchins paid the price," another man said.

"Hutchins was sloppy. I warned him… warned all of you… that having a set schedule makes targeting you very simple."

"The werewolf who slaughtered him?"

Price clicked the remote. A picture from a hotel security camera showed a woman with strawberry blonde hair walking down a hall. "It took us a few days to identify her: former Navy Corpsman Tamara Cochran, age 28." The picture changed to show a woman lying in a hospital bed. "Seven years ago, an IED in Afghanistan blew off her left leg, left arm, half of her right arm, and caused third degree burns over 60% of her body."

"Mein Gott, these lobos can perform miracles such as this?" A woman whispered.

"Yes," Price said. "Evidently she was one of Karen Arthur's finds in a VA hospital."

"Has she been dealt with?" A man asked.

"No." Price stared at the man. "First of all, she disappeared immediately after partially consuming Peter Hutchins. We're dealing with creatures who are very comfortable running off into the deep woods, at thirty-five miles per hour, and staying there for weeks, if not months, at a time. Second... ladies and gentlemen, we now face an enemy numbering in the thousands, soon to be in the tens of thousands, who can walk among us undetected and are downright compulsively vindictive. They are perfect assassins. I believe Karen Arthur when she says they will destroy us all if we harm even one lobo."

"So, they just get away with killing one of us?" A man asked.

"For now," Price said. "We need a way of detecting them. For now, make sure everyone in your inner circles has no issue with touching items made of silver."

There were nods of agreement around the table.

"How badly are we exposed with Dr. Geffman at large?" A woman asked.

"We're not. I kept Geffman in the dark as much as possible. However, finding her must be a top priority: she is the foremost expert on lobo physiology. I'm afraid her background in genetic manipulation might lead to an even stronger form of lobo - perhaps one that lacks the silver allergy."

A man leaned back in his chair. "So, that's it? Project Lobo is over and now, because of it, we face the most dangerous foe in our history? I expected better from you, Edward."

Price smiled. "I have a solution. Project Draugr."

The others began talking amongst themselves.

"You must be joking, Edward," the man leaning back in his chair said. "You said yourself the Draugr were uncontrollable."

"They are; however, after the massacre in Rural Retreat, Virginia, I made some inroads with the Draugr who survived. They can't be controlled but they can be bargained with."

"What will they want in exchange for handling our wolf problem?"

Price shrugged. "They like the cold. They'll want someplace in the north where they can live without fear of reprisal. You might be able to convince them to take Greenland. Perhaps northern Sweden and Norway. But Alaska and parts of Canada should be on the table."

***

Kootenai National Forest
Montana

Dr. Joseph Marlow hiked through the rugged terrain using only a map and compass. Karen had warned against using a GPS. The trees formed a massive canopy above him dwarfing the trees of Virginia.

He breathed deep, smelling the pine and cedar.

Joseph hadn't seen Paula in three days.

She did that sometimes, disappearing for a day or two and then returning. When he asked her what she had been doing, there was always an excuse. 'Chasing elk,' she would say. 'Running with wolves', 'Shadowing a bear'.

Hunting.

She was hunting here in the deep woods so far away from humans that she couldn't even catch their scent.

The hair on the back of his neck stood up.

He was being stalked.

Six months trekking the backwoods with Paula had sharpened his senses.

He knelt by a stream and began filling his canteen.

Insects stopped making noise behind him to the left.

Birds flew away directly to his left.

Paula didn't make a sound when she leapt on him, rolling him onto his back beside the stream.

She growled softly, opening her wolf jaws and lowering them to his throat.

Her teeth touched his neck.

And then he shoved her over, pinning her shoulders to the moss. His sunglasses fell off as he rolled.

His new, blue eyes glowed even in the bright sun.

His jaws lengthened and he opened them wide, closing on her throat.

He felt her change beneath him, fur receding, becoming soft skin.

306

Paula smiled up at him, her yellow eyes bright with only the slightest tinge of red.

He took human form once again.

Joseph Marlow had been right.

When had Karen Arthur looked at his soul in the hangar on that last day? She had known he was right as well.

Paula was cured.

She would always be dangerous but no one worth loving ever wasn't dangerous.

Soon, they would return to civilization.

He kissed her deeply and shrugged off the rest of his clothes.

Yes, soon, they would return to civilization.

But not today.

**The Nine Fingers Saga will continue in
Nine Fingers: Bedford Blues**

About the Author

At the time of this publication, Tony Bowman has written eight novels. He lives in North Carolina with his gorgeous wife, Laurie, his beautiful daughter, Sara, and a hundred pound Catahoula Leopard dog.

Born in the Appalachian Mountains of southwest Virginia, he will tell you he was born and raised a hillbilly. The hills of his Russell County home are a part of him, as tangible as his fingers or toes. Not a day goes by that he does not miss the steep hills and the dense, fragrant forests of pine and cedar.

He has lived all over the country, from North Carolina to the Amish Country of Pennsylvania, to the San Francisco Bay, and the bright lights of Las Vegas. But, the lure of travel is lost on him now, and he longs for the view of the mountains of his youth and the cool taste of water from a limestone well.

Mr. Bowman writes stories of Horror, Science Fiction, and Suspense.

Horror seems a strange genre for someone who grew up in such an idyllic setting. But, horror stories are woven into the fabric of Appalachian life, whether they are tales of ghosts, or witches, or things that prowl the hills at night – hungry things that snatch away the unwary or unwise. He is merely carrying on the tradition of telling stories in the dark, albeit with a twenty-first-century outlook.

Mr. Bowman welcomes your comments. Contact him via:

Email: thattonybowman@gmail.com
Webpage: https://thattonybowman.com
Facebook: https://www.facebook.com/tony.bowman.14289

Other Works by Tony Bowman

Appalachian Horrors Sequence
    Nine Fingers: The Tucson Ripper (Short Story)
    Nine Fingers (Novel)
    Nine Fingers: The Beast of Bray Road (Novel)
    Nine Fingers: The Good Wolves (Novel)
    The House on the Hill (Novel)
    Nine Fingers: Bedford Blues (Upcoming)
    Dark on the Mountain (Upcoming)
    Coal Fire (Upcoming)
    Redbud Revue (Upcoming)
    Nine Fingers: Apocalypse (Upcoming)

Turning the Darkness Sequence
    Turning the Darkness (Novel)
    Valkyrie: Rat in the Dumpster (Short Story)
    Valkyrie: The Road (Novel)
    Valkyrie: The Three Witches (Upcoming)
    Valkyrie: The Cannibal War (Upcoming)
    Valkyrie: The Dawn (Upcoming)

Lawman (Novel)

Vales Hollow (Novel)